Vaughan Kest

The Hand of the Mighty and Other Stories

Vaughan Kester

The Hand of the Mighty and Other Stories

1st Edition | ISBN: 978-3-75234-901-6

Place of Publication: Frankfurt am Main, Germany

Year of Publication: 2020

Outlook Verlag GmbH, Germany.

THE HAND OF THE MIGHTY AND OTHER STORIES

By Vaughan Kester

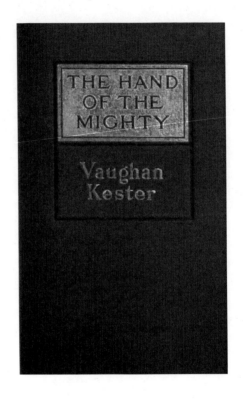

VAUGHAN KESTER

THE HAND OF THE MIGHTY

AND OTHER STORIES

By
VAUGHAN KESTER

Author of
THE PRODIGAL JUDGE, THE JUST AND THE UNJUST
THE FORTUNES OF THE LANDRAYS, ETC.

WITH PORTRAIT, AND A SKETCH OF THE AUTHOR
BY PAUL KESTER

INDIANAPOLIS
THE BOBBS-MERRILL COMPANY
PUBLISHERS

Acknowledgments are due to Short Stories, Munsey's Magazine, The Century Magazine, The Bellman and The American Magazine for permission to reprint certain stories included in this volume.

VAUGHAN KESTER

Vaughan Rester was born in New Brunswick, New Jersey, but the greater part of his boyhood was spent in Mount Vernon, Ohio.

Among our earliest and most vivid recollections were the long railway journeys which we took with our father and mother back and forth between our home in the East and my grandmother's house in Mount Vernon. It was in Mount Vernon that my brother contracted the severe cold that resulted in a hoarseness of speech from which he never entirely recovered, and that finally developed into the condition which occasioned his most untimely death.

Despite this difficulty of speech, his boyhood was a very happy one. My grandmother's house was near the edge of the town and we knew all the short cuts to the woods and the river. We played games, took long tramps, and lived healthy and delightful lives. We went barefoot, we swam and played with all the boys in the town. Indeed, my brother was an absolute democrat all his life.

We went to a little private school kept by Miss Plummer, a friend of the family. Miss Plummer had an original method of teaching, and expanded our minds and won our affection, but I doubt if we were good students. I know I had great difficulty in learning to read, and Vaughan also had his struggles.

At home our mother made a practise of reading aloud to us books of all sorts—ancient history, science, biography, the Bible—anything in which she was interested. For a long time I think it was the sound of her voice which held our attention, but soon we followed with more or less comprehension the words we heard. This formed a most valuable part of our education.

We were very fortunate, too, in our friendships as little boys. We had charming friends who exercised a lasting influence upon us.

When a little older we went to a private school kept by Mrs. Charles Curtis. Here again we had the personal care of a woman of culture. Her instruction was individual and helpful to us both. Later we attended the public school for one term.

By this time Vaughan had become a great reader. He read everything and forgot nothing. All his life he was astonishing us by the things he knew. At last it came to be a commonplace when any one in the family was in doubt upon any point in history or general knowledge, to hear some one say, "Ask Vaughan"—and almost always Vaughan knew.

When Vaughan was about twelve years old our mother, with her friend,

Mrs. Kimball, and others, established the School of Design for Women—now the School of Art—in Cleveland, Ohio—and for the greater part of the next seven years we lived in that city. The school was established on original and useful lines, and its rapid growth was as interesting to Vaughan and me as it was to Mrs. Kimball and our mother.

Much of this time was spent in Mrs. Kimball's house, 1265 Euclid Avenue. If we had been at school in Mount Vernon, here in Cleveland was our university. Everything was discussed before us, and we constantly visited our mother's school, which soon grew to such proportions that it occupied half of the top floor of the vast dingy old City Hall. At that time we attended a private school kept by Mrs. Bierce, and later we had for tutor a young man to whom we recited at Adelbert College.

I think our mother wished Vaughan to enter Adelbert regularly, but he became at this time possessed of a great desire to "go west." My uncle had recently purchased a ranch on the River Platte, near Denver, and Vaughan was not content until consent was given to his trying the life there.

I did not go west with my brother, and only know from what he wrote, and from what he told us on his return, that the plains and mountains and the Denver of those days made a deep impression upon him. Looking back now I wish that he might have spent a longer time in Colorado. The West appealed to him strongly. He had the large elements of the pioneer in his nature, and a deep and peculiar sympathy with the native American in any primitive condition. Certain chapters in *The Fortunes of the Landrays* are so vivid and so real that one knows how well he used his opportunities for observation and absorption in the months he spent on the ranch at the foot of the splendid mountains.

It was while we were living in Cleveland that my brother first developed a spasmodic and not very deep interest in writing. With a friend he got out an edition of a highly interesting paper called *The Athlete and Quirk*, devoted almost wholly to prize fighting. My mother financed the venture. I doubt if a copy remains in existence. The enterprise was abandoned not because our mother's faith declined, but because Vaughan and his fellow editor were too lazy, or too busy with something else, ever to get out a second copy. I don't think Vaughan's contributions were of much value. I know he was terribly bored whenever we reminded him of them.

By this time I was trying to write plays, but it was not for some years that Vaughan took seriously to writing. When he was nineteen our mother resigned from her school and we went to Florida, where we spent six months camping and cruising on the gulf coast, a delectable time for Vaughan, who especially loved salt water and boats.

We camped for many weeks on Sea Horse Key six miles out in the Gulf of Mexico from Cedar Keys. Here Parsons Lathrop, and had been breakfasted by our mother's cousin, William Dean Howells, who then and thenceforth showed us both the utmost kindness. I think meeting Mr. Howells had much to do with firing Vaughan's ambitions. From that time on Mr. Howells was our guide, philosopher and friend, our sponsor and our supporter. We hoarded our funny stories in the hope—generally successful, for his good nature is unfailing—of making him laugh, and he lent an equally willing ear to all our troubles. Two young men never had a kinder friend, nor a wiser. From the first Mr. Howells had faith in Vaughan, and Mrs. Howells, whose rare discrimination we learned to value so highly, and whose generous interest was so unfailing and so helpful, at once saw qualities in him. Her appreciation of him was immediate and intuitive. She sensed at once not only what he was, but what he might become, and I think to her he was always of the stature which he was just consciously attaining when he died.

During one of Vaughan's long visits to his grandmother in Mount Vernon, Ohio, he heard a vague report that Dan Emmett, the composer of *Dixie*, was living north of the town. He hunted up the famous minstrel, and found him, nearly eighty years old, chopping wood for a living.

Mr. Emmett had been a man of some means, and was well connected, but he had drifted away from his people and was living a hermit's life in a little house he had built, unknown for the most part to his townspeople.

This meeting with Emmett was important to both my brother and to the old composer. They became great friends, and the result was that Vaughan wrote several articles for the papers—accounts of Emmett's career as a composer and as one of the Christy Minstrels. *Kate Field's Washington* printed the first of these articles. These sketches marked the beginning of Vaughan's career as a writer. It was his first real appearance in print. The money he received for this work he gave to Mr. Emmett, who had furnished him with the facts the articles embodied.

I remember very well how distressed Vaughan was at the thought of leaving Emmett when he should return to Virginia.

He induced me to write to A. M. Palmer, at that time head of the Actors' Fund, stating Mr. Emmett's case and explaining that Emmett was unwilling to make any appeal for himself. The response was immediate. Fifty dollars was telegraphed to my brother for Mr. Emmett, and a letter followed promising a pension of five dollars a week. This pension—and one was never better deserved—was paid to the old composer as long as he lived.

This little success with his pen inspired Vaughan to more serious effort. It was also the direct means of his meeting with Paul Wilstach, who was so long and so intimately associated with us, and whom, indeed, we came to regard as one of our family. Paul Wilstach was collecting autographs at the time Vaughan's article on Emmett appeared in *Kate Field's Washington*. He wrote, asking Vaughan to secure an autograph copy of *Dixie* for his collection. Vaughan replied that he would obtain the autograph if Mr. Wilstach would send him a check for five dollars for Mr. Emmett. The check was sent, a correspondence ensued, and when Paul Wilstach came east he visited us at Ben Venue, the house above the Potomac in which he now lives.

Paul Wilstach and my brother wrote some farces together, and aided each other to keep alive their literary enthusiasms. When a little later we were living in the big white house on Riverside Drive in New York, Paul Wilstach frequently made the place his home.

Vaughan was about twenty-three when we went to New York, settling ourselves on Riverside Drive in The Big White House, as the place came to be called by our friends. Here my brother and I wrote a two-act play together —*The Cousin of the King*—which was published in *The Looker-On*, and afterward played by Walker Whiteside. This was the only play in which Vaughan had a hand that was ever acted. But he was keenly interested in the theater and most sympathetically and helpfully interested in my various ventures as a playwright.

Not long after we settled in New York he wrote a short story, *The Mills of the Little Tin Gods*, which Mr. Walker accepted for publication in the *Cosmopolitan* magazine. Mr. Walker was enthusiastic about the story, and sent for Vaughan, who returned from Irvington with an offer to go on the staff of the magazine and the news syndicate which Mr. Walker was at that time conducting in connection with the *Cosmopolitan*. Vaughan enjoyed his work at Irvington. It was a novel experience and it brought him into contact with men of ability. He saw a magazine in the making and he helped to make it. He also did a great deal of hard work for the syndicate, and he obtained special articles from others. For a short time I joined my brother on Mr. Walker's editorial staff, and we would go up to Irvington together for the early Monday morning conferences.

After this there was never any doubt as to the career my brother meant to follow. It was while he was associated with the *Cosmopolitan* that he obtained a short leave of absence from his duties and returning to Mount Vernon, Ohio, was married to Miss Jennings. My brother's wife was deeply interested in his literary career, and devoted herself to him and to his work. His marriage was undoubtedly an added incentive to his ambition and it was at this time, or soon after, that he began the writing of his first novel.

8

It was after Vaughan left the *Cosmopolitan* that he joined me in promoting a special performance of Ibsen's *Ghosts*, which our friend John Blair gave at the Carnegie Lyceum. Charles Henry Meltzer was the other active worker behind the scenes. The whole affair was so distinguished and interesting that Mr. Blair conceived the idea of devoting the following winter to a series of modern plays. Vaughan and I, with Mr. Meltzer, volunteered our services, and we were joined by Mr. George Eustis, who by his generosity made a rather elaborate program possible. Performances of each of the five plays were given in New York, in Boston, and in Washington. The series was brilliantly successful; the genius of Miss Florence Kahn, now Mrs. Max Beerbohm, quite dazzled the critics, to Vaughan's great delight. He gave all his time, and did more, perhaps, than any other single individual to make the season a success. This was his only experience in actual theatricals. He knew, however, many noted actors and actresses. Indeed, our house was much frequented by artists of all sorts.

It was through Mr. Howells' influence that my brother obtained a position with Harper and Brothers. I have no very definite knowledge of the work he did for them, except that I know he read many manuscripts during his association with this publishing house, and that he met a number of men famous in the literary world. I think his whole association with the Harpers, though it did not extend over many months, was a pleasant one for him. It culminated in their acceptance of his first novel, *The Manager of the B. & A.*

In the spring of 1900 we returned to Virginia, taking up our residence at Woodlawn Mansion, about eight miles distant by road from Gunston Hall, and three miles from Mount Vernon. Woodlawn was built on what had been a part of George Washington's plantation. Washington himself drew the plans for the house, and they were afterward perfected by Doctor William Thornton, the architect of the Capitol.

Soon after we had established ourselves again in Virginia, *The Manager of the B. & A.* appeared as one of the American novel series the Harpers were then issuing. It was very generously received by the critics.

During the five years we lived at Woodlawn my brother was seldom absent from home. He was deeply interested in the restoration of the house, and even more interested in bringing up the worn-out farm lands.

He had much of the spirit of the backwoodsman. He was tall and powerful, standing six feet two without his shoes. He was very fond of wearing old, easy-fitting clothes—as he was of smoking old pipes. His affection for his old hats was remarkable. To see him about the place tinkering at any odd job which proved too much for the ingenuity of others, delighting in saws and hammers, and pounding his fingers, fond of gardening, and all the rough industries of a large country place, the last idea a stranger would have associated with him was that of authorship.

Vaughan found many types at hand which later offered not a few suggestions for some of the figures in *The Prodigal Judge*. Bob Yancey in particular had his prototype in Kelly Dove. Mr. Dove and my brother were great cronies, and I remember when years later he was reading the first chapters of *The Prodigal Judge* to us at Gunston Hall, we instantly recognized Mr. Dove in the character of Bob Yancey.

Farming the land and restoring the house were fascinating and time-engrossing occupations, but Vaughan still continued his writing, and it was at Woodlawn that he wrote his second novel, *The Fortunes of the Landrays*, which the McClures published.

Always a most deliberate and unhurried worker, he grew even more deliberate and unhastening as time went on. He worked hard, but did not work rapidly. There were times when a chapter would seem to write itself, but I fancy he was a little suspicious of easy composition so far as it concerned his own work.

He was always at his desk when not engaged in some congenial outdoor occupation. He wrote a great deal on scraps, throwing much away. He seldom or never crossed a "t" nor dotted an "i". Often he left great blank spaces and half pages without a line upon them, covering others closely with his fine writing. In their externals his methods of composition seemed rather slovenly, and his manuscripts would have been the despair of any copyist but his wife; but he knew what he was about, and it was utterly useless to attempt any reformation in his habits. He had great patience. He did not satisfy himself easily. He wrote and rewrote and polished and polished again.

Not infrequently he would put aside his work on a novel to write a short story. He wrote a dozen or more, all of which found their way into print except one, *Mollie Darling*, written not long before his death, which appears in this volume for the first time.

Just before the publication of *The Fortunes of the Landrays*, Woodlawn Mansion was sold and I bought a place in the north of England. In England Vaughan met with an understanding a little more complete than he had known in America, except from Mrs. Howells. He made friends immediately, and fitted into the easy agreeable country-house life as perfectly as he had fitted into the different phases of American life he had known. *The Fortunes of the Landrays* came out while we were at Augill Castle.

Vaughan's throat causing him some concern, we went to London, taking Lady Florence Boyle's little house in Victoria Square, just back of

Buckingham Palace. He had begun a new novel at Augill Castle, but he did little or no writing in London. Later it was thought best for him to return to America. Some months were spent at Ben Venue and then we moved into Gunston Hall, which remained my brother's home until his death.

While we were in Ben Venue, Vaughan wrote his one romantic novel, *John o' Jamestown*. Contrary to his usual custom he wrote this book rapidly; but he compensated himself by taking more time than was usual over his work on a new novel, afterward published under the title of *The Just and the Unjust*.

He had almost completed this book when he was seized with the idea which resulted in the writing of his best known and most popular story, *The Prodigal Judge*. He had submitted the incomplete manuscript of *The Just and the Unjust* to one or two friends, who suggested rewriting certain parts. For this work at the time he had no inclination, so put the book aside and plunged into his work on *The Prodigal Judge* with a great deal of enthusiasm. At last he had hit on a theme in which he could employ his wonderful sense of humor. His wit was spontaneous; but while it was a constant delight to those who knew him intimately, he had never regarded it as an asset of any value. I think at the last he began to appreciate that it was his best medium, and that with him the line of least resistance was the safest and wisest to follow.

During the three or four years he lived at Gunston Hall, his work was constantly interrupted by journeys to Washington for slight operations upon his throat. He had great singleness of purpose or he could not have successfully continued his work in the face of such disadvantages. But there was nothing of the invalid about my brother. He diffused an atmosphere of wholesome strength, good nature and health, and until the very last weeks of his life he maintained the attitude of a strong well man.

We were confident that *The Prodigal Judge* would meet a ready acceptance and would find favor with the public. My brother hoped so, too, but there was sufficient doubt in his mind for him to be relieved intensely by the very generous words in which the publishers accepted the book.

The book was well under way and the proofs read, when my brother's physicians decided that an operation of a somewhat serious character was necessary. He met the ordeal bravely and came through it well. We had a pleasant Christmas together at Gunston Hall, and he was recommencing work on *The Just and the Unjust*, when another very serious operation was determined upon. Two weeks after the second operation a third operation was performed. My brother rallied, and in March was able to return to Gunston Hall. He had the satisfaction of knowing that his book had achieved all the success he could possibly have hoped for it. He died at Gunston Hall on the night of the fourth of July, 1911.

Paul Kester.

THE HAND OF THE MIGHTY

SIMPLE and genuine, that's the way Thomas R. Pendagrast impressed the valley. You really might have felt, after listenin' to his innocent chatter, that he'd barely got under the wire. He wasn't much to look at, either. Plain in the face, but comfortable-lookin', as if he was well fed, and with the winnin'est smile that ever come into the valley. You'd never have picked him out of any crowd for a millionaire, he was such a simple soul. That was the key-note of his character as we have read it. For takin' him all in all, I never seen but one simpler soul, and that was Silas Quinby.

No, we never called Silas Si. That would have been too much like intrudin' on his privacy. You see, you felt instinctive Quinby couldn't stand for no reductions; that he hadn't anything to lose without great personal sufferin'. Silas lived at the head of the valley. His was a white frame house with green blinds and a dornick-bordered walk leadin' down to the front gate. When you knew Silas and seen his house, you realized he was like that; that if there'd been a way to look into his soul, you'd have found it was painted white, with green blinds, and had a straight and narrow path leadin' off to travel in.

We had a heap more respect for Silas than confidence in him. He was a man who looked like he'd stand indefinite without hitchin'. He was a lawyer, but he hadn't no practise, because no one in the valley had ever been able to make up his mind to let Silas practise on him. There was some reckless characters here, just like there is in every neighborhood, but none of 'em had ever been that reckless. So at the end of forty years Silas was still waitin' for his first case.

He done better as a notary public, which ain't a perfession callin' for much independent judgment. We figured it that havin' been through college and the law school, Silas's natural parts were sufficiently improved so as he could witness an oath. But beyond this no one had ever taken chances. So he kept chickens by way of helpin' out his professional earnin's. He was successful at that. Even folks who affected to sneer at him for bein' such a simple soul owned up that he had hen sense. No, his parts couldn't have appeared brilliant on the surface when you realize that after livin' all them years elbow to elbow with him, the most we could find to say was that he had hensense.

Socially he was of them poor unfortunates that never gets a chance to finish anything they start to say. About the time folks was willin' to listen to him somebody changed the subject. He was always bein' broke off in the middle and serialized. It was as if some one got nervous waitin', and turned the page.

From what I am sayin' you may gather that Silas was at the tail-end of the procession. But that was hardly it. He was more like a man who'd missed the procession entirely. But he was a simple soul all right, and he never bore malice with folks for bein' short with him or showin' plain that they didn't care a cuss for what he thought.

But to go back to Thomas R. Pendagrast. He come into the valley in a great, big, yellow tourin'-car along late one afternoon in dog-days. It was me seen him first. His car was standin' in the road, and he seemed to be examinin' a daisy he had in his hand. None of your ox-eyes, but just one of those ornery white-and-yellow kind same as are such a pest.

"Ain't it wonderful—the white and the deep, deep yellow, like gold?" he says, smilin' at me kind of shy. "Do you think any artist could paint such a golden yellow?" he says. "I don't."

"I wish they didn't seed so powerful energetic," I says.

"But who made 'em?" he asks, smilin' quaint.

"Blamed if I know. Burbank didn't; he's got better sense."

"Yes, you know," he says, sinkin' his voice and smilin' awful sweet.

"I know they run out a mowin' meadow mighty quick," I says. "If anybody made 'em, I wish to blazes they'd been about something useful instead."

"My friend," he says, lookin' pained, "don't say that. God made 'em; they are His flowers. Are you a church-member?"

"I'm a deacon at the Fork's Meetin'-house," I says.

"My brother!" he says gentle-like, and smilin' winnin' and friendly.

"Here's another simple soul," I thought as we shook hands, "another soft pedal like Silas Quinby, dotty and rockin' on his base, but well-meanin' and harmless."

But I misjudged him. You see, he lived his religion; that was it—it was a part of his everyday life. Most folks go about hidin' their religion as if it was a private matter; but that wasn't Thomas R. Pendagrast's style. He was willin' you should know just how good he was.

Just then one of the men in the car spoke his name. Say, you could have knocked me down with the daisy in his hand, I was that outdone! But I knew it was him from havin' seen his picture so often in the papers. Well, he climbed back into his car after we'd shook hands again, and I took off acrost the fields as hard as I could run. I beat the car down to the valley and spread the news that Pendagrast, the millionaire, was comin', that I'd seen him and shook hands with him.

At first folks didn't believe me, but when his big yellow car rolled in slow over the Fork's road,—the first one that had been seen in the valley,—people realized that we had uncommon visitors with us. And later there was his name on the hotel register, good for no tellin' how many millions. Folks came and looked at it, silent and awed, and then walked away on tiptoe.

One of the gentlemen of Pendagrast's party gave out a statement that the financier was seekin' rest and quiet. No wonder, after the way he must 'a' been workin' to pile up all the money he had. The gentleman said, too, in private conversation with several of us that Mr. Pendagrast was a much misunderstood man, that his aims and purposes were bein' constantly misrepresented by his enemies. He said he was merely one of them Christian business men in whose hands an all-seein' Providence had seen fit to place the temporal welfare of our country. What you noticed at once about Pendagrast and his friends was the religious tone of all their remarks; yet they were cheerful—cheerful without bein' vulgar.

Right from the first Pendagrast liked the valley; and when he seen we kep' out of his way and didn't try to intrude on him, he got awful friendly, and to such an extent that he'd stop and speak to any man he met on the road. He'd ask him his name most likely, how many acres he farmed, if he was married, and how many children, and was he a church-member. You could see he was all balm and oil and gentleness and thoughtfulness. He appeared to overflow with the milk of human kindness. He was as sweet as a cat with sirup on its paws, always soundin' the soft note in his talk, and always moral and improvin'.

Well, sir, his friends just seemed to love him. It was beautiful to watch the way they sort of hung on his words. And when he told a funny joke, you could see them fix their faces, and then they'd laugh and laugh, and slap each other on the back.

It wasn't no time at all until we knew he was just such another simple soul as Silas Quinby. He was simple in his pleasures, in what he et, and in his thoughts, like Silas was. Folks commented on this. But while Pendagrast got a chance to finish all his remarks, poor old Silas had never been trusted with much beside the weather, and even there he had to be mighty careful not to overstay his time.

But the most astonishin' thing was the way Silas Quinby and Pendagrast became friends. It was like two streams of molasses flowin' together and makin' one sweetness. It was because they was both such simple souls, you see. I doubt if Pendagrast had ever met any one like Silas, which was sayin'

15

just like himself.

He said Silas was the most genuine man he had ever met with, and that some day he must come and visit him at his city home. He spent hours with Silas lookin' over the chickens or drinkin' buttermilk and eatin' doughnuts Mrs. Quinby fed 'em at the back door like two happy lads.

You bet it made us feel good. There was the master of millions and our Silas like brothers. Why, we began to talk of runnin' Silas for justice of the peace. He'd wanted the office for years, but no one had felt he'd care to have a case tried before Silas. Not that he was not well meanin'. No; it was his mind we feared, not his heart.

Then Pendagrast and his friends must see the p'ints of interest about the valley. Silas was their guide. No one knew the country better than he did, whose land they was on, and all about the folks that owned it. It was beautiful to see those two simple souls goin' around gatherin' flowers or pickin' up curious rocks and pebbles. You see, they was both so genuine anything that was innocent could charm 'em. They'd come home to the hotel, their arms bulgin' with wild blooms and half a hundred of broken rock mebby stowed away under their feet in the car. I never knew a millionaire's pleasures could be so harmless or so inexpensive.

Nights Silas used to fetch him down to Miller Brothers' store so he could get acquainted with folks. Sociable? The most sociable man I ever met with. Mebby he'd borrow five cents off one of his friends and lay it all out in crackers and cheese; then he'd set on the counter and dangle his legs and talk and munch and munch and talk. He never seemed to carry no money. I suppose, havin' so many millions, he didn't want to appear ostentatious; and when he'd ask for the nickel his friends would laugh and laugh; and it *was* comical, him having to borrow five cents like that. Once he brought some picture-cards down to the store he'd had taken the year before when he was in the Holy Land. There was views of him at the Tomb, him on the shores of Galilee, him at the Mount of Olives, but no olives.

The first Sunday he spent in the valley he attended church right there in the old Fork's Meetin'-house, and after the service the minister asked him if he wouldn't favor us with a few remarks. Say, I ain't ever forgot that meetin'. What do you think that simple soul done? He got up, his eyes shinin' and tears in his voice like he was gettin' ready to leak, and told us about his early struggles.

Joe Whittaker said afterward he hadn't known whether he was attendin' divine service or night session of a business college. As we left the church, I says to Joe:

"How you can bring yourself to criticize a simple soul like that is more than I can understand."

"All the same," says Joe, "he's got God and mammon confused in his mind. Savin's and salvation are pretty much one and the same to him. I don't want to be told how to make twenty-five dollars to start on,——I know that much,——but I'd be grateful if the old man had told me how to make a million or two."

"Well, he deserves a lot of credit," I says.

"What for?" asks Joe.

"For bein' successful and sacrificin' himself to make money," I says, heated.

"Do you respect a hog for taking on fat?" says Joe.

"No, I don't," I says. "That's a hog's nature, to take on fat."

"Well, it's his nature to make money," says Joe. "He ain't never gone outside of his natural instincts. But where you and me has got various instincts, like bein' careless in our spendin' and lazy, he's never been able to let go a dollar once he's got his hands on it. I bet you the Indian yells with pain when his fingers touch a penny."

Well, Pendagrast stayed ten days in the valley, and then he went away, promisin' to come back the first chance he got. When he left it was just like the sun had gone down for good. We'd been thinkin' in the hundred millions, dreamin' of motor-cars and steam-yachts, and we was suddenly dumped back on the Miller brothers, our richest family, who mebby made two thousand dollars a year sellin' groceries and calicoes, and speculatin' in hoop-poles and shingles.

The night after the big yellow tourin'-car had gone hootin' good-by down the valley road, Silas Quinby come to see me. I seen he had something on his mind. Finally he got me out to the woodpile. When a man had something very private to say to his neighbor, he always got him out to the wood-pile. It was an old valley custom.

"You're missin' him, Silas?" I says, meanin' Pendagrast.

"Yes," says Silas, sighin', "a wonderful man, simple and genuine, and all his goodness on the surface, where it counts," he says. "And yet I don't know as it's so much on the surface as underneath," he adds.

"It's all around," I says.

"And yet he's a terribly misjudged man. Have you read them awful libelous attacks on his character in the magazines and newspapers? It makes my heart bleed for him," says Silas, moved.

Then Silas asked me about some wild land I owned. He wanted to know if I'd ever thought of sellin' it. I'd been tryin' to sell it for thirty years, but couldn't. There was six hundred acres all told, mostly broke rock and scrub-timber. I'd been offerin' it for two-fifty an acre.

"Yes," I says. "I'll sell fast enough if I get the chance."

"Well, I've had inquiries," says Silas.

You see, he was a real-estate agent, though he'd never sold any land. But it's easy to be a real-estate agent. You can start with a sign. And Silas had started twenty years before.

"I wish you'd put your land in my hands to sell," he kept on. "All I want is a ten per cent, commission if I make a sale. But you must give me a year's time."

"Why," I says, "that's an awful long time to take, Silas."

"Well," he says, "you've taken thirty years, ain't you, George? And your lowest price is two-fifty?"

"That's my askin' price. I'll accept two," I says.

"Or as much more as you can get?" he says, laughin' in his simple way.

"Don't be foolish, Silas. If you got anybody feeble-minded enough to think he can farm that land, don't you try to dicker with him," I says getting anxious.

The upshot of it was I signed a paper giving Silas a sort of option, him to be exclusive agent for one year. Then he handed me a dollar.

"What's this for, Silas?" I asked.

"Why, to bind the bargain," he says, smilin' at me simple.

"Why, that's all right, Silas; I trust you," I says, humorin' his fancy.

He made me promise I'd not tell a soul about the option. But that was reasonable, because if anybody in the valley could have got hold of his buyer, first thing they would have done would have been to tell him he'd starve to death on that land, that it was so thin a turkey-buzzard didn't make a shadow flyin' over it. Yes, it was some poor as far as fertility went.

Of course I kept still, but one night as I was walkin' home from the store with the youngest of the Miller brothers,—we married sisters,—it sort of come out that Silas had been to him about land, and they'd give him an option on two thousand acres of cut-over mountainside.

"We'll watch Silas," I said. "He's losin' his mind."

"Well, it ain't much to lose," says Miller. "He's got nothing he'll be less likely to miss."

"Yes, but he's such a simple soul," I says. "I don't know but we'd ought to make up a purse and send him off to see a brain specialist. It's a mania he's sufferin' from, for no man in his health would ever think he could sell twenty-six hundred acres of this cut-over land," I says, appalled at the extent of Silas's hallucination.

"We must watch him," says Miller. "He may turn violent any moment. These manias grow on a man until he ain't any control over himself. We must watch out for Silas," he says.

The next day Miller took me aside and told me that Joe Whittaker had told him in confidence that Silas had got an option out of him for his farm.

"What did I tell you?" says Miller. "He's mad, stark starin' mad."

"That's it, Miller; his poor simple nature has give way at last. Associating with multi-millionaire's was too much for him. I knew his brain was thin in spots, and it's let him through at last. That's over three thousand acres he's goin' to sell—more land than's changed hands in the valley in eighty years."

"Don't you think we'd ought to get him committed to an asylum right off, and not wait?" says Miller, anxious. "I got a house full of children, and he's my nearest neighbor. I've had new strong locks put on my doors and windows, and I've told my wife if she ever hears Silas give a whoop, not to wait for nothin', but to go inside and lock all the doors."

Well, we kept on investigatin' Silas, and we got on the track of something like fifty thousand acres of mountain land he was holdin' on option! When me and Miller footed it up, Miller turned white as a sheet, and I felt sick all over.

"Poor, poor Silas!" I says.

"Fifty thousand acres—think of that!" gasps Miller. "Why, you couldn't give it away in an ordinary lifetime. There's never been any one crazier than him, and here he is walkin' the roads without a keeper! It's awful!" The sweat was pourin' off Miller's face. "George," he says, "with a madman like him, even a strong fellow like you wouldn't be safe. They have awful unnatural strength, these maniacs. Why, you'd be a child in his hands. I bet there ain't no twenty men in the valley could handle him, thin and peaked as he looks. George, it's awful; we're living over a slumberin' volcano."

"Poor Silas!" I says. "His mind's diseased, all right."

But we could see plain that Silas had all that terrible cunnin' the mad has. He talked just as rational and simple like he'd always done. He seemed still to have plenty of hen sense, which was the only kind of sense we'd ever credited him with havin'. Yet me and Miller was like men setting over the crater of a volcano,—if that's where you set,—which we was expectin' any moment to bust wide open.

Then one day a stranger drove into the valley. He was a lightnin'-rodder, and he came to me to talk rods. I was cold on the proposition, but he was a clever sociable chap, and one thing led to another, and before long he says.

"You've got a lovely valley; what's land worth here?"

I told him all the way from two an acre for stumpage up to thirty for the best valley farms. He seemed to think them figures mighty reasonable, for he asked me if I had any broke land that 'u'd do to clear for sheep. The upshot of it was that I told him about that six hundred acres I'd been tryin' to sell for such a time, and he made me an offer of two an acre cash out of hand. I wanted to kick myself, for I remembered that fool option I'd give Silas.

"Wait," said Silas, when I'd hunted him up and explained matters. "Don't be too hasty."

"Hasty! I can't be half quick enough. I want you to tear up that blame paper, and let me sell my land now I got the chance, Silas."

He wouldn't do it. He said that wasn't enough for the land, and that I mustn't think of sellin', for he wouldn't agree to it. Stubborn? I never knew he could be so downright mulish. Argument and entreaty didn't budge him.

That same night down to the store Miller took me aside. It seems the lightnin'-rod man had been soundin' him. It really appeared he was more anxious to buy land than he was to sell rods. He'd made Miller the same offer he'd made me, and Miller was crazy to sell. He said he never expected to get so good an offer again, but that fool paper of Silas's stood in the way, and he couldn't do a thing with Silas.

"If I only hadn't taken his blame dollar, I'd tell him to whistle!" said Miller, groanin'.

"Did that simple cuss give you a dollar, too?" I says.

"Simple? Why, George, his option is almost as good as a deed. It's a contract for sale, him to fix the price at any figure he chooses to name above two an acre. We've accepted a consideration. I ain't sure he's so simple, after all."

"What can we do, Miller?" I asked.

"There's only one thing, George, that I know of," says Miller. "We must get him adjudged insane, and recover them options that way; and we mustn't lose no time about it, either, or that sucker will buy other land."

It looked like what Miller feared would happen, for when the lightnin'-rod man found he couldn't do business with me or Miller, he went to Whittaker. Naturally Whittaker was wild to sell, but he was up against Silas.

The lightnin'-rodder was a sport, all right. He said he'd always counted it a fair test of a man's ability to sell rods, but he was findin' there was stiffer business propositions, and he couldn't afford to let no transaction get the better of him. He was goin' to squat right there and buy his sheep farm if it took all summer. You see he had his nerve with him.

And through all them days of stress, when it looked like his neighbors might mob him any minute, Silas preserved the even tenor of his way, like the fellow says, mindin' his chickens, and goin' around serene and ca'm, at perfect peace with the world.

But of course things couldn't go on like that long. Something had to be done. It was Miller thought of what he had ought to do—Miller and his lightnin'-rod man. They got up a petition and sent it to Pendagrast. They reminded him how friendly he'd be'n with Silas, and urged him to join us in sendin' our poor friend to a private asylum for the insane, where he could have the medical attention he was requirin' so much, and be restored to such hen sense as the Creator had endowed him with in the beginnin'.

It showed what a simple genuine soul Pendagrast was when inside of a week his big yellow car came scootin' into the valley and drawed up in front of Miller Brothers' store.

"Where's my poor friend?" he says, after we had shook hands all round. "Yes," he says, wipin' his eyes, "it's best I should take him where he can be confined and have medical attention."

We sent for Silas. Say, it was touchin' to see them two meet and clasp hands, each lookin' innocenter and simpler than the other, and like butter would keep indefinite in their mouths.

"Are you well, Silas?" asks Pendagrast, with his arm thrown acrost Silas's shoulder. "And how's Mrs. Quinby and her good doughnuts?" smacking his lips. "And the chickens, and your vegetable garden—all doin' nicely, I hope. Well, you must make up your mind to leave these simple joys for a spell; I want you should visit me in my city home. I've come to fetch you away." And he winks at Miller.

21

They'd arranged the doctors was to be introduced to Silas there without his knowin' who they was, so as he wouldn't be on his guard. You see we hadn't been able to do nothing with old Doctor Smith, the valley physician; he said Silas had just as many brains as he ever had, and a heap more than the folks who had put their land in his hands to sell.

But Silas said he couldn't leave home. He was awful firm about stayin' just where he was. He couldn't think of moving.

"It's that dreadful cunnin' insane folks have," whispers Miller to me. "He's suspicious of his best friend."

It was just beautiful the way Pendagrast talked with Silas, humorin' him like a little child, pleadin' with him to visit him in his city home, where there'd be prayer-meetin' every Thursday night and two regular services on Sunday. He held out every inducement he could think of, but Silas was as firm as he was gentle. It was plain he was set against leavin' the valley. Presently Pendagrast took him by the arm and says:

"Gentlemen, I must go down and pay my respects to Mrs. Quinby, and beg one of those nice doughnuts off'n her. Me and my friend will return soon, I hope, to say that he has reconsidered his decision, and will go with me to pay me the visit I want him to." And they locked arms and walked off, two as simple-souled men as you'd wish to see.

We owe it to Mrs. Quinby for a knowledge of what happened down to Silas's. She listened at the keyhole after she'd fed Pendagrast a plate of doughnuts and some buttermilk.

"You're actin' very wrong, Silas, to keep them folks from sellin' their land when they got the chance," Pendagrast says, after a little friendly talk. "Yes, Mr. Miller's told me all about it. They are thinkin' of havin' you locked up in an asylum somewhere, and you'd better destroy them papers. I doubt if they are legal—"

"They're legal," says Silas, smilin' his sweetest. "I'd stake my life on that."

"Have you ever thought of them poor fellows and their bitter disappointment?" says Pendagrast, his voice tremblin'. "Have you put yourself in their place, my friend? Have you applied that great moral test to the situation? Before we go any further, would you like to kneel down beside me and say your prayers?" he says. "I know the temptations of greed, that money's the root of all evil. It can do no hurt," he urged in that gentle winnin' voice of his.

And Mrs. Quinby, beyond the door, covered her head with her apron, she was that moved by the simple soul's eloquence. She missed Silas's answer, but she heard Pendagrast go on.

"I tremble for your safety here, Silas—even your temporal safety, my friend. Every man in the valley's got land to sell, and now it looks like their opportunity has come, and you're blockin' the deal. It's cruel of you, Silas," he says. "And they're a rough lot—rough, but gentle, and they may do you bodily harm, like tarrin' and featherin' you without meanin' to. I can't bear to think of that, Silas; it hurts me here," he said, restin' his hand on his wish-bone. "And you can't pray, my friend. It's a bad sign, Silas, when a man loses the power to pray; it shows he's walked afar with false gods," he says.

"They don't know what's best for them," says Silas. "I got a buyer for their land. It'll be sold in good time—"

"What!" gasps Pendagrast, turnin' white.

"I say I've found a purchaser for their land."

"Who, Silas?" says Pendagrast.

And Mrs. Quinby, watchin' through the keyhole, seen that he spoke with effort.

"It's a group of capitalists in New York. All I got to do is to wire 'em, and their representative will be here on the first train to close the deal," says Silas.

There was a silence, then Pendagrast says:

"Why didn't you let me know of your havin' this land to sell, my friend? Suppose we form a partnership, Silas. We'll close your options out at once at two an acre, and I'll personally guarantee you your commission, which I understand is ten per cent. That'll be ten thousand dollars for you."

"No," says Silas, "I must do better than two dollars an acre. These folks are my neighbors. I want to do the best I can by them."

"You're wrong there, Silas," says Pendagrast. "Business is different from most other things, and it's a good rule to think of yourself first."

"Mebby so," says Silas; "but it's foolish any way you look at it to sell the best coal land in the state for two an acre. And when you get your railroad built along the line of that old survey that was made twenty years ago, you'll need the gap on the Whittaker place, or you can't get your line acrost the mountains without goin' clean around," he says.

Mrs. Quinby said Pendagrast pretty near fell off his chair, hearin' this, he was that outdone. Presently he commands himself so as he could speak, and says, sighin' deep:

"I see it's as Mr. Miller said it was, and as I feared, but hoped it was not.

23

There ain't no railroad, and I never heard of no old survey—nor coal," he says. "My poor friend, I would gladly have stood between you and your neighbors, but I see now the law will have to deal with you, and the sooner the better, so these poor folks can sell their land and get their money."

"What law?" says Silas.

"A lunacy commission," says Pendagrast.

"Wait a bit," says Silas. "Do you remember that roll of papers you lost on the mountain? Well, I found it. I don't need to tell you it contained your plans and a copy of the old survey, as well as the location of the coal that your engineers, who come here two years ago trout-fishin', had checked up for you."

"Quinby," says Pendagrast,—he was dealin' now,—"I'll take them options off your hands and give you a bonus of fifty thousand dollars; but you must agree to keep still until after I've dealt with these folks—"

"No," says Silas; "I'm askin' two hundred an acre for the land."

Pendagrast groaned.

"Two hundred! Why, that's what it's worth!" he says in a shocked tone.

"Of course," says Silas. "That's what I want to get for these folks—all their land's worth."

"But that ain't business," urges Pendagrast, almost moved to tears. "Silas, my friend—" he began, conjurin' back that old winnin' smile.

But Silas shook his head.

"Two hundred, or I wire them New York parties I've been dickerin' with."

And Pendagrast seen that he was like adamant—like adamant covered up with cotton-batting.

"No," cries Pendagrast, "rather than have you do that, I'll pay what the land's worth."

"Two hundred," says Silas, gentle but firm.

Mrs. Quinby, looking through the keyhole, says she seen something like a mortal agony wrench Pendagrast; then he groaned horrid, showin' the whites of his eyes, and says weak:

"Fetch pen and paper. It's highway robbery, but I'll sign—I got to," he says.

"I've the papers ready for you," says Silas.

Pendagrast signed them, then he drawed himself up.

"I shudder for your future, Quinby," he says. "No, I won't shake hands with you; I don't feel cordial."

And he groped his way out to where his big tourin'-car was drawed up under the maples.

And that was how Silas Quinby saved the valley folks something like ten million dollars just by bein' such a simple soul.

The lightnin'-rod man? Oh, he was Pendagrast's agent.

THE BAD MAN OF LAS VEGAS

WHEN the Bad Man of Las Vegas left Baker's ranch, taking himself reluctantly from the midst of the unrighteous revel that was being held there, day was just breaking.

It was about mid-morning and the sun was high in the heavens when his horse stepped gingerly over the cactus bushes and into the well worn trail that led down to Las Vegas.

The Bad Man drew rein. He was having a moment with his conscience; one of the consequences of the early ride; or it may have been the unavoidable aftermath of Baker's whisky, which had been not only abundant but vile.

He recalled how he had come to Las Vegas, a raw lad of twenty. He saw himself as he was then, lank and wondering, with factory bleached skin. He had come West to make his fortune. When that was accomplished he was to return and settle down in the old home where his godly forefathers had dwelt since Pilgrim times, self-respecting and respected.

Las Vegas had been notorious for its wickedness when he first drifted there. For a while he had kept clear of it all, then the experience of a single night had changed the whole after current of his life. Entering one of the gambling hells in search of a friend, he had found him at cards with the bully of the place. He had tried to get him from the room, there had been words, a quarrel, and then all was a blank until he awoke from the delirium of his fear and anger to find himself in the center of the room, beneath the flaring kerosene lamps, with the bully dead in the shadow at his feet.

He lived the years swiftly after that, in a sort of mad, blood-letting frenzy. Every man has friends, and one killing involves other killings. It was not enough that he had killed one bad man; he must keep on killing bad men or else fall himself.

He had preferred to keep on. He speedily acquired a fatal handiness with his weapons, in a few months growing into the strong alert man capable of holding his own against all comers.

He knew, though the change came slowly and almost imperceptibly, that he was none the less surely living toward that day when he would be hunted out of Las Vegas; when the advancing tide of civilization would touch and pause there, and his career would culminate with one murder too many.

He took off his hat to let the wind fan his forehead. It was like the springs

26

he had known in the East.

He seemed to catch the odor of roses and honeysuckle—he remembered his first and only love. Their parting came back to him with vivid minuteness of detail. It had all been infinitely bitter to them, but he was going where a man had a chance, and he would return.

He had scarcely thought of it in years, and now there was only the scent of the flowers and her face rising out of the gray plain before him. She had done her part faithfully and then she had married, to live her days amid the hard commonplaceness of the little eastern village where she was born.

The Bad Man gathered up the reins, which had fallen from his hand to the horn of the saddle, and was about to apply the spur to his horse's flank, when, glancing back over his shoulder, he saw a wagon coming down the trail, the center of a moving cloud of dust. Influenced by a sudden impulse he could not explain, he permitted the reins to fall slack again.

As the wagon came nearer he saw that it was a homesteader's outfit drawn by a single horse that was dark with sweat and dust and flecked here and there with white splotches of foam. A man was driving, and at his back a woman's face was visible.

As the wagon drew up alongside of the Bad Man the homesteader reined in his horse. Las Vegas' questionable hero spoke first. He merely remarked that it was a fine day. The homesteader inspected him narrowly before answering the greeting, then he said—and his tone was one of surly reserve, while his manner was neither easy nor gracious—"It is a fine day."

He was a round-shouldered man of thirty-five with a sallow unhealthy skin and a scanty ill-kept beard. He had put aside his coat and wore only a faded, much mended cotton shirt and overalls—once blue, but now showing white at the seams—tucked carelessly into the tops of heavy boots.

The woman peered out anxiously and fearfully at the stranger.

The latter said by way of continuing the conversation:

"Where are you bound for, pardner?"

"Sunken River Valley. Got a brother there," was the gruff response.

The Bad Man looked him over carefully and critically, then the wagon, and last of all the horse. He noted that the wagon showed the effects of the roads and a long journey. The jingle it sent forth whenever the horse moved spoke eloquently for repairs. The horse, however, though it had been driven hard, was comparatively fresh and able. The gentleman from Las Vegas lived in a community where men were largely judged by their horses, and he decided that the animal before him was a recent purchase.

"Where are you from?" he asked, when done with his scrutiny.

"Western Kansas. It's a hell of a country. Grasshoppers one year and no water the next. About cleaned me out." Then he added surlily: "If you are done looking me over, I guess I'll be moving."

Meantime the woman had disappeared from view, but she could be heard speaking to some one inside the wagon. Then a child's voice, fretful and tired, answered hers.

The homesteader's manner, even more than his words, was an affront to the Bad Man, who was perhaps unduly sensitive in such matters. He was debating whether he should not interpose, some objections to his continuing on his road, when the woman called out querulously: "Do drive on, Joe. It seems as though we shall never get there!"

The man saluted with his whip. "So long." And the wagon with a creak and a rattle rolled off, jangling as it went.

The Bad Man touched his horse with the spur. "I'm going your way," he said.

For a time they rode on in silence. Every now and then the homesteader stole a glance of doubt and mistrust at his insistent and evidently unwelcome companion. Clearly he was far from being at ease. Finally he said:

"You weren't wanting to say anything in particular to me, were you?"

The Bad Man regarded him with mild surprise. "I reckon not," he answered.

"I didn't know. Only you seemed so all-fired set on stickin' close to me, that's all; I didn't mean no offense."

There was a pause. The Bad Man turned the matter slowly over in his wind. He had formed a very unfavorable opinion of the homesteader, and was wondering whether it was not a duty he owed society to tell him so frankly. He allowed a certain latitude because of the different sense of humor different men have, but there was nothing funny about the homesteader. He was just plain uncivil.

"Yes, sir-ee," said the homesteader, "western Kansas is a hell of a place. It ain't worth the powder it would take to blow it to blazes. I wish I'd never seen it. When I made up my mind to come West, my wife sort of persuaded me to stop there. She didn't want to go any farther. Sort of wanted to keep somewhere near the folks in old Vermont. Then she was taken sick; she was ailing before we started West. Then our two boys up and died, and now the young un's down. It's mighty hard on her ma. I got a brother in Sunken River Valley, and some of the folks from back East moved out there while we were in Kansas. My wife will be mighty well satisfied when she gets among her own sort again. Women get lonely so darn easy."

They could hear the mother singing softly to the sick child. The Bad Man jerked his thumb over his shoulder.

"What's the matter?"

"Fever," said the other laconically.

"So you are from Vermont?"

"Yes. Wish I was there now, you bet. It's God's own country."

"What part of the state do you come from?"

"Central part. Barrettsville."

The Bad Man started violently, but recovered himself on the instant.

"I suppose you are pretty well acquainted there?" he asked, with studied indifference.

"I ought to be. Lived there most of my life."

"That's singular. I met a fellow from Vermont just the other day, from Barrettsville, too."

"Lots of our folks have come West. They're scattered all over out here. Some of 'em are doing mighty well, too."

"You didn't happen to know the Thomases, did you?"—with elaborate carelessness. "Which?"

"I guess the man I am asking about had something to do with the mills. There are mills there, ain't there?"

"Well, I declare! That's funny!" and the homesteader laughed a mirthless cackle. "Should say I did know the Thomases. My wife was a Thomas—old French Thomas' daughter. But"—lowering his voice—"the old man's been dead five years come next May."

The Bad Man turned his face away.

So that was the woman he had loved!

There was silence again, undisturbed save for the clatter of the horses' hoofs and the rattle of the wagon. The child was asleep, and its mother no longer sang to it.

29

The homesteader thrust aside the flaps and glanced in. The woman, with the child in her arms, was seated on a mattress at the back of the wagon, looking out at the long dusty streak that wound over the range and lost itself in the gray distance of the plain.

Craning his neck the Bad Man saw her, and then as her husband dropped the flaps, he pulled up his horse and drew in behind the wagon. The woman raised her eyes.

"Is the little one asleep?" he asked, his voice shaking with an awkward tenderness.

"Yes. She's just pining away for green fields and trees."

He surveyed the woman before him with a certain wonder. He would never have recognized her, she was so changed, so altered from the likeness he had carried in his heart; but now, knowing who she was, he could trace where she had fallen from that likeness. He was quite sure she could not recognize him, for he had changed, too, but in a different way.

"If he'd drive slower, wouldn't it be easier for her?"

The woman looked into his face in alarm.

"We want to get there as quick as we can. Seems as though we'd never get there!"

"You can't make it to-day."

"My husband says he'll drive till he gets there if it takes all night."

"There'll be a dead horse between the shafts if he tries it," said the Bad Man in a tone of calm conviction.

"The horse——" and the woman stopped.

"I don't reckon he sets much value on the brute from the way he drives."

The woman gazed fixedly into his face. "Did he tell you?" she questioned in a frightened whisper.

In a flash he realized what the trouble was. "He shouldn't have done it," he said gravely. "I know that," she answered breathlessly. "But what could he do? Our own horse had died. We had no money, and with the baby sick we just couldn't stop! If he is found out, what then?" The Bad Man shook his head dubiously. "I'd rather not say."

"Do they hang men for horse stealing?"

"They have," he answered shortly.

Further conversation was interrupted by the sudden stopping of the wagon.

"Darnation! Which trail do I take?"

The Bad Man pointed to the right.

"There's your road. You'll find it plain enough."

"Much obliged to you, stranger. I don't reckon you're going over to Sunken River Valley yourself?"

"Hold on;" and a detaining hand was placed upon the lines the homesteader held. "That's a good horse you're driving, pardner, but if you keep this pace you'll take only his hide and bones into Sunken River Valley with you."

"I've got to get there, horse or no horse," answered the man nervously.

"How'd you like to trade? I've taken a fancy to that animal of yours, and if you're bent on killing a horse I don't, know but I'd rather have you kill the one I'm riding."

The homesteader leaped from his seat on the instant.

"I'll do it!" Then he bethought him that perhaps some little display of reluctance might be seemly and natural. "Your horse is sound, of course?"

"Sound as a dollar. Look it over if you don't think so."

The woman came to the front of the wagon, listening breathlessly. Now she put the flaps aside and looked out.

Her husband turned to her. "We're going to swap horses—you don't care, do you?"

She tried to meet the glance of the Bad Man, but could not.

"It's all right, wife?"

"Yes," she answered in a low voice; "it's all right."

The animal was already free from the shafts, and at her word he led it out from between them. The Bad Man threw himself astride the stolen horse.

"I'll say good day to you, pardner—and to—you"—to the woman, and without a word more he was galloping off down the trail toward Las Vegas. |

"I guess I was darn lucky to get rid of that horse," the homesteader remarked, as he gazed after the Bad Man.

The woman said nothing. She only wondered.

MOLLIE DARLING

OUT of the warm distance came the song:

> "Do you love me, Mollie darling?
>
> Say you love none else but me—"

The man seated in the cabin door raised a battered face and listened, as down the trail came the singer and the song.

> "Mollie, sweetest, fairest, dearest;
>
> Look up, darling, tell me this.
>
> Do you love me, Mollie darling?
>
> Let your answer be a kiss!"

The dog at the man's feet cocked his head knowingly on one side and seemed to listen, too. The man addressed the dog.

"Duffer, that's a right sweet old song, ain't it?—a right plaintive air. When you're fifty odd, Duffer, them old songs dig holes in your memory." As he spoke he gently caressed the dog. It was yellow and palpably of uncertain breed, but just as palpably of distinguished social qualities. "Duffer, I'll bet you what you like he ain't fifty,—and that his Mollie's within safe walking distance!"

Around a turn in the trail, a winding path that led up and up, and from behind a big boulder, came the singer in blue work-stained overalls and blouse. He swung a tin dinner pail with one hand and his cap with the other. His years were plainly a scanty half of fifty. Catching sight of the man in the cabin door, he paused, while the song died abruptly on his lips.

"Hullo!" he said.

"Evening," responded the man. Middle age had put its stamp upon him; hard-lived years apparently, for he was lean and muscular, with the brown skin of perpetual sunburn. A long scar slashed the bridge of his beak-like nose and halved a shaggy iron-gray eyebrow with a white welt. The eye beneath was fixed and staring, yet it served to mitigate and soften the somewhat severe expression that lurked across the way, as it were, on the other side of his face; for his good eye was dark and piercing, and held a deep spark.

Duffer, wagging his tail, investigated the newcomer. He sniffed at the blue overalls that kept the rancid odor of smoke and oil and machinery. The young man clapped his cap on his thick mop of black curls, opened his dinner pail and found a crust.

"Think he'd like this?" he asked of the dog's master, who nodded. Duffer made short work of the crust, and then, wise and inquiring, nosed the bottom of the dinner pail.

"What do you call this place?" inquired the elder man. There were sixteen houses on the bench below.

"Sunset,—Sunset Limited, some of us calls it. Say, Alvarado's knocked the spots out of us,—so's Last Pan, so's Buffalo Bend. Sunset Limited,—yes, sir, and that ain't no joke either!"

"Quiet?"

"You can hear a pin drop during rush hours. This is one of the rush hours, me going home to supper. That gives you the dimensions of the rush." The young man laughed pleasantly. "My name's Johnny Severance," he added, by way of introduction.

"Mine's Brown."

"Huh," said Johnny. "That's Brown's Peak you're looking at. Brown was an old-time scout; he stood off a bunch of Apaches here way back in the early days. They named the mountain after him."

"You'll always meet plenty of Browns wherever you go," said the owner of that name, in impartial judgment of its merits.

"It is awful common," agreed Johnny. "You prospecting?"

Brown shook his head.

"Health, mebby?"

But Brown's appearance was strongly against this supposition. "I don't want no more health than I got," he said.

"Well, you do look hearty," admitted Johnny. "But every now and then they blow in here for their health. That was the way with the last fellow who had this cabin. He croaked." And young Mr. Severance sank his voice in decent recognition of the universal tragedy. He continued: "I'm keeping the pumps up at the Red Bird sucking. The stockholders are suffering from cold feet.

Well, so long, Mr. Brown!" and he moved off in the direction of the sixteen houses that constituted Sunset.

He passed fifteen of these houses, whose back doors looked boldly out across an arid valley to a distant line of jagged peaks that saw-toothed the horizon under flaming bands of color. No one of the fifteen but breathed an air of dilapidation and neglect, for they sepulchered dead hopes. The sixteenth was in pleasing contrast; it was newly painted and two stories high. A sign announced this the Mountain House,—M. Ferguson, Proprietor.

Johnny passed about a corner of the Mountain House and paused beside the kitchen door, where there was a barrel, a bench, a tin basin, a roller towel, a cake of soap and a sixty-mile view set under the splendid arch of the heavens. He filled the basin at the barrel, tossed aside his blouse, and began the removal of such evidences of honest toil as he had brought away from the Red Bird.

A window overlooked the bench, and he was presently aware that a slender bit of a girl was gazing down on him with serious blue eyes and smiling warm red lips; a fresh color the mountain wind had blown there was in her soft round cheeks, which held a dimple that came and went tantalizingly, and her hair curled in golden disarray about her pretty face. Johnny stared up at her through a mist compounded of soap and water.

"My eyes are chuck-full of suds, but I can see good enough to know you're the sweetest thing that ever was, Mollie,—honest you are!" he said.

The girl laughed, disclosing a row of white even teeth.

"Well, will you just get on to them dimples!" cried Johnny.

"Now, Johnny,—honest?"

"Honest, what?"

"The sweetest thing——"

"Wish I may die if you ain't!" said Johnny fervently.

He made great haste with the towel, then he stepped close to the window. His mop of black curls was raised toward the yellow head, there was a soft sound and Mr. Severance seemed greatly cheered and refreshed by something.

"Mollie, you got the sweetest lips to kiss,—honest you have," he said.

The girl laughed shyly.

"You always say that."

"You want I should aways tell you the truth, don't you?" he demanded, his arm about her shoulders.

"Can't you say something different?" asked Mollie, puckering her brows and then dimpling at him.

"What's the use of trying? You bet you I don't want to think no different," and Johnny looked at her with adoring eyes, their faces very close together. Finally he released her. "Any news, Mollie?" he asked.

"The gentleman that's bought the Pay Streak over at Alvarado was here for lunch. He come in a big touring-car with his wife and baby, and its nurse. They seemed awful nice people, Johnny."

"I wish I had his bank roll. They say he's a millionaire all right," said Johnny.

"Mollie!" a voice called from within, and Mollie said hastily as she turned away:

"Supper's on the table; you can come in when you get ready."

M. Ferguson was another Mollie, the younger Mollie's aunt. Years before while Sunset was still a prosperous mining camp, she had come West to make her home with her brother and to take charge of his motherless child. The brother had died in that evil time when the bottom was dropping out of Sunset. She had given the best years of her life to her niece; singlehanded she had fought a long fight with adverse circumstances and had won a modest victory. Now one can not live an utterly self-sacrificing life to no purpose, so Miss Mollie had a certain sweet dignity that came of much goodness, and a soul at peace with itself.

The Mountain House was a part of the niece's heritage. It was kept alive by chance tourists. Johnny was the regular, the star boarder, and frequently the only one, and at all times so much at home that he usually wiped the supper dishes. Mollie washed them. Johnny was the trusted man up at the Red Bird, the very right hand of a soulless corporation whose only symptoms of life were in its feet and even they were undeniably cold. He pulled down seventy dollars a month just as easy! With all this wealth pouring in upon him every thirty days, with money saved, too, and Mollie flitting in and out of those big bare rooms at the Mountain House, why, no wonder he was intent on matrimony!

That night after the dishes had been duly washed and as duly dried in the intervals between sundry breathless moments when Johnny's black curls and Mollie's golden head were very close together, they strolled out upon what had once been Sunset's long main street, past the houses that still fronted it and up the trail toward the Red Bird.

Miss Mollie sat in the doorway of the Mountain House in the warm twilight and watched them as they went slowly forward arm in arm. They brought back the sentiment of youth, and she shared vicariously in its romance. Yet there was a heartache scarcely stilled in the realization that the imperceptible gradations of time had swept her away from the morning world in which youth dwells; that for her, beginning to be visible down the pathway of the years, were the silences—the solitudes that she must before long enter alone.

The twilight deepened. The last vestige of color faded from the sky. The white cap of Brown's Peak sank into the gloom, merged with the blue of the heavens and was lost to sight. There was a footfall on the path as a tall shadow detached itself from the night, and Mr. Brown, with his dog Duffer at his heels, paused on the step. Seeing a woman in the doorway of the lighted office, he removed his hat.

"Evening," he said.

"Won't you step in?" asked Miss Mollie, slipping aside her chair which blocked the entrance. "I guess you're Mr. Brown Johnny was telling us about at supper?" she added.

"Yes, ma'am." Mr. Brown looked severe and even purposeful, but his voice held a shy deferential note.

"He's not used to women," thought Miss Mollie.

From under the flapping brim of his hat Brown stole a covert glance in her direction. She was very good to look at, he decided, with her soft brown hair drawn smoothly back from her comely face, and her dark eyes that held just the hint of a sorrow lightly borne.

Subsequently he negotiated for one meal a day at the Mountain House. He elected that this meal should be supper, because he would then have the moral support of Mr. Severance's presence.

When he had tested it he found that Sunset yielded a superior article of peace. Save for Johnny, who passed his cabin twice a day, he was undisturbed. Usually it was Johnny's morning song that brought him awake, —Johnny on his way toward the gaping hole at the timber line with Mollie's farewell kiss sweet upon his lips. Yet Mr. Brown did not succumb to the charms of Sunset without a struggle. He told Duffer each morning:

"I guess we'll pull out of here to-morrow, old sport!"

But the to-morrows became a respectable division of time, and presently as a concession to some inherent love of accuracy Mr. Brown changed his formula.

"I guess we'll be leaving here along about day after to-morrow!"

But the days after to-morrow went to join the to-morrows, and Brown still lingered in Sunset.

Into this Eden, like another serpent, came Mr. Bunny, his hair slicked low across his forehead and tastefully roached back over one ear. He breathed an air of profound sophistication. Johnny and he met at the bench by the kitchen door where Mr. Bunny was bestowing certain deft touches to his toilet.

"Say, pardner, this million-dollar palace hotel seems to be mainly in the hands of the suffragettes, don't it?" he remarked.

Johnny surveyed him without favor.

"Huh!" he said, and scooped up a basin of water from the barrel. Mr. Bunny, not easily discouraged, waited.

"What's your name, pardner?" he presently asked.

"Severance," said Johnny shortly.

"Say, I knowed a fellow of that name in the Klondike,—I'm a liar if I didn't. He was a card-player. We was awful intimate—"

"Huh!" said Johnny again. He was not impressed with Mr. Bunny nor Mr. Bunny's friend.

Mollie appeared at the window, but catching sight of Mr. Bunny she vanished into the inner regions of the Mountain House.

"Mama! mama!—what was that?" cried Mr. Bunny softly, in admiration.

"Look here!" said Johnny, wheeling on him. "You cut that out!"

"It's the climate, pardner. These here high altitudes braces a man up most amazin'——"

"The climate's all right, but you can get just as rank here as anywhere else," warned Johnny. Mr. Bunny gave him a sidelong glance. Johnny completed his toilet in silence.

"Going in to supper now, Mr. Severance?" asked Mr. Bunny affably.

Johnny nodded, led the way around the building, in through the office, and on into the diningroom where sat Miss Mollie, inoffensive Mr. Brown and Mollie at supper. He presented Mr. Bunny with no little formality.

Mr. Bunny's company manners immediately developed one striking merit. They seemed to afford their fortunate possessor the greatest possible satisfaction and confidence. Also when you tapped Mr. Bunny you tapped an unfailing spring. Moreover he had a generous and withal a thoughtful nature, had Mr. Bunny, especially *was it* thoughtful.

"Miss Ferguson will try them pickles, Mr. Severance. Just chase the butter down this way, Mr. Brown,—Miss Mollie's aimin' her eye at it. Mr. Severance, 'low me to shoot a slice of bread on to your plate..." This and much more of a similar character in the interval of agreeable and easy conversation, the burden of which Mr. Bunny lightly sustained. And while he talked, his small wicked eyes, close-set under their low brows and of an indeterminable color, slid around in a furtive circle. They took in everything, but they came back and back to Mollie.

"Say, Denver, Albuquerque, Dawson, 'Frisco,—I've seen 'em all; and say, I've seen a lot of life, too,—and me only twenty-five. How many fellows do you reckon have been about as much as me? But I'm giving it to you straight when I say it's good to hit a place like this where you feel at home, and where you can wash out of a tin basin at the back door like you done at mother's!"

Johnny listened abashed to Mr. Bunny's easy flow of words. It might have occurred to him that this fascinating stranger never spoke of anybody but himself; that his own moods, emotions, ambitions, thoughts so called, occupied him entirely and to the exclusion of all else, for he moved in a world of men rock walled by his own towering egotism. It was wasted labor to try to change the drift of the conversation. Whatever was said instantly reminded Mr. Bunny of himself. At the most, one merely opened up fresh and inviting fields for him to enter and claim his place in the foreground.

After supper he cornered quiet Mr. Brown in the office. That gentleman's bad eye had attracted his attention, and he seized the first opportunity to ask Brown how he came by that scar, thus artfully framing a question that covered the eye as well.

"Knife slipped while I was picking my teeth," said Brown, regarding him malevolently.

"Say, I thought you might have bit yourself accidental," responded Mr. Bunny.

In the kitchen Johnny was talking earnestly with Mollie, as they washed and dried the supper dishes.

"Don't you have nothing to do with that fellow, Mollie——"

"Why, Johnny?"

"Well, mainly because he's no good. He's the rankest proposition I even stacked up' against, and I've seen 'em as rank as they make 'em."

Mollie puckered her brows thoughtfully. She was fond of Johnny and they were engaged, but all the same she had the very human quality of disliking orders, and Johnny's voice smacked of command.

"I thought he was entertaining, and that he had nice table manners," she said.

"Well, I didn't notice 'em if he had. I hate these smart geezers!"

"He was awful polite, Johnny." She wished Johnny to be fair to the stranger; at the same time she felt affronted by his foolish jealousy.

"Fresh," said Johnny, "if you call that being polite."

No more was said then, but somehow when they walked up the trail there was this between them, and they walked farther apart than usual. They were silent, too, a good deal of the time. Moreover it was a short walk; but before they reached the hotel Johnny had returned to the vexed subject of Mr. Bunny and the treatment Mollie was to accord him.

"Mollie, you are not going to talk to that fellow any more, are you?"

"Certainly I shall talk to him. I am not going to be impolite just because you are," rejoined Mollie, with a little toss of her head.

Johnny flushed hotly, then the color faded from his face.

"All right then, if you'd rather talk to him than me, you can, but I won't be here to listen to it—I can tell you that!"

They had reached the door by this time, and Mollie, holding her chin very high, said coldly:

"Good night, Mr. Severance,—I think I must go in. Thank you for your company."

Johnny gasped, then he said politely:

"Good night, Miss Ferguson," and turned away, while Mollie went up to her room with burning cheeks and smarting eyes.

But it was not until she was safe in bed that she shed a few surreptitious tears.

"He might have known… that I care more for his little finger—than for all the Mr. Bunnys in the world!" she whispered tremulously to herself under cover of the friendly darkness.

Mr. Bunny, for reasons of his own, remained in Sunset. He discovered that M. Ferguson desired to introduce water on her premises. She designed to have flowers, a kitchen garden and grass. This involved a half-mile of ditch. He let it be known that for a proper consideration he might be induced to betake himself to ditching, though he also let it be known that this was a pursuit he should never look back upon with any feeling even remotely approaching pride. He further gave M. Ferguson to understand that he had recently lifted a mortgage on his widowed mother's quarter-section back in Nebraska. This had taken his last cent. He drove a much better bargain in consequence, did artless Mr. Bunny.

To Johnny he had already explained that he had impoverished himself in Albuquerque; his attentions to a handsome brunette having been the immediate cause of his financial undoing. Later she had proved unworthy of his generosity. He was hitting the high places now mainly because of the throw-down she had given him. He indicated that this throw-down had been cruel and perfidious beyond words. Brown had heard the same story from Mr. Bunny's own authentic lips, but in his case Mr. Bunny had added:

"Say, I put my coin on the black. You watch me make my next play on the red. That ought to fetch a change of luck."

Then one morning Johnny's song failed to rouse Mr. Brown, but its very absence at the accustomed hour brought him wide awake. He heard Johnny's step on the path, and looking from his window saw Johnny go by, his curly head bowed and his shoulders rounded.

Mr. Brown sat in his cabin door and considered the situation over his morning pipe. Subsequently he sought out Mr. Bunny, peacefully ditching, gun on hip. Not that Mr. Bunny was actually ditching; truth compels the statement that he was seated on a flat rock with his spade within easy reach. Mr. Brown addressed the ditcher:

"Ain't you finding this a mighty sedentary job?" he asked.

"Shucks! I've made big money in my time,—ten a day in the Klondike tending bar——"

"What you getting here?"

"A dollar fifty, and my board," said Mr. Bunny sheepishly.

"Why, she's doing you—ain't she?" cried Brown. "Robbing you right along! No wonder you're warming them rocks. A dollar fifty to a high-priced man like you hardly pays for the trouble of drawing your wages!"

Mr. Bunny looked off, got up, dug his spade disconsolately into the bank, threw a couple of shovelfuls from him with disdain; and sat down once more. Brown regarded him earnestly.

"And your mother back in Nebraska on that quarter-section, like I heard you tellin' Miss Ferguson at supper last night, looking anxious to you to remit… and that handsome brunette down in Albuquerque that cost you such a pot of money…. Say, Mr. Bunny, you got to do some mighty close figurin', ain't you, to make both ends meet?"

"Just between ourselves, Brown, you can cut out the mother,—but I was giving it to you straight about the other."

"Well, I see you got all the feelings of a high-priced man; it naturally fusses you to think how Miss Ferguson's taken advantage of you. Dollar fifty,—why, that ain't whisky money for an ambitious fellow like you."

"You're right, it ain't," said Mr. Bunny, shaking his head ominously. "I'm going to pull out of here soon. Say, Brown,—" he continued confidentially, "I could take her away from him—" and he nodded in the direction of the Mountain House. Mr. Brown understood he was referring to Mollie now. "Just as easy as nothing. All I got to do is just to crook my finger at her,— see?" said Mr. Bunny. "But pshaw! I don't marry. They none of 'em ketch me. I'll have my fun with a fair-looker, spend my money on her, but there ain't an ounce of matrimony in my system." And into Brown's ears he poured a tale of triumphant sin, giving Mr. Brown to understand that he, Bunny, was a bee among the flowers.

Brown was viewing the gun on Bunny's manly hip with a wistful eye. It had been years since he had renounced such vanities. Bunny leaned over to pick up a stone.

"Say,—what in blazes you up to?" he cried, for Brown had deftly slipped the gun from its holster. He fell back a step and gave Bunny the benefit of his good eye. Mr. Bunny was instantly conscious of a cold feeling at the pit of his stomach. "Say, you give me back my gun!" And he began to bluster.

"Forget it!" said Mr. Brown softly. "If a man took that trail and kept moving, he'd be in Alvarado by to-morrow night——"

"Give me back my gun, Mr. Brown——"

"I never did believe in these here private irrigation projects," said Brown. "And I don't believe you're the man to put this one through." He drew back the hammer of the gun.

"Say—it's loaded, Mr. Brown—" cried Bunny. "Look out!"

"Of course it's loaded. I wouldn't insult you by thinking you packed an empty gun. You keep moving at a reasonable rate of speed and you can be counting the lamp-posts in Alvarado tomorrow night,—seven on Main Street, and four on Prairie Avenue. You're wasting your time here…. No,—you don't need to go down to the Mountain House—you can start here!"

"Say, she's owing me money, Mr. Brown. A man wants what lie's earned, don't he?" said Bunny meekly, but disposed to raise an issue.

"Of course he does,—but he don't want what he ain't earned." Brown looked at him with weary petulance. "Ain't you open to a hunch?" The muzzle of the gun menaced Bunny, who fell back a step in consternation, ducked, turned and fled shamelessly.

Brown returned to his cabin feeling that he had permanently eliminated the fascinating Mr. Bunny, and evidences of a certain austere pleasure radiated from his damaged features. But though the hour arrived when Johnny Severance should have come striding down the path from the Red Bird, head thrown back and shoulders squared as he swung his cap and dinner pail, it brought no Johnny; and Brown, disturbed and wondering, set out alone for the straggle of buildings on the bench.

He found two anxious-faced women at the Mountain House; the eyes of each were red from much weeping, and he surmised that there had been a crisis—that his well-intentioned interference had been too long delayed—and he suffered a moment of intense humiliation. He had figured creditably in more than one strenuous human drama, but never before had he to reproach himself with being dilatory. It gave him a unique sensation.

Supper was eaten in dreary silence. At first Miss Mollie had attempted to talk to her guest, but her voice was forced and unnatural and now and again trailed off into what sounded very like a sob, while Mollie's big blue eyes were misted lakes of sorrow. In the presence of their grief Brown was stricken into speechless shyness. He felt that the feminine soul was a curious and an awesome thing; he stood close to it with trepidation. But he did not lack a certain deep integrity,—he would see this thing through to a finish.

After supper he hung around the office, where presently Miss Mollie joined him. He sensed it that his hostess was only anxious to have him go, yet he lingered, perturbed and ill at ease. At last he cleared his throat.

"I don't see nothing of Mr. Severance," he remarked with diffidence, as one who had encroached on a forbidden subject.

The tears swiftly gathered in Miss Mollie's soft brown eyes.

"I'm afraid he's gone," she said.

There was a pause. Brown followed a crack in the floor from the desk to the wall opposite and back again with his embarrassed glance.

"Anything happened?" he at length asked, and the very bluntness of his query threw him into a state of intense and painful confusion, but he gripped himself hard and went on. "She"—he jerked his thumb in the direction of the diningroom where Mollie could be heard clearing away the supper dishes —"she's feeling pretty bad," he hazarded, and once more was stricken dumb.

"Yes, she's feeling awful bad, Mr. Brown. Johnny's gone. He sent down word—a good-by—from the Red Bird this afternoon, and said he was going."

Brown considered.

"He should be fetched back," he presently observed with conviction.

"Where is Mr. Bunny?" asked Miss Mollie, and her tone betrayed anxiety.

Brown flushed under his sunburn.

"He's left Sunset. He went sudden."

"Did they—did he and Johnny meet?—was there trouble?" began Miss Mollie.

"No, ma'am. Bunny had his reasons for going. They looked good to him and nothing was holding him, so he just went. I seen him when he went. It looked like it come over him all at once that he had ought to go," explained Mr. Brown considerately and at length.

"I am so glad! I was afraid that perhaps they had met."

"Where's Johnny gone?" inquired Brown.

"We think to Alvarado."

Mollie had appeared in the dining-room doorway and was listening, but Brown's back was turned toward her.

"What's to hinder my going there after him?" asked Brown. "I can produce an argument he'll listen to." Unconsciously his hand rested on Mr. Bunny's gun.

"It's awful kind of you to suggest it, but perhaps you shouldn't go; it may make trouble for you," said Miss Mollie. It was the habit of a lifetime with her to think of others.

"You're a good kind man!" cried Mollie fervently through her tears, advancing. "You tell him that I just hate and despise that Bunny.... I didn't mean anything I said.... I'm sorry—sorry!" She seized one of his hands in both of hers. "Oh, he must come back!—tell him to come back, Mr. Brown ——"

"I'm aimin' to tell him just that,—and he'll come back all right," Brown assured her.

"Do you think he will?—do you... do you?"

"I was never surer of anything in my life."

Mollie relinquished his hand, and throwing her arms about his neck, kissed him. An instant later and she had buried her face on his shoulder and was sobbing aloud.

Mr. Brown's unhandsome face flushed scarlet. Never in all his varied experience had he known anything like this. Then his face grew white, and he shook as he had never shaken in the presence of danger, violence, or the risk of sudden death.

Johnny Severance had quitted the Red Bird and turned his face in the direction of Alvarado. Two years of perfect happiness had vanished in the cataclysm that had overwhelmed him and Mollie.

A sudden mist swam before his eyes. Well, she hadn't treated him right, but he hoped she would find peace,—he was man enough to wish no less. He must shape his own future out of the wreck she had made; though this didn't matter greatly, since he was sure life held nothing for him,—indeed, he rather gloated in the thought of an existence, bleak, purposeless and incomparably lonely,—and again the mist seemed to burn his very eyeballs, while it sent the gray valley and the line of purple peaks deep into the distance.

He kept the trail for Alvarado all that day and at nightfall went into camp. Necessity now drove him to the lunch he had brought away from the Red Bird. He choked over each mouthful, for Mollie's small deft hands had been busy here. He reflected bitterly that never again was this to be.

"It'll be up to some chuck-house cook to fill my dinner pail!" he murmured sadly. With the final mouthful he felt that he had destroyed the last link that bound him to the past.

Morning found him sorely tempted to pocket his pride and go back,—back to Mollie, his pumps at the Red Bird and the Mountain House; but he sternly repressed this ignoble weakness. No, sir! She had cast him off. Yet he sat a long time with his head bowed in his hands and watched the light flood the valley. Then again he took the trail. His steps lagged. Not that he was tired, but the cataclysm was somehow seeming less complete than it had seemed the day before.

He went forward, steadily resolute, with his chin sunk on his breast and his glance lowered. Suddenly he became aware that some one was coming along the trail toward him and looked to find himself face to face with Mr. Bunny. There was a strained moment, then Bunny, eying him askance, put out his hand.

44

"Why, how are you, pardner?" he said. Johnny ignored the hand. "Say, what's your grouch?" inquired Mr. Bunny in a tone of affected astonishment. Johnny gave him a look of scorn. "Oh, that,—well, see here, Mr. Severance, I ain't no plaster saint, but say, I'm on the level. Yes, sir,—I didn't interfere none between you and your girl——"

"Who said you did?" demanded Johnny, angry with himself for allowing such a thought to gain a place in Mr. Bunny's mind.

"Then why don't you shake hands?"

"I'm willing enough to shake hands," responded Johnny sourly.

"You didn't look like you was," said Bunny. There was a moment's silence. Mr. Bunny's original idea had been that Johnny had followed him with sinister intent; since this was evidently not the case, what was he doing here? While he was debating this point, a somewhat similar problem was occupying Johnny. He had supposed Bunny still at Sunset. "It's mighty agreeable to meet old friends, ain't it, Mr. Severance? You going on to Alvarado?"

Johnny signified that this was not unlikely.

"Say, when did you leave Sunset, pardner?" continued Bunny.

"Yesterday," said Johnny briefly.

"Say, if we'd knowed what was in each other's minds we might have come away together," observed Bunny.

"You going on to Alvarado?" inquired Johnny.

"Not immediate," said Bunny hastily. "Yesterday I run into a old friend who's been doing a bit of prospecting. He's pulled down a grubstake. Say, I'm considering a proposition he's made me. He's back yonder a spell." And Bunny nodded indefinitely.

"Well, so long!" said Johnny.

"So long, pardner," responded Bunny. They shook hands and separated.

Mr. Bunny passed back along the trail and was presently lost to sight behind a gray fold of the hills. Johnny found a convenient boulder and sat down to consider this meeting from every point of view.

"I reckon he lied about that grub-stake,—I reckon he's going back to Sunset!" was his definite conclusion. "Honest, he's the most ambitious liar I ever listened to!"

He quitted his boulder and went forward, but very slowly now. Memories of Sunset, memories of Mollie, were tugging at his heart-strings. All at once, breaking in upon the silence in which he moved, he heard his name called, and turning, was again gladdened by the sight of Mr. Bunny, who was coming along the trail at a brisk run.

"Say, pardner," he panted, when he had gained a place at Johnny's side, "would you be willing to help a fellow creature in distress? Oh, not me,—a fellow named Graham; a intimate friend of mine, and a fellow in the hardest sort of luck. It'd make a wooden Indian shed tears to hear his hard-luck story; and he's met with a accident. Say, you're a western man,—I reckon you wouldn't turn your back on no fellow being in real eighteen-carat distress the way Bob Graham is!"

"What's the matter of him?" asked Johnny, with a striking lack of interest.

"One thing, he's got a hurt leg; spraint it on these here rocks and he's sufferin' something awful. But what he's sufferin' in his spraint leg ain't a circumstance to what he's sufferin' in his mind. You bet you, that's what gets a fellow every time! I know, 'cause I know what I went through with when that brunette throwed me down in Albuquerque after getting all my coin. I don't pose as no blighted being, but say, it was agony—yes, sir, agony!"

"Is this the fellow you were telling me about first? Look here, Bunny, you began pleasant enough with a grub-stake, and now I'm hearing all about a spraint leg," said Johnny.

"Well, what's to keep a man from having a grub-stake and a spraint leg simultaneous? You come with me, and I'll show you Bob Graham who's got both."

"Huh!" said Johnny.

"I can't tell you all Bob's story, but there's a woman into it, his wife,—yes, sir. Say, talk about throw-downs! Why, he's got yours and mine beat to a pulp. Ain't it tough the way women do?—how they show you the high places and then give you the laugh? Say, Mr. Severance, there was reasons why I couldn't give it to you straight about Bob without consulting him. If you feel afraid of anything——"

"What of?" demanded Johnny quickly.

"Durned if I know, but some people are timider than others," said Bunny, with an oblique glance.

"You show me this friend of yours," said Johnny.

Mr. Bunny led the way back down the trail to the point where Johnny had previously seen him disappear. They climbed a hill and entered a small bottom. Here, prone on his back and gazing peacefully up at the hot sky, was a gentleman of singularly unprepossessing exterior. When aware that his solitude was being invaded he uttered sundry heartrending groans and fell to nursing his right leg, which was elaborately bandaged in strips torn from a blanket.

"Sh—" said Bunny, over his shoulder to Johnny. "Sh—ain't it pitiful?"

The groans were continued with increasing vigor.

"Bob!" whispered Mr. Bunny. "Bob,—old pardner!"

"Is that you, Bunny? I reckon I must have fell asleep," said the sufferer weakly.

"Say, Bob, I want you should shake hands with Mr. Severance."

Bob raised himself with apparent difficulty on one elbow, and extended his hand.

"How are you, Bob?" continued Mr. Bunny with anxious solicitude. "But I can see it's painin' you something awful!"

"Folks, I've spraint my leg,—mebby she's broke—" and Bob groaned.

"You want a doctor—" said Johnny. Mr. Bunny and the sufferer exchanged significant glances.

"Folks, it ain't my leg that's hurtin' me most,—it's here—" and Bob rested his hand on the bosom of his shirt.

"Stomach?" said Johnny innocently.

"Sh,—heart!" said Bunny quickly.

"My feelin's are raisin' hell inside of me. This spraint leg ain't nothin'." But Mr. Graham groaned lustily. "Mebby if you two was to help me, I could manage to hobble to my shack…. No, stranger"—to Johnny, as they set out —"I don't want no doctor. He might set my leg, but he couldn't cure me. Folks, I'm hard hit where no pills can ever get to."

They helped him back into the hills, but had Johnny been a little less disposed to confidence he might have doubted the integrity of that sprained leg, for Bob had a curious way of forgetting and then suddenly remembering it with many groans. If Johnny noticed this at all it only went to prove Mr. Bunny's statement that the mind of man was capable of furnishing a very superior article of suffering.

Mr. Graham's retreat was a shack set down in a grove of young pines. As far as Johnny could see, his grub-stake seemed to be in a convenient liquid form.

"Put the bottle down beside me, Bunny, where I'll have it handy," said Bob, when they had helped him to his bed on the floor in a corner of the room.

"He needs a stimulant," explained fluent Mr. Bunny. "When you're sufferin' like Bob is, you got to take a stimulant."

"Folks, I've knocked around a heap," said Bob. "I've drunk whatever can be got through the bung-hole of a barrel or out of the neck of a bottle; but when a man's really sufferin', whisky's got all the other souse skinned a mile!"

"What did I tell you?" asked Bunny of Johnny, with a glance of commiseration.

"Besides, I don't have no doctor from Alvarado,—my enemy's got the everlasting drop on me, that's why! If my leg's spraint she can stay spraint—if she's broke she can stay broke!" added Bob with resolute stoicism.

"You certainly talk like a man, Bob!" said Bunny admiringly.

"If I could only jest see my child—" said Bob, and passed the back of his hand before his eyes.

"It's them domestic feelin's that's hurtin' him so," whispered Bunny to Johnny. Aloud he said: "I'm in favor of tellin' Mr. Severance just how you stand, Bob,—why you can't have no doctor."

"Kin you vouch for Mr. Severance?"

"Of course I can vouch for him. Ain't I told you he was a hundred per cent, all right?" cried Bunny warmly. He fixed Johnny with his shifty glance and went on.

"When I first knowed Bob it was in Ogden. He was a residin' snug and makin' a good livin', ownin' a saloon. There was no business man there thought higher of. He had a nice trade and plenty of friends because he was always aimin' to please. He was a married man, was Bob, and had a wife and kid.... Say, when you know what a woman can do to a man! You bet you if I get many more throw-downs like I got in Albuquerque I'm going to cut 'em out! Well, Bob had the happiest home you about ever see. He owned a piano and a fast-steppin' buggy horse,—and talk about your family man! I often says to him, I says, 'Say, Bob, this looks awful good to me and I don't know but you are to be envied, yet it comes over me, ain't a man takin' long chances when he centers all his happiness on a woman like this?' I says, 'Say, it's mighty nice to set here in your parlor and listen to Mrs. Bob hit the hurdy-gurdy, but,' I says, 'are you sure of her?—as sure of her as you are of yourself?'

"Say, I must have had a hunch,—for along comes a Boston man. Say, she was fascinated! Here was steady-goin' old Bob doin' a nice business and never dreamin' that a spider was gettin' ready to drop into his sirup! Well, one day Mrs. Bob and the kid were missin'. Next Bob heard she was up at that stylish place in Nevada where the divorces come from. Bob just sacrificed everything. He wanted his boy back. He was willin' to pass the mother up if she felt like that, but he wanted the boy. Well, say, he followed 'em from place to place, and finally the Boston man come here and bought the Pay Streak over at Alvarado. Bob followed 'em, but the Boston man had the sheriff fixed. He showed Bob the outside of the town—that's what he done!"

Johnny had heard of the Boston man and the purchase of the Pay Streak. He permitted his glance to stray in Bob's direction. He had not liked Mr. Graham's looks from the first, and he was liking them even less as time went on.

"I don't care a cuss for nothin' but the boy," said Bob the business man. "She can stick to her millionaire,—she's throwed me down,—but I want to see the boy just once and kiss him on his little lips, and say good-by and get out. Folks, I know when I been hit by the trolley."

"Ain't it pitiful?—and him with his spraint leg?" murmured Mr. Bunny. "Just wantin' to say good-by to his kid before he fans it on out of here."

"It ain't much to ask," said Bob gloomily. "And yet I dunno as I shall ever see him again, or hear his sweet little voice call me daddy like he done in Ogden. I reckon they've learnt him to call the Boston man that afore this."

"Ain't that heart-breakin' for you?" cried Mr. Bunny.

"If he could just be fetched out here so I could kiss him good-by, I'd feel a heap better, folks. But I dassant go into Alvarado. And you don't go there either—they'd spot you for my friend."

"Ain't that a frame-up for you, pardner?" Bunny appealed to Johnny. "And yet nothing could be easier according to what Bob's told me than to fetch the kid out here. His nurse trundles him to the Pay Streak every morning in his little buggy when his imitation daddy goes up there,—see? And she trundles him back alone,—it's a good mile.—Say, Bob, I wished I could help you!"

"I only wants to kiss him just once or mebby twict," said Bob mournfully.

A brief pause ensued. Johnny moved uneasily in his seat. He felt curiously committed to Mr. Bunny and his afflicted friend. For some reason, which he obscurely sensed, it was apparently up to him to produce the child for that farewell kiss on which Mr. Graham's happiness seemed so largely to depend.

"I hate to see a western man downed!" resumed Bunny. "Say, Mr. Severance, when I met Bob last night I told him about you—I'm a liar if I didn't!—I says to Bob, I says, 'Say, Bob, we don't want no yearlin's in this.' I says, 'There's a fellow back yonder I'd give a heap to have with us.' I wouldn't insult you by offerin' money for the job!" concluded Bunny with generous enthusiasm.

"No," said Johnny hastily. "I ain't lookin' to earn no money that way." He appeared entirely credulous, since he felt it to be his best protection, but he was deeply regretting the alacrity with which he had followed Mr. Bunny.

"There weren't many husbands like Bob here,—that gentle and considerate and always aimin' to please. Say, pardner, you take it straight from me,—it ain't the man any more, it's the bank roll the dolls are after! That Boston man was a ingrate,—I told you so, Bob,—you remember?—I says, 'Bob, he acts white on the surface, but he's a ingrate all the same!—and I hate a ingrate!' Say, I suppose it's because I'm a conservative."

After tying himself up in this verbal knot, Bunny heaved a sigh.

Johnny glanced about him. He was meditating flight. The ideal parent had sniffed audibly at Bunny's moving peroration.

"Sh—" said Bunny softly. "Ain't it rank, the affection a man feels for his own child?—how it kin make him suffer and suffer?"

Certain sounds issued from Bob's vexed interior which were supposed to be indicative of the anguish of soul that shook him.

"Say, Bob," said Bunny, "I'm in favor of lettin' Mr. Severance in on this with us. I got a heap of confidence in him,—and if it's agreeable to you I'm willin' he should fetch your child out here. We'll fix it this way: He'll be on the watch when the nurse and the Boston man takes the kid up to the Pay Streak, like you say they do every mornin',—see?—he'll wait until she gets half-way back to Alvarado, then he meets her strollin' casual along like he was goin' up to the mine. He snatches the kid out of his little buggy and skips with him, does Mr. Severance. I'll be hid back in the hills a ways and when he gets to me I'll take the kid off his hands—see?"

But Johnny did not see. He suddenly placed his veto on this ingenious scheme.

"What!" cried Mr. Bunny in hurt astonishment. "You mean you ain't with us, pardner?—after we've took you into our confidence like this... and you a western man?"

"No," said Johnny. "I never had no luck in pickin' up strange babies. Seems there's something in the way I take hold of 'em that makes 'em holler."

"And say, you call yourself a western man?" said Bunny in a tone midway between pity and contempt.

"I'm awful sorry,—honest! He's been treated tough all right." And Johnny glanced inquiringly at Bob.

"And you don't put out your hand to help a fellow creature up who's down?" demanded Bunny. "Here you go wormin' your way into other folk's confidence and then you give 'em the laugh,—you're a peach of a fellow!" The glance of his shifty eyes became suddenly wicked and vindictive. "Say, you'd ought to be beat up some,—a reptile like you!"

"I'm in favor of givin' Mr. Severance another chance to show there's good stuff in him, Bunny," said Bob. "I'm in favor of offerin' him money for the job. What's a few dollars to come between a parent and his love for his child?"

"What's your price, pardner?" asked Bunny.

"No," said Johnny. "If I seen a way open to help Mr. Graham I wouldn't want money for doin' him a good turn,—honest I wouldn't." He quitted his seat.

"Say, you set still!" warned Bunny menacingly. "We ain't through with you. We've took your measure, and your dimensions don't suit!"

Johnny was unarmed, while Mr. Bunny wore a gun on his hip, a spare weapon he had borrowed from Graham to replace the one of which Brown had despoiled him. He half drew it, then, changing his mind, he snatched up a stick of fire-wood. Johnny backed hastily into a corner.

"Shoot his feet out from under him, Bunny!" advised Bob.

"I use a stick on snakes!" Bunny heaved up his club.

But just here a notable interruption occurred. The door of the shack yielded to a man's hand, and swunk back plainly disclosing Brown's gaunt figure.

Bob, in the exigencies of the moment, forgetting his sprained leg, sprang to his feet, while Bunny dropped his stick and reached for his gun. Indeed, the motion being made nimbly, his fingers even touched it. They did no more. There was a shot and he emitted a howl of anguish. Simultaneously with Bunny, Bob had reached for his weapon with confidence and speed, for in certain select circles he enjoyed something of a reputation as a gun-fighter; but he was no more fortunate than his friend. He was quick, but Brown was quicker. His hand traveled with the speed of light. Apparently he had no use for sights. He pointed his gun as casually as a man points his finger at an object and with the same instinctive accuracy. In this particular instance Bob was the object.

"You travel!" said Brown to Johnny, who backed from the shack. Brown lingered to say a few fervent words. When he was gone, Bunny glanced at Bob, who was cursing while he nursed a shattered wrist; he himself was shot in the shoulder.

"Say, it was a man named Brown—" said he weakly.

Johnny and his rescuer moved rapidly off in the direction of the trail.

"It was awful unexpected the way you showed up," said Johnny. He glanced at Brown, dazed and wondering. "Why, I didn't think you were within thirty miles of here... you've got the full use of your two hands! You've been considerable of a man in your day,—and I wouldn't recommend no one to fool with your remains——"

"Was you hunting trouble, Johnny? I seen that fellow with the tied-up leg sentenced two years ago for a hold-up he'd pulled off in Alvarado. Incidental I'd like to ask you did you believe what they told you about his wife and child? They were aimin' to use you in a kidnaping scheme. Young man, they say a fool's born every minute. I reckon you arrived punctual on the clock tick all right."

"You don't think I believed 'em, Mr. Brown—honest?" protested Johnny.

"They weren't taking chances—they were willin' to pass them along to you. It looked like you'd feed right out of their hands, sonny!"

"I couldn't see no other way out of it. Where are we going now, Mr. Brown?"

"To Sunset."

"I can't go back there,—honest, I can't!"

"Why not?"

"Well,—just because I can't. She—Mollie—" began Johnny doggedly, and paused abruptly.

"Naturally she's feeling some annoyed the way you've acted, but if you go back humble... Look here,—you don't know the first thing about a woman's love. It don't go by merit. Just look at a woman,—take her as a mother,—it's a boy, or a girl, or it's twins,—and she's there with her love. She never makes a kick, not she! That boy, or that girl, or them twins, suit her apparently down to the ground. It's pretty much the same when it's a case of man. You come along and you're what she loves; not because you're any good—which you ain't—but you're what life's offerin' her and it's up to her to make the best of her chances. Does she notice any rake-off when she sizes you up? Nope, she don't. It's her nature to make mistakes and have poor judgment. She just loves you because you happen to be you. That there's a sixty dollar a month limit to the game you'll play, don't bother her none, for she's got a heap more courage than sense; she takes her fightin' chance. She's ready to believe in the luck you'll never taste, and through it all think you're a good man but unfortunate."

"I wonder feeling that way about women, you ain't never married," said Johnny.

"I respect 'em too highly. But if I ever had any idea of that kind, I wouldn't be like you, young man! I'd never go further than the Mountain House,—M. Ferguson, Proprietor."

It was a week later. A crescent moon swung low in the heavens and lighted up the trail that led past Brown's cabin. Its faint radiance showed Johnny and his Mollie walking very close together, as was their wont, while they talked in ecstatic whispers in the intervals of tender silences that brought them dim night sounds from the valley below.

In their wake, but at a discreet distance, for youth was having its right of way upon the mountainside, came Miss Mollie and inoffensive Mr. Brown, with Duffer at their heels. Miss Mollie's unaccustomed hand rested lightly, shyly, on Brown's arm. She was scarcely trusting her happiness. Those solitudes she had once feared were to be shared with the man at her side, whom Johnny had not ceased to exalt as a singularly capable gentleman, and that quick—my!—one who undertook to keep engagements with him was likely to experience a terrible sense of being late. Miss Mollie was already realizing this. She moved as one in a dream. The heart of youth had quickened in her breast, the hard years were forgotten.

Why, the very mountain seemed to nod a benediction in the half light.

"You're a mighty good woman, Mollie," said Brown. He seemed to expand with an austere joy. "If there are any crowns in the next world you'll be wearin' one instead of the sunbonnet you've worn in this."

"You're a good man, too. Just look what you've done for those two children, Mr. Brown."

"Joseph—" corrected Mr. Brown gently, "or just Joe, when you get more used to the idea."

THE BLOOD OF HIS ANCESTORS

W HEN he told me his story, prefacing it with a scrap of philosophy, John Norton assured me it differed from that of scores of other men of his class but in one or two unimportant particulars. He gave it as his opinion that one need not necessarily be a genius to get ahead in this world; there are other qualities almost any man can cultivate which command opportunity, and in spite of the fact that he spoke with the authority of a rather conspicuous success, he disclaimed the possession of any special ability above the average.

To begin with, Norton had much of the cheerful ambition characteristic of the average American. He had been thoroughly drilled in the idea that the one thing needful, if one wished to get on, was industry,—given this, the results were as certain as that two and two make four.

He was a broad-shouldered young fellow, more than commonly prepossessing, with an utter absence of any ability for sharp practise; indeed, he was inclined to view his fellows with a gentle kindly confidence that proved costly until he learned caution, and even then he was not bitter, only a little hurt.

He came of honest stock and of people in comfortable circumstances, proud of their traditions and their respectability and rather regretful of the fortune old General Norton had somehow lost when he emigrated from Virginia to Ohio in 1814.

Perhaps John would not have felt called upon to make the plunge into business had his father kept his name off the notes of his neighbors; as a consequence of his indiscretions the broad acres he had inherited slipped away piecemeal.

John was the eldest of four boys and the first to leave home. At twenty he went East. He recognized that he would probably have a good many ups and downs before he finally got placed, and he was thankful his career was to be among strangers.

He was not much worried in the beginning over ways and means, for his father sent him money each week, and small as the sums were they gave him a pleasing sense of security. He soon discovered that merely to make a living can be a difficult problem; it also dawned upon him that he reached the solving of the problem in a roundabout fashion through a haze of uncertainty.

After his father's death, when it became necessary for him to make his own way unaided, he brought to the task a sad earnestness. He was, he felt, without business tact—indeed, the word business comprehended all of which he was most ignorant. He could never impress people with the importance of those benefits they would derive from thinking as he wished them to think, for he was never quite sure about the benefits. He could feel himself shrink and dwindle and grow limp, when what he needed was a convincing force. Still it continued part of his faith that there was some work he could do well, and that sooner or later he would have the opportunity to do it. He was a little shocked to find that there was no particular merit in being well-born and well-bred.

He was in rapid succession clerk, traveling salesman, bookkeeper, advertising solicitor and real-estate agent; he went from place to place hoping each time he made a change, that now he was nearer success.

Meanwhile his mother died, and the home had been sold to pay his father's debts. His brothers had scattered,—one was in California, a clerk in a store, another was a miner in Colorado, a third has gone to South America, while Tom, the youngest, was editor of a country newspaper in Texas.

At thirty John married, and wisely concluded that the day for experiments was past. The idea that he was to acquire riches he put resolutely aside; if he could make a decent living it was all he dared expect.

It remained for Mr. Thomas Haviland, of Bliss, Haviland and Company, to give him his opportunity. When he got with this concern, John felt the connection to be a really notable one. The position carried a salary of twenty dollars a week with a fortnight's vacation each summer on full pay. There was one drawback. The managing director had the reputation of being exacting and hard to please, with a disagreeable temper and variable moods, but John was fully prepared to make some sacrifices to obtain steady employment. He wanted to be thrifty and sensible. One of the first things he did was to have his life insured. This gave him a solid and substantial feeling, alike new and comfortable. Later, perhaps, he would be able to open a bank-account.

He was relieved to find he could do this work, about which he had had many misgivings, as well as there was any need for it to be done. He was fortunate in the start in escaping all personal contact with Haviland, or his satisfaction with himself and his lot might have been less pronounced. The managing director had a genius for taking the very marrow out of a man's bones and the hope out of his heart. On principle he never respected those in his employ. He would probably have explained his attitude by saying it was impossible to respect men who were content to earn beggarly salaries of from fifteen to thirty-five dollars a week. Even at these prices it must be owned he contrived to surround himself by an uncommonly low grade of business intelligence.

Perhaps he liked the contrast it offered to the vigorous grasp he always maintained on affairs.

The clerks carried on their work in fear and trembling, conscious that at any moment Haviland might come out of the private office, purplefaced and furious over a trifling blunder, to lash them with sarcasms that cut like a knife, —or even worse, some poor devil would be summoned into the private office to explain; an utterly hopeless proposition, as Haviland could not sit quietly through an explanation. He made mistakes himself, but he refused to recognize the right of others to do so; at least he would not listen to their excuses. He complained continually that the clerks wasted his time, which he valued at a fabulous figure, but he would spend half a morning criticizing the mental equipment of a shaking, underfed, five-dollar-a-week man, and then dismiss him as if he were the scum of the earth,—a mere thing.

John saw and heard a good deal that filled him with astonishment the first few weeks he spent in the office of Bliss, Haviland and Company, and he decided that Haviland was not a gentleman, and when he discussed his character with Alice at home of an evening he said a good many hard and bitter things, for they talked of him incessantly; he was the one topic in the homes of all the men in the office; he lowered the tone of their lives, and brought servility and fear into the lives of their wives and children. That John escaped insult, he attributed to luck; apparently there was no protection in the fact that he was earnest and conscientious. Gordon, the old bookkeeper, who had been with the firm forty years, was a model of industry and exactness, yet he was in hot water pretty much all the time when he was not in deep water and trembling for his position.

To be sure Haviland had his own disappointments and his nerves were on edge most of the time. He was greedy of gain, but more greedy of fame,—or the irresponsible notoriety which he mistook for fame, and which was perhaps sweeter to him than a responsible fame would have been with its obligations, and he hated the directors, who seemed in league to limit him to a conservative business with reasonable profits.

John, whose ancestors since the days of the Norman Conquest had taken a hand in almost every war in Anglo-Saxon history, resolved that if Haviland ever "went for him" as he did for the rest, he would let him have the ink-well or some similarly convenient missile, but he was more and more grateful as the days ran into weeks and the weeks into months, that nothing unpleasant occurred involving him.

He had been with Bliss, Haviland and Company almost a year when one afternoon, Gordon, the bookkeeper, came out of the private office a dull tallowy white, with blue-drawn lips. He stopped beside John's desk.

"Mr. Haviland wants to see you," he said. "You are to go in now,—right away."

As John turned to obey the summons he ran over uneasily all those matters that had gone wrong in his department and for which he could possibly be held responsible. As he raised his hand to knock on the door of the private office he decided that happen what might he could not afford to lose his temper. He reached this decision quickly, and when he heard Haviland call "Come in," pushed open the door. Haviland was seated at his desk, and the expression on his face was not reassuring.

"Oh! It's you, Norton; take a seat,—I want to speak to you."

John closed the door and at a sign from Haviland sat down in the chair at the managing director's elbow, which one of the clerks who retained a sense of humor had christened "The Mourners' Bench." Haviland swung round and faced him squarely.

"I shall have to send Gordon away," he said. "How would you like his place?"

John knew that the bookkeeper received twenty-five hundred dollars a year, and he drew in his breath quickly.

"You do your work well," Haviland continued graciously, without giving John a chance to reply. "I have never had occasion to find any fault with you; of course, you understand we shan't pay you what we are paying Gordon,— he has been with the house forty years. It's a very fine opening for a young man, Norton, and I am glad to be able to offer it to you. It will mean an advance of two hundred a year at once."

"I shouldn't like to feel I was taking Gordon's place—" John said.

The red line of Haviland's neck with its heavy veins swelled out over the top of his collar; there was a moment's silence, and then he said curtly: "You are not taking Gordon's place;—he is to stay on until the end of the month. That will give him ample time to look up another place."

"I doubt it," John retorted, unconsciously imitating his employer's tone and manner. "He's an old man, Mr. Haviland, and I don't think any one will care to make an opening for him." Haviland frowned.

"I should be sorry to believe that, Norton,—very sorry, indeed. I shall advise him to take a less responsible position—one more suited to his years," expanding cheerfully, as though his advice would be of incalculable value to Gordon. "Will you take the place?"

Norton hesitated. It would have pleased him to tell Haviland just what he thought of him, but he remembered Alice and said, "Yes," instead, adding grudgingly, "I shall be glad to accept it."

"At twelve hundred a year?"

"Yes."

"Very well, then,—that's all."

As John went back to his desk he knew that Gordon's glance followed him from the door of the private office. He mounted his stool and took up his pen.

The old bookkeeper slunk over to his side and placed a trembling hand on one corner of the ledger above which John was bending intently.

"What sort of a mood was he in, Norton,—nasty?"

John nodded.

"Did he have anything to say about me?" Without lifting his head John nodded again. Gordon fingered the corner of the big book nervously.

"I never got such a calling down from him before. But then, you know, you've got to stand his temper if you want to get along with him, and what's the odds,—we're paid for it, and it's all in a lifetime." He studied John's face guardedly. "What did he say, Norton?"

"I am awfully sorry," John began, "but perhaps you'd as soon hear it from me as from him——"

"He didn't tell you I must go, did he? He didn't say that—I thought he didn't mean it——"

"That's what he said."

Gordon leaned heavily against the desk.

"I knew he was wanting to get rid of me, but I didn't think it would come yet a while;—I—I was hoping I could hold on a little longer. Why! I have been here forty years—I'm not fit for anything else!"

Unconsciously in his excitement he raised his voice, and the last word was almost a cry. He choked down his emotion. "He'll get his deserts one of these days! A man can't go on forever, as he's gone on, walking over people, and prosper, and he'll find it so!"

John stole a glance over the room.

"I wouldn't speak so loud," he cautioned. "They will hear you."

"I don't care!" fiercely. "I don't care what they hear!" but he sank his voice to a hoarse whisper. "I—it isn't right, Norton,—it isn't right!" He paused an instant to let his gaze wander about the long bare room with its rows of desks, and a sudden mist came before his eyes. "Why! I haven't missed half a dozen days since I started in here. Summer and winter every morning at eight I've pulled off my coat and hung it with my hat on that nail over there,—it's been 'Gordon's nail' for forty years!" Then he broke down completely.

The office grew very hushed and still. The clerks stopped in their work and took in the scene with eager silent curiosity.

Fifteen minutes later they were working away again as though nothing unusual had happened. Gordon, at his desk, was trying to add a long column of figures, while every now and then something fell upon the pages of the ledger before him that raised a round blister or blurred the ink.

That day marked the beginning of the change with John Norton. He felt that this new position of his was held at the expense of manhood and self-respect. This left its mark on his character. Alertness and energy seemed to leave him as the ambition faded out of his life. In his despair he became morbid. His was the uncertainty of a man who feels he has failed without knowing how or where. He told himself the day was coming to him just as it had come to Gordon, when his services would no longer be of value to any one,—his little contribution to the world's progress having been made he would be discarded, he would drift farther and farther out of the moving current of things until he finally reached the great Sargasso of human energy where the wrecks stay, a derelict.

At first he had preferred to look upon the position as temporary, as a convenience to serve his end until a better offered, but nothing better did offer and he finally lost all idea of another place. His only fear was that he might be discharged, and he knew that a week's idleness would be a calamity.

Try as he would he could not get ahead. It was with difficulty that he managed to keep up his life insurance, which was the only provision he was able to make for the future.

It was probable that at this time neither his economies nor his expenditures were ordered with any particular intelligence or to any practical ends. His ability was that of the average man and he sacrificed himself to the average opinion. It was necessary for him to live in a certain way; his home must be in a respectable neighborhood, his wife and children must be well dressed. These were the essentials.

Sometimes he talked with Alice of giving up the struggle. He had a vague notion that if he went into the country, where he could work with his hands, he would do better and get larger returns for his toil. But it always ended in talk; nothing ever came of it; his point of view was the extreme one. He felt that he belonged to another race and time, with different ideals, different capacities and different aptitudes. The men he knew were all of the same sort. With the brawn of pioneers and soldiers wasting in their arms they were clutching pens pathetically enough, or selling silks and millinery when they had much rather be felling trees. But the trees are all felled, the worlds work as far as it can be done by hand is finished, and these primitive natures, who in a wilderness would have been all sufficient to themselves, retain but a doubtful utility.

Alice never really knew how difficult it was for him,—he kept that to himself.

He was held accountable for all the laxity on the part of those under him, and the office force was habitually indifferent, as men are apt to be who feel there is nothing to be gained by zeal and conscientiousness. Scarcely a day passed that he did not smart beneath the weight of Haviland's displeasure, nor could he rid himself of the terrible and degrading fear he had of the man. He would stand in dogged silence—abject, bruised and shaken—whenever Haviland chose to break the ready vials of wrath upon him. Haviland was not always disagreeable, however; he had his genial moments when it was wise to enter heartily into the spirit of his peculiar humor.

Norton's position was nominally at least, confidential. Once each year he made out a statement that found its way before the directors at their annual meeting. In preparing this statement it was necessary to go over the stocks, bonds and securities in the vaults with Haviland; then together they counted the cash in hand and John signed his name to the report, a formality having a certain significance in the mind of one of the directors at least, for he turned in his first statement unsigned, and had been called before the directors. Mr. Bliss, the largest individual stockholder in the company, had gravely interrogated him regarding the matter. The explanation was simple enough. Haviland had not told him to sign the statement. Upon learning this, Mr. Bliss had suggested that the managing director immediately inform the bookkeeper as to the exact nature of his duties. John was greatly impressed by the incident, so much so that afterward, when making out the annual statement, he was always troubled by an exaggerated sense of its importance.

He had been with Bliss, Haviland and Company three years, when he made a little discovery. Haviland was speculating,—in direct violation of his agreement with the company.

John had been in possession of this secret about five weeks when one morning he was summoned into the private office. He found Haviland looking rather disturbed.

"We'll have to be getting at our annual report," the managing director said. "Let me see,—this is the eighth of the month; I suppose you already have it well along."

"I've been at work on the books for the last two weeks."

"Make a full and complete showing, Norton."

"Yes, sir."

At eleven o'clock Haviland left the office hurriedly in response to a telephone message.

Half an hour later a spruce-looking youth with a small paper parcel under his arm walked into the business office and inquired for him. John went over to the railing where he stood.

"Mr. Haviland's out; can I do anything for you?"

"I am from Brown and Kemper," mentioning a well-known firm of brokers. "I want to leave these bonds for Mr. Haviland." He untied the parcel as he spoke. "Will you take their numbers and give me a receipt?"

John was too dazed to speak. Not only was Haviland speculating, but he was speculating with the funds of the company. He was vainly endeavoring to collect his scattered wits when Haviland came in, panting and in hot haste. He gave the broker's clerk a shove that sent him spinning toward the wall, then with a single furious ejaculation he snatched up the bonds and disappeared into the private office.

During the next two or three days John in fancy lived through all the agony of an unsuccessful search for another position, and at last awoke to a proper understanding of the case. Haviland was afraid to dismiss him.

The directors' meeting was called for the twenty-ninth, and late in the afternoon of the twenty-fourth, as John was closing his desk, Haviland came out of the private office and strode to his side.

"I want you to come up to my house to-night, Norton; it's about that statement I want to see you. Can you come?"

John did not look at Haviland; he felt embarrassed and ill at ease. They had avoided each other for days.

"I am sorry to bother you, Norton. Won't you come up to dinner? I am all alone."

"No," hastily. "I guess I'd better not; my wife will be expecting me."

"Just as you like. I can look for you about eight?"

"Yes."

Haviland moved away a step. He was mopping his face with his handkerchief. He seemed old and broken. His aggressive arrogance of manner had entirely deserted him.

"Everything was all right to-day?" he inquired aimlessly.

"I think so."

"Then I'll look for you at eight." Haviland turned and went slowly into the private office. As John passed the door on his way out he caught a glimpse of the managing director; he was sitting with his elbows resting on his desk and his chin sunk in his hands.

When John mounted the steps at Haviland's that night, it was with a good deal of reluctance. The butler admitted him and showed him into the library, where Haviland welcomed him with an effusive cordiality that only served to increase his desire to escape from the house. A table stood in the center of the room, with cigars and decanters on it. Haviland had evidently been drinking; his face was flushed and his manner confident. John put aside the glass he pushed toward him.

"I'll have a cigar, if you don't mind—thanks."

Haviland leaned back in his chair.

"Well, how's the statement coming on? The business makes a pretty good showing, eh?"

"It's been the biggest year in the history of the house."

"If they'd let me alone, I'd make Bliss, Haviland and Company a power," with something of his old self-assertiveness. "But they don't see it my way."

John looked his assent. Haviland filled his glass.

"You won't join me?"

"No, I thank you."

"I am going to have your salary put back to the old figure, Norton. I'll have to get the directors' consent, but you can tell your wife when you go home that you have a raise to twenty-five hundred." He turned expectantly toward his bookkeeper; he was counting on enthusiasm—gratitude, even, but he saw no trace of either on John's face.

Their relations had undergone a great change. Haviland was no longer the despot John had known in the private office; he no longer inspired fear; he never could again. He was simply a redfaced vulgar man who was seeking to bribe an employee to betray his business associates. John had brooded over the possibilities of this interview; he had thought of the sarcasms he would hurl in his tyrant's face—but the tyrant was no longer a tyrant, he was only a guilty man, more or less pathetic to look upon, as guilty men are apt to be when retribution is in sight.

To cover his losses, Haviland had taken almost half a million dollars from the company, consequently the necessity for a statement that would satisfy the directors and leave no room for inconvenient questioning was imperative. Provided it was forthcoming, it would give him a year in which to return all the securities he had hypothecated. Personally, he felt quite safe; he had gone deep enough into the funds of the company while he was about it to protect himself effectually,—at the worst he could always effect a compromise. He could turn over his property; carefully handled, it would easily reach half a million, and there was his stock in the concern besides. But he had no notion of compromising if he could help it, for what would he do without money, his credit and reputation gone! He grew sick. It all rested with the bookkeeper, who promised to be difficult to manipulate. He silently added five thousand dollars to the sum he was willing to offer as a last recourse. He cleared his throat.

"Now about that report, Norton; I suppose you will want my help to-morrow."

John looked distressed.

Haviland hitched his chair nearer and dropped his voice to a confidential whisper.

"You know how busy I am,—you are ready to sign that statement—what's the use—"

With a calmness he was conscious he did not feel, John took the cigar from between his teeth and said slowly:

"I am not so sure about that."

Haviland looked at him blankly for a moment. He laughed shortly, and remarked: "I guess you are not such a fool, after all."

He drew his check book from his pocket, took a pen from the table, and dipping it in the ink, dated a check and signed it.

"For what amount shall I make it, Norton?" The pen hovered above the blank space on the check.

John shook his head.

"No," doggedly. "I can't do it,—I'm sorry for you, but I can't. What's the use?—it will be about as hard on me as on you,—I'll lose my place."

But Haviland was not heeding him.

"If I make it ten thousand, will that satisfy you?"

It was John's turn to look blank. Ten thousand dollars! He turned faint and giddy; he tried to speak; he saw the pen circle and then sweep down toward the check. He put out his hand and caught Haviland by the wrist.

"No, don't!" he gasped.

"Shall I make it fifteen thousand?"

"No." And this time there was no irresolution.

Haviland groaned aloud; the sweat clung in beads to his forehead. He rose from his chair.

"I am offering you fifteen thousand dollars for the stroke of your pen,—if it is not enough, name your own price," he added hoarsely.

"I can't do it."

"Do you mean you won't come to terms?"

"Yes."

"Why?" His face was livid.

"Because I can't do what you ask of me,—I can't shield you, and I can't take your money. I don't suppose you understand,—it wouldn't do me any good—I should feel as though I had robbed some one—I could never tell my wife how I got the money; there would always be that between us. I'll finish what I can of the statement to-morrow and hand in my resignation."

As he spoke he came slowly to his feet.

Haviland only half heard what John said. He was standing with his hands resting on the table, staring straight ahead into vacancy. The whole world would know! This stupidly honest fool, whose intelligence he had always put at zero, was the Nemesis in his path. For the first time in his life he was cowed. He turned to John with a dumb fear in his eyes.

"For God's sake, Norton—do you realize what this means?" he cried brokenly. "You must stand by me; I'll come out all right! Don't go over to them—they will never do for you what I will!"

"I hadn't thought of them, or what they'll do."

"No!" with something of his old explosive manner. "You are looking to them for your reward when you have betrayed me! But what will it amount to? A few hundred a year, perhaps!"

"That was what you offered me first."

"Oh, you'll get it from them! It's easy enough to see what your game is!" Then, as a last appeal, he cried: "You know nothing positively. All I ask you to do is to take your money—the money I am willing to give you, no matter why—and clear out—go where you choose—do as you please—"

But John moved toward the door, and Haviland read in the tense set lines of his face his decision.

John went down the steps slowly, like a man in a daze. It had been the most dramatic moment of his life; it left him confused and stunned, and with an inexplicable fear of the future.

Soon this fear took a definite form. He quickened his pace. He must hurry home and tell Alice the whole circumstance and ask her advice. Perhaps he had already committed himself by going to see Haviland! He revolved the matter in his mind. What could Haviland do—would he dare accuse *him?* He could run no risks—he owed it to Alice and the children to take every precaution. But how was he to protect himself?

John turned sharply, with a new idea. Above all other claims, above the consideration of self, he owed a duty to the stockholders. They had a right to know what he knew; he could not shield Haviland with his silence. He must see one of the directors. He paused uncertainly on a street corner. To whom should he go? At the board meetings he had been impressed with Mr. Bliss' kindliness of manner; he would go to him rather than to any of the others, and tell him what he knew of the situation, and resign. He was sick of the whole business and felt himself unequal to it. He glanced around, hoping he might see a belated cab, but the street was silent and deserted.

It was three o'clock when he reached Mr. Bliss'. Four times he halted doubtfully before the door; four times he felt his courage ebb and flow, and four times he wandered aimlessly down the block. The fifth time he mounted the steps; there was a momentary irresolution, and then he rang the bell with a firm hand. He felt like a criminal, a conspirator, as he stood there, for, after all, Haviland had his good points—only one would never have supposed it merely from associating with him. He was on the point of abandoning his project, when the sickening fear returned that in some way he might be implicated. He thought of Alice and the children, and set his lips in grim determination; he dared not do less than protect himself. At last a sleepy half-dressed footman opened the door.

"What do you want?" he asked crossly.

"I must see Mr. Bliss," and John pushed past him into the hall.

"Come in the morning."

"I must see him now."

"Well, you can't! He's in bed."

At that moment Mr. Bliss himself appeared at the head of the stairs, dimly visible in a long white sexless garment.

"What is it, Martin?" he asked. "A telegram?"

"It's I, Mr. Bliss,—Norton—the bookkeeper from Bliss, Haviland and Company. I must see you! It's a matter of the utmost importance," he said earnestly.

"Martin, light the gas in the library. I'll be down in a moment, Mr. Norton."

Ten minutes later he joined John down-stairs in the library.

"Now, what is it, Mr. Norton?" he asked cheerfully.

"It's about the directors' statement," said John with a troubled air.

"Well?" his companion interrogated, while he bent upon the young man a shrewd glance. He wondered if the bookkeeper had been purloining the funds of the company.

"I have just come from Mr. Haviland," John explained. "I want to resign. He expects me to make up the statement without going over the securities. He has offered me fifteen thousand dollars for the kind of a statement he wants."

He paused uncertainly, and then went on hurriedly: "Last week securities to the value of thirty thousand dollars, which I supposed were in the safe and which should have been there, were returned from a broker's office. Mr. Haviland has been speculating. I have known this for some time, but I did not know that it was with the funds of the company until these securities were handed me by mistake."

"You are quite sure of what you say, Norton?" the director asked. "These are very grave charges you are making."

"I am quite sure, Mr. Bliss. I suppose he expects to return every dollar he has taken," John added. It was a comfort to be able to say a good word for Haviland.

"No doubt,—every man who speculates with money not his own intends to do that. Haviland will be called on to make good within twenty-four hours, and if he can't—why—" The pause was eloquent. He was silent for a moment; then he said: "Tell me as nearly as you can just what passed between you to-night."

Slowly and carefully John gave the substance of his interview with Haviland, while Mr. Bliss watched him narrowly.

"And you want to resign, Norton?" he asked at length.

"Yes."

Bliss laughed shortly.

"Why don't you ask for an increase of salary,—you'll be more apt to get that."

"I haven't told you what I have with any hope of that sort, Mr. Bliss," said John a little stiffly.

"No—of course not. But put the notion that you are to resign out of your head. More likely you'll be asked to help reorganize the company under my direction,—for Bliss, Haviland and Company can't go under, no matter what ducks and drakes Haviland has made of our money."

John came slowly to his feet.

"I must go home to my wife now," he said, "she will be wondering what has kept me so late."

"Wait a moment," said Bliss. "I'll go with you. Let me call a cab," and he summoned the footman.

"It is very kind of you," said John. "But is there any reason for it?"

"It's just as well. We must see the directors before nine o'clock."

As John leaned back in his seat in the cab, Bliss said kindly:

"You look worn out, Norton."

"I am tired," he admitted; but beyond his fatigue and weariness he was feeling a sense of peace, security and hope. His old ambition, long dead, as he told himself, stirred within him. After all,—after all the waiting and doubt and fear, success had come at last when he least expected it. The cab drew up before the dingy flat-house where he lived, and John sprang lightly to the pavement. They entered the building. It was still quite dark in the narrow halls, but as they came to the landing before his own door John gave a start. Two men were standing there; one was Haviland, and the other a stranger. Over their shoulders he caught a glimpse of Alice's white scared face. Hearing his steps, Haviland turned with a hungry wolfish look.

"This is the man," he said shortly. "Arrest him."

The stranger moved forward, but Bliss, coming slowly up the dark stairs, said gently:

"It's too late. It's no use—I wouldn't do that!"

He took the warrant from the detective's hand and tore it into long strips, while he and Haviland gazed into each other's eyes.

WHEN WE HAVE WAITED

OH! I beg your pardon," some one said politely from before me in the darkness.

This I thought was remarkably handsome, as I must have all but knocked the speaker off his feet.

Then, in an instant, I was wondering who had spoken.

If it were Jackson he would have said—I knew, for I had heard him more than once on occasions when I was endeavoring to mount the narrow stairs at the identical moment he was trying to descend them—"Get out of the way, you beast! What the devil do you mean by walking all over me?"

Therefore, being vastly amazed at the politeness emanating from the blackness in front of me, I put up my hand to find the gas-jet—we were on the second-floor landing—and having found it, fumbled in my pocket for a match and lighted the gas.

This enabled me to see who had ventured to introduce civility into the atmosphere of mild ruffianism that prevailed among the outcasts at Mrs. Tauton's.

Standing jammed rather close against the wall, where he had evidently considered it safe and expedient to withdraw in view of my hurried ascent of the steps, was a young man with a round boyish face.

"I really beg your pardon," he repeated. I was so astonished at his continued politeness that, with the mistaken intention of turning on the gas still farther, I turned it out altogether, and we were a part of the surrounding gloom again. But in the momentary brightness lent by the flickering flame I saw Gavan for the first time.

From this not entirely favorable beginning there came about a speaking acquaintance that soon ripened into friendship.

I was a clerk in a down-town office, and had by a series of misfortunes gravitated from the outskirts of cheap respectability to the dingy apartments that Mrs. Tauton kept for the exclusive use of single gentlemen of uniformly large hopes and small means, and I took my meals—they had a marked tendency to cast a cloud over any sunniness of temper I might have originally possessed—with wretches of my kind at the same low-priced resort just around the corner.

In after years some of us will remember the dyspepsia, there acquired, particularly young Tompkins, who ruined a fine constitution in a vain endeavor to subsist on a diet of pie interspersed with milk.

Tompkins subsequently made a million or two by a singularly soulless operation in railway shares. I have never blamed him for his consciousless greed, as I attribute it to the food his early poverty compelled him to live on in the effort to keep body and soul together.

I simply think he failed in his object.

It was on the steps at Mrs. Tauton's that I first met Gavan. It was not long until he gave me his complete confidence and I was permitted to know his aims and ambitions.

He desired to write plays and to dispose of those he had already written.

It soon became his custom to make nightly reports to me, giving me detailed accounts of his doings, and I came to know what actor or manager had promised to read his work.

His appearance was so youthful, I do not question but that it condemned him unheard in the minds of most. I think it prevented his being taken seriously.

When the people he wished to reach were kind and considerate, it was because they were amused and regarded the whole thing as a joke.

In any event his plays were being returned to him with almost every mail, accompanied by letters more or less encouraging, as they reflected various degrees of kindliness on the writer's part.

I had not known him for many months before I was aware of a change. His face wore an anxious look, but he retained his cheerfulness, which was, however, more a habit than a condition of thought. I knew that he was wretchedly lonely and that disappointment came to end each hope he dared indulge in.

It was a mighty step from the sleepy little southern town where he had lived, to New York, with its supreme indifference to so small a unit in the struggling mass.

With his grave earnest eyes, which were almost pathetic in their seriousness, and the face, that the days of waiting had stamped with lines— markings of the hand that was empty for him—he was only one of many.

His mother was an invalid, his father had long been dead, and they were very poor. This bit of information he imparted with the utmost reluctance. I guessed at it without the telling, as no one, unless there was the grim incentive of pressing poverty, ever braved the terrors of life at Mrs. Tauton's.

Little by little he told me of his mother, and I saw that love for her was the one strong passion of his heart. She lived—none too happily—with relatives in the town that had been the home of his family for a great many generations.

He seldom or never spoke of what he would do for himself when he should achieve success; it was his mother who was to profit by it.

One night he came into my room and dropped dejectedly down on the edge of the bed, that answered all the purposes of a chair when not in actual use as a couch.

"What is it, Gavan?" I asked.

"Nothing much. Only my first year in New York is about at an end, and there is no gain of any sort to show for it. The whole thing has been miserably discouraging."

"Why, Gavan, you are making important acquaintances all the time, who will aid you on to what you want."

"It is deadly slow. It's forever and eternally to-morrow."

He made a troubled little gesture with his hand.

"They say my work is good, that it is eminently clever—sometimes even that it's great; but that is not enough, and I try again. Try to be more like—not myself—but some one else; for it seems they don't want me on any terms. I wonder if there is such a thing as a man's being absolutely unavailable in the world—being of such an odd size and shape of both soul and mind that there is no niche he can fill. Do you know, I am beginning to think it of myself, that I don't fit—just don't fit anywhere."

And he looked at me questioningly. I had never seen him so despondent before.

He must have understood my thought, for he continued:

"I am ashamed to burden you with my woes. If I were the only one concerned it wouldn't be so bad,—I could stand it."

A wistful far-away look came into his eyes as he said softly:

"But there's my mother. It's for her I am working much more than for myself. Her life is so hard, with poverty and the contemptible pettiness of those about her."

He turned from me to hide the tears that would gather against his will.

"And there she sits," his voice sank to a whisper, "counting the days till I shall come and take her away. And what if I never can,—what if I end in failure! We wouldn't require much for perfect happiness, but small as the sum needed is, I can't make it. I shan't stay here much longer. I'll go home and settle down at something else."

"You wouldn't give up your work!" I cried.

"I can't keep her on the ragged side of uncertainty. I'll go back; unless soon there is a change for the better in my prospects." There was an abrupt pause. His voice had broken on the last word.

For a time we sat in silence, and when he spoke again it was cheerfully and of other things.

A few days later Gavan left the shelter of Mrs. Tauton's roof and went farther down-town, where he had rooms with an old shoemaker and his wife, who were "just as good and kind as could be," he informed me; and I think they were, but the apartments he had quitted were palatial by comparison with those he now had.

About the same time I made a move in the opposite direction toward my former mild respectability.

One Sunday he came to my lodgings, his face radiant. At last a play was accepted. There were only a few minor changes to be made; he could do them in a week or so, and then the company would begin to get up in their parts.

"I shan't have to quit and go home after all," he said. "I've written mother all about it. I'd give a good deal to be there and enjoy it with her. It would be such fun! Perhaps it isn't many months off till she can join me here, and then, old fellow, you are to come and live with us."

This last was one of his favorite ideas for the future. When he felt elated or particularly hopeful it was always broached, and it was characteristic of his general goodness that he wished to share all he had, or was to have, with his friends.

When I saw him a week later his work was progressing and the play would surely go on before the season ended. But by our next meeting his hope had evidently moderated, for he looked downcast and troubled as he explained the production had to be deferred. "They haven't the money it will take. A heavy outlay for scenery is involved, you know. It will go on the first of the coming season, and that's about the most I can expect under the circumstances. In the meantime there's a lot of work I wish to do, so it doesn't much matter. I can wait, only"—and his glance became tender—"it will go hard with mother. She won't understand why it's not as I said it was going to be."

Unfortunately, when the manager returned from his summer trip abroad, he brought with him from Paris the success of a thousand nights.

"He will do that at once, and then try mine. He really prefers my work, but thinks that more immediate profits are to be expected from the French piece," Gavan told me, and this was all he had to say.

The imported play had a long run in New York, half the winter and better. Then it was taken on tour.

"They can't drop a sure thing," he explained nervously when he informed me of the new arrangement. "However, the very first opening is to belong to me; no telling or guessing when it will come, but scarcely until next year. I'll have to do what I can meanwhile to drag out an existence. I can't give up. I've done so much it would be foolish even to think of stopping. If there is only a decent bit of luck in the end, a few months will pay up for the two years of misery. Of course, it's tiresome, this everlasting putting off, but if I wait long enough and don't starve, I am sure to see the play go on. The manager has said over and over that he wanted to stage it, and I think he does. It wouldn't be so rough if I were the only one concerned, but there's my mother. I know she is feeling it keenly, though she tries not to show it."

He was still brave, but the deep secret joy was gone from his eyes. He was slowly drifting back to the despondency that had marked the last weeks of his stay at Mrs. Tauton's.

"I don't suppose," he added, "that mother can comprehend how slow a matter it is, and I don't know that I make it clear to her."

How he lived through the winter and the spring that followed, I never knew.

When summer came I tried to induce him to go into the country with me for an outing.

He was profuse in his expressions of gratitude, but felt that he must remain in the city. The season was almost over and soon everybody would be there. It was his opportunity.

"I don't know why it is," he wound up reflectively, "but I seem to have a harder pull of it than most do. I wish I didn't look so young. Then, too, my work is original, and I find originality is an offense to most people. I can't do clever trifles."

No, his work was not clever; I appreciated that. It was only great.

On my return from the country he met me in Jersey City.

"I didn't write you about it, old fellow," he said, as we crossed on the ferry.

"My time comes in a month. Everything is in shape for the production—scenery painted and costumes made. I've hung around for three years, but my day has come at last!"

He took my congratulations with the graciousness that was characteristic of him.

"It isn't unmitigated bliss," he remarked. "I have had to all but ruin the piece to get it on. I guess it will pass muster and that's all I care for now. Three years such as I have spent are warranted to take the pride out of any man's soul."

Lightly as he spoke, I knew he was staking all his future on the event.

"Drop in for the first night," he said, as he left me at my lodgings. "I want your opinion. I have great faith in your judgment," he added politely.

I knew he hadn't, but he was invariably kind, even at the expense of truth.

During the month, the last one of waiting, I saw him frequently. The many interests relating to the presentation went forward with unexpected smoothness, and there was but one drop of bitterness in Gavan's cup. His mother was unwell. He had observed a decided change in the tone of her letters, something that was deeper than mere sorrow at his absence. One of his relatives (for like a true Southerner he had a surpassingly large number of them) had written that it was his duty to come home at his earliest possible convenience.

When Gavan told me this, he said:

"And it's the truth; I have been away a long while. Once the first night's over with, I turn my back on New York. My mother needs me."

I could see that he was very much exercised about his mother's condition.

"You know she may be a lot worse than they say. I have no idea that they would go into detail even if it were a serious matter, and mother herself would be the last person in the world to expect information of that sort from."

The eventful night came. I was late, having been detained at my office, and the first act was ended when I reached the theater, but I was in time to see Gavan bow his thanks to those in front from the stage. This I saw through the blur of lights and the mist that swam before my eyes.

The curtain had gone down on the last act when I made my way around back and joined him.

"Come," he said, as I took his hand. "Come, let's go home. I am tired—and I am satisfied."

He was silent until we reached his door.

"Come in,—don't leave me yet."

And I followed him up to his room.

He had again relapsed into silence, but I could see that he was happy. Finally he roused himself from his reverie to say:

"You don't mind if I go to bed, do you?—and stay a little longer; I want to talk to you. It's such a comfort to have you here."

I said I would stay all night if he desired it. I was too excited to sleep.

He was soon in bed, and I drew up a chair close beside him.

Then he began to talk of his mother, to tell me of what he would do for her. "For I fancy the turning point is past," he said. "I signed contracts to-night for more work, and now money goes to bind the bargain. They are not the barren formality they were when I put my name to the first one two years ago. I'll go home and see how mother is before I do anything else, and take a rest of a month or so. I can afford it, for the play's a big hit. There can be no mistake about it. Now that success has come, somehow it's not quite all I anticipated. A part of the satisfaction has been lost in the struggle, and a part of my ambition as well. I've served my apprenticeship to art. I have starved, hoping against hope, for three years, and now I'll be content with the money it will mean. After all, it narrows down to this: We begin with different aims before we have exhausted ourselves in trying to overcome the ignorance and prejudice of others."

When I left him he was sleeping with his head upon his arm. The boyish roundness seemed to have returned to his face and the anxious look was gone. He was as I remembered him in the old days at Mrs. Tauton's.

The night was at an end when I went into the street. Boys were calling the morning papers and the city was wide awake. I made a collection of the various papers and left them with the old shoemaker, who was already at work in his little basement shop, to give Gavan when he should have had out his sleep. Then I went uptown to breakfast in my own rooms.

It was late in the afternoon when I started back to see him, and as I reached the house the old shoemaker met me at the street-door. I saw his kind face was grave and serious, with lines of grief upon it.

"Is he sick?" I asked.

The old man motioned me to follow and without a word we went up the stairs. In the bare desolate hall above, with its unpalliated hideousness now garishly alight with day and sun, stood a policeman, the center of a group of curious men and women.

Still I did not comprehend.

I entered the room. Gavan was lying upon the bed just as I had left him. In his hand was clutched a crushed and torn scrap of yellow paper.

As I paused, looking stupidly down at the bed and its burden, I became dimly conscious that the old man was standing at my side speaking to me, telling me how it had happened.

"He got a message from home. His mother died last night. It's that he's holding so tight in his hand. Poor lad! a power of promise and real goodness went out of the world with him."

There were dark stains upon the bed-clothes, and he lay in the midst of the papers that told him of his triumph.

THE DESERTER

PRIVATE AUSTIN sat languidly upon his cot and slowly raised a cloud above his head from the disreputable black pipe firmly clenched between his teeth. His eyes, wandering aimlessly, finally rested upon a shotgun leaning against the opposite wall,—one of two furnished by a kind and benignant government for the sole and exclusive use of the sportively inclined members of Company A—and his vague unrest took form in a desire to spend the day with that gun upon the prairie in a search for solitude and game.

To gain this privilege, the consent of the officer on duty was indispensable, and Private Austin who had seen much pack-drill and who had acquired a valuable familiarity with the inside of the guard-house, knew that this consent was not for him. However he arose, giving himself a vigorous shake, and his attire, previously wrinkled into a thousand twists and creases, became the undress uniform of a private of remarkably neat appearance.

Passing along the narrow gangway between the long line of cots, taking care in doing so not to awaken the sweltering tossing figures slumbering uneasily upon them, he reached the door and stepped out into the open air.

For an instant as he inhaled the fresh morning air and gazed upon the blue hills rising from the level stretch of plain, their dusky outlines now tipped as with gold by the sun, his own mean life—his rough companions—were forgotten. Then as slowly and reluctantly his eyes turned from their distant point of vision and roamed around the circle of accustomed objects,—the white frame cottages of the officers' quarters, the bleak, stern, uncompromising walls of the too familiar guardhouse, the well beaten earth of the abhorred parade ground, the very stunted trees that seemed to have lost all graceful form and to stand in stiff unbending ranks as though nature itself felt the control of a military despotism,—he was once more a soldier, common and unclean, with an unquenchable thirst for beer and a loathing for all discipline.

As he stood alone with his disgust, his attention centered itself upon Lieutenant Parsons who was returning at breakneck speed from his morning canter. As the lieutenant drew near the post he reined in his horse. This gave Private Austin an opportunity to approach and make his petition.

Lieutenant Parsons turned in his saddle and looked at the soldier in utter and unmitigated contempt. To the disciplined well-trained West Pointer the general conduct of Private Austin could only be accounted for by a moral turpitude and a state of original sin shocking to all well-ordered minds, and his present highly audacious request was but one of those constitutional aberrations arising from that condition.

A prompt and vigorous expression of his opinion was on his tongue's end, but contenting himself with a brief answer in the negative, half deadened by the bugle-call which rang out at the moment, he continued on his way to headquarters.

Private Austin followed with his glance the figure of his superior until he had reached a distance that made comment safe and pleasant, when he proceeded to express himself in such crisp and belligerent English as only the resident of a military post would be able to appreciate. He continued as he reentered the barracks to voice his indignation in a fashion both edifying and pleasing to the aroused soldiers. Then suddenly he picked up a shotgun and made his way to the rear of the room, heedless alike of the sergeant's sharp command to stop his noise and fall in line and the wondering gaze of his fellows. With a vicious jerk he tossed open a window and carefully deposited the gun without, immediately following with other government property, namely, Private Austin, of Company A.

As the others emerged upon the open space before the barracks, he shouldered his gun and walked off in a deliberate and unconcerned manner, taking care, however, to maneuver a course that brought the barracks between himself and the rapidly assembling regiment upon the parade ground. But the deliberateness of his march was pure bravado, for no sooner had he reached a sheltering cluster of trees that offered concealment from the curious eyes of any of his comrades who might be watching his movements, than bending low he started on a swift run.

At last his breath failed him and he threw himself down at full length upon the scant verdure of the prairie. And now he thought for the first time of the penalty of his act. There were two courses open to him: either to obtain all the pleasure that could be obtained from his unwonted liberty and then return to the post, there to spend many a day in the guard-house as a consequence of having been absent without leave; or he might attempt to make his way across the plains and there lose himself. But this was an almost impossible project as he knew, since the reward the government offers for the return of each of her straying defenders keeps the border sheriffs on the alert. No, it would be wiser to return and face the consequences at the post, than to risk spending the next five years of his life in the military prison at Leavenworth. He would surrender within the specified twelve hours, beyond which time the comparatively innocent "absent without leave" would become the dreaded "deserter".

Having now recovered his breath and his customary spirits, which had been rather damped by his reflections, he started to made a wide circuit with the mingled determination' of spilling the blood of every living thing that should be so unfortunate as to come within the range of his gun, and of arriving at the post before nightfall.

A prairie schooner, drawn by a pair of meager oxen and driven by a sad-faced woman, was toiling over the sandy ridges. A half-grown boy, barefoot and ragged, led the way, shading his eyes from time to time with his sunburnt hands, and gazing eagerly on all sides in a vain hope that each moment might bring to view the longed-for haven of their march. On the seat beside the woman two children crouched, so weary of it all that they seemed involuntarily to avoid looking at anything save their own brown feet. Within the wagon among the poor belongings of the family was a rude bed and on this bed lay a man, gaunt and hollow-cheeked. By his side a young girl watched.

The man turned feebly toward her.

"The post?" he asked fretfully, reiterating the question that never left his lips. "Can you see it yet?" There was an age of suffering, endurance and longing in his voice.

"Not yet, father," replied the girl soothingly. "But we will surely reach it before night."

"If we have not already passed it," said the man. "It is impossible that Frank has kept the trail."

"He has done his best, father."

Without replying the man turned away, and in a few moments either slept or had sunk into a stupor.

The stretch of prairie was at last broken to the west by a strip of timber. The oxen turned toward it longingly. Instinct told them that where there were trees there must be water. Even the stolid lad in front quickened his pace, and disappeared in the undergrowth that skirted the edge of the grove. Close following came the oxen.

The woman's face had not changed, but the children's, before so indifferent, now seemed alive with cheerfulness and expectation. Then suddenly they heard the boy give a shout of warning. But all too late, for like a streak of gray light a skulking coyote went flying past. The report of a gun sounded, and one of the sad-eyed oxen breathed a sigh of relief, bowed its knees and then fell gently forward upon its side.

At the sight of this great calamity all else was forgotten. The woman moaned dismally, while the girl looked over her shoulder so stupefied that she paid no attention to the sick man who in querulous tones demanded the cause of the excitement.

This was the scene that presented itself to Private Austin's astonished gaze, when, gun in hand, he emerged from the thicket in the hope of getting another shot at the coyote. He saw the dying ox, the dismayed faces, the tearful eyes, and he wished devoutly from the bottom of his heart that Private Austin, heavily ironed, was again within the walls of the most dismal prison that in his varied life he had ever known.

Approaching slowly he spoke a few words half apologetic, half sullen. He would have been glad to arouse a fury, more easy to meet than their calm despair. Stepping forward he unhitched the remaining ox, and promised a prompt and sufficient recompense for their loss. The night was closing in upon them, the distance to the post was great, they must make their camp where they were, and in the morning he and the boy could go for assistance.

A busy man that night was Private Austin. He brought a smile to the woman's worn face, he caused the children's merry voices to ring out in the darkness as they drew round the camp-fire. His arms gently shifted the sick man from his hard bed in the wagon to one of gathered leaves and grass that was as down to his tired limbs. He made the girl smile and blush and turn away, only to come again. But a change came over him when all was hushed and silent, when he alone kept watch beside the smoldering campfire. Three times he arose and strode off into the night with his face toward the east, and then turned back.

It was well toward morning and the boy Frank lay sleeping beneath the protecting shelter of the wagon-bed, when a heavy hand was placed upon his shoulder and he awoke. Crimson streaks of light told that the day was near. With a finger on his lips as a sign not to disturb the others, Private Austin motioned the lad to follow him.

"A reward is offered by the government for the return of Private Austin, deserter, late of Company A," read the placard nailed upon the barrack walls. "A reward is offered by the government for the return of Private Austin, deserter, late of Company A," read the telegrams that sent out a thrill of greed through the veins of half a score of sleepy sheriffs. "A reward is offered by the government for the return of Private Austin, deserter, late of Company A," read the colonel in front of the gathered regiment. And then a strange thing happened: across the open space came Private Austin, his hands tied behind him with his own belt, and by his side a half-grown boy with Private Austin's shotgun held in his grasp. To the waiting colonel came the pair.

"Colonel, the boy took me. He gets the reward," said Private Austin.

WHAT REARTON SAW

REARTON dropped down in the chair I pushed forward.

"Can you give me a moment or two?" he asked.

"As many as you like," I answered. "Just wait till I put my name to this—" and I signed the letter before me.

He watched me fold and slip it into an envelope, then he said:

"I want your opinion on certain matters."

"Come now, Rearton," I entreated. "Let me off if it's to be another talk on spiritualism!"

"Confound it! Why will you persist in calling my beliefs by what to me is the most offensive of names? I recognize the existence of the supernatural. Every intelligent man must."

"Then, praise heaven, I am not intelligent."

"I want to ask you this. How much more than you actually see would you be willing to believe?"

"A great deal less,—and even then I question not I'd be pretty well deceived. The evidences of the senses are no evidences at all. They are a cheat ninety-nine times out of a hundred. The testimony of no two witnesses ever tallied exactly, even though they stood side by side looking on the same event."

"Come, that's a broad statement," he objected. "Of a very general truth," I supplemented. "And it holds good from the crucifixion down to the present day, whether the occasion was most momentous or most trivial."

I was aware that my friend was dabbling in the occult, and if any thing I could say would throw discredit on it I was anxious it should not be left unsaid.

"Look here," he continued, "supposing I should state to you as a fact susceptible of positive proof, that the future can be made visible to a man."

"Oh, come!" I interposed. "Let's drop this."

"No, I can't." He had become suddenly grave. "I want you to promise me that if I send for you during the next week you will respond to the summons."

"See here, Rearton,—what folly are you about to engage in?"

"My dear boy, it's not folly! If what I expect happens, I shall be able to gratify a rational desire to read the future,—my own particularly."

"When you do," I burst out, "I hope I'll be there to see how the thing's done!"

"That's exactly the favor I'm asking."

We sat silently looking at each other for a moment. I felt vaguely that my friend was not the man for such experiments. He was far too likely to be the dupe of another's cunning, being sensitive almost to the verge of weakness, essentially a dreamer with all a dreamer's love of the unreal.

"What does Miss Kent say?—does she know?" I asked.

"Miss Kent is quite willing."

"Probably she agrees with me that it's all a pack of nonsense."

"There you're mistaken," he said quickly.

"Faith,—supreme faith,—must be dominant in her character then. Few women would care to have the man they expect to marry forestall time in the fashion you propose."

"Miss Kent is not the ordinary woman. Her willingness shows sublime faith in our affection."

"Quite so,—that is if she really thinks it possible."

"I assure you"—and his pale face flushed—"I assure you she shares my beliefs fully. Why shouldn't the future be as plain as the past?"

"Now see here, Rearton," I said, "I'm not especially fond of argument, and if I can't swear my way through a dispute it is rather apt to languish as far as I am concerned. One thing I am sure of,—if bare one-half of your good fortune was mine I'd be amply satisfied with the present. Nothing so remote as the future would trouble me."

Rearton, seeing that I was not inclined to discuss the question he had propounded, took his leave of me.

A day or so later I received a note from him requesting my immediate presence at his apartments. I hastened there. He opened the door himself in response to my knock and I followed him into his room. I could see he was laboring under some great excitement. His first words were evidently intended to explain matters.

"He will be here in a moment." He spoke hurriedly and in a low voice as though he feared a listener. "The reason I sent for you is because of all my friends I think you are the least likely to be imposed on. I have the uneasy feeling that many of my investigations were not conducted with absolute fairness,—an uncomfortable sensation of having been tricked. Understand me, my faith in the great principle remains unaltered, but the methods used in its demonstration have been unworthy."

I made a gesture of ridicule and dissent, and he added:

"Your unbelief and doubt are my mainstay. I trust to you to see that what is to follow is carried out in the spirit of truth that prompts the undertaking."

I was about to make a reply when some one said in a voice of marvelous sweetness and culture:

"If you are ready, gentlemen."

I turned hastily. Standing beside the door that gave access to my friend's dressing-room was a man in a loose robe of dark and curious fabric. Not the habit, but the man, riveted my attention. I saw a colorless face devoid of beard or mustache, a face incontestably perfect as to feature and outline, but the very antithesis of handsome. The mouth was fine and cruel, the forehead serene and broad, with wonderful eyes that burned and glowed with a peculiar lusterless fire as they met mine. The whole effect was distinctly unpleasant. The man was of the kind that one might imagine murdered from love of crime as an art, to whom profit was secondary to pleasure. I instinctively knew that the quality of his mind, though incomparably acute, was debased and diseased far beyond the limits of the rational, yet nothing could be further removed from insanity nor madness.

Rearton said, "This is my friend," placing his hand on my arm as he spoke.

The man, having advanced to the center of the room, and acknowledged the introduction by an inclination of the head, said, "Let us begin." I observed the same quality in his speech that had arrested my attention in his face. Soft and sweet as the tones of his voice were, they were entirely divorced from feeling. It was a soulless perfection.

In the center of the room was a table with three chairs drawn about it. Rearton took the one at the head, and in response to his bidding I seated myself at the foot. The man—medium or whatever he might be—dividing the space between us.

For a moment or two I kept my glance fastened upon him, then I turned to Rearton. A marked change had taken place in his appearance. He had sunk down in his chair in a heap like a drunken man or an imbecile in a period of bodily degeneracy corresponding to the mental. The white of his eyes showed through their half opened lids a dull lead color. His skin was splotched and yellow. He seemed scarcely to breathe. It was altogether horrible!

As I gazed, slowly he straightened up, the lids rolled back, and with a convulsive motion—a nervous tremor—he sat erect, staring at the man. The latter began to sway from side to side, and as the needle follows the magnet, so Rearton's body moved in unison. He was dumbly obedient.

All this while I was far from being unaffected. I don't know that I can better describe my sensations than by saying that flashes of cold coursed through my veins. I had an uncomfortable and cowardly desire to turn and see who was behind me. This continued until I was absolutely chilled and shivering. My head began to swim, a sickening nausea lay hold of me, and still those wonderful eyes against my will and reason held me spellbound. I could not draw away my own from them. I followed their search into futurity.

At last, in desperation, placing my hands upon the table, I sought with the aid of the support it gave to rise. It was all folly! I must throw off this influence—it was a cheat—a swindle... strange that I should be powerless to resist.

Suddenly as I struggled to retain the mastery over my senses a cry of pain escaped my lips. I had received a shock as though the base of my brain had been seared with a red-hot iron. I felt my head go down upon my breast, and then another mind than mine swayed me.

Without any effort on my part, uninfluenced by will or force self-expressed, I turned to Rear-ton; and as I looked at him he grew indistinct—far removed and distant—and yet I knew that by putting out my hand I could touch him. There began to be strange faces that peered on me from out the mist that had fallen on us. They came and went like passing shadows.

This phase of my experience ceased abruptly. Once more I saw Rearton, his glance fixed and unwavering, his lips moving as if in speech. It was the vision of his future that he saw, and what he saw was shown me.

I seemed to know that he was married, and to Miss Kent. This I knew, not as an onlooker, but as his second self; and yet in what was to follow I suffered simply as one suffers with those whom he loves, who bears a portion of their grief through sympathy.

He was living in the rapture of his joy, and obedient to his deep desire, her presence stole from among the shadows that surrounded us and came so near that she stood beside his chair. She was so beautiful with youth and innocence that I heard him murmur her name in an ecstacy of love and tenderness, putting forth his arms as though to take her into his embrace.

Vagueness closed in, shutting out the picture, but only for an instant. It was cleared away, and Rearton was seen kneeling at the foot of a low bed. Hers was the pale face on the pillow. My first thought was that she would die; but it was the beginning, not the end, of life.

As the days came that were made manifest to us, the story was carried on. We saw the child against her breast, she softly singing it to sleep. A thousand gracious things we beheld in those glad days of love.

By slow degrees a change came into their lives. The note of harmony that had been struck, sounded for the last time, and was silent. It was the gradual decay of affection, but so insidious was the transition—so covert the difference—that neither could have said, "Here the evil started." Soon neglect mounted up and stood for wrong. Again and again they parted, she in tears—he angry and dissatisfied.

Staining the cheeks of Rearton's real self were tears, too. He strove to speak—to contradict the false evidence, to say it should not be as foretold—to comfort her, but his lips refused him utterance.

Slow growing came the change until at last they had drifted far apart, each with separate interests; the only bond between them, the child.

With startling rapidity the pictures flashed back and forth in front of me. She was seated alone before a window that opened out upon a vine-covered balcony. The sweet odor of honeysuckle filled the air. She was a mature woman now,—no longer the girl, no longer the young mother, but the matron whose ripened charms had reached their full perfection. Yet in the gain of years and experience there was plainly evinced a loss to her. She had gained the bitter wisdom that hardens the heart and soul of its possessor.

A man appeared at the window. He seemed to speak her name, for she arose and went to him. At first I thought it might be Rearton, for his head was turned from me, but it was not. It was one whom I had never seen. I did not have to wonder much what brought him there. They were lovers. By gesture and the visible semblance of speech I knew that he entreated her to go with him. She half yielded, only to hesitate. Something held her—some memory—the thought of some duty—not love for her husband. That was dead,—long dead.

At my side the real Rearton sat with hands resting on the table, staring wildly into vacancy. Great drops of sweat stood on his forehead, and the muscles of his throat were knotted as from the mighty but unavailing effort he was making to speak. With merciless strength and cruelty he was chained down to the sight.

He saw the woman he adored, through his neglect and indifference, about to cast away her life. She had all but yielded, when she ran back into the room and paused beneath a picture that hung on the wall. It was of herself when she was a bride. She compared herself with it. They were the same in look and feature,—and yet she had lost so much! Standing on tiptoe, with her small white hand she struck the canvas until it was torn and marred. She would leave no record of the past to mock at her—to tell what she had been!

A few moments sufficed for the work of destruction, and she rejoined the man who had waited for her the while by the window. Together they were advancing toward it, when a figure glided from behind the curtains that closed an inner door. It was Rearton's future self. A polished bit of steel glittered in his hand. He came between them and the balcony.

Thus confronted, the woman sank into a chair, bowing her head in her hands; but more from shame than fright. The two men gazed sternly at each other. Slowly, steadily, Rearton raised the gleaming piece of metal, there was a puff of smoke—another—and another—

With the first one the woman had sprung to her feet and darted forward, throwing herself before the man she loved. With the last puff of smoke she slipped from his arms—for she had sought a refuge there,—falling swiftly to the floor with a little sob of mingled pain and relief that compassed all contentment, for it was distinctly audible, stealing through the silence of the unborn years. A spot of purple darkened the whiteness of her breast.

Seeing what he had done, Rearton fell on his knees beside her and took the heavy head on his shoulder, trying to call her back to life and love. When he saw that all hope was vain, he covered his face with his hands.

Once more the shadows came. Once more the faces filled the air, and the scene had shifted. The signs of unspeakable suffering were stamped upon Rearton's brow when I again saw distinctly. He stood on the deck of a ship, his son at his side. I divined that he had escaped punishment, and was seeking forgetfulness—the unfound—in wanderings to the far ends of the earth. Hiding in his cabin aboard the same ship, they unconscious of his presence, but he conscious of theirs, was the man who had loved Rearton's wife. By what chance they were brought so near was unknown to me. For an instant I observed the three and then they were gone. Space swallowed them up, and only the ocean lay climbing to the moon.

Then came wind and storm, and the waters throbbed against the night, beating its black bosom; but the first streaks of dawn showed both sea and shore,—the sea still vexed by memory of the gale,—and a mighty stretch of sand that rolled before the wind as did the waves. The sun rose red, and showed dark on its crimson rim the solitary figure of a man edging the desert.

It was Rearton. He was alone. I saw that his dress was torn and discolored, stained and wet.

All day long, beginning with the dawn, he paced the shores of a little land-locked bay, never taking his eyes from its glassy surface save to search among the wreckage that littered the beach. All day he came and went. All day,—searching,—always searching. Day gave place to night, and the day was born again, and still he passed back and forth scanning the bay with intent glance that sought no relief from the hot reflection of sky and water.

Finally thirst drove him inland to where the starved stream, that gave the greater part of its moisture to the dry and hungry earth, was untainted by the ocean's salt. Across the hot sands each day at evening he made his lonely pilgrimage for the means whereby he might sustain life.

When the waters of the bay were quiet and untroubled, huge bubbles could be seen to rise and break, bursting when the air was reached. Whenever this happened, the watcher would mark the spot with his eye and swim out, diving repeatedly as though seeking for something that lay in the slime at the bottom. But on each occasion he came back empty-handed. Still he waited, making no effort to leave the desolation of which he had become a part.

Many days passed in this manner. One evening when he had gone to the stream, a black and bloated object rose with a single bubble on the bay. And then one by one up came the dead, until a hundred floated on the slack of the tide, or moved lightly, influenced by the imperceptible current. They were the bodies of men and women, with streaming knotted hair to which the seaweed clung. As the tide came in, they drifted to and fro,—ever faster with its increasing flow. Each seemed to hurry in itself,—a silly parody on life and haste. Lashed by the wind, the surf disturbed the smoothness of their resting place. Then a strange thing happened. As the bodies followed back and forth, they smote one against the other, darting from spot to spot, bobbing up and down, or rolling from side to side. At one point when the tide boiled over a sunken ledge of rocks, they had a wild fashion of making the pass so close together that the hindmost would strike those before them with such force in the swiftening current that they would leap their length from the water, or come erect, standing knee-deep in the waves with much waving of stiffened arms. It was the dead at play.

The wind and the waves were going down, sinking with the sun. Still the bodies kept up the chase in the swirling rush of the waters. The moon came up. The tide reached its fulness and stood spreading out on the beach, and the dead were at rest.

Rearton returned and saw the dark things that were black in the shadows of the shore. He waded in among them, pushing his way through the rotting mass that seemed to sob and sigh as they struck one another,—for his progress in their midst created movement. Hours he searched, turning over those that floated face down that he might see their features and miss none. All through the night, aided by the moon's rays, he continued his ghastly quest until it was day.

He, himself, was changing rapidly. The wild light of delirium and madness shone in his bloodshot eyes. As he thrust the drowned bodies from him, I could see him laugh with a foolish hanging of the lip from which the saliva dripped and frothed.

At last when he was on the point of abandoning the search, one body drifted out from the shore until it was fair beneath the moon, and he saw, within the circle of mildew that clung to hair and garment, his son's face. A white film covered the open eyes, the flesh was blue and horribly swollen. Without hesitation he took the hideous reeking mass into his arms and carried it ashore.

I looked again to see the waters, the moon and all beneath the night the bodies of the dead, but they were blotted out. I could see Rearton alone where he had taken the body back from the beach. He had placed it upon the ground and covered it with his coat. Not far off he was on his knees, digging in the loose earth. This was all I saw in the somber grayness of the dawn. Skulking in the gloom that foretold the day came a shape across the waste. It paused upon a hill of sand that the wind had blown together, and with head erect and ears drawn up, sniffed the air. Then it followed the scent.

It came near where Rearton dug with bare hands and a fragment of plank from the wreck. Came near, and squatting down, watched him for a space as he labored. Then with stealthy tread it went forward.

A growl of greedy satisfaction attracted Rear-ton's notice. He looked up and saw the hyena tearing at his son. Snatching up the piece of plank with which he had been digging, he rushed at it. Man and beast met with a shock, and I saw the animal leap repeatedly at Rearton's throat, its teeth tearing and lacerating his face and throat. With the desperate strength born of peril and his madness, he wielded his weapon and succeeded in beating off his furious antagonist. Then a single blow dealt with savage fervor stretched it lifeless at his feet. Without stopping to tie up his wounds he resumed his work upon the grave.

Soon the hole was sufficiently deep, and he placed the body in it and covered it with earth. To make sure that the grave would not be molested, he brought what portions of twisted beams he could carry away from the wreckage that strewed the beach and piled upon it until a great heap marked the place of burial.

Twice the sun sank, and twice it made radiant the heavens before the task was completed to his liking.

He had been mad, crazed by grief and misery, before he found the body of his son. He was further poisoned by the wounds he had received, and because of them he had gone mad as a beast and not as a man. Flakes of foam were thick and white upon his beard; he had a frightful manner of swinging his head from side to side, snapping with his teeth at whatever came within reach.

It was the third day since he had been so. He remained in the vicinity of the solitary grave, not even leaving it to go for water,—that he no longer needed. The grave continued to hold a meaning, though he was far beyond the saying or the knowing why he stayed. It was blind obedience to an impulse or an emotion that survived the extinction of the last spark of human intelligence, in him quenched forever.

His roving glance that shifted constantly, happened to see a cloud of smoke that ascended from a point a mile or so farther up the coast than he had yet gone. For a space this wonder fixed his vacillating interest. A dulled intelligence stirred within him. It drew him in that direction. He went slowly at first, on hands and feet, then standing, he hurried forward at a run almost.

On a tongue of land that projected out boldly into the ocean, a great bonfire had been built and set alight. As the maniac approached, he saw the builder of the fire where he stood between it and the sea, his eyes fastened upon a passing ship. At first the maniac paid no heed to him, but walked around and around the blazing pile. He was unseen, for the man had no thought but for the ship that drew in, guided by flame and smoke. Finally he became aware that he was not alone. He moved back to the fire and Rear-ton saw his face,— the face he had seen last when he had bent over his dead wife where she had fallen. He gazed at his former friend stolidly for a time with unwavering insistence, but by degrees a partial capacity for reason dawned upon him and with it came a measure of memory and hate.

Meanwhile the man was frozen to the spot, horror-stricken by fright of what was revealed to him.

It may have been a minute, it may have been ten, that the maniac and man stood staring at each other; the former with foaming lips that sweated drops of blood; the latter with cheeks that blanched and paled. The man turned toward the ship. Its coming promised safety, should it come in season; and while he did so Rearton advanced a single step, pausing when the man faced him again.

There was power in sanity. It exercised a certain mastery over him. Man and beast stood looking fixedly each at the other, but he could not resist the desire to turn and see from time to time the movements of the ship, and whenever he did so Rearton, crouching low, came closer. For an hour this was the fashion of his advance, and in that hour the man had looked at the approaching ship just thirty times. The maniac had made just thirty forward steps that counted thirty yards. Perhaps there remained ten that separated them.

The ship was stationary, and a boat had left its side and started in. Strong as was his temptation the man dared not look. He kept his face turned to the maniac. He put one foot behind him and fell back in the direction of the beach, moving with the utmost caution. With equal caution the maniac followed.

They had almost reached the water. They heard the distant splash of oars disturb the stillness,—and giving way to weakness, the man withdrew his eyes that he might see the boat. Instantly, with a bound, the maniac darted at him. He gave a smothered cry of rage as he hurled himself on the man, bearing him to earth. There was a short terrific struggle as they wrenched to and fro, his teeth were buried in the man's throat, and mouthing closer with vise-like grips he strangled him to death.

As this was doing the sailors landed, and armed with their oars came near the place where the two men were. Rearton relaxed his hold on the dead man's throat and with an angry snarl sprang at the foremost. With their oars the sailors beat him off and hastily retreating to the boat pushed afloat, still defending themselves against his mad attacks.

When sufficient space was between them, they paused to look and marvel. They could see him alone now in the desert, down on his hands and feet, chasing and biting at the cloud shadows that drifted over the waste and sandy plain and fruitless earth.

Slowly, lurching forward by stealth and cunning across the table, came Rearton's actual self. He was frothing at the mouth, his face showed red with livid scars. Nearer—nearer he came, until I felt his hot breath touch me. I could not move... but fear gave me power... by a mighty effort I sprang to my feet, breaking the spell. Still he followed me on hands and knees over the table. It was no fancy. I saw him with unclouded senses. I could see the flakes of foam upon his lips,—for there they were!—I could see the livid cuts and bloodshot eyes. He was mad. The vision had become the reality. So bestial was he, so awful and inhuman, that without a thought of pity for him I snatched up the chair in which I had been sitting, and swung it up above my head. He crept nearer in his hideousness. The chair quivered in my clutch, ready to fall. It was his life or mine,—and he was mad.

But I was saved the after pain and remorse that would have been mine had he taken hurt or harm at my hands. 'The man who had done this thing, who was destined to answer for this sin of his committing, glided in between us. Rearton, where he crouched in readiness to spring at me, glanced up, his interest diverted for the moment, and his eyes met those that were so strangely dark and luminous. He wavered beneath the compelling force they exercised,—wavered for one brief instant and then with a whine like a dog's for mercy, fell down at the man's feet, licking the floor with his black and swollen tongue.

I waited to see no more, but rushed from the room out in the street. I had no conception of the time we had spent together, but it must have been hours and hours, for the streets were deserted and empty. I judged it to be long after midnight.

For a while I walked aimlessly about, seeking to calm and rid myself of a portion of my horror. Eventually pride and a sense of affectionate pity for Rearton returned. Maybe it was all a vision,—the last as false and unreal as the first! Though I tried to convince myself of this, it was only by the strongest exertion of will that I was enabled to mount the flight of stairs that led to my friend's apartments.

I listened in front of the door for an instant. No sound came from within. With a hand that trembled violently, I pushed it open and entered the room. There on the floor were Rearton and the man,—now the victim of his victim. Rear-ton's teeth had torn his face and breast in a shocking manner, and their last fatal hold was at his throat, on which they were firmly set. Both were dead. About the room the broken furniture gave every evidence of a frightful and prolonged struggle.

HOW MR. RATHBURN WAS BROUGHT IN

R ATHBURN paced the room with noiseless tread, now and then stopping to look at the tossing figure of the boy upon the cot or to listen to the words he spoke in his delirium.

Once he thought he caught the sound of hoofs upon the trail and he halted abruptly as his hand stole beneath the tails of his long English coat.

Mr. Rathburn's nerves were unstrung by the strain imposed upon them by recent and painful events. As he had expressed it to himself half a hundred times that day, "The gentleman who brings me in, whether it's afoot or in a pine box, goes just five thousand dollars to the good," and each time his thoughts reverted to the powerful inducement the general public had to "bring him in," his hand had stolen beneath the tails of his long English coat; and the comfort he derived from so doing had enabled him to say, "It won't be the first who tries nor the first six who try, but the seventh gets the pot."

Mr. Rathburn had left Denver the morning previous in great and pressing haste, and with a careful avoidance of human kind. He had never been a social man and the reward of five thousand dollars that was "out" for the man who would bring him in only served to intensify the natural austerity of his character.

The difficulties that beset Mr. Rathburn arose indirectly out of a quiet little game of poker when the stakes had been high, and when the game had ended (two gentlemen going broke), the tempers of all concerned had been even higher than the stakes.

Mr. Rathburn's honor had been called into question. Certain remarks, chiefly notable because of their extreme brevity and almost brutal frankness, had been directed at him.

What followed was hasty and unpremeditated.

Now that time had given opportunity for reflection, Mr. Rathburn consoled himself with the thought that it was in self-defense. In his view of the matter he stood at variance with that of the public, which was "wilful murder".

Fear of public sentiment had, however, never been a potent factor in Mr. Rathburn's career, but now, for the first time in his life, this sentiment of disapproval was backed by money, and he was aware that several bands of men were patrolling the country and that the various individuals composing those bands were anxious to get within speaking, or, to be more exact, shooting distance of him.

Rathburn had been making the best of his way over the range that afternoon in the usual unostentatious manner of a man fleeing from justice, when young Gordon saw him from his ranch near the trail and rushed in pursuit. Young Gordon will never know how near he was to death, for Mr. Rathburn turned and faced him, his hand beneath the tails of his long English coat. As a general thing, when people saw Mr. Rathburn's hand disappear behind him, they left precipitately, for that motion and the one that followed it were known to be singularly fatal to human life.

Young Gordon, in ignorance of this fact, had continued his approach, which, after all, was the best and safest thing he could have done, for Rathburn got a view of his face, and being a student of faces, he instantly decided that young Gordon was not looking for trouble.

The news of Mr. Rathburn's latest shooting affray had not reached the Foot Hill Ranch, and young Gordon did not know that the governor of Colorado had deemed it expedient to offer a large reward to the man who would put a check upon Mr. Rathburn's further independent action and hand him over to the proper authorities in Denver. Whether or not Mr. Rathburn was to be turned in alive or dead was left to the taste and judgment of his captor; the prevailing tone of the proclamation suggested, however, that Mr. Rathburn dead was easier to handle than Mr. Rathburn alive, and at present there were bets pending as to the probable appearance Mr. Rathburn would present to the community when on view at the undertaker's shop; for the opinion that he was "a goner" was strong.

Young Gordon's face, white and drawn with sorrow and apprehension, was more eloquent than any words. His brother was sick—dying for all he knew. Would Rathburn remain at the ranch while he went for a doctor? He dared not leave his brother alone. Would Rathburn remain until morning?

Mr. Rathburn had looked down the trail. He was quite sure that somewhere behind him were a number of enterprising gentlemen, and that the reward of five thousand dollars had stimulated a degree of activity that would be his ruin if he lingered. He looked at the mountains beyond, which, when reached, promised safety, and they were very near.

An elevation and generosity of conception characterized many of Mr. Rathburn's acts. Outside of his profession, and when removed from the unworthy and corrupting influence of the flesh, he was not without a certain nobility of soul.

He cast one longing look at the mountains, wavered and was lost.

Just ten minutes later young Gordon was galloping down the trail at breakneck speed, while Mr. Rathburn remained in attendance upon the sick boy.

As long as there was light in the sky he had turned frequently to the window and followed with his eyes the dusty streak of gray across the range that marked the windings of the trail, but from without the distance there came neither sound nor sight of life.

By turns, as the night wore on, Mr. Rathburn was nervous and reflective, now sitting in a chair beside the cot, now pacing the floor restlessly. The present experience was a new one for him. To be sure, at various periods of his eventful and not entirely blameless life he had found it both safe and necessary to deprive certain localities of his presence. Perhaps the necessity would again occur if he succeeded in spite of the delay in making good his escape; but he was not prying into the future, the present was enough for him, quite enough.

It was not long before he had forgotten his own troubles in his interest in the boy upon the cot, and it was borne upon his consciousness that the boy was very sick indeed, that his fever had reached a crisis and that unless a change for the better came before morning he would no longer need the doctor's aid.

The boy was very young, sixteen or seventeen at most.

Mr. Rathburn smoothed his pillow with gentle touch, and seating himself beside the cot, took the boy's hand in his own. The boy tossed to and fro, his eyes open and glassy, his skin hot and burning. Mr. Rathburn placed his disengaged hand upon the boy's brow and set himself to work to control and quiet his ravings by his own force of will.

The hours wore on. One, two, three. The little clock on the shelf beside the door ticked them off; still the boy tossed from side to side. But the watcher noticed that from time to time there came moments of quiet to the sufferer. They grew in length and frequency as the hours passed.

"We are getting the better of it," murmured Rathburn hopefully. "On the whole I am not sorry I stayed."

The hands of the clock were pointing to four, and the cold gray of dawn was stealing over the range, shot with rays of light in the east, when Mr. Rathburn pushed back his chair.

The boy was sleeping peacefully, his breath coming soft and regular. For the first time that night Mr. Rathburn discovered that he himself was both tired and sleepy.

He pushed back his chair until he reached the center of the room, then bringing his feet to an equal elevation with his head by means of a table, he, too, slept.

The sunlight was streaming into the room when sounds on the trail aroused him. He awoke with a start. His first glance was at the boy who was still sleeping. Then he arose and walked to the door.

Four men were cautiously approaching the house, while a fifth held the horses of the party.

Mr. Rathburn recognized the sheriff of Arapahoe County and his deputies, and his hand stole beneath the tails of his long English coat.

Then he remembered the sleeping boy upon the cot.

Mr. Rathburn stepped into the yard.

"Don't shoot," he said softly, "I give myself up."

MISS CAXTON'. FATHER

I F Miss Caxton's father had been called on to give a detailed account of Miss Caxton's life, he would have described it as a perpetual round of gaiety. By what process of reasoning he arrived at any such conclusion is known only to himself; but from out the depths of his ignorance this belief had sprung, and it bore fruit in an inclination to curtail any pleasure other than the purely domestic in which Miss Caxton might have desired to indulge.

It was his custom to observe that if one had a good home, that home was decidedly the best place for one, and on occasions when he knew Miss Caxton was desirous of spending an evening out, it was his wont to introduce this statement at the supper table, as the moral to sundry fables.

Likewise he manufactured numerous fictitious conversations supposed to have taken place between himself and others, in which Miss Caxton was held up as a shining example of domesticity; then he would light his cigar and saunter downtown to play at whist until a late hour of the night.

That there was anything incongruous in his conduct or any discrepancy between his words and his acts never occurred to him.

Once, when Miss Caxton ventured to point out this apparent difference in word and deed, he had explained that the noise the children made wore upon his nerves—but he was quite sure that no man loved his home more than he did, and that when Thaddeus, Roderick and Leander, the twin, grew up and attained a decent age, he would greatly enjoy spending an evening now and then with his family. Nothing could have induced him to believe that the noise wore upon Miss Caxton's nerves. He knew very well that women liked that sort of thing immensely.

He was not a man of imaginative temperament, or he might have wondered what he would have done had there been no elder sister to look after the children when Miss Caxton's mother followed the youthful Leander's mate out of this world. If this thought ever gained a place in his mind, he had put it aside with the convincing argument that in supplying the little boys with an elder sister he had placed himself beyond reproach. Miss Caxton was a living proof of that forethought that marked the serious operations of his life; nor was Miss Caxton overlooked in this happy adjustment; she had Thaddeus and Roderick, not to mention the twin—and even half a twin was better than no twin at all.

This satisfactory arrangement had continued for some years, when the advent of The Fool upon the scene disturbed the serenity of the Caxton household. Of course The Fool was not the name bestowed upon him by his sponsors in baptism; it was an appellation conferred by Miss Caxton's indignant parent, and he only made use of it in his daughter's hearing. That any one else should slip in and supplant him in his daughter's affection—while he was away playing whist, filled him with indignation. He also was astonished that his daughter should seem to care for The Fool. Though he seldom saw him, he was aware that most of his unoccupied time was spent in Miss Caxton's society, and he also knew that each night, as he came in at one door The Fool was taking his leave of Miss Caxton at another. But the young man's departure was so nicely timed with reference to the charms of whist that he had never actually set eyes upon him in Miss Caxton's presence.

Never before having come in contact with the inevitable, Miss Caxton's father had a poor opinion of it. He began a vigorous campaign, in which he was uniformly worsted. They had Bunker Hill for breakfast, Miss Caxton triumphantly crossed the Delaware for dinner and Cornwallis surrendered at supper time, and withdrew to play whist, leaving Miss Caxton and The Fool in possession of the field.

Miss Caxton's ability to keep her temper and preserve that equanimity which was her most marked characteristic, gave her undoubted eminence in this species of warfare—for the cloud of battle hung forever over the house. Her calmness exasperated her father more than any words could have done.

Under these trying circumstances a man of less fixed habits would have taken to drink as a means of relief—Miss Caxton's father took to abusing the children. The little boys and the twin began to lead a dog's life, particularly the youthful Leander, who seemed to possess a great though unconscious power of enraging his parent far in excess of all endurance. At dinner and supper, the only meals they took with their father, they were barely permitted to speak in whispers, and then only to make known their wants in the most direct English at their command. This had a repressing tendency on youthful spirit.

How long it would have been possible for this happy state of affairs to have continued there is no telling. Miss Caxton saw fit to firing matters to a crisis. One day, in company with The Fool, she left the paternal roof; at the same time she despatched a communication to her father, requesting his immediate presence at home. When he received the summons it had a mystifying effect upon him, but in obedience to the request, he repaired to the scene of his domestic joys. He had no sooner crossed the threshold than something within him corresponding to intuition made manifest to his mind's eye that all was not right. The little boys were not visible; even Leander's voice was hushed.

Most assuredly something was wrong.

But what?

Miss Caxton's father inspected the various rooms comprising his establishment. In his own room he found, conspicuously tucked in one corner of his looking-glass, a neatly folded note, directed to himself in Miss Caxton's familiar hand. This evidently was meant to explain the mystery. He tore it open. He read it. Then he read it over.

That the contents of the note were exercising a powerful and not wholly pacifying influence upon him was easy to be seen. Miss Caxton had eloped with The Fool.

She asked him to look after the children until she should return, which would be as soon as she was married. Miss Caxton's father held the note out toward his angry reflection in the glass:

"Here's gratitude for you! Well, she needn't come back home,—I'm done with her!"

Then, being only a man, he swore; and while he swore he made up his mind to a course of action that he intended should very much astonish Miss Caxton, when that young lady returned as Mrs. Some-body-else.

"Does she think I'll stand this? I see myself forgiving her. If I lay my hands on The Fool he'll spend his honeymoon with broken bones!"

Suddenly he bethought him of the little boys. They no doubt had availed themselves of the absence of all restraining force to do as they pleased. As this flashed through his mind he turned a trifle pale. He rather regretted that he had been so severe with Leander, for supposing—

He ran down-stairs and into the yard, only stopping to glance at the kitchen stove with a vague dread lest Leander had crawled into it and been cremated. On reaching the yard he examined the well, and was greatly relieved to find it empty of everything except water.

Then he espied the little boys with the twin between them perched upon the roof of a convenient coal shed in the rear of the house, whither they had withdrawn, knowing that something unusual was about to happen. The instant his eyes fell upon him his habitual acrimony for the twin asserted itself:

"Come down off of that! Do you want to break your necks?" he gasped. "Come down, I say!"

This the little boys were reluctant to do. They knew their father as an exceedingly irate gentleman. Therefore, when they caught sight of him, it begot no special joy in their hearts. Roderick and Thaddeus started to descend

100

from the roof, while the twin, lifting up his voice, howled forth his dismay.

"Hold on to the twin!" called Miss Caxton's father. "Do you wish him to fall?"

What activity the little boys possessed was dispelled by their father's evident anger. They sat upon the ridge of the roof, motionless and speechless. Their parent inspected the premises.

"How in the name of sense did you get up there?"

A sob from Leander was the only answer. Thaddeus and Roderick maintained a discreet silence.

Miss Caxton's father was a very busy man for the next fifteen minutes. He obtained a long pole and poked the little boys off the roof, one at a time, beginning with the twin; then as they rolled from the shed he ran and caught them. A good deal of physical energy was required in the operation, and when Roderick was dislodged, he being the last, Miss Caxton's parent was hot and exhausted; there was also a baleful gleam in his eyes, suggestive of the wrath to come.

He picked up the twin, whose small lungs seemed to distil shrieks, and followed by the little boys who sulked at his side, entered the house. During the next hour or two he gained a larger experience in the pure joys of domestic life than are usually crowded into so brief a period.

He gave Roderick and Thaddeus their supper—and something else as well —and put them to bed. Then he took Leander in hand, and tried to get his faculties into a condition for sleep.

The twin refused to be comforted; he wanted Miss Caxton, and Miss Caxton only. It was the burden of his woes. His father looked at him. In his glance paternal love seemed to be in abeyance.

"You'd better make up your mind to going to bed without her, for she's put you to sleep for the last time."

Whereat Leander howled afresh.

"If you don't stop and let me have a moment's quiet, I shall punish you. You hear?"

Leander choked down a sob and was silent.

"There," said his father approvingly, "I guess we can get along all right. Now, you go to sleep—right off."

Leander's sobs broke forth again.

"What's the matter now?"

More sobs and a howl.

"I thought I told you to keep still. Why don't you?"

Then he grew persuasive.

"Don't you love your papa?"

The twin looked at him with wide eyes.

"I am appealing to his better self," reflected Miss Caxton's parent. "The instinct of affection that a child has is a most wonderful thing, a wonderful thing."

Leander dissolved into tears.

"Hang the brat! What's got into him now?"

Miss Caxton's parent arose and paced the floor. Leander's grief continued unchecked. His father regarded him in amazement; the twin's capacity for sorrow was very astonishing; and his anger merged into something akin to wonder.

"He must be very wet inside," he thought

He addressed the twin in conciliatory tones.

"See here, Leander, do you think it safe to cry like that?"

But Leander, unheeding him, wept on, in a highly original manner. His father grew uneasy.

"Why doesn't he stop? Hush! There! There! To please papa, who loves you so much. Confound you! How long is this going to last—will it be all night?" he asked himself.

His resentment was weakening. Each sob of the twin lessened the enormity of Miss Caxton's crime. Her father was willing to take her back at any price— and The Fool into the bargain. In desperation he brought the sugar bowl and placed it as an offering of peace at Leander's feet.

"That should stop him," he muttered.

But it didn't. With a guilty blush he went down upon his knees in a vain effort to seduce the twin in the belief that he was a horse. He was in this interesting position when Miss Caxton opened the door and entered, smiling and serene. The Fool was with her, but he was by no means so serene as he could have wished to be and his smile was not an easy one.

Miss Caxton mastered the situation at a glance. Without a word she possessed herself of the twin's small person.

"I am sorry, papa, that you missed your game of whist, but it won't occur again," she said, as she walked from the room.

When she returned twenty minutes later, after having put Leander to bed, she found her father peacefully drinking cold tea—"to restore the tone to his nervous system," as he explained—while he gave The Fool a detailed and truthful account of his adventure with the twin.

THE HALF-BREED

John LE BO YEN was an Indian half-breed; the son of a whisky-drinking white man and a slovenly whisky-drinking squaw. Fate, which decreed he should have a copper skin, lifted him into temporary and unsavory prominence only as the perpetrator of certain vulgar atrocities, yet because there had been peace on sea and land for a decade, history once paused to give him a brief paragraph. Balancing the books, after another decade, she dropped him out of her record of events.

As a boy, Le Boyen had been taken in hand by the government and sent to school, where he mastered a little reading and less spelling with infinite difficulty. Later he was turned back on his reservation, given land, together with a yearly allowance in supplies, and told to shift for himself.

Now the grazing lands of Le Boyen's reservation were particularly fine and the neighborhood ranchmen rented the range from the Indians for their cattle. All went well until the stockmen sent in a petition to Congress praying that virtuous body to remove the Indians, as they interfered materially with the cattle business. Congress despatched a commission to inquire into the matter.

The tribe had been given their land just fifteen years previous, with the solemn assurance that they should not be molested. They had before that been moved exactly three times. These moves had each involved a little war, and the government had shot a few of the rebellious tribesmen at a cost of several thousand dollars apiece, which was expensive, but had proved profitable in the long run, for, once dead, they cost nothing to maintain. This was indeed the cheapest mode of procedure.

The commissioners came upon the scene and they found the Indian very much in the way. He was dirty, wasteful and not to be tolerated. When they had seen these things, they returned to Washington to deliberate. This last consisted mainly in discussing the next election—the true essence of statesmanship. A month or so later the Indians were informed that the great white father, who had his home toward the rising sun and who was chiefly notable because of his insatiate appetite for land, desired their reservation. The tribe voiced a feeble protest, but the pressure brought to bear upon the white father was rather more than he had the moral backbone to withstand. Troops were massed in the vicinity preparatory to a summary dumping of the Indians farther west.

The threatened calamity had brought the savages together in one corner of the reservation. They buzzed like a swarm of angry bees. The young men danced strange dances, and chanted songs their fathers had chanted when there were buffaloes on the plains; but the old men, the men who had gone out in seventy-three with Captain Jack, shook their heads. They had known the white father to devour whole tribes, simply that he might call a few rods of sage brush and buffalo grass his own.

When night settled down the chiefs gathered around the council fire. After the weak and ineffectual manner of savages, they wished to test the forbearance of the dominant race; they might make a harmless little dash into the cow country and then, before the troops were fairly on their trail, slip back to the agency. Under similar circumstances the white father had been known to display a prodigal generosity in the matter of lean contract steers, which were turned out to be slaughtered and gorged on.

In the midst of these deliberations, a man strode into the circle of light. It was Le Boyen, who silently raised his arm high above his head. The reeking trophies his hand held brought the shadowy figures pressing close about him, while a sullen murmur grew up out of the tense stillness that had fallen on the tribe. The half-breed had precipitated an unexpected crisis. Already mounted men were spurring over the range spreading the news of another Indian outrage. As this sure knowledge took hold of the savages, the murmur swelled into a roar.

All in a second the group resolved itself into a sea of tossing arms and waving hands, and a portion of the straining mob became detached, wrenching and tearing itself away from the rest. In the center of the detached band was Le Boyen. About him were twenty or thirty men who were ready to put their fortunes to the hazard of war, and following them came their wives and children. These fell back unhindered upon the tents, struck camp, got together their horses and rode away. To state the case exactly, Le Boyen, with perhaps thirty men and an equal number of women and children, had taken preliminary steps to declaring war against the United States of America.

During the next ten days he and his followers were a fruitful source of newspaper interest. His experience had taught him, among other things worth remembering, that if you kill a man he is done for. Had his education taught him proportion he would have known it was wasted labor on his part to begin the extermination of sixty odd millions of human beings with the means and men he had at hand. Not appreciating this, he began his ambitious undertaking at once, moving across the plains with no fixed plan or destination, gathering in the settlers along his line of march; and the gathering in was attended by horrors not to be told. Then he took himself off toward the mountains with the most complete and extensive collection of scalps made in many years.

Through all these days of success his interest in the total destruction of the white race never flagged; but certain of his followers were not so constituted that they cherished a lofty ideal purely for the ideal's sake. These, after the first flush of war had paled its glow for them, began to think sadly of consequences. The hard life, the thirst and starvation of the foray, grew stale and tedious; they longed for the ease and sloth of the reservation, where water was plenty and rations had the noble quality of regularity.

Two Indians in particular wished to be taken back into the fold; and as the days came full of effort and hunger, this wish thrived apace, and they agreed that the white father would doubtless pay well for a little information as to Le Boyen's whereabouts. To furnish him with the coveted knowledge it would be necessary for one to remain with the band, while the other deserted. Their plan was no sooner perfected than it was acted upon, and Le Boyen, suspecting the meaning though not the extent of the disaffection, put his people on forced marches. For four days they toiled into the mountains, while the traitor in their midst left his fatal marks on every rod of land they crossed. On the fourth day the band went into camp, that Le Boyen might have time in which to mature plans for the future.

Day had scarcely dawned again when the traitor stole out to inspect his surroundings. All the warriors slept, even to the guards, who, as they sat about the ashes of the fires, nodded over the guns in their laps. The only ones astir were a few Indian mothers, who were already lashing their babies to the travaux strapped to their lean dogs. The traitor had mounted a rugged bluff that overhung the canyon leading back into the valley where the temporary encampment was made, and straining his eyes to the farthest distance he saw what he yearned to see, a long line of mounted men. Rations were destined to be regular and his heart was glad. Without a backward glance toward the camp he started on a run in the direction of the approaching horsemen.

In the valley the band slumbered on. The fagged ponies nipped the grass. The squaws moved quickly to and fro among the tents. Then one of the dozing sentries awoke with a start and stood erect. Black against the crimson disk of the rising sun he saw the solitary figure of a man; and even as he gazed another and another filed into view. He knew they were mounted men, though a rise in the ground hid the horses from his sight. While he stood looking at them in stupid and speechless amazement, they wheeled over the intervening hillock with the sharp clang of steel on stirrup iron, and with a wild hurrah raced down the hill upon the camp. What the savages first knew, roused from their sleep, was that a hundred men were riding furiously among the tents with blazing carbines. The surprise was so complete that the Indians offered no resistance; those who could, men, women and children, rushed toward the ponies, stimulated by a vague hope that they might escape; and as they ran they were shot down.

Foremost among those who strove to reach the horses was Le Boyen. His war pony, saddled and bridled in constant readiness for alarms, grazed apart from the tired mounts of his party. He reached and threw himself astride of it, and with a yell whirled through the ranks of the slaughtering whites. In the stupendous strain of the few short seconds while he was flying through their midst he was absolute master of himself, and in a cloud of dust and smoke, a score of men firing at his half-naked figure, he dashed up the trail unscathed, away from the horror of total annihilation that lurked in the valley.

Ahead of him the trail dipped into a narrow bottom. Crossing this it wound up a steep ascent and disappeared in a rocky gorge. Le Boyen gained the bottom and the partial cover of its timber, when his horse stumbled. He drew it up with a savage jerk. The next instant it collapsed in a heap under him. He cleared his feet from the stirrups and leaped from the saddle, and with his cartridge belt in one hand and his rifle in the other, plunged through the brush toward the ascent. At his back the mounted men came crashing through the timber, and as Le Boyen sprang out of the cover and bounded up the ascent, the bullets of his pursuers flecked up the earth at his feet; but he gained the entrance of the gorge in safety, and threw himself down behind the first shelter that offered, a great square of granite.

He had his revolvers to fall back upon, so he emptied the magazine of his repeater. When the smoke cleared away he saw that his fire had been eminently successful. Two men lay dead at the base of the ascent, and a third, wounded, was endeavoring to crawl away. Le Boyen knew that his case was hopeless. He wondered what was back of him, if it were not possible to enter the gorge farther along. In fancy he saw his own hurried rush for a fresh cover. It would be the last episode in the clenching of a victory destined in point of conclusiveness to be little short of a massacre.

A medley of sounds came from the camp. He heard the voices of the white men; an occasional order given; the piteous yelping of the dogs; now and then a stray shot. A glance in the direction of the valley told him what this last meant: the soldiers were shooting the dogs, who, faithful to their tiny charges, would not allow the white men to approach them. Wary and thoroughly frightened, they circled about the camp, stopping at intervals to howl dismally. An officer had suggested the expedient of shooting the dogs as the only means of saving the babies; but this was not proving successful, for sometimes the dogs moved at the wrong moment or the soldier's aim would prove uncertain, and the baby and not the dog would be shot.

In the timbered bottom a gray-haired colonel was listening to the reports of several soldiers, who, according to the fertility of their imagination, variously estimated that there were from ten to twenty Indians secreted among the rocks.

"Then they are very saving of their ammunition," commented the colonel dryly. He turned to the officer at his side: "What do the scouts say, Captain? Is there any way of getting at the rear of the redskins?"

"Yes, Colonel."

"How long will it take?"

"About two hours."

"Very well. Detail Lieutenant Brookes and twenty of our men to make the ditour. We'll keep the volunteers here." The colonel looked annoyed. "I don't like this, Gordon," he said. "I wish it might have come six months hence, when I shall be retired and growing roses in California with my wife on that bit of a ranch I've told you of.... Do be careful about those dogs; detail two or three of the best shots for that work."

A bullet from Le Boyen's Winchester cut a leaf from just over the colonel's head.

"Better fall back, Colonel," suggested Gordon, on the point of turning away.

There was another report from among the rocks, and the colonel sat down very stiffly on the trunk of a fallen tree, the expression of his face one of utter astonishment.

"Are you hit?" cried Gordon.

"I believe I am," said the colonel in a whisper. He raised his hand to his breast as he spoke; then he coughed, and Gordon saw that there was blood on his lips. Before he could reach him, the colonel had fallen and lay quite still among the tangled underbrush.

They made a place for him on the edge of the timber, and Gordon covered him with his own coat.

"Poor old colonel!" he said sadly to his lieutenant. "He always wanted to grow a garden, poor fellow, and in six months he would have been free to amuse himself in his own way." There was a pause. "Well, make up the ditour party and get it started; I'll give those redskins something to think of while Brookes is getting to their rear."

During the next half-hour, from his place of concealment, the half-breed did much excellent shooting, now and again changing his position, while the bullets of the command flattened themselves on the rocks that hid him.

When the lieutenant rejoined his superior after Brookes' departure, he found that Gordon had taken up his station near the spot where the colonel had been killed. It overlooked the edge of the timber where he had stationed his men. The lieutenant, who was fresh from the East, was palpably nervous; while the captain's manner indicated long familiarity with just such affairs as the one in hand.

"Brookes has gone?" he queried, without waiting for the lieutenant to speak.

"Yes, half an hour ago."

"And there's nothing stirring in the camp back of us? That was a pretty clean sweep. How about Sergeant Porter and the dogs?"

"He thinks he's got them all, sir."

"That's good; that's very good!"

Gordon took the young man by the arm, and side by side they fell to pacing back and forth. The captain was well pleased with the situation.

"Brookes and his party will soon be behind the redskins," he observed; "and when they break for fresh cover we shall have a good chance to test the new guns and ammunition."

The lieutenant smiled. It was not a mirthful smile; but then he was between the captain and the gorge, and anything like enthusiasm over gunshot wounds was beyond him.

"Do you count on the home talent standing if the Indians try for this cover?" he asked.

"Certainly. The cowboys don't have much of an open season in which to shoot Indians. We'll wind 'em up in the open." Levelling his field-glass, the captain took a hasty survey of the gorge. "I guess they are coming now. Yes, it's Brookes and his men!"

Le Boyen, among the rocks, was also aware of the approach of Brookes. He was also aware that the captain was getting his men in hand. He had found time to roll a boulder or two to the rear of the position he had originally assumed, and now, on the top of one of these, he placed his two revolvers. On the whole, he was not particularly desirous of living since the destruction of his band; but he was desirous of doing as much hurt to his enemies as he could.

The volleys of the men from below and the volleys of the men in his rear now swept his hiding-place. It would have been fatal to expose a hand or an arm even. He would wait until the two parties had advanced so close that they must discontinue their fire, then there would be a brief second or two in which one who was really indifferent about living could do much harm. And so it happened that Brookes and his men were face to face with the rest of the command, scarcely fifty yards separating them, when Le Boyen picked up a revolver in each hand and rose from his lair. Before the startled troopers knew what he meant to do, he was emptying them in their faces.

The captain had been the last man up the ascent, owing to the shortness of his legs. He found Brookes and his men clustered about a solitary figure on the ground, a figure riddled and torn with bullets.

"Humph!" with a glance at the half-breed. "Where are the rest, men?" he added.

"That's all, sir," said Brookes.

"Nonsense; you don't mean that he stood us off alone?"

The lieutenant looked at the figure on the ground.

"It's just about the right proportion, don't you think?" he ventured.

"Well, I wouldn't say that for the credit of the race," said the captain. "Poor old colonel; think of getting shot in an affair of this kind!"

WILLIE

THEY say The Pines is a great place to feed. I thought you'd be tickled to death with the assignment!" said Chisholm.

Bentley Ames' glance came back from the dome of the capitol, seen now through the closing mists of a rainy day and the falling twilight, to rest on his chief's face with a lurking suspicion of disfavor.

"I supposed you'd let me cover the convention," he said. "What's Carveth going down to Little Mountain for?—if he wants the nomination why doesn't he get busy?"

"He's made his canvass. You see, Ames, he runs a factory in one of the western counties,—makes shirts,—the business office gets a thousand a year out of him and the News has got to treat him right." And the following morning, Ames, the expression of whose face told of the spirit of resignation that possessed him, boarded the train for Little Mountain.

He expected to reach his destination by ten o'clock, but there was a freight wreck on the road. As a result he spent five hours at a sad little way station, and when the line resumed its functions as a common carrier, he took the afternoon train that had just pulled in. He first sought the parlor-car, which he found occupied by three ladies; then in rather low spirits, his mind divided between thoughts of the luncheon he had not had and the dinner he would order at The Pines, he wandered on into the smoker. Near the door were four men playing cards. There next fell under his scrutiny a young fellow of five or six and twenty, who was reading a shabby volume of Emerson. Three seats farther on was the only other passenger in the car, a solidly built man of sixty with a pleasant ruddy face; he was dressed in black broadcloth and wore a high silk hat, and as Ames dropped into the seat opposite him he gave the News man a half smile of friendly recognition. There was something so genial and winning in his very air that Ames smiled in return.

"Sightly, ain't it?" and the silk hat dipped in the direction of the autumn landscape, where the brown fields yielded at intervals to gorgeous reds and russets set in a murky haze. Ames admitted the beauty, and the stranger took the cigar from between his strong even teeth. "Fond of nature?" he inquired.

In a general way Mr. Ames was, but he was not enthusiastic about it; indeed, he was so profoundly sophisticated that sensation of any sort reached him in a very diluted form. The elder man scanned the younger; then he drew from the region of his hip a flat leather pocketbook. It yielded up a square of pasteboard which he passed across the aisle to Ames, who read: "Jeremiah Carveth. Originator Plymouth Rock Dollar Shirt. 'Made on Honor.'.rdquo;

"By Jove!" cried Ames. "You're just the man I want to see, Mr. Carveth. I'm from the News."

"Are you now?" Mr. Carveth was frankly pleased. "What's your name?"

"Ames—Bentley Ames."

"Excuse me—" and Mr. Carveth turned in his seat. "Willie, step here!" he called, and the reader of Emerson put aside his book. "Mr. Ames, I want you should know my secretary, W. C. B. McPherson, William Cullen Bryant McPherson," said Mr. Carveth, when the secretary stood at his elbow. "He's a newspaper boy, too—does the locals on the Marysville Clarion. Mr. Ames, of the Capital City News, Willie."

W. G. B. McPherson gave Ames an embarrassed smile.

"Not a newspaper man in the sense that Mr. Ames is." It was evident he stood in awe of this more metropolitan member of the craft.

"I don't know about that," said Mr. Carveth. "I've always considered the *Clarion* a mighty clean sheet."

Ames smiled enigmatically. He was thinking of Mr. Carveth's rival, General Pogue, "Slippery Dick, who lived with his ear next the ground," and of James Cartwright Smith, who was back of the general. Carveth resumed the conversation.

"Ever been to Marysville? It's named after my wife; my factory's there."

Ames had not been to Marysville; he admitted, however, that he had heard of the place.

The landscape beyond the car windows had changed its characteristic aspect. The fields had grown smaller, the goldenrod and immortelles waved over heaps of stones in the fence-rows, while the russets and reds and browns had given place to the somber green of pine and hemlock. And now the train drew up at a tiny ornate station. The three men climbed into the coach that was waiting for them and were soon toiling up a winding road, from which they presently emerged upon the single street of a sleepy village. Beyond the village and crowning the mountain's summit they could distinguish the long stone and timber façade of The Pines in the shadow of the sinking sun.

Ames dined with the candidate and his secretary; afterward he interviewed Mr. Carveth. His story off his hands, he was lounging about the office with only the night clerk for company, when suddenly McPherson appeared; he was in his shirt-sleeves, while his feet were thrust into worsted bed-slippers;

in his hand he carried a pitcher. It was evident he did not see the two men in the corner by the news-stand, for after glancing about to get his bearings he disappeared down the corridor leading to the dining-room. A moment later they heard him rattle a locked door, then again the patter of his slippered feet sounded on the tessellated pavement, and he reappeared in the lobby. Ames heard him say "Dang it!" but rather in disappointment than in anger; and then the clerk emitted a shrill cackle of mirth, and McPherson, being thus made aware of the presence of the two men, faced them.

"Excuse me," he said. "But will you kindly tell me where I'll find the pump?"

Gray shadows invaded the darkness of the pines that clothed the slopes of Little Mountain, and through the open, eastward looking window of his room the morning sun shone in upon the News man. Perhaps he missed the clang of the trolley's gong, the early milk wagon's clatter on the paved street; perhaps it was the silence, scarce disturbed by the song of birds and the murmur of the wind in the pines, that roused him; but Bentley Ames emerged from his slumber and without changing his position, looked from his window into the red eye of the sun. He dressed and slipping out into the hall, tapped on McPherson's door.

"Come in," called the secretary, and Ames entered the room. McPherson was seated at his table, writing. "Oh, Mr. Ames—" he said. He seemed both pleased and embarrassed.

"Don't get up;" and Ames, establishing himself on the edge of McPherson's bed, began to roll a cigarette. "Suppose you tell me how Mr. Carveth broke into politics," he suggested.

McPherson's face lighted instantly with enthusiasm.

"There's a wonderful man, Mr. Ames; a splendid type of the American business man! You should go through his factory; you should see the hundreds of busy operators. You would understand then what Mr. Carveth means to Marysville. Marysville," added the secretary, "is pledged to Mr. Carveth."

"I dare say." But Ames was not impressed by the loyalty of Marysville.

"You don't think much of his chances?" ventured McPherson.

"What I think of them wouldn't be fit to print," said Ames candidly. "Dick Pogue's rather a hot proposition for your man to stack up against, and back of Pogue is J. C. Smith." Ames slipped off the edge of the bed and took a turn about the room.

"You must admit, Mr. Ames, that nobody has any confidence in either General Pogue or Mr. Smith," said McPherson.

"They can get along without it," said Ames with calm cynicism.

"I shouldn't like to think that any public man could go far without the trust of his fellow citizens," observed McPherson.

"With those ideas you should keep clear of politics. You and Mr. Carveth may as well retire to the classic regions of Susansville."

"Marysville," corrected McPherson mildly.

"Marysville, then," said Ames. He paused by the corner of McPherson's desk. "Well, the occasion will be interesting as a souvenir of public life, eh, McPherson?" and he smiled down pityingly on the top of the secretary's slightly bald head, for McPherson was looking into the pictured face of a young girl whose photograph, framed in red plush, decorated his desk. Ames extended his hand and possessed himself of the photograph, which he proceeded to examine. "Your sister?" he asked, after a moment's silence.

"Miss Carveth," said W. C. B. McPherson, but his voice had lost much of its agreeable quality.

"I beg your pardon," said Ames, flushing as he hastily returned the photograph to its place on the desk. McPherson quitted his chair.

"I think we had better go down-stairs," he observed stiffly.

They found Carveth waiting for them in the office.

"I been lookin' over the paper," he told Ames, as they seated themselves at the breakfast table. He turned to his secretary. "I can't see that we occupy so darn much space, Willie. The world seems unaware of the fact that Jeremiah Carveth and W. C. B. McPherson are willing to act as a kind providence in shaping the destiny of a freeborn people. I'm getting a sickenin' consciousness that there's tall timber growing for me." He laughed in McPherson's face, which had gone from white to red. "Cheer up, Willie, cheer up. It's good to be alive, and the rest is dividends. You mayn't land me in office, but what's the odds? Crisp and bright, Willie, crisp and bright!" he urged with kindly concern.

But the thought of defeat was a bitter thing to McPherson, and presently he excused himself and quitted the table.

"I want a meetin'-house talk with you, Ames," said Carveth, the moment the secretary was out of hearing. "I was all for private life, the privater the better, until Willie smoked me out. It's this way, I got a daughter—" Mr. Carveth paused; in spite of his habitual frankness he was struggling with a sudden sense of diffidence. "We got only the one child, and naturally her mother and I center everything on her; and we've been fortunate, for we've been able to give her a good many advantages. Now Willie's interested in Nellie; and Nellie's interested in Willie. It's a match her ma and I desire; but Willie's chuck-full of pride. He's got nothing but a salary of fifteen dollars a week, and he says he can't regard marriage as a commercial asset; and there you are." Mr. Carveth gave Ames an expressive smile. "I don't say but what Willie's right. He says if he can get me elected governor he'll feel that he ain't just an experiment. I guess you gather, from what I say, that I'm in politics to oblige Willie; and that's the situation."

The state convention met on the tenth of the month, and when the morning of the tenth dawned Ames was conscious of a feeling of disquietude. He rather took it out on Mr. Carveth's secretary.

"You'll see what a gilt-edged snap does for a man, Mr. McPherson," he observed. "Your little delegation and all the other little delegations will be given their little say, then Smith will quietly proceed to nominate his bunch; and it will dawn on a few enlightened minds that the business could have been transacted by just getting him on the phone in the first place." And having eased himself of this depressing prophecy, Ames began a perusal of the News.

Some two hours later the secretary hurried into the hotel office.

"In strict confidence, Mr. Ames," he said, and thrust a telegram into Ames' hand. It proved to be from James Cartwright Smith, and requested an immediate interview with Mr. Carveth.

"He'll take the first train to town?" asked Ames.

"I have just sent Mr. Carveth's answer. He will see Mr. Smith—here," said McPherson.

The next morning, when Smith descended from his car, Ames was on the platform, but as the *News* man advanced toward him the party leader shook his head.

"Nothing doing, Ames," he said.

"I didn't know but you'd come down to see Carveth," insinuated Ames.

"Carveth, Carveth? Oh, yes—merely a coincidence;" and he turned away to enter the coach.

"Interesting, but not true," murmured Ames. He let the coach drive off and then set out briskly in pursuit.

Reaching the hotel, he hurried up-stairs to a room on the second floor that immediately adjoined the one occupied by Mr. Carveth. There was a connecting door. Over this door was a transom and below the transom Ames had placed a table, on the table a rug, and on the rug a chair.

"I interpreted your wire as signifying your willingness to accept the nomination at the hands of the party organization," Smith was saying as Ames mounted to his post.

"Well—yes," answered the creator of the Plymouth Rock Dollar Shirt cautiously.

"We're going to read Dick Pogue out of meeting, Mr. Carveth; he's been fed from the public crib about long enough. I suppose you've seen in the Washington despatches that Senator Burke is ill? One of the first jobs the next governor will have will be to appoint his successor."

"That's so; but you ain't told me where the hitch comes in."

"Ain't I?" rasped out the boss. "It's just here: Pogue's got his eye on his brother for the place, yet when Burke was made senator it was agreed I was to follow him. Isn't it plain to you why I came down here? I want your word that I'm to succeed Burke; then I'll shake hands with the next governor."

"When it's business I'll dicker for anything I can swap, use myself, or give away; but I got a different feeling about politics," remarked Mr. Carveth.

This came with such a shock to Ames that he almost fell off his seat.

"Quite right, Mr. Carveth," said Smith pleasantly. "But a few pledges——"

"I won't promise nothin'," said Jeremiah Carveth with sudden stubbornness. "If I go to office I'm going there a free man. Otherwise Marysville's good enough for me."

"Not pledged in any offensive sense, Mr. Carveth," Smith urged. "We would never attempt to dictate a course of action to you——"

"I guess you wouldn't—more than once," said Carveth shortly.

Mr. Smith gasped audibly, and Ames surmised he was hearing the distant roar of the convention, the first rumble of that landslide he had prematurely set going, which was to bury Slippery Dick while it uncovered Jeremiah Carveth.

"I'm offering you the place at the head of the ticket," began Smith quietly. "That's tantamount to election; all I want is your promise that if Burke dies you'll appoint me to fill out his term——"

"Ain't you read any of my speeches?" asked Carveth. "Haven't you noticed that I take pretty firm ground in the matter of boss rule? Mr. Smith, you're the

116

last man I'd ever think of making senator. I don't want to seem rude, but, well, I've told you Marysville's good enough for me."

"Don't worry;" said Smith. "I had determined to support you; I could not imagine that you would be so blind to your own interests as not to meet me half-way; but a dozen telegrams will change the program—you'll go back to Marysville all right."

McPherson had slipped from the room, and Ames abandoned his post and hurried in pursuit. He was just in time to see the secretary's long legs vanishing around a turn in the corridor. Keeping them in sight he descended to the office floor. McPherson was now speaking directly to the clerk.

"Will you go personally to Mr. Carveth's room and interrupt the conference there between him and Mr. Smith? Mr. Smith wishes particularly to catch the eleven-ten train."

Ames retired to the check-room. As the clerk's footsteps died out in the hall overhead, he heard a chair dragged across the tessellated floor, and peering out from his place of hiding, he saw McPherson by the aid of this chair reach the office clock and resolutely turn the hands back twenty minutes. This accomplished, McPherson took himself into the open air. He raced down the road toward the telegraph office. Here Ames found him fifteen minutes later scribbling away at one corner of the operator's deal table. He glanced up as Ames entered the room.

"Oh, Mr. Ames," he said, "look from the window and tell me when the coach from the hotel arrives." Even as he spoke they heard the shriek of the engine's whistle. McPherson sighed softly. "I'm afraid Mr. Smith has missed his train," he said. "And I think he was quite anxious to catch it."

Twenty minutes slipped by and there was a hasty step upon the threshold, and James Cartwright Smith burst into the room.

"Here, rush these telegrams!" he roared, and tossed a dozen sheets of paper in front of the operator.

"The wire's busy, Mr. Smith," said McPherson mildly, so mildly there was almost a touch of sadness in his tone.

The great man turned to the operator.

"Throw this stuff out of the window, or I will, and send those wires."

McPherson measured the politician with a large prominent eye, then he said in a tone that would have carried conviction to a less excited man than Smith:

"If you do that, you'll go after it, and it's twenty feet to the ground."

For answer Smith made a grab at the pile of copy in front of the operator. McPherson shot up to his full height of six feet, and extending a long arm, seized him by the wrist.

"It's twenty feet to the ground, Mr. Smith," he remonstrated. Smith swung about on his heel.

"How can I get away from here, Ames?" he asked.

"You'll have to wait until eleven-ten to-morrow," said Ames cheerfully. The leader groaned aloud. "Come," Ames added, "you go to the hotel with me, and we'll be back here after lunch." But once he had coaxed Smith back to The Pines, he abandoned him and hurried again to the telegraph office.

"See here, McPherson," he expostulated, "it's all right where Smith is concerned, but how about me?"

"I'd love to oblige you, Mr. Ames; later, perhaps."

"But that won't do any good," urged Ames impatiently.

"No, I suppose not, since the News is an evening paper."

"And what's the *Clarion?*"

"Semi-weekly," said the secretary pleasantly.

The secretary wrote telegrams to the *Clarion* until he wearied of that pastime; then he began to tear pages out of his copy of Emerson. Incidentally he and Ames had passed to a state of siege. It became necessary to spike the office door fast to the jamb to keep out James Cartwright Smith, who, supported by a bell boy and the night watchman from The Pines, had established himself in the narrow hall, where he kept the air thick with threats and curses.

Six o'clock came and McPherson was still flashing the Concord sage's wisdom into Marysville. Mr. Smith was still on the stairs, but the boss no longer swore nor threatened; his tone was one of entreaty, his words abject. Two hours later and he was offering McPherson any sum he chose to name for five minutes' use of the wire. At ten o'clock he was heard to descend the stairs and pass up the road in the direction of The Pines; whereupon Ames knocked the spikes out of the jamb and opened the office door on a sleeping world; then he turned to McPherson.

"I suppose you are going to hold on to your end of the wire until the convention adjourns?" he observed. The secretary nodded and flipped a fresh page of Emerson across the table.

"Wait a bit, boss," said the operator. "I got to take off a message for you."

The message was from the leader of the Carveth delegation. As McPherson slowly absorbed its meaning a smile of intense satisfaction overspread his features. He passed it on to Ames, who read: "Carveth nominated. Hip—hip —hurrah!"

"This means a great deal to me, Mr. Ames," said McPherson softly. "Indeed, it means everything." Quite unconsciously he had slipped his hand into the breast pocket of his coat, and Ames caught sight of the plush frame that held Miss Carveth's picture.

MR. FEENY'. SOCIAL EXPERIMENT

ON the street some one had handed Mike Feeny an oblong of pasteboard. Mr. Feeny stoked with the Gulf and Mexican Transportation Line.

"Is it a ticket to a show?" he asked, removing his pipe.

"It is; go on in and enjoy yourself." And the donor laughed. He was a pleasant-looking young fellow in evening dress, much like the young fellows Mr. Feeny sometimes saw on the awning-covered promenade deck.

"I'm beholden to you," said he, being a person of manners when sober.

And pocketing his blackened pipe, he strode into the brilliant foyer of the Music Hall where the many lights fully disclosed him as a stoop-shouldered man of large muscular development, clothed in respectable shore-going garments recently purchased at a bargain of a Jewish gentleman on the river-front. A great shock of violently red hair formed an aureole about his long sad face, and the drooping ends of a blond mustache reached well back toward the freckled lobes of his ears. Mr. Feeny was strictly Irish, with the large potentialities of his race.

Now Mr. Feeny did not know that the International Congress of Economics had assembled there to give expert testimony, and charting a careful course in new shoes that pinched somewhat, he followed the trickle of well-dressed humanity into the building, where an usher showed him to an aisle seat in the last row of orchestra chairs. The orchestra was finishing a classic prelude. This first attracted Mr. Feeny's attention. It was displeasing to his musical tastes, and he remarked in a husky whisper to the gentleman on his left:

"Say, buddy, them fiddles is on the bum——"

"Hush!" said the gentleman, raising a warning finger.

"What for should I hush?" demanded Mr. Feeny. "Cheese it yourself!"

Feeling the incident closed, Mr. Feeny's glance shifted in the direction of the stage, where a number of men and women were seated in a wide half circle.

"'Tis a white-faced minstrel show! But, oh, heavens, ain't them girls the hard-featured huzzies?" thought Mr. Feeny.

A gentleman had risen and was making a few introductory remarks, the exact drift of which was lost on Mr. Feeny, but as he subsided, his place was taken by another gentleman who smilingly acknowledged the decorous ripple of applause his name had evoked. He commenced to speak and Mr. Feeny gave him his undivided attention.

"He's a grand flow of words. I wonder he don't choke," was his mental comment.

Eventually he became aware that he was listening to an account of the decay of the cottage industries of France. Laboriously following the speaker he possessed himself of this concrete fact in segments and was moved to instant contempt of the speaker's conclusions. He had never noticed this decay in industry; his personal observations led him to believe that while jobs were sometimes hard to obtain, there was always plenty of work after you got them.

He prepared to quit that spot with expedition, since he felt that any more economics would constitute a surfeit. But as he slid from his chair, the first gentleman advanced again to the center of the stage, and Mr. Feeny caught a name he knew, the magical name of MacCandlish.

"I'll see the next turn," he told himself, as amidst a perfect storm of applause a cheerful little man of a portly presence approached the footlights.

"It's him all right, I seen him onct through the bull's-eye window of the smoking-room afore the mate cussed me out forward,—and him worth his hundred millions!" Mr. Feeny breathed hard.

There was the hush of expectancy. The little man smiled kindly, tolerantly, while the lights seemed to cast a golden halo about him.

"It is my privilege to appear before this congress to speak on the uses of wealth," he began in a soft purring voice. "And I only regret that I have not had the leisure in which to prepare a paper on so interesting a theme. However—a few thoughts occur to me——"

Mr. MacCandlish paused for a brief space, and then once more that kindly voice flowed across the footlights. "It has always been my conviction that those who have lacked the opportunity to examine the operations of wealth are frequently led astray. In the first place, riches are invariably the direct result of great economic services undertaken for the good of mankind!"—and thus launched, Mr. MacCandlish began to deal not with the dead and dry of theories and panaceas, but with the living actualities of trade and production.

"Ain't it grand what the likes of him does for the likes of me!" thought Mr. Feeny in a pause, and then again that soft voice opened up fresh regions for him.

He saw that what Mr. MacCandlish called the law of supply and demand—

which he seemed to hold in the very tenderest regard—regulated things. He saw, too, that millionaires were only far-sighted individuals who had mastered the fact that what the world tossed aside to-day it would urgently need to-morrow, and garnered this waste, exacting a small margin of profit for the service.

"It's great!" Mr. Feeny told himself in a spent whisper. "I go somewhere as far as I can get, and raise things—no matter what—and then one of these here capitalists comes along and says: 'Feeny, me boy, how are your crops? I've one end of a thousand miles of railroad track at your front gate for to haul 'em away with.' No wonder they're well paid... 'tis right they should be,—I begrudge 'em nothing."

"And after all"—it was Mr. MacCandlish speaking—"let us see what actual advantages the millionaire has, what does his money buy him in excess of what another may have? A little better shelter perhaps, more costly clothes, and his three meals a day!"

"'Tis true," thought Mr. Feeny. "They'd bust if they et oftener, the way they feed; and as for clothes, I've seen their lady friends with far less on than a workin' man's wife'd think decent."

Mr. Feeny had entered that building a rather heedless person who got drunk at every port of call, and who knew the inside of every calaboose in every flea-bitten center of civilization along the Caribbean, but he was to quit it a groping intellectualist with a germ lodged in his brain that was to fructify.

Mr. Feeny boarded the *Orinoco* of the Gulf and Mexican Transportation Line a chastened spirit. His last hours ashore, and the last of his wages, had been spent in a second-hand book-shop where he had acquired three books that, under various titles, dealt with the burning question of why the other fellow happens to have it all; a condition that is much older than political economy, just as language is older than grammar. Now the *Orinoco*, newly scraped and painted as to staterooms and gilded saloons where the eye and foot of Mr. Feeny never penetrated, had been chartered for a mid-winter cruise. Mr. Feeny heard this directly from one of his mates, Tom Murphy, who had it from an oiler, who had it from the second assistant engineer.

"It's a party of magnates," he explained. "We're to have close on to a billion dollars aboard,—live weight, you understand. MacCandlish, the big railroad man—you've heard of him in the papers, Feeny—is one of the bunch, and they've got a Protestant bishop along,—but I don't think much of the likes of him!" In theory, at least, Mr. Murphy was an ardent churchman.

"For what are they usin' this old hooker?" demanded Feeny.

"They're goin' down to have a look at mines in Mexico," said Murphy.

Mr. Feeny's first keen lust for wisdom survived the days of heavy toil that were his portion.

"But I've read hotter stuff," he told himself one black night when he had been at sea ten days. He lay in his bunk and listened to the heavy seas break under the *Orinoco's* quarter. This was varied by mighty shivers when the racing screw fanned the air. And then suddenly it was as if tons and tons of water with the weight of lead, and driven by some vast power, had dropped on the *Orinoco*. Mr. Feeny sprang from his bunk. His first instinct was to rush for the deck, but thoughts of his mates in the stoke-hole sent him down the iron ladders that gave access to the vitals of the ship. As he gained the engine-room, the stokers burst out of their steel-walled pen, and after them came a rush of steam.

"All out?" roared Feeny.

"All out," some one bellowed in return, and they began swarming up the ladders, Feeny leaping from round to round in advance. At last, spent and breathless, they issued into the black night.

Then came a second shock. A mighty sea lifted the *Orinoco*, three thousand tons of steel and wood, and tossed her like a cork against something that did not yield to the terrific impact. Mr. Feeny picked himself up from among his fellows.

"She's aground,—and no thanks to her!" he bawled.

"The crew's gone with the boats!" said some one in his ear.

"Is that you, Tom Murphy? Let's see what's come of the millionaires!"

Mr. Feeny, chastely garmented in an undershirt, and with a wind-blown halo of red hair, invaded the smoking-room. His mates, naked to the waist and grimy from their toil, but showing patches of white skin here and there where the waves had touched them, slouched at his heels. They found that Capital was just getting on its feet. MacCandlish, his ruddy cheeks the color of Carrara marble, was crawling out from under a table where he had been thrown; the others of his party were variously scattered about the room.

"Yer left," said Feeny dispassionately. "Like us, yer left,—for the captain's gone with his crew. I'd recommend you lifted the large armchair off the stomach of the fat gentleman on the floor in the corner, he's breathing hard and quite purple," and Mr. Feeny having thus delivered himself, withdrew with his mates.

"'Twas a shame for the captain to leave 'em. I hope he drowns…" said

Feeny. "For duty's duty,—which reminds me that I'm the oldest man in the stoke-hole with more tons of coal to my credit than you'll equal even if you're given length of days, so I'll serve notice on ye, one and all,—I'm skipper!"

A wan light was lifting out of the east. It spread over the tossing seas and under the low ragged clouds that the gale sent hurrying into the south.

"There's land!" cried Mr. Feeny. Peering through the saline reek of the storm, they saw first a narrow spit of land, and here and there a stunted palmetto. Then as the light spread, higher ground, dense with a tropic growth; while beyond was the sea again, a long restless line of blue that backed against the horizon.

Mr. MacCandlish and his friends issued from the saloon and worked their way along the bulwark to the group of stokers.

"Well?" said the millionaire, and he addressed himself to Feeny.

"I'm thinking, sir, we'd best leave the old hooker when the sea ca'ms down a bit. Yonder's one of the life-boats hanging to its davits. Presently we'll h'ist it over the side and go ashore," said Feeny.

"Then you don't think we are in any imminent peril?" asked Mr. MacCandlish.

"That feelin' you got comes mainly from an empty stomach," said Mr. Feeny soothingly. "Here, Tom Murphy! you see if you can get these gentlemen their breakfast." He himself went below and accumulated a pair of trousers.

Then under his immediate direction breakfast was served in the saloon, while the stokers browsed about the forward deck. With hot coffee life took on a changed aspect; also Mr. Feeny's assured manner and the close proximity of the island combined to contribute their measure of hope to the minds and hearts of all. It was mid-morning, however, before Mr. Feeny declared it was not too great a hazard to attempt a landing, and to his "Easy, Murphy... easy, I say, Tom Murphy... Easy!" in a rising crescendo, the boat dropped into the water.

"Hurroar!" cried Mr. Feeny.

"Well done, my men!—very well done, indeed!" said Mr. MacCandlish.

"Splendid, true lads,—all of them!" murmured the bishop.

"If you'll step lively, sir, we'll have you dry shod on terry-firmy in a jiffy!" said Feeny.

Within an hour after they had effected a landing it had been definitely ascertained that the island was not inhabited.

"That bein' the case," said Mr. Feeny, "I think I would best put the b'ys to work fetchin' off supplies. What do you think, sir?"

"Oh, by all means." It was Mr. MacCandlish who answered him. He and his friends were peacefully resting in the shade of a group of palms. "And will you have an eye to our personal belongings? Our trunks and hand-bags, I mean?"

"I'll have them fetched off immediate," said Mr. Feeny.

All that afternoon he and his mates tugged at boxes and bales, or sweated at the oars. At dusk they stopped for a bite to eat, and to rig up a shelter of awnings for the millionaires.

"I'm doubtful about the weather," Mr. Feeny explained as he came up from the boat, his shoulders piled high with mattresses. "And bein' as there's a full moon to-night, we'll just bring off what more of the stores we can."

And at midnight when Mr. MacCandlish strolled out under the tropic moon for a last look about before turning in, he heard the voice of Feeny and the voices of Feeny's mates as they raged at their work. If the stokers slept that night, none of the millionaires could have told the space of time Mr. Feeny allotted to them for repose; for in the rosy dawn, when they ran down to the shore for a plunge in the surf, there midway between the wreck and the island was the life-boat piled high with stores. And all that day the work went on without pause. Only Murphy, with frying pan and coffee pot, snatched a few moments from his toil to minister to the comfort of the party under the awnings.

That night the wind slued round to the south and blew a gale; and when morning broke, the *Orinoco* had vanished finally from the sight of men.

"'Tis organization I'm teachin' the b'ys," explained Mr. Feeny.

"Ah!... organization," said Mr. MacCandlish.

"I've knowed about it since that night in New York when I heard you give 'em the talk in the theayter. It was great!"

"Were you there, Feeny?" asked MacCandlish.

This was the most subtle flattery he had ever known.

"Was I there? Drunk or sober, it was Mike Feeny's best day ashore! I been a understandin', reasonin' man ever since I listened to you. Supply and demand,—the problem of civilization, the problem of distribution,—bearin' this in mind I've divided the work. Tom Murphy's something of a cook, so I've app'inted him to the grub division, with Sullivan and the Portuguese to help. Corrigan, and Pete, the Swede, will bring our supplies up as we need 'em from the point where the salvage is stored. And I've put O'.ara to oysterin' for the good of the community. The other lads will work as comes handiest."

"You are showing excellent judgment, my man," said MacCandlish warmly.

Just at dusk that night, Mr. Feeny, in the presence of the stokers, hoisted a queer-looking flag down by the camp where he and his mates lived. Then standing with bared head beneath the fluttering pennant, he said:

"I pronounce these here the United States of Ireland!... In conference with Mister Murphy, I've decided on a Declaration of Independence and a Constitution which you can ask about if you're at all curious. If you ain't— I'll say this much for it,—we're opposed to anarchy, communism and socialism. We believe in the sacred rights of property—which is only another name for salvage. We believe, too, that the law of supply and demand is a great law, and well adapted for to take healthy root in this climate. We will now proceed to vote for Mike Feeny for president; Tom Murphy, police judge; Jack Corrigan, alderman; and Pete, the Swede, cop. 'Tis right the foreigners we have should hold some of the jobs. And now the elections bein' happily over, we'll just leave the public at large to discover what's been done for to make life brighter and easier for it."

Knowing nothing of those vicissitudes through which the island was passing, the public slept soundly, and after a refreshing plunge in the sea was ready for breakfast. But no smiling Murphy appeared. No Sullivan and no Portuguese came to do its bidding. Presently Mr. Feeny hove in sight swinging along the sands.

"Hurroar!" he cried. "We're organized,—completely organized! The law of supply and demand had adjusted herself to her surroundings, and Mike Feeny's the student of political economy what's done it!"

"Eh? What's all this, Feeny? And what's become of that loafer Murphy?" demanded Mr. MacCandlish.

"You go down with me to the new hotel tent, the St. Murphy-Feeny we call it, to typify the spiritual as well as the spirituous needs of man. Cooks is scarce,—they perform a necessary and useful function. So do waiters,— pickin' up food in the kitchen and distributin' it under the pa'ms. I hope you have your wads handy, for Mister Murphy's now doin' a cash business. Says he: 'We're a prosperous people. Things is naturally high; they'll be higher yet, by the grace of Heaven!'.rdquo;

"What is this crazy drivel?" said MacCandlish petulantly.

"Why hasn't breakfast been served us?" inquired the bishop, with marked asperity of manner. Feeny had fallen in his esteem.

"I am telling you what Mister Murphy says down at the Murphy-Feeny. Says he: 'Them great staples, Scotch whisky and bottled beer, is scarce, while such luxuries as bread and tinned stuff is reasonably abundant but firm in price, with every indication of a sharp advance. But,' says he, 'the per capita wealth of this nation's phenomenal, and it's evenly distributed—or will be in the near future.'.rdquo;

Mr. MacCandlish's brother-in-law laughed aloud at this. Since his marriage to the millionaire's sister, prices had not greatly troubled him; the cost of living could soar or sink, it was all one, and this cheerful optimism had packed the fat on his ample frame. But Mr. MacCandlish's business associates were built on more meager lines, and were of sterner stuff. They had, when expedient, ordered shut-downs and lock-outs with entire composure; and they had not scorned to profit by short crops to boost the price of bread. But MacCandlish shook his head. Feeny continued:

"I've vaccinated this coal-heavin' bunch with this here political economy serum, and it's took with every mother's son of 'em. They were ignorant cusses five days back, but now they are practical men of affairs."

"If this is a joke—" began Mr. MacCandlish.

"Do I look like I'd joke?" demanded Mr. Feeny. "It's system I'm telling you about,—the elimination of haphazard methods of distribution, for one thing. Now there's Corrigan, a husky lad with a good back and a strong pair of arms, him and Pete, the Swede, has become common carriers for the good of all,—you'll find none commoner anywhere. The Portuguese's buildin' a fence about the bananas and cocoanuts preparatory to puttin' a price on 'em. He's a taste for farmin' and is aimin' to develop the natural resources of this island. By the same token, Corrigan's gone into the poultry business with them turtles, and O'.ara's adopted the oyster beds. He says there's a future in oysters. He looks for a short crop, as he's got no gum boots and is timid about gettin' his feet wet,—but with prices fair, and constantly tendin' higher round the R in February."

They had reached what Mr. Feeny called the hotel tent. The *Orinoco's* awnings had been used with admirable effect, and across the front of the canvas edifice was displayed a sign with letters two feet high, "St. Murphy-Feeny. European Plan." The humor of the situation seemed lost on Mr.

MacCandlish and his party; only the stout brother-in-law laughed, but a hostile glance from the eye of a friend caused him to repress his mirth.

"Mister Murphy's prepared to cater for you at them prices that has the indorsement of the Hotel Trust," said Mr. Feeny.

"I denounce this as an iniquitous outrage! It's downright piracy!" sputtered Mr. MacCandlish, very red in the face.

"Easy," said Mr. Feeny soothingly. "We made a fair split with the salvage, but feelin' that you'd prefer to have the whole of your personal belongin's we let 'em offset the ship's stores. Now do you be reasonable! Mr. Murphy says he'll have no rough-house for his. Any man that's white and willin' to behave himself can feed here. For such as can't conform to these simple rules, Pete, the Swede, will do the bouncin'. 'twill be one, two, three and out ye go to the inquest. I little thought, Mr. MacCandlish, sir, I'd have to p'int out to you of all men the fairness of this arrangement," continued Mr. Feeny severely. "Ain't it highly necessary you should be fed and looked after? You can't well do that for yourself, havin' outgrowed the habit; and you're too busy playing poker, when you ain't eatin' and sleepin', to rightly know what you do need ____"

"Bridge!" snapped Mr. MacCandlish.

"It's cards, ain't it? Well, the b'ys and me have agreed to take the job of caring for you off your hands. Having saved the salvage from the sea, we are minded to turn an honest penny with it, but owin' to the scarcity of the necessities of life and bein' aware that none know better than yourselves that the value of a thing depends on how hard it is to get, the St. Murphy-Feeny will adopt a scale of prices that will compare favorably with what you're used to in New York, at them places that's run for the millionaire trade. I've heard in the papers of your eatin' meals costin' twenty dollars a plate, and that sometimes your lady friends dissolves pearls and di'monds in the apple vinegar for to take away that cheap taste; we can't give you di'monds and pearls, nor yet 'lectric lights, but we can give you prices—" Mr. Feeny rested a long forefinger against the side of his nose. "Maybe we can go 'em one better—Mister Murphy, how is it with ham and eggs this day?"

"With two eggs?" asked Murphy.

"With two eggs," said Mr. Feeny.

"To be served one person?"

"To be served one person. I hope you'd have too much self-respect for to let a customer split his order!" said Mr. Feeny.

"I would,—I'd bust his crust," said Murphy. "Twenty dollars if the eggs is fried on one side, thirty dollars if they're fried on both sides. The extra labor makes this slight difference in price. I would mention, too, that the privilege of shakin' the pepper castor onced on your vittles is five dollars. Rates for more extended service on application."

"Well, no one has to eat here unless he wants to," said Mr. Feeny.

"You never said a truer word, Mike Feeny. They can go hungry if they like."

Now finance is a big subject, but Mr. Feeny and his mates attacked it' with the same energy they would have attacked a bunker of coal, consequently prices performed miracles in the way of change; but as Mr. Feeny had prophesied, they constantly tended higher; also their prevalence was wide-spread; for that red-headed student of political economy resolutely fixed a value to each service and to every necessity.

At first MacCandlish had been disposed to negotiate checks, with the disingenuous intention of later stopping payment on them, but Feeny held out firmly for cash.

"When that's all gone, we'll take over your paper," he said. "I'm thinkin' of starting a bank for to accommodate it; but as long as your money lasts we'll just keep on doin' a nice cash business."

And MacCandlish submitted, but with a very bad grace, to what he regarded as the iniquitous exactions of the stokers. Always before when prices had been high, he had directly benefited; indeed, high prices and good times had been synonymous terms with him.

It was an added strain that the castaways were his guests. Under the circumstances it required all that decision of character for which he was rightly famous to suggest that they stop eating. But he pointed out that if they did this, there must come inevitable collapse to Feeny's elaborate commercial system; it was merely a matter of principle, he explained; and early one morning he led his friends to the far end of the island, where they would be remote from temptation and the allurements of the St. Murphy-Feeny.

"We'll presently bring those scoundrels to their senses," he said. "We'll freeze 'em out and dictate our own terms."

"I think you've managed this all wrong!" said his brother-in-law gloomily.

"How so?" snapped the great man.

"I'd have started the boycott after breakfast. If we must starve for a principle, I for one should prefer not to do it on an empty stomach. I've always regarded breakfast as a most important meal—the keystone of the day, as it were. No, certainly I should not think of beginning to go hungry until after I had breakfasted,—it's an awful handicap!"

The bishop spoke dreamily of lunch. He made it clear that he rather sided with the brother-inlaw. He admitted that he had frequently gone without lunch; it could be managed where one had anticipated such a contingency—but breakfast and dinner—the good man sighed deeply.

"You'll probably have an opportunity to try going without both," said MacCandlish tartly.

The bishop groaned outright at this, and fell to gathering wild flowers for his herbarium. He wandered farther and farther afield in his quest. After a time the brother-in-law observed that he had disappeared along the sands. A gleam of quiet intelligence flashed from his eyes. He rose languidly from the fallen log on which he had been sitting and sauntered off without so much as a glance at MacCandlish.

"Where are you going?" demanded MacCandlish sharply.

"I am going to look for the bishop," said his brother-in-law with dignity, and he, too, vanished along the sands.

The sun soared higher and higher above the palms and burned splendidly in the blue western arch of the heavens. MacCandlish, watching its flight, reflected grimly but with satisfaction that he had shepherded his little flock safely past the luncheon hour. Presently one of the castaways expressed great anxiety concerning the bishop, and declared his purpose of going immediately in search of him. Two others of the party were quickened to sympathetic interest in this project and announced their willingness to share in it.

The sun sank toward the heaving restless blue of the ocean. In distant peaceful centers of life, happy millionaires were beginning to think of dinner. Realizing this, Mr. MacCandlish experienced a poignant moment, and felt his Spartan fortitude go from him. He turned to speak to one of his friends, and discovered that he was entirely alone. He glanced warily about him, and then stole off through the jungle in the direction of the St. Murphy-Feeny.

He was not wholly surprised when he found that his friends had preceded him thither. They were clustered sadly about Mr. Feeny, who was explaining that the St. Murphy-Feeny was temporarily closed to the public.

"They've gone on a strike, the b'ys have. Capital's in the kitchen and labor's out under the pa'ms, both full of principle and strong drink. It's a private matter between the two, only it's my belief you'll get no dinner this day. 'Compromise,' says I to Murphy. 'Compromise—nothin'.' says Murphy to me. 'I'll teach them dogs they can't run my business,—it's me private affair.' 'Think of your public,' says I. 'The public be damned!' says he. And there you are! It's the conflict of two opposin' ideas,—as they say in one of me books. Just like it is when the trolley's tied up and you have to walk five miles to get home."

Mr. Feeny sighed. "I'm thinkin' Mister Murphy will have to h'ist his prices to make good this day's loss. 'Tis wonderful how easy political economy is to learn when you put your mind to it... but dinner's got a black eye."

"What's the row about, Feeny?" asked Mr. MacCandlish. Hunger tempered the visible manifestations of his indignation, but a hard steely glitter lurked in the corners of his eyes. It boded ill for Mr. Feeny when they left that island.

"You upset the delicate balance holdin' supply and demand steady on their jobs, when you quit eatin' this mornin', Mr. MacCandlish. It immejiately provoked hard feelin's between Mister Murphy of the Hotel Trust and Mr. Sullivan and the Portuguese of the Labor Combine. As I've just been explainin' to your friends,—I hate these strikes,—there's the loss in wages to labor, and the cripplin' effect on capital. The Portuguese and Mister O'.ara of the Oyster Trust are figuring up what it's cost them, and Mister Corrigan of the Poultry Trust is hoppin' mad. Eggs is a natural breakfast food, he says, and he's the heaviest loser. They tell me, too, that he so far forgot himself as to put his foot in the Swede's face, closin' one eye and giving his nose a strong list to starboard. Just why he done so I ain't rightly learned, but it must have been along of feelin' peevish about the outlook for the poultry business. You see, *I* can do nothing,—and, anyhow, I'm thinkin' of foundin' a library where you can go for to improve your minds.... 'The Feeny Foundation,— Established by Michael Feeny, 1910. A University of the People, endowed by Michael Feeny.' Can you think where the name could be introduced again without seemin' a mere repetition? Mister Murphy's decided to have a 'Ospital for his. 'What's a Captain of Industry without his little fad?' says he. 'Vittles may cost a trifle more, but I'll have my 'Ospital,' he says."

Mr. MacCandlish had forsaken the group that clustered about Feeny, and stolen to the back door of the St. Murphy-Feeny with burglarious intent; but he heard the voices of men within and the clink of glasses, and turned mournfully away. As he hid so his glance fell on Mister Murphy's garbage can. In that instant hunger overcame him. He snatched up the can and fled with it. He had almost reached a sheltering growth of palms when Feeny caught sight of him and raised the alarm.

Mr. MacCandlish's Marathon was soon run, for as he bounded into the bush he heard Feeny close at his heels, and a second later the stoker's muscular hand seized him by the collar of his coat.

"No violence!" panted the bishop, as, purplefaced, he gained a place at Feeny's side.

Mr. Feeny surveyed the millionaire with a glance of scornful pity.

"I little thought that you'd be the first to ignore the sacred rights of property, Mr. Mac-Candlish, sir," he said. "'Tis no excuse that you're hungry. What's moral on a full stomach remains moral on a empty stomach. The eternal principles of right and wrong ain't made to fit the shape of a man's belly,—and the likes of you... the friend of presidents and kings... to swipe a garbage can!" concluded Feeny, but more in sorrow than in anger.

In the golden dawn a week later, a rapturous shout from Mr. MacCandlish called his friends from their tent. He was standing on the beach, frozen into a tense and rigid attitude.

"Look!" he gasped, pointing.

There, anchored off the end of the island, was a small and dingy-looking steamer, but the sight of it gladdened the hearts of the castaways. Pajama clad, they cavorted along the sands, whooping gleefully. Then, as they rounded a wooded point, they came on the stokers. Near at hand a ship's boat was beached, and two barelegged sailors were hunting turtle eggs; while a third stranger was engaged in earnest conversation with Feeny. Mr. MacCandlish swore.

"My dear friend...," admonished the bishop, greatly shocked.

"It's an English tramp—the *Nairn*," said Feeny pleasantly, as he turned toward them. "We sighted her along afore day and h'isted signals. This gentleman's her skipper. He was bound for Para, but he's taken a fresh charter and'll land us in New York inside of two weeks, barring the risk of the high seas and the acts of Providence—No, no, Mr. MacCandlish," as the millionaire edged toward the *Nairn's* skipper, "a bargain's a bargain,—and the contract's signed. The ship's already under charter. But you'll find Mike Feeny always ready for to do business when he sees a chance to turn an honest dollar. I'm as willin' to speculate in transportation as in vittles. The *Nairn* ain't a Cunarder,—far from it,—but she'll land you in New York at two thousand a head; which gives us a nice profit."

Two hours later the *Nairn* was steaming north, and Feeny was watching the island as it merged with the blue obscurity of sky and sea; while from the after deck Mr. MacCandlish cast menacing glances in his direction. It was evident that his feelings toward that self-taught political economist were unbenevolent in the extreme. Somewhere about him was concealed much cash, and those many, many checks, which he intended to recover when they reached New York and he could invoke the aid of the law.

Now Mr. Feeny cherished no illusions on this point; and one night, as the *Nairn* was steaming up the Jersey coast, he called his mates about him.

"I misdoubt me philantrophic friend, Mr. Mac-Candlish. He's showin' a peevish spirit, I'm thinkin'. After all, he's no real political economist, but just a cheap skate who's played a sure thing so long he's got no sportin' blood left. If we put them bits of paper in at the bank for to take our money out, we'll get pinched instead,—he told me as much."

"What might you have it in your mind to suggest, Mister Feeny?" asked Mr. Corrigan.

"Go to some tall buildin' on Broadway, and have a talk with one of them big lawyers."

Thus it came about that as Mr. Hargrew, whose specialty was corporation law, was glancing over his mail the next morning, a low-voiced clerk informed him that one Feeny earnestly desired speech with him.

"He's Irish, and has a couple of men with him. It looks like the executive council of some labor union," the clerk added.

"Show them in," said the lawyer.

"Mornin'," said Mr. Feeny.

"Good morning," said the lawyer.

"Feeny's me name, and I'm a retired Captain of Industry from the United States of Ireland. If you've read the mornin' papers you've seen how that other great Captain of Industry, Mr. MacCandlish, and a party of friends was picked up off an island in the Gulf of Mexico."

The lawyer nodded.

"Yes, I've read about that," he said.

"We was the *Orinoco's* coal heavers. It's us that saved the lives of them babes of millionaires. We stood by them when the sailors had quit the ship, we salvaged the wreck, and fed and tended 'em. We done all the hard work, and organized a government, and made that island so homelike you couldn't have told it from New York. Everything was legal, and I ask you if the rise in the price of staples wasn't a natural rise, owin' to the law of supply and demand?"

The lawyer laughed and shook his head. "Wait!" said Mr. Feeny. "I'll say nothin' of the trouble it was to care for 'em, nor the spirit they showed,—how Mr. MacCandlish was caught escapin' into the pa'ms with a can from the back door of the St. Murphy-Feeny, where Mister Murphy of the Hotel Trust chucked his broken vittles—you might call it garbage and not misname it. When he was captured and fetched back penitent, I said to him: 'Mr. MacCandlish, I never thought you'd be one of the first to ignore the sacred rights of property,' and what he answered would be a case for libel if I had the mind to push it. Now, if stealin' isn't stealin', what is it?" The lawyer appeared to consider.

"I got a roll of their checks as big round as a strong man's arm, and I'm lookin' for a way to get 'em cashed without gettin' pinched meself," said Mr. Feeny.

"And you wish me to arrange this if possible?" said the lawyer, smiling. "I am not sure I can, but if you like you may leave those checks with me and I'll see what I can do; wait a moment until I run them over, and give you an acknowledgment." When he had done so, he looked up into Mr. Feeny's long sad face and whistled softly. Then he looked again at the bundle of checks and again at Mr. Feeny, who seemed to understand.

"We was a prosperous people," he said.

"You were, indeed. Is this all, Mr. Feeny?"

"There was some cash... all they had, I remember to have heard them say," answered Mr. Feeny.

"You may come this afternoon somewhere about four."

And that afternoon when Mr. Feeny, punctual to the second, presented himself with Mr. Corrigan and Mr. Murphy, the first thing his sad eyes saw was a neat pile of bills on the corner of Mr. Hargrew's desk.

"The full amount is here, Mr. Feeny," said the lawyer. "That incident of the garbage can was an important point in the adjustment of your claim. Yours must have been a profoundly interesting social experiment."

"I dunno as I should call it that," said Mr. Feeny modestly. "For it's my opinion there's nothin' easier than political economy. The mistake most people makes is in havin' the demands instead of the supply," and Mr. Feeny permitted himself to smile.

ALL THAT A MAN HATH

I

THE pen slipped from Philip's fingers and unheeded rolled across the table, while with a sigh of weariness he abandoned himself to idleness. Resting his elbows upon the table, he sunk his chin into the palms of his hands and gazed listlessly out of the window on the street below. The cold gray light of the dull October afternoon was almost at an end; already the street-lamps were beginning to flare forth redly in bold relief against the gathering gloom of the coming night.

To Philip it was a dispiriting and cheerless prospect, heightened by the winter's first chill breath. He had seen it all so often; if he could only see the last of it. Each year brought back those same dull days, with their leaden skies to fit into his worst mood of despair and longing and unfulfillment. He felt himself starved in mind and experience. He was conscious always of a fierce desire for something different—that broader life to which he could not go, and which would not come to him.

*Written at the age of 20.

Slowly his eyes came back to the table and a settled seriousness stole into them as he looked at the manuscript lying upon it.

"I fancy it will be a go this time," he thought, "but"—a bit sadly—"I have thought that so many times, and somehow I am just where I was in the start. No nearer success, no nearer anything—except perhaps the end of my hope and faith in myself."

He had risen and now stood looking down at the table with its litter of paper, pens and letters... and rising from the midst of the disorder—a mountain of hope—the pile of manuscript. It had meant days and weeks of labor: days when he had striven with enthusiasm for its completion; days, too, that had been given up to the savage denying of his mistrust and doubt. Through these and his varying moods he had toiled, and at last his task was approaching its end.

Turning, Philip left the room and descended to the narrow hall below. Here it was already quite dark. He fumbled about until he found his hat and overcoat, and after getting into them made his way back through the parlor and sitting-room to the dining-room where his mother was arranging the supper table.

"Oh, it is you, Philip," she said, glancing up from her work. "I heard you in the hall and thought it must be the girls returning."

Mrs. Southard was a woman of fifty with a strong placid face that had taken comparatively few lines. Her dress was of the simplest black, and severely plain. It had been black ever since Philip could remember, for his father had died when he was a baby.

While Philip was conscious that his small world had changed much in the years that marked the limits of his memory, his mother was still precisely the same as he recalled her, returning to his first vague impression of people and things. She was not and had never been an intellectual woman perhaps, but to him she stood for that which was most steadfast and purposeful. Nor was she hard with all her splendid strength. Her judgments were infinitely more generous than those of most women.

"You are not going out, Philip?" his mother asked, observing that he was ready for the street. "It's almost supper-time."

"I won't keep you waiting, mother; I am just going down-town to post some letters."

"Yes, dear, but do be here for supper."

"I shall be."

He turned back into the sitting-room, intending to leave the house by the side door. His mother followed him, and on the threshold he faced her again.

"What is it?" he asked, "anything you want from down-town?"

"No, dear, only I haven't told you, and I wish to now. I expect Anson home to-night. He will remain over Sunday. Do be nice to him."

She spoke appealingly, for Philip's face darkened at the news.

"Am I not always nice to him? I mean to be for your sake."

"Yes, but you seem so far apart, and you are brothers."

"Oh, it's all right, mother, and we get along peaceably enough, considering how we hate each other. There, dear, you can't reconcile the utterly unreconcilable, so don't spend your precious strength in trying to."

And Philip, closing the door after him, went down the steps and into the street. "So," he muttered, "Anson will be here to-morrow and I shall have to endure his presence for at least a part of one penitential day."

The one cordial emotion that the brothers shared in common was hatred one for the other. As children they had eased this rancor by a frequent exchange of blows, but now, unhappily for their peace of mind, they were past that sort of thing.

The street Philip was following took him straight to the center of the town and into the midst of Saturday's crowd. It was such a gathering as one might see in almost any country town on the last day of the week: self-conscious and uncomfortable, in ugly ill-fitting "best clothes". The business of the day was over, and the crowd paraded up and down the main street, or back and forth across the Square. Philip pushed his way into it with assertive elbows. He crossed the squalid Square with its soldier's monument and its few stunted trees that stubbornly declined to grow and as stubbornly refused to die. From the Square he turned into a side street that led past the post-office. Here he posted his letters and paused in front of the building, undecided where next to go. As he stood there a man who had been leaning against an iron railing that surrounded an area way left his position and slouched up to Philip's side. The latter scanned the shabby figure with some uncertainty, then he said: "Oh, it's you, Lester?"—and held out his hand. His greeting was so lacking in cordiality, however, that Lester ignored the proffered hand.

"If you prefer to be alone," he growled, "why don't you say so?"

Where they stood the lamplight fell upon his face—the face of a lad of twenty-two or three—stupid and sullen and debased. But Philip saw a look of such abject loneliness in his eyes that he placed his hand on the boy's shoulder: "Come on, Lester," he said, and together they went down the street and away from the town. "What are you doing?" Philip asked presently.

"What I have always done—nothing."

"When one hasn't anything else to do it's about the most agreeable of all occupations," Philip observed. He noticed that his companion's unsteady gait indicated a recent debauch, but this did not prejudice him since he attributed all moral delinquencies to a lack of sense, and so readily condoned them on the grounds of inferior judgment.

A boyish friendship, almost forgotten, was all they had in common. Philip searched his mind for some topic of conversation that might interest his companion, but finally gave it up and they trudged along in silence.

They reached the outskirts of the town in this manner and Philip was about to turn back.

"Let's go on to the end of the road," said Lester with sudden interest. "It isn't far," he added, for his companion hesitated.

"Oh, all right, only I hope you don't take this walk often, Lester," Philip said with a laugh, for the road ended at the graveyard.

Five minutes later and they were standing before the cemetery gates. The pale light of the October moon fell among the naked trees, while the dead leaves rustled in the wind. There was the ghostly white of tombstone and monument and the dismal black of contrasting pine trees. Philip leaned against the fence and surveyed it all critically. He owned that he was grateful to Lester for having brought him there. It gave him a distinct sensation.

"I am rather set against graveyards as a rule, but this is nice and curious and lonely," he said. Lester did not answer him and Philip continued: "I haven't been out here in years. I guess not since we buried Mr. Benedict. Do you remember when we buried Mr. Benedict, Lester? I recall it as one of the most gratifying events of my childhood. I got a whole day from school in honor of the affair." Philip raised himself on tiptoe and peered over the fence.

Lester paid no heed to Philip nor to what he was saying. He leaned silent and sullen against a tree that stood by the path, and gazed off into the frosty distance in the direction of the town. Out of this distance there floated a confusion of sounds—harmonized and softened by time and place; while through it all, clinging to the heavy atmosphere, drifted the odor of burning leaves and the musty scent of dying vegetation. There was a touch of sad regret in the night as though something that had been beautiful was ended. The boy felt this in its kinship to the ruin he had wrought in his own life.

"You are no doubt wondering why I spoke to you," he said at last.

Philip nodded his head: "You know, Lester, we haven't had much to do with each other in some while."

"I want to talk with you."

"Well, go ahead, for it has just occurred to me that I promised to be home in time for supper."

Lester turned a pair of bloodshot eyes full on Philip and asked: "You think I have been a fool, don't you?"

Philip shifted his feet uneasily. He felt that truth played such an insignificant part in the exercise of civility.

"You think I have been a fool?" Lester repeated.

"Before I answer that I'd like to know why you ask. You see the reason that prompts an inquiry is more than apt to determine its answer with me. I always wish to give satisfaction."

"I ask because I'd like to know what you think of me. I don't suppose you have any sort of use for me. You don't know, Philip, how bad I have wanted some one to talk to for days and days—some one who is not like myself. And when I saw you to-night, I made up my mind that you should hear what I have to say. I can't keep it any longer—my head will burst if I do—can you listen?"

"Go ahead,—I'm listening."

"For the most part it's nothing but what you know. It's just about my being such a fool. Yes, yes—and it's more than that!"

Philip saw that he was powerfully excited, that there were tears in the eyes of this boy, with a man's heavy burden of sin on his shoulders.

"You know about the money I got when I came of age; the money my father left me when he died. I—you know what a circus I made of myself. How every last cent of it is gone?"

"Yes, it's the gossip—and I hear it."

Lester paced back and forth in front of Philip for a moment, and then leaned dejectedly against a tree.

"When you talked about how it used to be when we were boys, I could have choked you. I wish I were back to it, with these last years to live over!" He paused, trembling with excitement and sorrow. "When I got hold of my money you shook me off and would have nothing more to do with me."

"I hadn't the time, Lester. I was busy and you were not. Our tastes had ceased to be the same, that was all. You should not bear me a grudge on that score."

"I don't—I like you the better for it—you are the only fellow I can talk to. I know if you have any sympathy for me it rests on what I was when we tramped around the country in vacation time. How I wish I might go back to it and be a boy once more—once more!"

With a gesture of anguish he drew his hand across his face. Perhaps he sought to hide some part of the pain that was plainly stamped upon his woebegone visage. He had been so proud of his very misdeeds—and now

———

"I have a lot of sympathy for you, Lester; just a lot, and I am sorry for you, too."

"Thank you, Philip; I suppose I deserve all I get. I have been such a cad!—such a cub! I spent in two years and less what it took my father all his life to save. It will be a long while before I get hold of such a lump again, and if I have to make it, probably never. You know how, when I came of age, I was taken up by fellows much older than myself. My head was completely turned by my popularity—well, it lasted for a while then quite suddenly I found myself with empty pockets and no friends. People discovered all at once that I was shockingly immoral. They might have known it all along if they had cared to. I never made any bones about it. I was no better and no worse than those I went with. Now I am an outcast. The fellows who helped me on to this don't see me any more. I have the road to myself when I go down-town: everybody gets out of my way, but this is nothing—if it were no more than this I should not mind."

"What else is it that's wrong?" said Philip, beginning to find the boy's confession interesting.

He was feeling a certain solicitude for the harvester of wild oats. They had been close friends once, and at not so very long ago either. Lester's plunge into folly had terminated their intimacy—the friendship had become irksome to both—for months they had scarcely exchanged more than greetings when they chanced to meet, and all in an instant Lester was sweeping him back to the years when they had been inseparable. With a palpable effort Lester continued:

"I've got all sorts of habits that are ruining me, as sure as I stand here—they are—and I can't stop. If I can get the money I am going away. Maybe it will be better then."

"Come, come—brace up! There is no good in running away. I doubt if it will improve matters."

"No, I can't stay."

"I should if I were you. I should wait for a fitting opportunity and get even with all my former acquaintances in some dazzling fashion."

Philip spoke cheerfully enough, but the tone of his voice was pleasantly suggestive of manslaughter as the method he would recommend.

"What do I care for the damned Judases!" Lester burst out. "All I want is to see the last of them." Then suddenly he relapsed into sullenness; "I don't know that it's worth the trouble," he said. "I might just as well finish it off and be done with the whole thing one time as another. I have thrown my money to the dogs and my chances with it. I may as well let the rest follow."

"Nonsense! You don't mean what you're saying. Stop drinking and behave yourself and you'll discover that you have plenty of friends left. It won't benefit you to whine about it. That you have played the fool concerns you alone. You can't make the town responsible for what you've done yourself."

Philip being the older, had always in a manner dominated Lester. Even in the days of their youth Lester had required a large amount of encouragement to keep within the wide limits of what Philip had marked off as the straight and narrow path in the field of his moral perceptions. For Philip had never aspired to any close companionship with the sterner virtues and he was consistent in advising no lines of conduct he was not himself willing to follow.

"Damn the town and everybody in it! There is not another such spot on the face of the earth."

Evidently Lester did not find being an outcast agreeable, and he viewed himself as an injured individual, since his behavior had offended no one, until his riches were gone. Philip passed his hand through Lester's arm and led him down the path.

"You go home and when morning comes, bringing with it a clear head, think it over and arrive at the only sensible conclusion within your reach... to go it straight and steady."

"Do you think I am soft to unburden myself to you like this?" Lester asked.

"My dear boy, I regard you as the opposite of soft."

On their entering the town, Lester reverted to his former silence and Philip, commenting on the change, thought: "It was the enlivening associations of the tomb that made him talkative." Neither spoke until they separated in front of Lester's home. Then Philip said: "Good night, don't worry, it won't help you in the least."

"Good night."

"If you should happen to want some one to discuss your affairs with, look me up. I shall always be at your service."

"Thanks,—I will."

Lester turned from the gate by which he had been standing and went toward the house. Philip followed him with a sympathetic glance.

"Poor boy," he thought, "he's in hard luck, and though there is no one to blame but himself, it doesn't make it easier to bear."

Then he called aloud: "Good night. I'll expect to see you soon."

Lester waved his hand as he paused in the sudden burst of light from the opened door. Then the door closed, and Philip stood alone, staring thoughtfully at the darkness where but a moment before the streaming light had been: "I am sorry for him—but, suppose he avails himself of the proffer of companionship I was rash enough to make and eats up hours and hours of my precious time—what's going to become of my work? This won't do. A wretched creature who has squandered his fortune in riotous living comes along, makes a brutal assault on my feelings, and I weakly succumb—amiable ass that I am!"

There never was a bridge Philip did not cross in advance of his coming to it —never a bridge he did not go back to and recross after he was once safely over. So he stood thinking of the hours he was no doubt destined to waste on the unhappy Lester. At last he went his way reproaching himself with the unwisdom of having displayed a tender and susceptible nature.

He reached home while still engaged in abusing himself; with his hand upon the knob he halted a moment before opening the door. He wished to put his faculties in a state of repose so that he could meet his brother pleasantly and with no outward sign that he desired to kick him. This generally demanded a previous arrangement with himself. Assured that it was accomplished, he pushed open the door. The sitting-room was empty, but the noise coming from the dining-room told him that the family was at supper. His mother, hearing him enter, called: "Is it you, Philip?"

"Yes, mother. I'm late. I really meant to be back long ago." Then to Anson as he passed from one room to the other: "How are you, old fellow?"

Their mother's eye was upon them and the brothers exchanged greetings in a friendly enough fashion. Anson even declared himself as delighted to see Philip:—a gratuitous bit of lying for which the latter thanked him profusely as he took his seat. About the table was grouped the entire Southard family. Philip, his mother, Anson and the two girls—Katherine and Florence. The "inharmonious whole"—as Philip was wont to call them. Anson was the eldest—his brother's senior by five or six years and verging close on thirty— handsome, too, in his way, by all odds the most prepossessing member of the family. But his original advantages were somewhat marred by his unfortunate mannerisms, the result in part of his occupation—that of confidential clerk in the office of a manufacturing concern. His every act, serious or the reverse, was performed with a petty and aggravating secrecy. It was displayed in everything he did. He even ate in a confidential manner, seeming to tell a business secret to each mouthful he swallowed. Philip, stealing covert glances at him, decided that he had never seen him quite so abominable. Yet, it struck him for the first time that Anson was a disappointed man—the world had not yielded him all that he had been coached to think it would. He had been brought up in the belief that he was a marvel of human perfectibility. As a child, he had been so precocious in pursuit of the virtues, great and small, that much had been predicted of him. Now when the glamour of youthful goodness was changing into the fixity of a shining light, he was held to be a model worthy of prayerful emulation by all right-minded people—and so he was. If he had been stuffed with straw, he could not have been freer from flesh-begotten sin.

Despite this he was a disappointed man. He had been such a remarkable boy that when he reached maturity he was in much the same unhappy plight as a little Alexander with no more worlds to conquer. That which had been so astonishing in the child, that uncanny goodness that caused elderly females to throw up their hands at the mere mention of his name and launch forth in praise of him, excited no especial comment in the man. It never occurred to him that he had been nourished on thin air. His whole education was such a mistake—such an injustice—How could any one thrive beneath the load of useless rectitude he had set out to carry like a fool,—mainly because it placed him in the ranks of other highly proper monstrosities.

Philip, slowly eating his supper, came to a realization of this and something not unlike pity stole into his heart.

It was such a remote chance, so removed from the realm of the possible that Anson would ever succeed in distinguishing himself more than he had done, and what would become of him?

As he speculated on the outcome, the two girls and Anson talked back and forth across the table, and he stopped thinking to listen.

It was the usual discussion of ways and means they carried on. This bill to be met—its fellow to be evaded until the end of the month. The evidences of a not over-lovely existence, but hard and precarious—close to the ragged edge of want. The much spent on the worthless shams—the little on the solid comforts of a good living.

"As if any one is deceived or thinks us richer than we are," Philip thought. "We are more or less like our neighbors and they estimate our income to the last penny, just as we do theirs." There was something so hopeless about the aspect life took on, something so perilously near to the perpetual grind of downright poverty, that it made him revolt and he burst out angrily: "Why, in heaven's name, don't you find some more cheerful subject to discuss! Must it forever be debts and bills, as if there was only the one purpose in living—to squirm through somehow until the end of the month!"

"I guess," Katherine, the elder of the girls, said, her eyes snapping viciously, "that some one has to think of such matters, though I am sure no one wants to; and Anson is here so seldom and he is the——"

"Katherine!" Her mother spoke sharply, warning her not to finish the sentence.

Philip looked down at his plate and bit his lips. He knew what his sister would have said had their mother not interfered—that Anson was the family's mainstay—but her mother's warning stopped her.

It was by no means a loving family, nor was there any special graciousness in their intercourse. Philip barely tolerated his sisters. Katherine was undeniably mean and spiteful. To her natural tendencies she had added an exceedingly bigoted habit of thought which she referred to as "her faith".

Its acquirement, if she was to be credited with telling the truth, had cost her many sleepless nights and great self-sacrifice. It was exercised chiefly in a rabid criticism of her species in which she recently delighted.

Florence was rather better in sweetness of temper and disposition, but to hear her talk was maddening torture to him. She had all a woman's misplaced and indiscriminate adjectives. Everything was "grand" to her, from hot popcorn to a clap of thunder.

The connecting link holding the four together was Mrs. Southard, whose force of will kept them united after love and affection had ceased to exist.

The first strong emotion they had known had been hate, one for the other. They were so different in every quality of soul and body; they saw and were on the opposite side of every conceivable question. But one thing they had in common, an admirable tenacity, which rendered them insensible to either courtesy or reason where their prejudices were at stake.

The home, such as it was, existed only by grace of Mrs. Southard's strength of character. For while their mutual dislike reached a degree of bitterness hard to comprehend, they all loved her, each in his or her own way.

"What detained you, Philip?" his mother asked when Katherine was restored to composure.

"I took a walk with Lester Royal."

"I don't think him a very good person to be seen with," Katherine interposed. She felt bound to raise a disturbance on moral grounds.

"Don't you?—why not?" Then as a happy after thought: "There are certain people who should be restrained from thinking."

Katherine ignored his remark and returned to the charge.

"What sort of a reputation has he, I should like to know! But of course you are superior to a trifle like that."

"I fancy it's what it should be."

"You know very well he has no reputation at all. But I suppose you don't mind—you are so liberal."

144

"Then I am sure there is nothing wrong with it since it doesn't exist."

"It does exist and is most unsavory!"

"Well, even an unsavory reputation is a decided improvement on no reputation at all."

"I don't think——" Katherine began.

"I am glad you don't, Kate; it was never intended you should," Philip made haste to say.

At this point Florence took up the cudgels against Philip:

"I should think you would have been ashamed to let people see you with him—he's simply horrid!"

"I wasn't seen with him, so don't distress your conscience with the idea that I was."

"No thanks to you that you weren't," said Katherine.

"Your penetration does you credit, Kate. I don't happen to possess your inordinate respect for appearances." He was waiting to make a telling retort. This always stimulated him.

"I suppose you can't select men of good character for your friends," Katherine snapped.

"Freedom from vice is more a question of ignorance than anything else." Unconsciously he glanced at Anson as he spoke.

"I should be ashamed to think it," said Katherine.

"Perhaps my spiritual insight has become blunted by my unfavorable surroundings."

"I suppose that's a covert slur at me and my religion," with heat. "The things you say are disgraceful!"

"I don't see how mother can permit it," Florence said, bent on being in the row.

"For pity's sake, girls, can't you let Philip finish his supper in peace, without going out of your way to complain of what is no affair of yours?" It was Mrs. Southard who spoke.

Philip pushed back his plate. "I am through and will take myself off," he said. He kissed his mother, and with an indifferent good night to the rest, left the room. A moment later the street door closed with a bang.

"I wish to gracious he was already married to Barbara. I'll bet he'd know pretty quick he wasn't any better off," said Florence.

"There—there," Mrs. Southard objected wearily. "Can't you find something else to talk about?"

II

The Southard's belonged to that great division of the human family—the eminently respectable. As far as they went they were above reproach—nor were they without a certain prestige. As Katherine was wont to remark: "They knew the best."

Furthermore, it was tradition that once upon a time they had been very rich, or rather their remote ancestors had been so blessed, and vouching for this former grandeur, there remained to them a considerable and distinguished connection.

These distinguished relatives, whom Philip hated cordially, were much addicted to the habit—while on their periodic gyrations about the country—of stopping with his mother, when by so doing they could break long and possibly fatiguing trips.

On these occasions the relatives spent most of their time in curl-papers or smoking jackets. Whenever Mrs. Southard ventured to suggest some mild festivity in their honor they refused to be entertained, with: "We beg you won't, Cousin Jane. We are here simply for a nice quiet visit with you and the children. Later on we shall be forced to be so very gay, you know...." On these occasions when the guests divided their time about equally between eating and sleeping, their entertainers' mode of living was ordered on such a scale of magnificence and reckless extravagance that they were almost invariably brought to the verge of ruin, and they generally atoned for the temporary burst of luxury by months of close economy. Then when the rich and distinguished relatives had taken their leave, the Southards would cut down expenses and try to convince themselves that the departed guests were the most charming people imaginable. Some little fiction of the kind was positively indispensable when the grocery bill came in.

One member of this contingent happening to die—the only disinterested action of a singularly selfish career—had bethought him of the Southards in his last moments and had strangely enough remembered them in his will with a legacy for each of the children. It was a matter of some hundreds apiece and the two girls and Anson had straightway spent their portions.

Philip, at the time of this windfall, was in business: it gave him the opportunity he had long coveted. He planned three years of liberty in which to follow up his inclination to write.

No one appreciated the courage this involved and Philip went his course without help from any one. He told himself that if he came to grief there would be but scant loss—a little money and the waste of days.

He had been by no means a success in commercial pursuits, and if he failed with his pen, why, it was no more than he was apt to do in other things. For a year his labors in the field of literature went unrewarded, and many times he was tempted to give up the struggle in disgust. Then at last, when his small legacy was all but gone, the first meager returns filled him with renewed hope and energy.

Slowly, very slowly, he saw his tiny bank balance swell until it reached the grand total of a thousand dollars. Upon that day there came to him the satisfying though distant vision of success.

It was not to be a selfish success he told himself: he would shirk no obligation when it came—all should profit by it. But he could do so much with a different environment. The appreciation his brother and sisters gave him was so tainted by an indiscriminate disapproval of his aims, and their recognition of his poor triumphs so niggardly, as though any reference to them was an acknowledgment of superiority on his part. In spite of this he would do what he could for them—when he could. Most of all would he do for his mother. She should have the thousand things, big and little, women loved and wanted. She had done so much for him—for all of them. She had brought them up unaided, through a struggle against poverty, the hardness of which he could only dimly divine. He would have counted it the blackest treachery not to have thought of her.

Then when the girls were married—and marry they must—he intended to get husbands for them, even if they had to be bought—she would come and live with him.

They had talked it over a hundred times—he and Barbara—and knew just how it was to be arranged.

He never questioned his ability to do all this, for his faith had become perfect and abiding.

In the kindly benevolence of his castle-building he even wished well to Anson. After all, they were brothers. Anson had a fondness for travel; he would give him the means to indulge that taste, he *should* travel—more than this, he should travel always—the farther away the better.

When he left home, Philip betook himself into the presence of his betrothed. As he entered the parlor where Barbara sat—idly turning the leaves of a book, she looked up at him and smiled.

"I am glad you came," she said. "I was just beginning to think I shouldn't see you to-night." Philip drew a chair near to hers as he answered. "So am I, but I should be at work."

"Guess who has called this afternoon?"

"Why do you make me exert myself—why don't you tell me at once if I am to know?"

"Mr. Shelden."

"Well, and what had he to say? Do you know, Barbara, I object, for it just occurs to me that he is without a wife... having already disposed of one. Truly I object to his calling on you."

"But he is papa's friend——"

"Oh, is he? Well, he is a precious old fool—that's my opinion of him."

Philip, conscious of the slightness of the claim he had upon her, dreaded a possible rival. He knew the sanction to his suit was only passive—the least thing might bring about the most pronounced opposition.

"He is not so very old: he is only forty-five. He regards himself as still youthful, for he assured me this was the age of the young man," said Barbara.

"It's the age of the damn fool," Philip grunted savagely, and then penitently: "That was a case of justifiable damn: it was wrung from me, Barbara. It's so exasperating to hear such twaddle."

"I believe you're jealous, Philip. I really believe you are!"

"Of course I am! I am no better than a pauper—and he——"

"How inconsistent of you. The other evening you said you should never care whom I saw. Do be consistent."

"Consistency is the last refuge of an idiot. Because I say or do a thing once, am I to be tied to it for the rest of my days?"

"But it is quite impossible to keep track of your beliefs."

"Pardon me, I have opinions, but no beliefs. What else did he say?"

"You mean Mr. Shelden?"

"Yes. What other shoddy nineteenth century-ism did he repeat?"

"He said any number of things. He spoke about you."

"Old gossip! What did he find to say about me?"

"He asked what you were doing."

"I hope you had the courage to tell him it was none of his business."

"I didn't do anything so rude. I told him you were writing. He seemed deeply impressed and said he had always liked you."

"Humph! He's a startling novelty."

"I thought it very lovely of him to be so sympathetic, for of course he knows. I have an idea papa tells him everything."

"What else, Barbara? Can't you tell me all?"

"I told him about your book—and then we discussed books in general. He reads a great deal, so he told me."

"Probably—*Thoughts for a Christian on Losing his Hair*—for I have observed he is getting bald."

"How mean of you!"

"Oh, Barbara, what in heaven's name is going to happen if some one comes between us—some one who has money and all that's worth while?"

"You know there is something that no one can have but you."

She leaned forward, holding out her hand for him to take. "I have given you so much love that you must have it all, or I shall keep it for you untouched forever."

And Philip, looking into the face so close to his, saw that she meant the words she spoke. But beyond the words he seemed to see that a cloud could not rest long upon her. She was created for love and brightness, and in his heart he knew that they must be together soon or he would lose her.

"What is it, Philip?" she asked after a short silence. "What are you thinking?"

"That I am happy," he answered, smiling. "Only that?"

"Could it be more? How glad I am that you are as you are. I would not have you changed."

"It's not because I am so good, is it? For you know I am not."

Before he could answer a door opened and closed in the adjoining room. The sound had an instantaneous effect on Philip.

"Here is your father, Barbara; we'll speak of the weather. It is a matter upon which I am disposed to agree with any one—always excepting the pious Anson."

"Why do you pretend to dislike your brother? I think him very nice,—very fine-looking."

"Hate is as essential to certain natures as love—and much more satisfying."

"But you can't *hate* him. You are far from honest."

"People form such queer notions of me. They are eternally thinking I am not sincere, and yet, Barbara, I mean all I say—while I am saying it. Could integrity carry me to greater lengths?" She looked at him with knitted brows. He was unlike any one she had ever known.

"Are you really afraid of him?—of papa?" she asked.

"The relations existing between us are strained; he may at any moment send me from the house for good and all."

Barbara laughed. "I am quite sure he is guiltless of any such intention."

"I regret to say that I am not."

Philip regarded Mr. Gerard as a person of one idea, and that invariably a wrong one. It was neither safe nor agreeable to be so at his mercy, for he held Philip's happiness in the hollow of his hand, and that young gentleman was much oppressed by the suspicion that he was not popular with Barbara's parent. When he questioned her she always assured him that her father respected him most thoroughly, but Philip doubted this.

It must be admitted that now and then he detected a pugnacious quality in Mr. Gerard's manner toward him, which he stubbornly declined to notice or take exception to, as every other consideration was minor to the great one of gaining time in which to place himself beyond the reach of interference, so he put his pride in his pocket and strove to prevent a clash.

Mr. Gerard appeared suddenly in the doorway.

"I wish you would come with me into the library, Philip," he said. "There is a little matter I should like to discuss with you. Barbara will, I am sure, excuse you for a few moments."

Philip came to his feet on the instant. The parable of the spider and the fly presented itself to him.

"How do you do," he said. He was not at his best when Mr. Gerard was about.

"Just follow me into the library, if you please." For Philip was gazing stupidly at him.

"Oh, certainly." From the door he glanced back at Barbara, and she saw that his face was clouded with apprehension.

While she was wondering what it all meant, and what her father could have to say to Philip, there drifted in to her the murmur of their lowered voices, coming from the room that had conferred upon it the name of library in recognition of the fact that its furniture consisted in the main of a desk, some leather-covered chairs given over to decay, and a bookcase, containing an encyclopedia, a dictionary, and by actual count ninety-six novels. The room was also adorned—as the complete triumph of intellectuality—by a bust of Shakespeare.

Here Mr. Gerard was supposed to do his thinking.

Barbara's mother was an invalid and seldom left her room. This was another tangle in the snarled arrangement of Philip's hopes, for Barbara's father had severe Spartan ideas on the duties of children to their parents. And Mrs. Gerard was so busy with her symptoms, real or imaginary, that she never concerned herself in domestic matters. She left all that to her husband, who ran things with a high and often heavy hand.

Barbara controlled her curiosity as best she could. Finally the conference was at an end. She heard her father remark in his ordinary strident tones:

"You appreciate the justice of my course, Philip."

A few minutes later, Philip reentered the parlor.

"What is it?" she asked quickly.

He crossed the room and stood leaning against the mantel, looking down at her in silence.

"What is it, Philip?" she repeated.

"Your father says that I must be ready to marry you within a year or else ——" he paused.

"Or else what?" she asked anxiously.

"The worst. I shall have to give you up."

Philip saw her face pale. She arose and stood at his side, her hand upon his shoulder, her head tilted so that she could look into his face.

"It shall be only you, Philip. If it is not you it shall be no other."

He gazed at her in silence, trying to read the depth of her faith in her eyes. The thought that she was beautiful and that he loved her came strongly to him.

"You believe in me, Philip; you trust me?"

"As I do no one else—as I never shall another. It is you and only you. Everything is centered or ends forever in you." And then he laughed lightly.

"After all, it is not so bad. Perhaps this will force our happiness upon us sooner than we have dared anticipate."

"How long did he say?"

"Within a year, and it is so short a time," he said, with a deep breath.

"Within a year," she repeated slowly. "But I can't be forced away from you. He can't make me give you up." And she shook her head in defiance.

"Can't he, Barbara? Can't he, dear?" And Philip bent toward her, speaking softly.

"I belong to you."

Philip straightened up, saying somewhat grimly: "I must work. I shall be forced to see you less often."

"Must you?"

"Yes. This admits of no delay. And no matter how hard I work... even then it's all doubt and uncertainty."

"Why do we have to wait?"—with a sigh. "I could help you so much if I were with you. I know I could."

Philip ground out between his set teeth the one word, "Money," and Barbara was silent.

"We are most unfortunate," he continued. "We both belong to what are called prosperous and well-to-do families and yet beyond a well defined point there is not an extra penny, every cent being swallowed up in the wretched sham of appearances. I own frankly I am poor, and as if this were not misfortune enough in itself, my poverty is allied to a worthless sneaking respectability that is maintained at the cost of constant sacrifice. I have the added ignominy of knowing that the very appearances on which is squandered everything, deceive no one. How destructive to self-respect to live a lie unbelieved even by the most credulous! If it accomplished its beneficent mission, there would be a worthy excuse for it, but to run the risk of damnation for the sake of a lot of unsuccessful deceits makes my soul sick."

"What do we care for people? If we are happy what does it matter?" She pressed close to his side. "What do we care?"

"Do you mean you would marry me now, if you could, and disregard the doubtfulness of the future?"

"But you haven't asked me yet... how can I tell?"

"Would you, dear?"... tenderly.

"Try me. It would be such fun to live just as we could, and not have to make believe. I imagine the worst of poverty is in the thought that some one else knows. Tell me what father said."

"I have already told you, Barbara."

"But tell me how it came about. How he led up to it and what you said."

Philip thought for a moment. When he spoke his manner suggested weariness, as if the recent ordeal had been too much for him.

"Really I am quite collapsed, quite annihilated. What a stunning advantage a young woman's father has over his daughter's 'young man.'.rdquo;

"Won't you answer me?—what was it papa said?"

"Well, we kept clear of sentiment from the start—we canvassed the situation from a purely business basis."

"But you know nothing about business."

"I talk intelligently enough on a good many subjects of which I know nothing."

"What else did he say?"

"Oh, that I was a very proper young man, and all that sort of thing."

"And then what?"

"After an exchange of compliments he gave me to understand that business was business. Then, Barbara, with startling brevity and great solemnity, tempered with severity, he informed me that this waiting was unjust to you, that it unduly compromised you, to all of which I agreed. He again alluded to my virtues; during their enumeration, my feelings were of the ghastly jolly order, for I thought that this formed the prelude to a blessing and dismissal— but it didn't. He wound up by asking me what my resources were. Of course I shuffled about and tried to daze him by a complicated explanation, filled with glittering generalities, though I own they did not glitter, for he held me to the subject in hand and I marshaled up my prospects for his inspection. I confess I was governed by no intention to be honest. I lied outright wherever I could and where I couldn't I maimed or strangled the facts. If I had only had warning—a little time for preparation, and the memorizing of imaginary statistics—I should have made a better showing. I simply could not stick to the truth; but it stuck to me in fragments. I felt as though I were pasted all over with it."

"But what did you say to papa?"

"I told him what my income was—I had to name a sum so small I am sure

153

he believed me at once. Lastly I told him of my expectations,—and there was where I lied. With the result that, providing I shall increase my earnings sufficiently to warrant such a course, I am to marry you within a year,— otherwise I don't."

And Philip dropped into a chair dejected in body and mind.

"Now, what the dickens does he expect? I can't become famous on twelve months' notice. However, I must work morning, noon and night with no let-up whatever."

"And what's going to become of me then?" asked Barbara.

"You know, dear, we can't sacrifice the future for the present. It's a beastly short time in which I am to make a substantial addition to my earn ings, and your father most expressly stipulates that I bring them up to some appropriate figure. In the event of my being able to do this he will entrust your happiness to my care, feeling assured I am and will continue to be worthy of the trust he reposes in me—and so on and so forth through the easy let-down that he gave me. On the whole he was fair… most fair."

Philip was silent for a moment, then he said:

"That I have a thousand dollars and better in the bank was a point in my favor—if it had not been for that the chances for a respectful hearing would have been slim."

"It is quite a sum," Barbara said. "Lots of people here, nice people, too, live on small salaries and never get anything ahead. Of course there are others, like the Perkinses, who are rich."

"It's pitifully small!" said Philip, and looked his disgust.

"I don't know—one can do lots with a thousand dollars. You can buy a very pretty little home here for that," said Barbara practically.

"Of course your father knows the money was left me and that I didn't make it. He hinted that it was about time that I got into something certain. He even said that as soon as I did we might marry. It's awfully lucky about that money. I hope to goodness nothing will happen to the bank, for if there should, I might just as well quit."

Both laughed at the idea.

"Isn't it absurd!" said Barbara dolefully.

"No, it's very serious, dear. Let's think what I can do to get a salary out of the town. I wish I could go away, but I simply can't do that. I must stay and help out at home. I suppose I'd better try and bone the papers for more work.

That's the only sure thing in sight. I can always get that in small doses, because it helps the sale. My friends are willing to pay something for the opportunity to criticize the drivel—it's about the only opportunity they have had yet. It's a great thing to be a literary man in a small town, Barbara!"

"I hate to think I am to be bought," Barbara said angrily. "That it all rests on money, as though love were valueless."

"It's a commercial age."

"You seem to believe in nothing." There was marked disfavor in her glance.

Philip raised his eyes to hers. "I believe in your happiness and mine if I succeed. I have every confidence in myself."

"But not in me—you never speak of that!"

"Yes, dear, in you, too!"

"You don't say it as if you meant it!"

"I am not accustomed to saying things I mean seriously."

"I wish you would pay me the compliment of being serious."

"I do."

And truly beneath all the flippancy his heart-was heavy—and as lead.

III

I t was Sunday morning. Philip pushed into the church as the congregation streamed out through the wide doors. He made his way up to the choir loft where a man had just risen from his seat before the organ. This was Franz Becker.

"You are late, Franz," he observed.

"It is Communion Sunday," Becker said in a deep beautiful voice. "That makes it late."

"See here," said Philip, "I wish you would ask me to dinner with you. Anson's home and I want to avoid him if possible."

"Certainly," answered Becker,—"by all means come with me."

They went down and out of the church: Philip, light and active in all his movements; Becker, ponderous and slow—but masterful always, a man for the big things of his art. A warm friendship existed between the two. Philip had an intense admiration for the musician, who seemed to dwell in a state pretty evenly divided between abject despondency and settled rage. He respected this temperamental constancy. They were both friendless in a marked degree, neither of them being calculated to invite an extensive or varied acquaintance. Few people enjoyed Philip's conversation. Indeed, it was a special point with him that they should not. Nor did Becker rejoice in any great popularity. He was wholly repellent in his attitude toward the small world in which he moved—with a savage pride that was ever on the alert. He might have been in a primitive sort of way something of a social lion, but his taming was too imperfect to admit of it. His rudeness and barbarities comprised the most interesting anecdotes the town could furnish. Becker came of a class where poverty was the unvarying rule—meanness and commonness had been his earliest companions and in a moderated form these two kept their place at his side, chaining and crippling him, running him to the earth where he would have soared—a clog upon his steps forever.

Just how he had acquired his mastery of music none could tell. It was part instinct—part study—that in its feverish intensity was all but incomprehensible. His father had been a musician of more than passing note in the little German capital where he had lived, hoped and died, leaving the promise of his genius unfulfilled. There, his mother, after a brief widowhood, had married again, a man much beneath her in every respect. The marriage was followed by a speedy emigration to America, where a brother of her second husband had settled. Franz's stepfather was a shoemaker and had wished Franz to follow his trade; but as the boy grew and as inclination became purpose, and purpose in turn work, that which was locked up within him found expression. He could think and feel and dream. Best of all, perhaps, he discovered that his rare talent had a moneyed value that he was quick to profit by—then came the rush of ambition that was to carry him on and place him with the masters. It spent itself and he was left where it had found him—exhausted and wearied by the fruitless effort he had made. He could only go so far and no farther—circumstances drew in like a narrow circle about him. He was a giant set to do a dwarf's labor. From the start his mother and stepfather had strenuously opposed him on every hand.

However, when he had proved that music possessed a money value that he turned readily to account, they ceased to object—for money, like religion, is sacred, and not to be made light of.

But his determination to rise above the dependent and precarious position of an instructor they persistently combated. Enough to live on comfortably to them represented enough for soul and body alike. That his art meant to him expression and development, they never guessed and he never sought to explain. He was very patient with them and forgiving.

So, silently and without complaint, he drudged away as teacher and organist, his burden made heavy by innumerable younger brothers and sisters whom he was pushing with him into humble respectability.

Going back into the past he could recall the hard bitter season that came in his childhood and youth: there were things done then, want endured and privation, that even in the comparative luxury of his success made his heart sick with a deadly sense of shame and humiliation.

He could remember the death of a little baby sister that happened shortly after the family's arrival in the town. The memory of that event stood forth distinct and minute down to the least particular. It was one of those hopelessly miserable experiences he would have liked to forget, but could not.

There were many little ones then and they were very poor, indeed. His stepfather had not been able to pay for the assistance which is customary at such times, but had shaped a coffin with his own hands for the little body, and when all was ready, borrowing a horse and wagon from a neighbor, had driven to the graveyard, holding the pine box across his knees. As his mother was ill, and could not go, Franz had ridden alone with the shoemaker, who, even then, to all appearances was an old man bent and gray from much confinement to his bench. The small boy rode crouching in the bottom of the wagon, for there was not room for him upon the seat. He was long haunted by the vision, ineffaceable and clear, of his father, as he drove along, bending sadly over the burden in his lap, gray and somber, with the poor dignity of grief.

Their way took them past his uncle's store, for in a squalid fashion the brother was well-to-do. As they passed his place the child who huddled drearily in the bed of the cart, oppressed by an indefinite sense of sorrow, saw his uncle standing beside his open door in his shirt-sleeves—the center of a lounging group of idlers—and when the man became conscious of the nearness of the two, the wide-eyed child and the father, driving the horse, the coffin in his lap, he laughed aloud.

It was years afterward, when his uncle had quitted the town for a larger field somewhere in the West that the brooding solitary boy comprehended the full meaning of that day's ride, and it gave him an insight into the quality of human sympathy that one can safely rely upon receiving in the hour of need, far beyond his age. It served to augment a peculiar harshness of belief—a wish to keep to himself and from contact with others.

The family's poverty, which was beyond denial or subterfuge, only intensified this characteristic. His pride was like a raw sore;—the kindest touch was positive pain for him. Anything that savored of patronage or of condescension met with an instant and rude rebuff.

The Beckers—for the family was known by this name—a tacit recognition of Franz's importance and the family's unimportance that offended no one more than it did Franz—were extremely imposing as to numbers, with a majority in favor of the sterner sex, and the old shoemaker's patriotism had been evinced in the naming of his numerous offspring.

On the particular Sunday in question the midday meal was rendered more cheerful than otherwise by Bismarck and Von Molke, the two most youthful of Franz's half-brothers, who upset divers mugs of milk as well as pretty thoroughly smearing their small features with chicken gravy. Bismarck was finally ordered from the table by his father in very broken English because of some flagrant breach of good manners.

His exodus was shortly followed by that of his brothers and sisters who were in transit through that state of physical incompleteness, the sign of which is seen in the combining of long legs with diffidence.

These had eaten as though on a wager and one by one as they finished their meal slipped from their seats and took themselves off, the last mouthful in process of mastication.

Soon there remained only the old shoemaker, his wife, Franz, Philip and Von Molke—who still toiled manfully, albeit wearily, with a spoon tight-clutched in his chubby fist at whatever came within reach.

Bismarck had reappeared upon the scene. Into his small soul neither modesty nor diffidence had ever seeped even in microscopic quantities and he skirmished noiselessly about the room, always heedful of his father's guttural command to "go away"—promptly exiting at one door to appear as promptly at another with recriminations hoarse upon his lips against Von Molke, whose appetite, generaled with a nice knowledge of its capacity, bade fair to outlast the pudding.

With cold malignancy the latter's periodic cry of, "More, please," would sound, and up would go his plate in spite of his brother's muffled entreaties that he should desist. In this manner Bismarck saw the last fragment of the pudding disposed of, which sight so maddened him that he forgot all caution and darted at Von Molke intent upon wresting the coveted prize from his possession.

In the moment of victory the strong arm of paternal law was interposed between the combatants and the assailant, hotly pursued by the assailed, was borne from the room in his father's arms to meet his punishment in the back yard.

"Come," Franz said, rising. "Come, let us go to my room."

And Philip followed him, hearing him mutter as he went: "Can he not wait when my friend is here?"

It was a large bare apartment they entered, carpetless and curtainless, with an iron bedstead at one side and a hideously ornate stove at the other.

Philip lounged down into a chair, searching in his pocket for pipe and tobacco.

Without—for the room overlooked the back yard—they could hear Bismarck and his father. The former was crying, while his parent was expostulating with him in mixed German and English, but the sounds of grief continued with no show of abatement.

"He has a vile temper," Franz said, "when he is angry. The little boys are not bad as such little beasts go."

"I think them amusing," Philip responded. "The way in which a child profits by the presence of guests to gorge himself on dainties is a fair example of uncontrolled human nature."

Just then they heard the patter of small feet beyond the door and a faint voice saying: "I want in!"

It was Bismarck, and he waited for no answer, but inserted himself ingratiatingly into the room, presenting a countenance whereon grief and gravy had combined with disastrous results.

He was still sobbing but managed to gasp:

"I ain't hurt. It ain't that—but I do hate to have a darned old foreigner bang me about—it hurts my feelings!"

And he made a dive into Franz's lap, burying his head against his breast where for exactly three minutes he remained with wriggling legs a victim of keen despair.

"There is Americanism for you with a vengeance, Franz," said Philip.

The three minutes having expired and native depravity having usurped the place of anguish, Bismarck was forcibly expelled from the room and withdrew to more congenial fellowship with his brothers.

Philip broke the silence that succeeded Bismarck's expulsion in which they had both been actively engaged.

"Well," he said, "I haven't seen you for a whole week, Franz. However, I don't suppose you have anything good to tell me." Franz made a savage gesture that fully expressed a large disgust.

"Do you know, Franz," Philip continued, "we haven't originated much over here except the Declaration of Independence and a beastly bargain-counter spirit in relation to the arts." He paused a moment, then added laughingly: "One knows so much at twenty-four. I am frequently astonished at the scope of my critical capacity. It must be hereditary with me,—you know my father was a minister. They are the only class of men who enjoy the delightful privilege of unrestricted judgment. In that profession simple ignorance is not a hindrance, but rather a help."

Franz was in no mood for frivolity. "You are more than apt to offend people by what you say. Of course with me it makes no difference. You should be more thoughtful."

"I offend people, my dear fellow; that's what I am living for."

Becker voiced the thought that was uppermost in his mind: "My father and mother think I am as successful as any man need be. They do not comprehend that what I am doing now is drudgery, a present makeshift only—that my career is all before me. The only opportunity I have had, and I should scarcely call it that, was five years ago when I went to New York, thinking, for I knew no better, that I might accomplish something there. I tramped the streets for days in my effort to get a hearing. I offered my manuscripts to any one who would print them, as a gift. Bah! it was the same always—native work had no value. If I could only get to Europe—there they know what is music and what is rubbish. My father and mother do not wish to be unkind but they are not informed in these matters, and when I came back beaten and more humiliated than I can say, I saw they were glad of my failure. Their thought was that I should have been satisfied, and their one regret was for the money I had expended in so vain an undertaking."

His strong face showed plainly the pain that was his—the hunger and the longing.

Philip thought of those innumerable younger brothers. It would be years before any of them could come to the front and ease the load that kept Franz's shoulder to the wheel; meanwhile he was chained to a spot that could only give him suffering. There was danger, too, in the waiting. He might lose the very power to utilize his liberty when it did come. Men sometimes survive their inspiration and their genius.

Becker threw himself back in his chair: "We spend years in toiling for a little money that we may purchase opportunity and then—then, we die. Bah! what a fool one is to hope when the chances are all against him."

"Did you ever speculate on the final adjustment? God's apology to man?"

Franz shook his head: "What presumption, to suppose God keeps any record of us—such atoms as we are!"

"Not at all. My religion holds the splendid comfort of conceit and is based on the thought that man—and by man I mean primarily myself—is all, that my work, my good resolutions—which are a source of constant annoyance and distress to me—entitle me to certain favors in this world and the world to come. To be sure, opposition to the divine will is rather useless—at best we can but squirm like very small fish over a hot fire. Still, I shall make reparation for the absurdity of my beliefs by the dignity and persistency of my revolt, on much the same principle that prompts me to swear when I hurt myself by a foolish attempt to walk through an obstructed doorway in the dark, not that it does any good, but just to express my contempt for the inexorable."

Franz smoked his pipe thoughtfully. Philip occasionally shocked even his liberal ideas of propriety. They sat looking at the hideous little stove for a space and neither spoke. At last Philip said:

"Why, I say, haven't you a sort of a half-uncle in the West who could help you if he would? Can't you bone him for a start?"

Franz's brow darkened instantly: "You mean my step-father's brother? Don't speak of him."

"Oh, I beg your pardon," Philip made haste to say. "The fact is, I can stand almost anything in the shape of misfortune myself, except my relatives, but I thought it might be different with you."

"You do not comprehend. This person I loathe. It is nothing to him, of course. He is a rich man. I wonder what good money can do a brute like that?"

He looked out of the window, watching the dead leaves the wind was blowing into drifts against the fence in the yard below, and added almost sadly: "I think hate has been a more potent factor in my growth than love—at least it has stirred my heart the deepest."

"So your uncle is out of the question even though he should be willing to aid you?"

Becker struck the ashes from his pipe, remarking as he did so: "What can I do that will give me the longed-for opportunity? You are usually prolific in good advice."

"You might marry money."

"Never!" Franz interposed quickly. His friend's love-affair met with his strongest disapproval.

Philip ignored the interruption: "Now there is Mrs. Monroe. I have young Perkins' word for it that she admires you immensely. I am creditably informed she enjoys a fair income and she is still handsome and shapely—thanks to God and her tailor! Even the tooth of time has been dulled on her hardy anatomy. Franz, there is your chance."

"Don't be a fool! Do you think I——"

Franz was interrupted by the sound of an exceedingly pleasant voice that arose from the hall below. The voice was assuring some one that its owner was perfectly familiar with the way to Franz's room and was declining all proffers of assistance in finding it, with profuse thanks.

Becker and Philip had paused to listen, and now the latter said: "I rather fancy it's Perkins." A moment after a gentle tap sounded on the door, accompanied by, "May I come in?"

In response to Becker's bidding the door opened and Perkins stood before them.

Now there are awful depths of oblivion that may be sounded in a small town, and not to know the Perkinses was one of these depths, for that was to argue yourself unknown. Yet, to his credit be it said that Perkins was a modest youth, despite his temptation to gloat in the fact that his family represented two generations of riches; which was by far the most splendid incident in their history.

Young Perkins was not adapted to gloating. He was a youth with a supersensitive conscience and sandy side-whiskers, which grew out stubbily from an equally sandy complexion, and he would be polite to everybody, which was a sheer weakness on his part and not to be excused on any plea whatever.

What Perkins did not do his mother in nowise remedied, for she quarreled with her kind on a footing of perfect equality charming to behold, setting herself up for no better than the rest.

Perkins stood before his friends, breathless from his run up the stairs, his whole appearance indicating unusual excitement. He dropped down into the chair Franz pushed toward him, saying:

"Wait a minute till I get my wind. I am quite floored because of several things that have taken place to-day."

He wiped his florid face vigorously with his handkerchief.

"I—you see—that is, my mother received word yesterday from Madame Dennie, of Paris—Paris, France, you know—that she is in America. In New York, I think. Madame Dennie is the widow of Gabrielle Honore Dennie, who was a very distinguished man in France, prior to his death. I am sure I don't know what he did and my mother has never told me, but whatever it was I am certain he did it and it was uncommon. There was a stack of money in it. He was a banker, you know."

"Look here, Perkins," Philip remonstrated. "What is this all about?"

"But, you don't catch what I am driving at," Perkins cried eagerly; "he married my mother's cousin."

"Who did?" Philip asked.

"Monsieur Dennie."

"Oh,—well, go ahead."

"That's exactly what I am trying to do. He married Miss Ballard, my mother's cousin. That was before he died, of course. My mother was a Ballard and as you are both aware, that's my first name, and they were very celebrated people."

Perkins was still polishing his freckled features till they fairly glistened. He finally tucked his handkerchief resolutely into his pocket and folded his hands.

"I must get this straight, I am quite excited. Permit me to get my breath."

And he gazed benignantly at his friends from under his white lashes, a beaming smile playing over his countenance and dying away in the stubby growth of his side-whiskers.

"You fellows must have mercy upon me a moment longer. What I wish to tell you is this: On Saturday Madame Dennie is supposed to have left New York for this place. I assure you we were completely overwhelmed by the news, for while we—my mother that is—is her only living relative in America, the family connection has been allowed to languish. Heretofore my mother has made it a point to fight industriously with every Ballard with whom she came in contact. That's a distinctly Ballard trait, and in addition to the inherited and warlike instincts of her race, my mother's element is hot water. Very hot, you know, and I must admit it is seldom you find a person who spends less time out of her element than my mother. However, she has told me it will be the proudest moment of her life when Madame Dennie enters her house, so I am hopeful the hatchet will be buried blade down." With a stifled gasp, Perkins came to a pause.

"See here, Perkins," Philip said, "what is it you are trying to tell us? Come, don't keep it all to yourself. Let us into the secret. That's a good fellow."

"My dear Philip, I pledge you my sacred word of honor my one wish is to enlighten you, but I appear little better than a candle whose light is placed under a bushel." He looked pathetically from one to the other of his auditors. "Allow me to get started right. I trust I have made it clear to you that I have a cousin, Madame Dennie and she is a widow lady."

"Widow alone is sufficient. It establishes her sex beyond dispute. Don't use the word lady when you can possibly avoid doing so. It's a hard worked word these days," Philip advised.

"Oh, pardon me. Well, Madame Dennie, who is a widow, has announced her intention of coming to us and we are overwhelmed by the honor, for of course my cousin is a woman of the greatest elegance and culture. Must be, you know. But what"—and his voice rose in a quaver of nervous objection—"but what have we to offer her either in our mode of living or in a social way that will please her? It will all seem so stupid here after what she has been accustomed to."

"Don't abuse the town," Franz said. "It will be a liberal education to her."

"Along a very illiberal line," Philip added.

"Oh, hang the town! It's how we are going to entertain her that gets me."

"You are a host in yourself, Perkins, and very funny," Becker remarked laughingly.

"When is she coming?" Philip asked.

"Oh, yes, I didn't tell you that, did I?" Perkins shook off his dejection. "The letter was received yesterday. In it she simply said she would like to visit us if convenient and be our guest for a little while. We were to wire our answer and our answer was, 'Come.' What the dickens else could we have said even if we had wanted to? All this that I have told you took place yesterday and since then consternation has reigned supreme. My mother's hair has been done up in curl-papers for the last thirty-six hours, tight twisted, and has given her a raging headache. The house is no better than a howling wilderness. I pledge you my sacred word of honor that I ate my supper last night on the back-stairs off a sewing-board held in my lap and I was mighty thankful to get it then. This morning I went without breakfast. Dinner I ate from a shelf in the back pantry with a soup ladle and all because Madame Dennie is somewhere between here and New York contemplating a descent upon us. I have taken curlpapers out of the water pitcher, and as I hope for mercy hereafter there was one in the cold soup forming the bulk of my dinner to-day."

Perkins became pensive for just the briefest space possible and a rather melancholy smile overspread his face.

"I say, did you fellows ever eat soup—cold soup—with curl-papers? Because if you never did—don't. It's about the most thoroughly revolutionary thing a man can do."

"You haven't told us yet when she is coming," Philip remarked. "When will it be, to-morrow?"

"That's what we are looking forward to."

"How old is she, anyhow?" And Philip propounded one of the inquiries a young man is almost sure to make sooner or later concerning a woman.

"Oh, dear me, I can't tell. Forty or fifty though, I should say at a guess."

Philip yawned. Madame's age made the whole affair seem very tame and unattractive to him. Perkins rambled on:

"That's the deuce of it. She will be old enough to take an interest in me. Women are forever taking an interest in me—a controlling interest you know —forever thinking I should be at work at something or other, just to keep me out of scrapes. And that's all bosh! I don't think there's any use for me to work, except perhaps to kill time, and I really couldn't do that, for in the end time will kill me and I shall be laid out stiff you know, quite dead, with tuberoses—"

"Limp you mean," growled Franz correctively. "Where the devil did you ever get the notion that you could be stiff?"

"I hope I didn't seem vain when I said women were interested in me, you know I mean those who are old enough to know better," Perkins ventured with much meekness, folding his hands over a stomach of which Philip was wont to remark, much to its owner's agony, that it was coming rapidly to the front.

"Of course you will invite us up to the house when your cousin comes," the latter said. "Franz and I shall be immensely happy to call."

Perkins brightened visibly. "I thought you rather slumped when I told you her age. To be sure you are to call. Did I ever speak of her brother to you— Geoffrey Ballard? I know a good deal more about him than I do about her. He has been in America frequently. In fact, as far as France goes, he is an exile: got into some difficulty and was forced to leave the country."

This was said with studied carelessness; nevertheless it was plainly discernible that Perkins was accessible to the mild glow of pride which a perfectly respectable and well conducted youth usually feels in those of his family who have won their laurels in the shaded realms of the disreputable.

"I guess he is a very bad lot. Once my father chanced to meet him in New York. My father was fascinated by him and on the strength of the good impression he had made, Ballard borrowed several hundred dollars. He told a very plausible tale about a remittance from home that he was expecting. No sooner had he obtained an advance on what was coming than he got out of the way and it was the last father ever saw of him. He must have been very clever though, because you know my father was never a very great hand to lend money."

His friends were too courteous to inform him of their perfect acquaintance with his father's posthumous reputation for close-fistedness, but Philip could not resist saying casually:

"I can readily believe that Ballard must be a very remarkable fellow."

"Oh, no," Perkins responded innocently, delighted that he was commanding Philip's attention; "we heard afterward he was a wild one—that he gambled and did all sorts of dishonorable things. Of course I wouldn't like to have either of you mention it, but once he pretty nearly killed a man in a duel. It was over a woman, you know."

And he looked highly scandalized—proud and happy, too, for it's not every day one can tell of a cousin who fights duels.

It was getting dark; the afternoon was drawing to an end and while Perkins was still giving the details of which he was master, that related to Geoffrey Ballard's career, Philip had arisen from his chair.

"I shall say good night," he remarked. "It is time I was on my way home."

IV

That afternoon while Perkins was busy discussing with his two friends the expected arrival of his mother's cousin, the Perkins' home, some six blocks distant, was the scene of violent Sabbath-breaking. It is but fair to state that the house-cleaning was done with a careful regard for the moral sentiment of the community, being of a secretive nature. In the house, in the midst of the disorder she had created, moved Mrs. Perkins, appareled in a gown decidedly the worse for wear and whose frayed train was momentarily collecting deposits of dust on its under edge.

Mrs. Perkins had been a beauty of the magnificent order. Perkins' sandy hair, complexion and freckles, were the gift of his father. The curlpapers to which her son had made honorable reference were conspicuous objects in her disordered costume, while her face was embellished with sundry dabs of dirt.

The Perkins' home was the finest in the town, but now it was in a state of wild confusion. The furnishings from the numerous rooms had been dragged into the halls where they accumulated in defiant heaps. Mrs. Perkins surveyed the ruin. "Where, where did it all come from?" she asked tragically.

At that moment had Mrs. Perkins lent a listening ear she might have heard, disturbing the Sunday quiet that filled the broad street outside with its peaceful repose, the distant rumble of wheels, foretelling the approach of some heavy vehicle.

"I think, Anna," and she addressed herself to her principal assistant, "I think, Anna, this will be a lesson to me!—a lesson I shall not soon forget. What are you looking at?" For Anna was staring fixedly out of the window paying no heed to her mistress' remarks.

Even as she spoke Mrs. Perkins caught the sound of wheels as they rolled over the hard gravel of the carriageway below the window.

"I believe they have come," Anna said, her nose against the glass. "I declare it looks like them. There are two of them and both are in black."

At the news Mrs. Perkins sank down upon a chair completely overcome. "No, you can't mean it, Anna! For heaven's sake, look again!"

"There's two of them," Anna answered triumphantly. "They're both getting out. It's them."

Whereat Mrs. Perkins let fall two tears which plowed their way through the dust upon her cheek and fell with a muddy splash to the folded hands in her lap.

"That I should have lived to see this day!" she moaned.

"Shan't I go down and let them in?" asked Anna.

"No. I shall go myself."

Mrs. Perkins arose, summoning up all the majesty of bearing at her command, and surveyed the faded silk wrapper that hung limply and dustily to her figure with profound disgust.

"I suppose I must—but, what an impression I shall give her. Run to her room and make sure all is right there. Thank heaven! I had the wisdom to see to that, and there is a quiet spot to which she can retire."

So speaking Mrs. Perkins hurried down-stairs in response to the bell that was sounding for the second time. With a final desperate clutch at the curl-papers, a hasty adjusting of her skirts together with a last shake to free them from dust and lint, she opened the door. Mrs. Perkins afterward described her sensations as startling.

In common with her son she had anticipated welcoming a woman of mature years: instead she saw two women. Both were in black, but one wore the especial garments custom has made the sign of widowhood. The heavy veil was thrown back, revealing a face at once youthful and beautiful but of an extremely pallid coloring though it was touched with just the faintest glow, born perhaps of expectancy and excitement.

This was all Mrs. Perkins' bewildered faculties had time to grasp for the stranger said with a sweet little dignity that became her well, advancing a step as she did so: "I am Margaret Dennie."

Her voice was beautifully soft, and in its enunciation suggestive of her foreign birth and education.

"I was expecting some one twice your age," Mrs. Perkins said, laughing in sheer surprise. Her astonishment had so much the better of any reserve she had decided to show in the company of her distinguished kinswoman, that she simply used the words that came most readily to her tongue.

"Why, you are nothing but a child, a mere child, and you are Madame Dennie?" As she spoke she held out her hand. "But do come in; the man wants to get by with your baggage." And she drew her into the hall, the maid following, leaving the steps to the driver and the trunks.

That evening was destined to remain forever more or less of a blank in Madame Dennie's memory. She was conscious only of the warmth of her welcome and an overpowering sense of fatigue.

Her real comprehension of events commenced on Monday morning when she was aroused from her sleep by the pelting of rain against the west windows of her room, accompanied by the steady and persistent drip, drip, of the water-spout's overflow beneath the eaves to the sodden ground below.

She had been in America ten days and in all that time had seen but one streak of murky sunshine stealing from behind the masses of vapor that drifted above the wet earth. Wind and rain had seemed to pursue her with absolute ill will as though the weather itself was determined to drive her out of the country and compel her to seek her usual winter's asylum in the south of France.

Raising her head from the pillows, she surveyed the room. A fire was burning brightly upon the hearth, the curtains at the windows were drawn, shutting out all evidences of the season's inclemency, save the steady and unceasing sound made by the storm.

Staying in bed offered superior advantages to getting up. With a sigh of contentment she nestled down drawing the covering about her, then closing her eyes and soothed by the contrast between the storm from without and the cheerful crackling of the fire upon the hearth, she gave herself up to thought.

The look upon the small face resting pallid and white against the whiteness of the pillows was far from happy, for madame dwelt much upon the unprofitableness of her past.

There were many reasons that might have induced the young girl to marry a man fifty years her senior—many reasons—and yet all of them were far removed from the realm of the affections. This Margaret Dennie knew well, and to her sorrow.

She would have liked to forget it all—indeed, the wish had extended over the last three years and resulted only in the positive knowledge that one can forget anything provided one wishes to remember it, or it is useful. Bitterness alone is defiant in the presence of forgetfulness.

She had at nineteen married Monsieur Dennie and had endured two years as his wife, then, mercifully for her, he had died.

A woman differently constituted would have thanked God for the release and set about enjoying herself, making merry with her late lord's wealth. In her case, however, three years had been spent in a vain effort to rid herself of some portion of the horror begotten in her soul by the sacrifice she had made. There had been but one governing motive in the ill-omened marriage—to get money for her brother.

Monsieur Dennie had promised to pay well for her charms and had kept his word with the result that Goeffrey Ballard had been freed from his pressing debts and given a new start and another chance to wreck himself—a chance of which he had availed himself most speedily, so that six months after the marriage no mortal could have said wherein lay the profits or where his condition was any better than before the crime had been consummated.

Margaret wondered often how she had survived those years of misery,—not that Monsieur Dennie was unkind; he had simply never succeeded in inspiring his young wife with one single spark of love. It had resolved itself from the first into dumb and uncomplaining sufferance on her part.

Nearness to him had caused her but one feeling—a dreadful repulsion—a horrible desire almost exceeding her control to cry out as if in pain, whenever he had touched her.

Under this strain she had lived for two long years, then came freedom; but the iron had entered her soul. Her whole nature was saddened and embittered beyond forgetfulness.

A morbid dread that she had confided to no one had taken possession of her; she was completely at the mercy of her own distressing fancies and had come to regard her marriage as a sin unpardonable, as something unforgivable in the eyes of God.

At best, marriage is an ordeal for any woman, and a loveless marriage is an abominable institution of torture. Not content with what could not be banished, try as she might to live away from it, she had some vague idea of a recompense to be made, an indefinite conception of earthly punishment which she was to inflict upon herself.

It was this conviction that prompted her to wear the deepest mourning as a matter of penance, for it reminded her of the awfulness of those years, accenting and keeping the recollection always before her as a sin she must not condone.

This was what drifted through her mind while she was in the drowsy state that is neither sleeping nor waking. With something like a sob she came to herself at last.

"Russell!" she called.

Her maid came from the adjoining apartment where for the last hour she had been busy unpacking trunks and arranging her mistress' wardrobe. She was a plain featured English woman who had served Margaret faithfully in the two capacities of nurse and maid.

"Will Madame dress?" she asked.

"Is it late?"

"The family has breakfasted."

"I hope you told them I did not care for anything before luncheon?"

"Yes, Madame."

"And it is raining again. It has done nothing but rain since we landed."

While they were speaking Margaret had got into a long loose gown and moved to the fire, where Russell had already placed an easy chair for her. Wrapped in the voluminous folds of the garment she had donned she seemed quite small and very slight. Her face was wholly lacking in color except for a faint flush that at times burned on either cheek. Her hair, in two massive braids that fell below her waist, was a rich warm brown in the shadow, and golden where the light touched it. Her hands were small and beautifully shaped.

Most apparent was a fragile quality of face and form as if a breath might wither her.

Sitting in the great armchair and shrinking down toward the fire for warmth, shivering too, in unison with every gust of wind or rain that spent its force against the window, one could but marvel that she had known so much of life.

Russell brushed her hair gently, taking care the strain should not rest upon the dainty little head.

Margaret gazed thoughtfully into the fire. A certain sad aloofness was expressed in her manner as though all her sorrows had been borne without friend or confidante.

"I wonder if it's like this every day—without sunshine or clear skies," she murmured.

Russell did not respond to the direct question, but finished dressing her hair and stepped to the door, saying:

"There is some one knocking. Perhaps ma-dame's cousin."

As she spoke, she opened it and Mrs. Perkins asked from the threshold: "May I come in?"

For answer Margaret, turning in her chair, extended her hand, a smile upon her lips: "If you don't mind my dressing. I fear you will think me lazy. It must be late."

Mrs. Perkins bustled to her side. A very becoming morning toilet contributed its due proportion to that lady's ease and comfort. "Really, my dear, I never felt so strongly drawn to any one as I am to you." As she spoke she bent and kissed Margaret with great stateliness and ceremony. "You are not at all like the Ballards who were military people and much given to combativeness. Your poor dear mother and I used to hold most violent controversies. We had such a capacity for differences; it always came to the surface when we were thrown much together. But then it was a family trait and I suppose I should revere it accordingly. To be sure, your mother was a Ballard only by marriage, but she was an active partaker in the traditional characteristics. Dear! dear! how antagonistic we were, and yet, a real affection existed between us. Now, can't you tell me something about yourself?"

Mrs. Perkins drew up a chair and Margaret took one of her hands caressingly in her own: "But what shall I tell you?"

"About yourself, my dear. About yourself, by all means."

"Ah!"—and she made a little depreciative gesture—"I am such an ordinary person. There is nothing more to tell."

Mrs. Perkins shifted her position: "You can't fancy how amazed I was when I saw you. I had understood always that Monsieur Dennie, your late husband, was a man of very—what shall I say?"—she paused looking into Margaret's eyes, seeking earnestly for the right word, but the allusion to Monsieur Dennie did not stimulate any great burst of animation on the part of his widow, and she was forced to finish her incomplete sentence with, "a man of very advanced age."

"He was seventy years old when we were married," Margaret said quietly.

Mrs. Perkins elevated her eyebrows. "Why, you are young enough to be his granddaughter!"

"I was nineteen." Her face had hardened perceptibly when Mrs. Perkins spoke her husband's name, and at the mention of her marriage this changed to a look of the keenest distress. Mrs. Perkins surmised that it had not been an occurrence of the utmost happiness to the girl-wife.

Intent upon getting away from what she conceived to be a disagreeable subject, though still with subdued inquisitiveness, she said:

"You have not been a widow then so very long?"

"Three years." With unmistakable relief—"I have lived in the south of France during that time, but my home is in Paris. Since Monsieur Dennie's death I have not cared to return to it." A pause followed.

Mrs. Perkins tapped the floor with her foot. She knew that any more questions would be in very bad form, as Margaret had shown that she was adverse to constituting herself the sole center of interest. Truth to tell, Mrs. Perkins was rather abashed. As a rule she had no compunctions when it came to catechising newcomers in the town as to their past and possible future. Her position, which was unassailable, made it quite safe to seek to put at rest all uncertainty under which she might be laboring. But Madame Dennie was distinctly of another world. Suddenly she bethought herself of her son. He was, as she knew, in the library engaged in stroking his immature side-whiskers and wondering if,—"she would like him, anyhow."

Sunday evening had been spent in the society of his friend Becker and when he had presented himself at his own door shortly after ten, he found his mother waiting for him, with a glowing account of the splendor, beauty and culture of their young relative who had just withdrawn for the night.

"I think I have not told you of Ballard, my son, you know," said Mrs. Perkins. "May I?"

172

Madame Dennie inclined her head by way of response, and Mrs. Perkins continued: "He is wild to meet you. For of course when he came in last evening, I had so much to tell him about you. He so regrets that he should have been absent. If we had only known when to look for you he would have been waiting for you at the train." Margaret entreated her to make no excuses. The kindness she had met with all but overwhelmed her as it was, she said, but Mrs. Perkins was not to be turned aside now that she had got a fresh start with plain sailing ahead of her.

"My dear, he so regrets he did not know of your coming in season to meet you. Not to have done so seems to us so very inhospitable."

Margaret pressed her hand gently. "You are most kind. I am sure I shall love you dearly and perhaps," wistfully, "perhaps, you will grow to like me."

"My dear, I do that already. I am drawn to you as I never was before to a —"

"A stranger you would say?"

"Yes, and no—for, after all, you are my cousin's child and that means much to me."

Madame Dennie appeared a trifle helpless and as though she was incapable of meeting these advances. A repellent feeling—a wish to keep from close friendships had grown up in her heart—springing from the sure consciousness that she stood in need of sympathy and love and would be weakly dependent upon it once it was hers; but fearing always that she might tell those things her mind most fed upon, she shrank from intimacies.

Mrs. Perkins vacated her chair, and said with a trace of self-denial in her voice: "I shall let you dress now."

With this she quitted the room and joined young Perkins in the library. She found him standing on a corner of the hearth-rug, lost in meditation.

"I hope she is all right, mother," he said.

"Oh, yes—she will be down presently."

"Is she much of a stunner by daylight?" he inquired.

"I wish you would be more select in your expressions, Ballard. She is a woman of the greatest elegance."

"You like her, don't you, a lot?"

"I confess I do. There is something indescribably winning in her manner. I think her marriage was not at all a happy one."

Perkins shook his head wisely: "He must have been too old for her, you know."

"He was fifty years her senior, she has told me."

Perkins was expressing his amazement at such a marriage, when the door opened and Margaret appeared on the scene. An embarrassed silence fell upon him at once. He barely managed to answer the greeting she gave him.

Long before that Monday was ended Ballard's interest in his cousin' had become tremendous. When night came he was her abject slave,—her worshipful admirer who demanded but one privilege, that he might still be allowed to worship—yet no one could have asked for less than she. She was almost timidly sensitive about being a care or burden to him or to his mother. Despite her habitual shrinking from nearer contact or sympathy, Perkins sat for the most of the day on a small corner of his chair, his knees tight together and his toes turned most resolutely in, like a plump little saffron-headed Trojan, heroically resolved on her amusement. The tension under which he put himself, was so stupendous that he absent-mindedly twisted every available button from his coat. He talked on innumerable topics: told her all about himself, "Not because I think myself at all unusual," he had been careful to explain, "but because I am so perfectly acquainted with the subject."

He racked his brain for fluent descriptions concerning his loftier emotions —told her his most cherished ambitions—"things I should never dream of telling any one else," he said very truthfully. "But don't you know, I guess you call for the best that is in me."

He launched forth in quest of miscellaneous data and was soon telling her of Franz Becker and Philip Southard. When he told her Becker was a musician and Margaret told him that music was the one thing she loved above all else, he felt as happy as though he had discovered a gold mine in the coal scuttle. So fascinated was he that during the ensuing half-hour he talked a good deal more music than he knew, and at last, in answer to a question she asked, he found himself manfully seeking to formulate a concise history of the United States.

In short, Perkins did much that day that a Solomon would have feared to undertake. Late in the afternoon the wind died down and the rain ceased. The clouds drifted from before the slowly sinking sun, and his crimson flames burned in the red west.

Together they went into the yard. It had become quite warm with the approach of the evening, but Margaret was folded in a great fur wrap. "I am always cold," she had said.

For a time they had strolled about the grounds, which were very extensive, and Ballard had taken her into the conservatory where the gardener—who with the rest fell immediately under her gentle sway—picked for her a bunch of lilies-of-the-val-ley. Then they had gone into the house again where she shared her bouquet with Ballard—giving him a spray of white for his buttonhole. Much to his sorrow Perkins found it necessary to leave her and go down-town. With his departure Margaret was left quite to herself. The repairing of the preceding days' havoc demanding Mrs. Perkins' supervision, and tempted by the outer brightness, she summoned Russell and wandered into the grounds about the house and from the grounds into the street. Both found much to wonder at in the little western city. It was so different from anything they had either of them ever known. As they passed down the street they came to a church—the door stood open and there came from within a burst of melody. Perhaps some service was in progress. Margaret turned, and followed by Russell, entered the building. They found it empty save for one man who was just visible as he sat with bowed head before the organ, his hands upon the keys.

Madame Dennie was no mean judge of music. She had heard the greatest masters of the world and she knew that this player, whoever he might be, was not one of the least. He was improvising and from his own fancies drifted into Bach's first prelude. While his fingers were wandering through the opening bars, a sound stole out of the vacancy behind him.

The player turned and saw her standing in the aisle—the little gloved hands folded in unconscious devotion—the head thrown back with its delicate halo of golden hair, while through a stained glass window, high up beneath the arched roof, a single beam of light came to touch and transform the upturned face that stood forth boldly outlined against the surrounding shadows and the darkness that was gathering swiftly.

The final note was dying away, lingering out its sweetness lovingly upon the silence and the expression of rapt intenseness was fading from her face, when for the first time her eyes met his to be withdrawn instantly. A moment later and Margaret with her companion stole noiselessly from the church. Within the organ was sounding again, throbbing like a great heart that had awakened from its sleep to life and love.

V

Madame Dennie had expressed the hope of avoiding all social obligations. And Perkins had barely ventured to ask her meekly if he might not invite his two most intimate friends to the house—he was "morally certain" she would like them immensely, they were such charming fellows. So in due season he had presented Franz and Philip, and to them Margaret was most gracious.

After their first meeting with Madame Dennie, the young men had walked home in a subdued frame of mind. They stopped at the Beckers' to smoke a farewell pipe and while under the stimulating influence of the weed Philip proceeded to analyze his emotions and indulge in critical comment.

"Didn't it strike you that Perkins was just a bit sappy to-night? How his tongue did rattle along and always about himself." Philip meditated for a moment. "Perhaps I am uncharitable. I think my main grudge against him rests on this—I wanted to talk about myself."

Franz was smoking his pipe. There was a faraway look in his eyes and he was paying little attention to what his companion said.

Philip continued: "How did you like Madame Dennie? She is very beautiful, don't you think? A woman of culture and great spirituality." Franz was still silent. "There is something about her that impressed me as being touchingly sad and pathetic—I can't describe it, but it's there. I should say though she had an infinite capacity for happiness."

Becker removed the pipe from his mouth. "I have seen her before," he said simply.

"Oh!" Philip regarded him curiously.

"It was at church. In the evening while I was at my practise." He paused abruptly.

"I am afraid Perkins is in a fair way to make a precious ass of himself," Philip observed. "He is at the beginning of a bad business and ought to saw off. Perkins is all right, you know, but even his own mother would have to admit that he is freckled and fat. If he goes to falling in love with his cousin —"

By a sharp decisive blow Franz knocked the ashes from his pipe: "I shall have to say good night, Philip. I don't propose to send you home but—"

"Oh, that's all right. What's wrong? Have I said anything I shouldn't?"

"Shall I go down or will you be able to find your way out by yourself?" Franz asked.

He held open the door and Philip passed from the room. At the foot of the stairs he turned and called back his good night. Becker answered him cordially enough. When he found himself in the street Philip came to a stand.

"I declare he fairly put me out. As I live," he finally cried, "as I live he is in love with her himself."

During the succeeding weeks they both saw much of Madame Dennie.

Usually Philip prided himself on his ability to shock people, but with her he carefully eschewed all levity. Nothing could have induced him to advance the sacrilegious theories with which he delighted to offend. Such was his unblushing apostasy that Mrs. Perkins, who had long viewed him as one of the lost sheep, (chiefly by reason of the fact that for some years her son had at intervals favored her with scattered gems from his friend's remarks as well as with his scandalously unorthodox criticisms of vital questions) presented him with a volume of sermons.

Philip accepted this token of unexpectedly kindled solicitude with a stately gravity far surpassing the donor's, while Ballard went off into a series of convulsions that brought with them unworthy prominence and attendant disgrace. Furthermore, he was detected by his mother in the shameless act of winking at Becker.

Philip derived great good from those sermons. They gave him a convenient supply of paper for the lighting of fires in his room.

Those were delightful evenings they spent together when Philip would drop in on his way home from Barbara,—for the Perkinses were nothing if not fashionable and kept later hours than any other family in the town.

The young men would form a half-circle about Madame Dennie, where she nestled in an easy chair beside the fire for the warmth she loved and needed, and they would stand, looking down at the slight black-robed figure and sweet pure face, talking the while very boyishly of their hopes and their aims. Philip and Perkins especially had much to say of themselves. Indeed, there existed at first a very pronounced rivalry as to who should say the more.

They told her their desires, their ambitions—everything, and to their confessions she listened with a certain quaint little display of friendliness and affection that completely captivated them.

There was this peculiar feature noticeable in the devotion she inspired,—it was unselfish always for it was possible to love her in a manner that exacted nothing in return; possible to lay all at her feet, and ask but the joy of giving.

The fall and early winter were unusually inclement and a troublesome cough kept Margaret confined within doors. Perhaps resulting from this and the anxious care Russell took of her, they divined that she was not strong. It was solely by indirection they came to know that the frail little body had worn itself out to the verge of exhaustion. But the undisturbed quietness in which her days were spent pleased her fancy vastly better than any gaiety could have done. The latter she had known to the point of surfeiting while her husband lived and she recalled it as something to be avoided.

Thus it came that the weeks covering her stay in the small western city were the happiest she had ever known.

She enjoyed her companionship with Perkins and Philip,—she could like them unreservedly and in return be treated to a sincere admiration not without its gratification to the starved little heart.

She stood more in awe of Franz, and he kept his thoughts of her a secret. She could not guess that they lay too close against his very soul for utterance; but there was a remarkable gentleness in his bearing when in her presence—a reverent quality far removed from his customary brusk-ness.

Cling as she would to the past, Margaret was slowly growing away from it. She was almost happy. In course of time she might have been entirely so, but for the existence of her brother Geoff, who skulked on the outskirts of decency—and who only indicated that he thought of her when he showered her with begging letters.

In all the mad indulgence of his worthless career he had done no generous deed. He had burdened some one always, taking to himself the lion's share of the fruits and shirking all the toil.

It was to pay his debts, to give him a fresh start, that Margaret had been coerced by her mother into marrying Monsieur Dennie. That sin occurred at a day when Geoffrey had squandered the last of his patrimony and had embarrassed his mother's and sister's fortune besides.

Then it was that Margaret, but little more than a child, was taken from the school near Brussels and brought to Paris that Geoff might play her as his last card in the losing game of chance that was swallowing up their possessions.

He had cast about that he might effect a suitable alliance (to him a suitable alliance meant one that should not be scant of profit to himself) and had fastened upon Monsieur Dennie, who yielded up the price of purchase with the utmost readiness. More than this, while he lived, Geoff' was well provided for and if he had not been a chronic spendthrift could have thrived exceedingly. Unfortunately, he had no intention to be on easy terms with his good luck, but was forever making unreasonable demands upon his elderly brother-in-law for money, and for yet more money. The result was that when the old banker came to die he put his property in such shape that by no scheming could Geoff get his hands upon it.

Monsieur Dennie's methodical bestowing of his worldly belongings did not stop there. He arranged that an annuity should be paid Geoffrey and his mother. It was further stipulated that in the event of the latter's death Geoff should also have her portion.

Mrs. Ballard had not long survived her son-inlaw, and though Geoff had availed himself of the addition to his means her death gave him, the doubled amount was as insufficient as had been his previous lesser allowance.

After her husband's death Margaret was left to live her lonely life without interference from her brother. He went his course and she hers, though it was his habit to appear from time to time a seedy, shabby beggar and take from her every cent she could get together. Then he would vanish, no one knew where, until he again needed money. Nor was this all. He had married—much as he did everything else—to gratify some vacillating whim, and when the novelty of the relation wore off he had forsaken his family with never a regret, leaving the broken home for his sister to maintain.

For years Margaret had cared for his wife and children—"Kate and the three boys" were always in difficulties, more or less pressing, difficulties of the sort only money—blessed balm that it is—could alleviate. In short, there were more drains, more attacks made upon the wealth of Monsieur Dennie, deceased, than one could enumerate in a long talk. These just referred to were of the unceasing, never-ending variety, that came clamorously with each month, came again until they were satisfied.

But of all, Geoffrey Ballard was much the worst. He was seldom stationary or confined to any place by tie or occupation. He came and went at will; there was never any getting away from him.

Had it not been for Russell, Margaret would have been utterly defenseless, but the maid was a strong and reliable character, who strenuously resisted the wholesale absorption of her mistress' property. When madame's bankers remitted her income, Russell would take into her keeping the sum she deemed adequate for their proper support, and no one could take this from her.

With the bulk of what remained Geoff generally made off.

One evening while Margaret was alone in the library at early dusk, the room unlighted by other flame than the glowing of coals upon the hearth, there came a tapping at a long French window opening upon the porch. She looked up quickly, startled by the sound, and saw a man standing in the half shadow.

One glance sufficed,—it was Geoff.

Frightened and trembling, she arose and went to the window, pushing it aside that he might enter. Without a word, he stepped into the room.

"How damnably cold it is," he grumbled. "Throw another lump of coal on the fire, will you? What a beastly climate—rough on a man who does not boast an overcoat. Thanks." For Margaret mutely complied with his bidding.

The flames leaped up, disclosing a man of nearly forty, shabbily dressed in garments once of the greatest elegance, but which from hard usage were now nearly ragged.

He was of fine physique with a handsome countenance that, like his clothes, showed unmistakable symptoms of wear, for a record of the degrading course he had pursued so assiduously was stamped upon it.

He glanced around the room, taking in its appointments. They met with his approval, for he said:

"This is not at all bad. You do get your share of the good gifts of this world while I spend most of my time standing in the rain waiting to gather up the crumbs you scatter. Here I traveled from New Orleans to New York, thinking of course I should find you there. Imagine my predicament. All I had went to the pawn-shops, and I just managed to scrape through."

This was said with an aggrieved air as though the fault was hers. "Now, what can you do for me?" he continued; "I want money. I think my dress bears out the statement—" And he took a disgusted survey of himself in a small mirror hanging above the chimneypiece.

On her deathbed, at the close of a very foolish life, Mrs. Ballard had wrung from her daughter the promise that she would never abandon her brother, and Margaret, who was the victim of sentimentality where her mother's last wish was concerned, had carried it out blindly without stopping to consider its injustice. The profligate brother now spread out his hands behind his back to catch the heat from the fire, and ensconced himself contentedly on the hearth-rug.

As his sister had vouchsafed him no response he returned to the charge. "I don't wish to force my needs upon you," he said. "You must know it's hard for a man of my age to get down on his knees for the money to keep himself going." Margaret raised her eyes to his, and stared at him, silent and miserable for a moment.

"Well?" Geoff asked impatiently, "what are you going to do for me—what may I count on?"

"When I saw you in New York, I told you distinctly what you were to expect, Geoff."

Her tone while not unkind was positive. Gentle as she was and tender in all her dealings and judgments, a show of firmness had to be maintained in her relationship with this spendthrift, and too, she felt as bitter a sense of injury as her forgiving nature could harbor for the wreck he had made of her girlhood. She added almost hesitatingly:

"I—I am so sorry you have followed me here." To him this seemed to denote such outrageous treachery that he was really hurt—and showed it. She went to his side, and placing an arm caressingly about his neck, said, "Forgive me, Geoff. I did not mean quite that, but I have been so happy here. If you could only be as I am then you would like it too, but you know you are so restless. That is what I meant."

He shook off her arm rudely. "I understand, this sort of thing is useless— I'm not deceived." She looked at him pityingly. How mistaken he was in every impulse and ideal.

"I have not tried to deceive you, Geoff. Why should I attempt to? But it is so sad that we should waste our lives, when there are such possibilities within us if we would only consent to make the most of them. We have both lived so untrue to what is best."

This elicited only a contemptuous shrug from Geoff.

Margaret clasped her hands, while a spot of red burned in each cheek. "Why can't we go back?—back into the past so far we shall forget the wretched years we have wasted so wickedly?"

Geoff was excessively bored.

"I presume you are referring to your marriage." He retorted angrily: "The utter thanklessness in which you hold that piece of luck amazes me. I should like to know what the devil would become of us if it wasn't for Dennie's money. Of course the old fool tied it up with such nasty restrictions one can just get at the income, but I am pleased to be able to assert that I am not ungrateful. I regard your marriage as the very best thing that could have fallen to your lot, and I consider that I did what was honorable. Therefore—your evident dissatisfaction rather astonishes me. Under the circumstances, I scarcely anticipated it."

He settled himself in a chair, stretching out his feet toward the fender. His handsome head, fine as to shape and size, was thrown back and the firelight fell upon the beautiful evil face. About the eyes were heavy circles. These were the visible traces dissipation had left. A few gray hairs showed among the profusion of dark curls.

"I don't intend to reproach you," Margaret said.

"I should think not, when you reflect what I have done for you," he answered coldly.

"But at what a cost—at what a dreadful cost!" she cried quickly, and her voice vibrated with the intensity of her grief.

Geoff was deeply resentful, but offered no further interruption. She would be more pliable with such treatment. He centered his rather sleepy vision earnestly upon the carpet and endeavored to gain relief in partial abstraction.

Margaret crouched on the floor beside his chair, watching the warm glow turn to ashes as in her own heart the gold had turned to gray. There was nothing left.

"I don't mean to reproach you, Geoff," she said at last. "I have never even told you how hard and unbearable it has been for me—the horror or the haunting sense of sin and shame. Perhaps you did mean it for the best. I hope you did for your own sake, not for mine; I hope you did!—but I have suffered so.

"There has been such a stain upon my soul since the days of my loveless marriage, it would not wear away, it has only grown less since I came here. I wish to forget—I wish to begin again and there is no one who should be so near as you, no one to whom I can so justly look for protection. Shall we not begin again, Geoff? I am so sure we may be happy if we only will, and the life you lead, dear, is such an awful mistake—it can bring you nothing but pain, and to have you come to me worn and jaded, drags me down more than I can tell. I am constantly fearing that serious trouble may overtake you, I live in continual apprehension about you. Is it right that I, who have so much to make amends for, should support this load, too? Can I not grow back into some measure of innocence, without having sin and evil brought forever to me—Geoff—Geoff!"

She looked up appealingly.

His eyes were closed and his breathing proclaimed him to be half asleep.

With a sudden uncontrollable feeling of repulsion she shrank away from his side; then she stood erect.

Her movement aroused him. With a yawn he opened his eyes and glanced about stupidly as though he could not quite remember where he was.

"Really, I beg your pardon," he said with lazy politeness. "But the heat made me drowsy. Positively I could not keep my eyes open."

He thought it about time to bring matters to a crisis. He drew himself together and made ready to terminate the interview.

"How much can you let me have? I am aware that your bankers won't remit for a while yet, but can't you do something for me temporarily? As you see, I am abominably shabby and it's no way for a gentleman to appear."

"How much do you need?" Margaret asked.

Geoff promptly dropped the whine in which he had previously spoken, becoming suddenly and wonderfully buoyant.

"Oh! a few hundreds. I'll spend them well, and I'll agree not to bother you again until your money gets here. I'll hang about quietly until it comes, then you can fix me up and I will bolt the place. Now I call that fair—and you would better"—he grew strangely sinister—"you would better do as I ask or you may get let in for more than the mere loss of cash."

"I will go to Russell and learn what can be spared."

"The old cat!"

Margaret left the room. In the hall she encountered Perkins.

183

"I was coming to find you," he said. "It's nearly dinner-time and dark as the deuce. I say," in surprise, "is anything the matter?"

For Madame Dennie's face was more than unusually pale—more than unusually sad.

"Where are you going, Ballard?"

"Into the library. That is I was going there, but if you don't mind, I'll just go along with you."

"Instead will you do me a service?"

Perkins instantly made a gesture of assent. "Whatever you ask," he said eagerly.

"It's very little. Please don't be curious, and don't allow your mother or the servants to enter the library while I am up-stairs." Perkins seemed mystified and she added: "Some one is there, some one I would rather not have you see."

At this his face cleared. He made haste to say, "I shall do exactly as you ask. Nobody shall enter the library until you are willing that they should."

"Thank you so very much." And she vanished up the stairs.

Perkins glared fixedly at the library door, his freckled features assuming a belligerent expression.

Margaret returned immediately and came down the stairs quite breathless.

"Shall I stay here and keep the rest away until he goes, you know?" he asked.

She gave him a thankful glance, and he added:

"There, don't you worry. No one shall disturb you."

He held open the door as he spoke and shut it carefully after her, so that no portion of a conversation clearly not for him should find its way to his ears.

Ten minutes later when Geoff had taken his leave Margaret found Perkins still at his post, pacing the hall with dignified step. Something akin to intuition informed him it would be well not to allude to recent happenings, so he remarked:

"I think dinner is waiting for us. Suppose we go see."

It was after dinner when Margaret was alone with Perkins and his mother that she crept close to the latter saying: "I think I shall have to go away."

Mrs. Perkins let fall her sewing and gazed at Margaret in blank astonishment.

"My dear, you surely don't mean it!" she cried at last.

Whatever traits Mrs. Perkins had inherited from her military ancestors, to Margaret she had been womanly and loving, and the friendless little wanderer had received from her more motherly care than she had ever before known.

"I think," she began again timidly, and her voice was perilously near to the point of breaking, "I think it is much better for me to go at once."

"But do you wish to go—that is—must you?" Mrs. Perkins insisted: "Dear! dear! I had never even thought of your leaving us, and yet it is scarcely probable you will be content to remain here always."

"I fear it is better for me to leave you, but I do not wish to go—it's not that —believe me it's not!"

"Then, my dear, Ballard and I will never hear to it."

It was then Margaret broke down entirely, and not knowing what else to do sought refuge in Mrs. Perkins' arms and from that safe vantage told of her brother.

"And he is coming back. I—I had hoped he would not, unkind and ungenerous as it may seem!"

"Very well. He shall come here," Mrs. Perkins said.

"Oh, no! oh, no! you must know—I must tell you that his actions may be hard to explain. They are often reckless in the extreme. I can not make my burden yours. You would grow to hate me if I did."

"Indeed we shan't," Perkins burst out. "I'll look after him when he comes. I can handle him. You have no idea how clever I am. You just turn him over to me—I'll manage him." And he shook his head knowingly, while under his breath he whispered: "If he cuts up and annoys her I'll punch his damned nose!"—which was very violent language for him.

"I so regret—" Margaret began again, but Mrs. Perkins would hear no more.

"There, my dear, we understand perfectly, so don't distress yourself at all about it. You are going to remain here, whatever happens."

"Of course you are!" Perkins chimed in. "We want you to feel that this is your home and that you are to stay here as long as ever you wish to. The idea! —the very idea—"

"You are so good," Madame Dennie murmured gratefully. "So kind! It is beautiful to be so loved."

"It is more beautiful to have you with us, you know," Perkins remarked, "and to be permitted to love you."

"If I remain you must grant me one favor in advance." And she looked at Perkins, seeing in him a victim for the wily Geoff.

"A million if you like," he answered rashly.

"You are not to lend my brother money. You must promise me this."

"I shall be guided wholly by you," Perkins assured her.

This ended all mention of Geoff, but late in the night when they had all retired, Mrs. Perkins was aroused by Russell rapping on her door and entreating her to come at once to Madame Dennie; who was very ill.

Mrs. Perkins found the poor persecuted one crouching down in her bed frightened and shivering, though her head burned as with a fever.

She had had a dreadful dream, and she could not free herself from the nameless fear.

While his mother was soothing Margaret, young Perkins in a disordered state as to costume, but even more so as to mind, skirmished about the hall demanding half-minute bulletins through the keyhole. He was eventually induced to withdraw when it was announced that his cousin was resting easily, and reluctantly sought his room, while his mother and Russell, sitting by Margaret's bedside, discussed the situation in muffled tones.

"It is nervousness," the maid said. "When you know her brother you will not wonder in the least why seeing him should so work upon madame." And needing sympathy herself she proceeded to give Geoff a character that made Mrs. Perkins shudder.

Russell was as sure as her mistress had been that he would come back, arguing that the remittance from Paris would prevent his removing himself to any distance until he had his grasp, "his greedy and rapacious grasp," as she termed it melodramatically, on the money. She also, warming up to her theme, repeated every disreputable anecdote, every questionable transaction with which his name had ever been associated. These, if properly compiled and edited, would have filled a large book and the contents would have been extremely spicy.

So startling was the narrative that Mrs. Perkins reproached herself because of the fatal promptitude with which she had undertaken his lodgment.

At such times, however, she had but to look at the slight figure tossing restlessly upon the bed to feel that for Margaret's sake she would gladly assume any risk.

VI

Philip had the street to himself as he walked up-town from the Perkins', where he had been spending the evening, but as he came to his own gate, he saw a man lounging beside it.

It was Lester Royal.

Since the night when they had met for the first time in months, Philip had not seen him, and he had ceased to command any portion of his thoughts in the pressure of work and newer interests, but the sight of the boy leaning dejectedly against the fence revived the memory of their former interview.

"Why, Lester, it's you, is it?" he said with a marked display of cordiality for he was not averse to a little human intercourse at that particular moment. "Beastly cold, isn't it?" he added.

"I am frozen," Lester said, and he shivered. "I have been waiting to see you for an hour or more. Take me indoors, will you, where it's warm?"

Philip took his hand. It was like ice. "I should say you are frozen. Come along with me!"

They turned into the yard and Philip with his night-key unlocked the house door and led the way up to his room where a bright fire burned in the grate— his one luxury. He pushed Lester down into a chair before it and said:

"Now what's up?"

He saw that his visitor was pale and worn, with dark haggard lines about his eyes, and the hands he held out toward the blaze were thin and tremulous.

"Have you been ill?" he questioned.

The younger boy shook his head.

"What's wrong then?"

For answer Lester cried hoarsely in a voice choked with emotion and grief, "I am done for, Philip—done for! I am dying by inches—I!—and a year ago I thought I should live forever."

He buried his face in his hands, sobbing like a child.

The spectacle of a man in tears was not at all soothing to Philip. Perhaps there might have been times when he would have done the same thing, but that was no excuse for Lester.

He had done and probably would continue to do a great many things that he could not pardon in another.

"Come! come! this won't do. Be a man," he said coldly.

He was really very sorry for the boy, but Lester had no earthly right to make such a violent assault upon his feelings; besides he had a lurking suspicion that he was harrowing up his sensibilities with the sole object of asking for a loan. Whatever his object, Lester paid no heed to him, and Philip, after taking a turn about the room, halted at his side.

"I say what's the matter, anyhow?"

"You think I am a baby as well as a fool!" came in stifled accents from the sufferer.

"Oh, no!" Philip remarked politely, "only it's rather unconventional, you know. Just a bit surprising—not to say startling. I am hardly prepared for it. If you could manage to slow up a little I should be very grateful."

Lester raised his head and looked up into his friend's face.

The suffering that Philip saw in the face before him caused him to push a chair close to the boy's and seat himself. Then with one hand half clasping Lester's, half resting on the arm of the chair, he said kindly: "Tell me, old fellow, what it is?"

"I can't! I can't! You will know some day. You will find out for yourself when—" He broke off abruptly, leaving the sentence unfinished.

"Very well, don't say more than you wish," Philip answered. It was too serious for any display of curiosity on his part he felt. He gazed pityingly at Lester who looked pale and wan. Thus for a time they sat, neither speaking. At last Lester said:

"I've got to talk with some one—my brain swims with it—for the one idea whirls and whirls till I am dizzy and blind. I am wretched, Philip, wretched; and there is no help for it. I've brought it all on myself. Do you think it very hard to die?"

"Easy, but not agreeable. Why do you ask such infernally gruesome questions?"

"I've got to die."

"I can't see where you are an exception to the rule. It's expected of everybody—the nasty act of termination. What a vulgar thing death is!"

Lester stood erect—the firelight flashing over his worn countenance. "It's different with me. I've got to die now—now!" With a groan of anguish he flung himself back into the chair while Philip looked at him in astonishment.

"See here. What morbid fancy has hold of you?" he asked. "I must admit I don't like this sort of talk."

But Lester's face was buried in his hands, only his dry hard gaspings were audible. He gained a degree of control over himself and again faced his companion, saying: "Don't you know what I mean?"

"No, I don't, and that's a fact."

Lester was silent. Some sentiment of reserve stood between him and the confession he was seeking to make.

"Have you been drinking lately?" Philip questioned gravely.

"Yes—but not to-day."

"You shouldn't do it. It's anything but good for you."

"Do you think I am fool enough not to know that?" Lester replied with almost savage earnestness.

"Then why in the name of sense don't you keep straight?"

"I resolve to, and then go and get drunk against my will. You don't know what it's like."

Philip regarded him sadly. There was a heavy melancholy in the boy's whole attitude that distressed him—a spirit as of dumb submission to the inevitable. It was only lifted when he indulged in his wild bursts of grief.

"What's the good!" Lester continued. "I can keep up for a day or two, but I go back to it every time."

Philip shrugged his shoulders, saying with a poor attempt at lightness: "I suppose one should not resist the flesh. Our most virtuous moments are those which come when we have tired the devil out within us and are basking in the splendor of the good resolutions that tread upon the heels of satiety." He would have given anything to recall the words once they were spoken, for Lester shrank from him.

"I didn't think you would talk to me so—not now," he said.

There was the dull glint of anger in his lack-luster eyes, but it faded away almost immediately. Once more he became stupidly quiet.

"Forgive me," Philip ventured penitently. "I didn't mean to wound you."

"It's all right," Lester said indifferently. "It's all right. I presume you are thoroughly sick of me."

"No, I am not. I'd like to help you if I knew how, but you don't tell me what your trouble is. It's blind guessing with me. I don't know how to give you a lift."

"It's too late, I tell you. I'm done for."

"Do you mind explaining just what you mean?"

"I've squandered what should have lasted me a lifetime. I am a bankrupt in brain, body and purse. My God!"—with a gesture eloquent of despair and misery—"I've ruined myself! There is nothing left for me but death."

And Philip, understanding something of the other's need, said: "It's not so bad as that. You can pull yourself around, but if it's as you declare it to be, you can't be too quick about it."

"The doctors say not. It's all up with me according to them."

"Damn the doctors! What do they know?"

"They say it's too late."

"Siuff. They lie! It's never too late."

"There, Philip, don't—don't let's discuss it. I am not afraid, but it's terrible. I have thought I had years and years before me, and they were all wasted in a day."

To his horror Philip saw that his friend was in a measure reconciled to death. This to a pagan like Philip, was incomprehensible.

Now that he had talked more freely, Lester was calmer and his dejection was not so pronounced as at first. Silence had fallen on them and they sat looking into the fire, each busy with his own thoughts.

"Let's talk about when we were boys," Lester finally said. "You do the talking just as you did when I saw you last. Do you know if I can't sleep nights—and I can't most of the time—I like to think about it: the past that stops where my folly began. In all the years since I came of age, there is nothing I want to remember—it's all agony to me. Talk about when we were boys, Philip—about what we did in vacation. You were always such a good old chap!"

He put his hand on Philip's arm and let it rest there affectionately while Philip in a low voice began to speak of the past,—and at the telling much that was hard in his own nature grew soft. A strange gentleness came into the hearts of both, as Philip talked of their boyhood. When the winding country roads knew the marks of their bare feet in the dust; when, stripped of clothing and shame, they lay lazily upon the hot sand by the river's brim, and afterward took the long walk for home through the scented dusk. Back to the days when they were dirty and happy—when respectability knew them not at all—Philip carried them. And Lester saw in the fire, the red of the sunshine; in the smoke, the darkness of night,—the warm summer nights that were filled with peace and sleep.

Surely, it was better then—and as he listened his head fell over on his shoulder, his eyes closed, while still as in a dream he heard the murmur of Philip's voice, saw the pictures he drew, and then he slept.

Philip moved noiselessly to the table where the lamp burned. This he blew out so that only the firelight filled the room, the firelight and the colder brightness the moon sent stealing in through the windows.

As the hours wore on, he kept his watch at the sleeper's side, thinking and wondering what it all meant and what the end would be.

It was almost day when Lester woke.

"Better, Lester?" he asked.

"Yes. I wish I were back to it. I wish I were a boy again. I am sick of the present, and the future has nothing for me. You know I can't keep from the very things that are killing me. I try and try and then I fail."

"You must keep from them if you are ever to be all you were, all you promised to be."

Lester shook his head.

"It will never be, Philip. It is too late—I am done for."

"That's absurd, Lester. There! I can tolerate any one except the man who differs from me in his opinions. For him I have the heartiest contempt."

"It's not all cowardice with me," Lester said miserably. "Now that the time has gone forever, I want what I have never had. I am desperately sick of myself."

He looked at Philip wistfully, and the remembrance was torture to Philip long afterward. "Did you ever want to be good? Can you imagine what this desire is in a fellow like me?"

"Why do you stir me up on these lines of sloppy sentiment?" Philip retorted. "No, I never want to be good. My digestion is perfect. Piety does very well for children and invalids."

Lester made no response to this and his friend added in an injured but more temperate tone: "You talk like a man on his death-bed. I can only give you temporal consolation. I can only tell you what seems to me the wisest course to pursue."

"Perhaps I am nearer that than you think for—nearer my death-bed," the boy answered, helplessly, drearily.

"Stuff!" Philip cried hotly.

Lester seemed to take small comfort from his words, but Philip made a last attempt to cheer him up. "As to the doctors," he said, "you can't depend on them; and that about your dying is rank nonsense. If folly and sin were so fatal, our race would have become extinct long ago. You may be in a very bad way—I don't say you are not, but anything is possible in this world. You are more apt to get well than to die. You made a mistake, though, when you consulted a doctor. As long as a man can remain in ignorance of those operations that are going on inside of him, he is in the enjoyment of a very considerable blessing."

Lester turned away.

"Well, I shall go home now if you will let me out," he said drearily.

"Are you going to keep clear of those indulgences that are, as you think, killing you?"

"If I can I shall."

"If you can—you must!" Lester's glance checked him:—"I'll walk home with you," he said gently, and as he saw Lester was going to protest, he made haste to add:

"It's no odds to me that it's late."

And together they left the house.

A week later it occurred to Philip that Lester had not lived up to the assurance he had given him at parting, that he would come around soon and report upon his troubles.

"Now I suppose I should go look him up," he thought, "and find out why he has dodged the agreement in this fashion. It's just my misfortune to be of an abominably conscientious temperament which causes me to feel morally responsible for his well-being. I really am conscientious,—even stupidity can not be urged in extenuation. In the present instance I know perfectly well what I should do: I should dismiss Lester from my mind. But I am too much of a conscientious ass."

In support of the truth of this Philip started at once in search of Lester.

First he visited his home, and found that he had not been there in several days, but it occasioned no alarm, as the boy's habits were decidedly those of a vagabond.

This was in the morning. At noon Philip was in such a state of preoccupation that he got through his dinner without an exchange of hostilities with either of his sisters.

In his search that morning he had encountered no one who seemed to remember having seen Lester recently.

He could not free himself from the belief that his disappearance was a serious matter. The recollection of their last meeting oppressed him with an unpleasant distinctness all at once. He roused himself from his abstraction to say to his mother: "Do you know, I am worried about poor Lester Royal."

Katherine sniffed aloud at this: "Lester Royal, indeed!"

"I've been looking for him all the morning and I can't get track of him," he continued.

"Perhaps he is too drunk to be seen. It would be no new thing if he were," said Katherine.

Philip was using such a character as his sister in some work he was doing, and he was interested in examining her capacity for abusive speech when spurred by anger. Here was an opportunity: "Well, if he wants to get drunk it's his privilege."

"He should be locked up instead of being allowed to disgrace himself and everybody else."

"Oh, no, Kate—you would be too severe. What you foolishly take to be a religious conviction is simply a woman's prejudice at seeing a man enjoy himself."

"Of course you call intoxication enjoyment. Your views are so broad."

"Are they?"

"You think they are, but if I were in your place I should exercise some selection in the choosing of my associates."

"Would you really? How nice!"

"My friends should be my equals. Neither low Germans nor drunkards."

"But men are only equal when they are drunk." From her seat at the head of the table, Mrs. Southard sent him a look of mute entreaty, and it struck him for the thousandth time that the wrangling in which he and Katherine indulged was hard for his mother to bear. He promptly abandoned the attack, finished his dinner in grim silence, and started out again, bent on finding Lester, but grumbling as he went that he should be so weak as to care about the boy.

He devoted an hour or so to investigating the various resorts Lester was known to frequent, and eventually learned that he had been seen very much the worse for drink on the day following the night they had spent together. Since then no one knew what had become of him. The opinion of the loafer who furnished the information was that he had gone off somewhere to sober up.

"The ass!" thought Philip bitterly. "The brainless ass! Here I get into a pretty state over his woes and this is the extent of his reformation. He goes and gets drunk, which is a good reason for his not going home or caring to see me."

It was a bright fall afternoon—brisk and bracing—with touches of winter in the air. Philip turned his back on the town. It was just the season for a tramp into the country, and since the greater part of the day had been wasted as far as writing was concerned he proposed to amuse himself.

As he strode along thoughts of Lester would come to him, and in the end pity had replaced his momentary bitterness toward him.

"Poor fellow!" he muttered. "Maybe he can't help it, after all. Unless one has ambition or hope there isn't much to keep one up. I wish I knew where he has hidden himself. If I just knew that, I wouldn't bother."

He crossed from the road he had followed since leaving the town and kept his way by the river's bank. In the gaunt leafless weeds and bushes choking the narrow path he seemed to see flitting on before him Lester's tragic face.

Soon the town was far in the distance behind him, only the smoke rolling up from the factory chimneys could be seen, and still he tramped on and on, going to the many favorite haunts where he fished or swam as a boy. Each turn in the road marked some event especially prominent in his memory.

In spite of the chilliness in the air he strolled slowly forward for a mile or two, when the yelping of a dog attracted his attention, suggesting possibilities of companionship. He went in the direction from which the sound came. The passing of a bend in the river brought the dog into view, a small yellow creature crouching on its haunches on the bank and howling dismally. When it saw Philip this was changed to short jerky barks and it bounded down the bank and began to tug at a dark object that lay in a thin scum of ice formed about it in the still water near the shore.

From where Philip stood, a little farther down the stream, a curve in the line of its flow placed him almost opposite the object.

"It's a bit of old clothing," he told himself. And he called aloud: "Bring it out, sir! Fetch it here!"

The dog, stimulated by his voice and presence, barked more furiously than ever, while Philip fell to throwing stones at the thing in the water with the double idea of encouraging the dog and cutting the ice that held it.

All at once the dog, as though frightened, put its tail between its legs and ran up the bank, where it squatted on its haunches and resumed its yelping.

"I wonder," thought Philip, "if it's my duty to go tear the thing loose, for my esteemed acquaintance, the yellow dog."

He armed himself with a stick. Thus prepared he made a circuit of the shore. The dog testified to its appreciation of his evident intention in a most unmistakable manner.

"Glad of a little help, are you?" said Philip aloud to the yellow dog as he went toward the object in the water.

"It has a funny look," he thought, "a very funny look."

With his stick he poked at it.

The object with a light silly motion bobbed up and down in the water. Philip poked more vigorously. "Come loose!" he insisted. "Come loose!"

Then all in an instant the stick slid from his grasp into the water and glided away 'beyond his reach.

The thing had turned—'turned with a ghastly sickening semblance of life, disclosing a blue discolored hand so poised that it was outstretched straight and stiff. As it swept past it touched Philip.

"It's a man!" he cried, shrinking away. "As I live it's a man!"

The object, turning farther, floated free upon its back and lay so, and he saw the bloated, hideously swollen face of Lester Royal. There was no mistaking it.

Philip uncovered his head and leaned back upon the shelving bank. The dog crept to his side, and he caressed it silently.

There was no sound save that of the river where it fretted against its gravelly bed and the call of crows from the deserted corn-fields.

"It's all up with him now," unconsciously Philip spoke aloud.

He paused and gazed down upon the body of his friend. The dog crept closer and would have licked his face. This roused Philip from his reverie.

There yet remained for him to summon aid,—men and a wagon, and accompanied by the idle throng that gathers at such times, to go back into the town.

VII

Geoff spent exactly a week in the East, where the money Margaret gave to him was judiciously used as the basis for certain operations of a shady nature, and he took to himself several large sums on which he had no shadow of a claim, viewed even from the broad latitudes of sport.

With this influx of wealth he had proceeded to enjoy himself, which duty discharged, he did what his sister had feared he would do, he came and overran the Perkins' household. He brought with him a valet, an accomplished rascal meagerly patterned on his master's more splendid dimensions. This, coupled to the many airs he gave himself, sufficed for a local sensation and Geoff's vanity was pleased in the supremest degree. To be stared at and to excite wide-eyed admiration and envy was one of the pinnacles of bliss he liked to scale when luck was with him. When it was not, he was more than content to slink through several grades of shabby genteel ruffianism, attracting just as little notice as possible. There were four people, however, who refused to accept him at the current valuation, and Perkins led the list— Perkins, who watched him as a cat does a mouse, and who fell foul of him innumerable times each day: while Mrs. Perkins, mindful of Russell's revelations, tried hard, but failed miserably, to be hospitable.

Nor did Philip and the prodigal prove congenial. They amused themselves by a frequent interchange of scantily veiled insults, staying perpetually and perilously near downright trouble of the head-breaking sort.

But the most pronounced ill will was felt by Franz.

No man fancies seeing the woman he loves controlled and commanded, with scant appreciation of her rights, by another, even when that other is her brother. This Franz had to witness, and his soul was not particularly prolific in patience either.

Just how often in the course of an evening he would have liked to take Geoff by the throat rose nightly into a handsome aggregate, for the impulse flourished mightily.

As for Geoff, his selfishness was on the alert. His sister had never known young men and here were three, and of the three, one was unmistakably in love with her, and supposing she should marry again. The thought was like a chilly devil. It gave him the shivers. Clearly Margaret must be removed from the Perkins' home and the Perkins' influence.

Fortunately, at this juncture, Madame Dennie's bankers in Paris forwarded a considerable sum of money, and notwithstanding his many resolutions to the contrary he permitted his habits to get the better of his purpose and with the major portion of the remittance in his possession, vanished from the quiet he had threatened to disturb.

Then was experienced a sense of relief by all. They had been happy until he came. Margaret had imparted to their intercourse the charm of refinement— the gentlest of companionship, and this is the best of friendship and the best of love.

It was a night or so after Geoff's departure. Perkins and Franz were in the library waiting for Margaret to join them. The former was worthily engaged in an attempt to improve the passing moments by vitriolic comments upon the morals of the profligate, a singularly congenial theme with him. He had aired his grievance against Geoff, and was basking in the agreeable glow of Franz's approval, when the door opened and Margaret entered the room. On seeing her he cried as if in astonishment:

"Why! What———-"

For Margaret was gowned entirely in some soft white fabric. He had never seen her in anything but black.

"Why!—I say—" It was Perkins who spoke, surveying her with the greatest admiration. "I say, you never looked half so dear or beautiful!"

Perkins was a privileged character, and said a good deal the rest could not but wish they might.

"Now," he began again plaintively, "I call this rough—very rough, indeed. I've got to go to the Monroes' and say good-by to Bessie's sister and her two young ones… but, I'll be back in three-quarters of an hour. You see, to-night her sister and the two young ones go home and I have rashly agreed to see that they get safely started on their journey. I don't and didn't want to do this, but Bessie's mother said it would be a nice thing for me to do, and she is a woman you can't say no to. One of these days I must tell you about Bessie's mother, as she is the most remarkable lady of my acquaintance. She is always wanting a franchise. When it isn't a franchise it's an amendment and that's something you add to something else to make it different. She is interested in abolishing whatever she disapproves of, which I think myself would be a fine way to get rid of what you don't like. She is a member of more societies than I can recall, and she won't wear song-birds in her hat—you simply couldn't induce her to. I think if she could she would manage everybody's business except her own, which doesn't interest her. It is currently reported that she talked Mr. Monroe, who was a very superior man with a cork leg, straight into his coffin—from all accounts the place for him, because he drank like a fish. I assure you it's with the utmost difficulty that I keep her from calling on you. I don't think I ever mentioned it, but where Bessie and her mother are concerned I am but little better than ripened fruit. Now I must go."

And before Margaret could reply to his outburst, Perkins was gone.

Franz had seated himself at the piano, idly fingering the keys. Margaret had taken her place beside the fire. She was rather wishing that Mrs. Perkins, who had slipped out an hour before, "to be gone five minutes," would return.

All at once, Franz turning from the piano, looked at her as if trying to solve some problem.

Was she still absorbed by thoughts of the past, or did the present speak louder to her? Did her change of dress bear any significance... could she possibly forget the social barriers that stood between them? What a fool he was not to know more of woman's ways. All the locked secrets of her heart were hidden from him, he could but guess and wonder.

"Won't you play for me?" Margaret asked.

It was a new experience, that of being left alone with Becker; she was not quite easy in it. Franz turned to the keyboard. "What would you like to have me play?" he asked.

"Whatever you are in the mood for."

Franz's fingers rested caressingly upon the keys. "I shall improvise for you."

Then low and soft, as though each note was a love word, he began—his fingers shaping into sound his thoughts. As he played these changed from doubt to certainty and the blood rushed tingling through his veins.

The all but imperceptible rustle of Margaret's dress caused him to look up. The song of doubt, entreaty and of triumph stopped abruptly. She was standing at his side, pale and breathless, as though drawn there by a spell.

Then the red burned upon her cheeks—she would have turned away.

"Don't go! Don't leave me—you must not! Not until I know!"

He caught one of her hands into his own and held it firmly, but she offered no resistance.

"You must tell me now—now," he said. "I can wait no longer, Margaret!—Margaret!"

"What shall I tell you?" she asked in tones so low he could scarcely hear. It gave him courage as hers seemed to ebb, for she was pale and trembling.

"That you love me!" he cried, "that you love me, Margaret! That you love me and will be my wife." And he drew her into his arms. "Margaret! Margaret!" repeating her name in an ecstacy of delight. "Is it so? Do you love me, dear?"

She put up her hand appealingly as if she entreated him to say no more.

Slowly he loosed his arms from about her and she sank down into a chair, while Franz regarded her with a troubled brow.

"Let me think!" she gasped. "Oh! let me think!" Then sadly: "I have lost my friend. I am so sorry—so sorry."

"Yes," Franz answered steadily, "you must choose now and forever between your friend and your lover."

On the table beside Margaret's chair lay the book she had been reading that afternoon. A black bordered handkerchief was visible where it rested in the leaves of the half-opened volume marking her place. In their nervous wanderings her eyes fell upon it and their roving glance was instantly arrested.

The memory of what had been fell like a cloud, blotting out the present.

Franz saw the handkerchief, too, saw that she shrank from it. He stretched forth his hand and took up the bit of black and white. He held it in his tightened grasp until it was a crushed and crumpled heap in his broad palm, then it was dropped to be whirled up in momentary brightness by the fire.

Margaret gave a little cry. What it meant he knew, for it was glad, free and bouyant, as if a load had been lifted from her by the single act.

She put out her arms and Franz sank down on his knees before her. A new feeling surged into his heart. He had felt a man's desire for possession—now, when the victory was won, this was changed to infinite tenderness. He looked up into her face and saw what a woman's love was like, and he was well content.

"Margaret," he said, "Margaret, has it all ended—the past? Has the new day dawned for us—for both of us?"

And Margaret, her hand resting on his shoulder, answered, "Yes."

How long they were together after that neither of them knew. The happy moments are those that are never counted. Only misery has time to note the flight of time and to curse its slowness, grumbling at the lagging seconds.

But she had space to tell him of the life she had lived, the life that took its place that night with the things to be forgotten.

Perkins, returning from seeing his friends started on their journey, chanced to open the library door quietly and saw something which he subsequently described to Philip as "paralyzing."

His face grew very red—so red, that the freckles on it looked white and sickly by comparison.

He closed the door softly and tiptoed to the opposite side of the hall where he stood for a long time lost in profound thought. He might have stood there for an indefinite period had he not heard some one come up the steps and fumble around in the outer darkness for the bell.

It was Philip, and before he succeeded in finding what he was searching for, the door was opened by young Perkins who, seizing him by the neck, whispered hoarsely in his ear:

"Don't utter a sound! Don't!—or I shall strangle you on the spot."

With no further explanation Philip was dragged back through the hall— Perkins executing a wild dance the while—and up to Perkins' apartments. Here he was relinquished from his friend's forceful grasp, becoming once more a free agent.

"What's got into you, Perkins?" he asked, adjusting his collar and cravat.

"It's settled!" Perkins said excitedly; "they have arranged it—and here I figured all along that I should have to do it for them, which just shows what a billy-goat I am. Aren't you glad, old fellow?"

"Look here, Perkins," Philip remonstrated reproachfully, "why don't you tell me what you are talking about?"

"You fool! Haven't you got any sense?—Franz has gone and done it!"

Whereat, instead of being offended at such unusual language as applied to himself, Philip clutched Perkins much as Perkins had previously clutched him and they danced madly back and forth across the room.

"I pledge you my sacred word of honor," Perkins managed to gasp in the midst of their careering, "I pledge you my sacred word of honor I felt as though I should faint—actually faint. I was paralyzed."

"Why, see here!" and Philip came to a stand, struck by an idea he had long cherished but had lost sight of for the moment—"I thought you were in love with her yourself."

"So I am. I adore her! positively adore her, you know, but what's a fellow to do when he feels himself thoroughly unworthy, like the dust beneath her feet?"

He folded his fat hands resignedly over the central region of his plump person—their favorite resting-place.

"You see, Philip, I could never satisfy her as Franz can and will; besides it's the most monstrous presumption to imagine even that she could care for a badly freckled specimen like myself. Dear old Franz! he will have his opportunity now, for you know she is very rich, has something tremendous a year, and she will gain a defender who will protect her from that blackguard of a brother of hers. Altogether, it is too lovely for words—quite ideal, you know."

Philip looked at him admiringly. "I declare you are a good little beggar!"

Perkins winced at the adjective "little". He did not like it applied to himself. He shook his head reflectively.

"My dear fellow, it could never have been me—and, too, there is Bessie. It has become solely a question of ripened fruit between us. Besides"—manfully —"I have from the first considered Margaret as so far above me that I have never wearied in my affection for Bessie—or her mother," he made haste to add.

Philip laughed.

"Particularly her mother."

"I simply include Mrs. Monroe, because it is impossible to leave her out. She is so accustomed to mixing in things."

"I suppose they will live abroad pretty much," Philip said. "It's the place for Franz."

"I say," Perkins burst out blankly, "that's so, isn't it? You know she thinks him a great composer."

"And so he is," Philip replied.

Perkins gazed at him mournfully, blinking his eyes, and when he spoke it was in gloomy accents.

"He will take her away, won't he? Having her here forever is all up. Do you know I hadn't thought of that—not till this minute. Really, it very much distresses me, just the mere thought." Vouching for the truth of what he said, a tear trickled languidly down his nose, and after hanging reluctant upon its very tip as though undecided as to its ultimate course, fell to his clasped hands where it glistened like a dewdrop in May.

"I—this is very overpowering. I had lost sight of the future entirely in my great pleasure at what has taken place. Bless me! I never speculated on the results—never once."

He raised his glance pathetically to his friend's face. "It's a damn poor showing for cousins, isn't it?"

The round face with its stubby fringe and blinking eyes shaded by their colorless lashes destroyed Philip's gravity.

"Why don't you get them to adopt you?" he said.

"Do you fancy they would?"—with a gleam of hope. Then as he saw the smile playing about the corners of Philip's mouth: "You are jollying. Please don't, old fellow—not now."

"We shall have to get our comfort from the belief that this is for their great good," Philip said.

"So we must," Perkins acquiesced cheerfully. "What a disgusting pig I am to think of myself when they are so happy."

Later, on going down-stairs, they encountered

Franz and Margaret in the hall, and Philip, glancing at Margaret as she stood just beneath the tempered light falling from the chandelier, decided he had never seen any one so beautiful—except Barbara, who was incomparable. He divined that now to her, life seemed to hold much—to be so fine a gift.

The two young men left the house together. Philip at first tried to talk, but Becker made his replies with such indifference that he soon abandoned the trial as useless.

Franz's elation was scarcely concealed by his silence or his reserve. It spoke in the exultant heaving of his breast, in his quick elastic step, in his every movement. As they came to his door he broke the silence with:

"I shall go on with you, Philip, and see you home."

"As you like, old fellow," Philip answered.

No more was said until they bade each other good night.

Franz turned back alone—but not to retrace his steps. Instead he rambled through the streets of the sleeping town—to find himself—he knew not how, a dozen times beneath her window. So he wore out the night, and when at last the day broke, it found him going in the direction of his home.

VIII

Philip was looking from his window out upon the street where the first snows of winter lay slowly melting in the sunshine, when a cab rattled up through the mud and slush. It stopped before the house and his interest became active.

"It's the saintly Anson! This is, indeed, penance for my sins."

Almost with the thought Anson stepped from the cab and was followed by a gentleman who had no small trouble in wriggling through the narrow door.

Philip, with a groan of disgust, recognized the junior member of the firm employing his brother.

"As if Anson were not affliction enough," he thought, "he brings Mr. Hale to bore us—especially me, by prosy recitals of his own worth."

He promptly put himself beyond his brother's range of vision, as he wished to avoid the necessity of going down-stairs until the last moment.

He resumed his work, and for an hour or more wrote steadily on, then he threw down his pen and was resting his eyes, his hands before them, when the door opened and his mother entered the room. He knew who it was without looking up, since she was the only one of all the family who ever invaded his privacy.

"What is it, mother?" he asked.

"May I see you, Philip? Are you very busy?"

There was something in her voice that caused him to glance around quickly. "Why, what is it, mother?"

He left his chair and went to her side. He saw that her face was red and swollen as though from much weeping. "What is it, dear?" He put his arms about her. "Does Anson bring bad news of any sort?"

By a sudden gesture she freed herself from his embrace, covering her face with her apron.

"Oh! Philip, it's awful." And she began to cry softly.

"But what is it—why don't you tell me?"

He tried to draw the apron away that he might see her face again, but she resisted his gentle force.

"What is it, dear? Is it Anson—is he ill?"

"It's worse than that! Oh! a million times worse!"

At her words the desperate sickening feeling begotten of some great and unknown calamity, the forerunner of actual knowledge, came into his heart.

"You must tell me, mother, or how can I ever help you?"

"I shall, only wait a minute until I am calm, for you must know—and you must save him!"

"I save him! What do you mean? What has happened to him?"

"You won't blame him? Promise me you won't be hard, now before I tell you. That you won't say of think unkind things of him? Promise me, promise me, Philip!" For he had hesitated.

"I promise, mother, for your sake."

"No! no! for his own."

"For his sake then. It is all one."

"It is difficult to tell even you, Philip."

He put his arms about her once more. "There, you don't mind me, you know," he said tenderly. "Dear little mother, so brave and good, you really can't mean you mind me?"

It was in a hushed strained voice, as though she feared the shameful secret she had to confide would find a listener in the very air, that she told Philip of his brother's fall from grace.

"He has taken money from the firm. A thousand dollars. It was not stealing." She was quick to shield him. "He expected—he fully expected to pay it back, down to the last penny, but the amount grew and grew, and soon it was beyond him. He meant to be honest. He has been so good always, no one would dare accuse him of stealing. You know it was not; say it was not! Say you don't think it!"

She had given way utterly to her grief, and to quiet her he said:

"Of course it wasn't stealing."

"There!" reassured and rendered almost happy. "There, I knew you would understand. Why, even Mr. Hale speaks of it in the kindest way. He knows Anson to be perfectly reliable—he doesn't dare question it. Everybody knows how good he is, he wouldn't think of doing wrong. He has explained it all. At first he took the money as an advance upon his salary and then the indebtedness grew. He was never able to make good what he had borrowed. It was so easy to take what he needed—so easy to think he could repay it. He meant to do what was right: I am sure of this. If I were not it would kill me." She paused for an instant. "It was unfair to put such a pitfall in any man's path, no matter how honest. It was unjust, and they should suffer, but—but"— looking up appealingly into his face—"we must save Anson, must we not? For if we don't—he will be arrested and then every one will know. The whole town. Think of the disgrace—the awful humiliation! We must save him. He is your brother, and deep in your heart you love him. Say you do!"

Philip, looking at her, bowed, broken, crushed, scarcely daring to raise her eyes to his, answered that he loved his brother, but in his soul he cursed him for the suffering he had caused.

"Mr. Hale assures me that if the money is returned at once, it shall be kept a secret—not even the girls need know. You are the only one who can do this, Philip. It all rests with you. Will you save him?"

"For his own sake and for yours—but, most of all for yours, dear, yes."

In an instant he remembered what that money was to do for him. More than money ever did before. The thought made him sick with a deadly nausea. He saw his hope sink lower and lower until it entirely ceased to be and despair stood in its place. He had all but won in the struggle, and now to have the fruits snatched from him at the last moment! *He had saved for another to scatter.*

"What will become of Anson?" he asked. "Where will he go? Of course he can't remain with the firm. It wouldn't be permitted, I suppose, nor pleasant."

"He has a friend in the West—some place in California—in business there. He has been urging Anson for months to come to him, and now, it is all most fortunate, he has decided to go. He can't very well stay here. If he should there is danger the secret might be discovered: he would have to get a new position and people would wonder, but once he is gone, they will forget all about him and then there will be no talk. No one will ever learn why he left."

Philip looked at her commiseratingly. With his hand he brushed away the white hair lying in disorder upon her forehead.

"Poor mother, poor mother! and you have been so proud of him!"

"As I shall always be. My poor Anson! As I shall always be—as I am of all of you." She smiled bravely through her tears.

"I shall go for the money. I'd better go at once or I may find the bank closed."

He spoke collectedly and his mother did not divine from any words of his that he was preparing to make the greatest sacrifice possible to him. Nor would he have her know. There was misery enough for her as it was. Yet the thought of what he had to do brought him unspeakable agony. It was not the loss of money, for money of itself was nothing to him, but everything in his little world was held in place by what he was giving up.

"I shall get the money," he repeated quietly. "I shall go for it at once."

"You are so good!" she cried. "You were always my comfort. I can rely upon you more than on the others."

She reached up and kissed him again and again. "Though no one ever knows of the sacrifice you make, Anson and I will, and we will honor you for it. Do not think that we undervalue it." He kissed her softly. No amount of praise could have wrung the money from him, but her tears had been more potent.

"You don't care," she questioned, "that the girls are not to be told of what you do for Anson?"

"No, dear. Glory of that sort does not in the least appeal to me. I have no objections to being deprived of it. What I do I do quite willingly. I am satisfied with your thanks and the consciousness that I have in a measure eased this burden for you." He smiled sadly down upon her. "Now I will go," and unclasping her arms from about his neck, he turned and left the room.

After a few moments' waiting to regain her composure, Mrs. Southard went down to the parlor where Anson and Hale sat, the former crestfallen and not over-confident of Philip's generosity.

To Hale she said: "My son will be back in a few moments with the sum you require. He has just gone for it."

Anson's face lit up with joy. He was safe! How lucky it was that Philip had kept his money instead of spending it!

They did not have to wait long for Philip's return. His mother, who had been watching from the window, saw him as he came into the yard, and quitting the room, joined him in the hall.

"You have it? You were in time?" she asked anxiously.

"Yes," he said, placing a bundle of bills in her hand. "It is a thousand dollars you need, is it not?"

"Yes. It is so good of you. How can I ever tell you what it means to me!"

With a heavy step, as if all the vigor had left him, Philip slowly mounted the stairs leading up to the floor above.

"Won't you come in and see Mr. Hale?" his mother called.

"I had rather not, dear," he answered.

He walked as one in a dream, mechanically closing the door behind him as he entered the room. Then he dropped wearily into his chair beside the table.

He was overwhelmed by the catastrophe. A comprehension of it all, and the probable results, began to come to him. He threw the few hundred dollars remaining of his little fortune on the table. They were worthless, so far as the purpose for which they had been saved was concerned.

Stunned and stupid he gazed at the little heap of paper. Each dollar represented some privation in his daily life.

With savage fervor he brought his clenched hand down on the little heap, while from between his set teeth he ground out curses, for now came a frenzy of disappointment.

It soon subsided, as all violent emotions are bound to do.

Only a dull pain remained. Still he kept his gaze fastened on the money before him. It reminded him of what the sum had once been—and was no longer. He must begin again,—go through the round of petty self-denial, the soul-stunting process of small economy.

"It will be so long—so very long until I get so much again," he thought. "While I am about it a thousand things may happen to rob me of the inspiration of her love. And all for the theft of a wretched paltry pittance, so small it could have done Anson no good, and yet so large it may be the ruin of my hopes. It is unjust that I should suffer for him! A thousand dollars! Bah! The commonplaceness of it!"

With his fist hard pressed upon the table and his eyes fixed on vacancy, he sat and thought; thought with a brain mad and drunk with grief. He would have liked to turn his face toward the wall and give up. He was worsted. The props with which he had sustained himself were gone.

How he hated Anson! The fool!—who had lived in a false world of pious frauds; whose manhood had failed at the one test to which he had been put; who had succumbed to temptation at the first opportunity.

To cover up this—to put a patch upon the torn garment of his brother's honesty he must suffer. How he hated him!

He heard Hale leave the house, but dared not look to see him go. He took all his hope, all his aspirations with him. And now how would it all end? Could he ask Barbara to wait much longer? How would he meet her father's exactions? What excuse was there to offer for the sudden vanishing of his savings? Mr. Gerard would think he had been lied to from the start.

Down-stairs the girls and Mrs. Southard were making ready for Anson's departure. It had been arranged that he should leave at once. They moved about noiselessly, talking in whispers, the girls wildly curious, yet not venturing to question their mother. The whole atmosphere was as though some one had died. It pervaded the entire house. Where he sat in his room, Philip felt it. In fancy he saw his mother packing Anson's trunk—saw her tears fall silently as she folded away his clothes—and as his fancy saw it, so he knew it must be in reality.

Despite the load that lay upon him crushing him to earth, he was glad she had been spared the greater humiliation and disgrace that but for him would have come to them. The realization of this lessened the extent of his own anguish somewhat, at least it was a consolation to feel that he had shielded her, no matter at what cost.

It was dark when his mother finally knocked at his door and told him that supper was ready.

"I'm not hungry," he answered.

She opened the door and came in, saying in some surprise as she did so, for his lamp was unlighted:

"Why, Philip, what's wrong?"

"Nothing, dear, nothing. Why do you ask?"

"You don't begrudge the money that kept us all from shame—you don't regret that?" She put her hand upon his shoulder.

"I regret nothing. For you I would have done a hundred times what I did to-day, and counted it a small recompense for what you have given me all these years."

"You mean it, Philip?"

"Certainly. I was sitting here in the dusk thinking it over—thinking how glad I am that it was in my power to do this for you—and him. No matter what the outcome may be, I shall not regret it for one instant."

Her hand caressed his cheek softly: "Won't you come down to supper?"

"What's the use? I couldn't eat now."

"But you will not see Anson again. It may be years before he comes back to us. Do come down."

"I shall go with him to the train. Won't that do just as well? I wish to think a while longer, here in the dark by myself."

"I know he will be delighted to have you," she said. "Poor Anson! It has been a terrible blow to him."

Philip smiled queerly to himself. He doubted the delight Anson would derive from his company just then, but he made no response.

"It seems unfair to ask any more of you," his mother said with reluctance, "but Anson is almost penniless. If you could only help just a little it might make it easier for him."

Philip gathered up the bills that still lay on the table where he had thrown them. "Here are one or two hundred dollars," he said, "he may as well have them. They are of no use to me, and you will feel so much better to have him go, if you know he has something to fall back on!"

She took the money gratefully. "He has promised to repay all he has had from you, so don't worry about not getting it back."

"Ah! dear," and he laughed, "that does not worry me in the least. I don't bother about what he will or will not do."

She turned to the door: "I shall call you then when he is ready." And she left him to his solitude.

Philip wondered when he was once more alone what his mother's action would have been had she known what that money was to do for him. On the whole he concluded it was just as well she did not know. He became reflective. With practise it might be possible for him to acquire a habit which would enable him to derive a melancholy pleasure from being miserable. He laughed aloud.

"I never knew that farce and tragedy touched hands," he thought.

It was quite late when his mother called from the foot of the stairs: "Anson is ready, Philip. If you will come, he will be so pleased to have you go down to the station with him."

He went down and found her waiting for him in the hall. "You will be kind," she whispered anxiously. "You won't say anything hard, when you are alone with him? Poor boy! he feels it so keenly. You will be considerate of him?"

"Yes, dear. Don't distress yourself. I shall be as kind as I know how."

They went into the sitting-room where Anson was bidding good-by to his sisters. Philip had no wish to witness his mother's farewells. He picked up a valise his brother was to carry with him, saying: "I shall start on ahead, Anson."

"All right. I shall be along presently," his brother answered.

Philip escaped into the open air. Soon he heard Anson coming, waited until he caught up, and the two brothers, without a word, set off for the station very much as though they were trying to run away from each other, but had foolishly elected to go in the same direction while about it.

Their destination was reached before either had framed a speech diplomatic enough for the occasion.

Anson went to ascertain how much time he had and returned almost immediately to say that he had ten minutes left.

"But," he added, "you needn't wait on my account."

"I'll see you off. I told mother I would."

"Of course—if you like. I thought you might want to go home."

They fell to pacing back and forth across the platform, still apparently trying to get away from each other. Neither spoke, and it was only when the train rushed in with a trailing echo of sound from out the darkness, that Anson found courage to say hurriedly from the door of his car:

"Mother told you, didn't she, that I would pay up all I have had from you? I intend to and shall, but I can't do it at once." The whistle of the engine broke in upon him. "I'll do it sure, Philip, I won't forget."

"There is no haste," his brother answered. "Don't sacrifice yourself because of me."

He extended his hand. "Good-by and good luck to you."

The train began to move.

"It was awfully good of you. You have done a lot for me. I——"

The train bore him swiftly away, but standing as he did on the rear platform of the last car, the door at his back, Philip saw him wave his handkerchief and he responded in a like fashion, wishing he were certain Anson could see him as plainly as he saw Anson.

And so he stood until long after the train had vanished, a miserable lonely feeling within him.

It was all hopeless—the whole affair.

His mother would never be quite the same again, she could never live beyond the memory of that day. At last he muttered:

"Poor devil! I am positive he didn't mean to harm any one, nor did he mean to be bad. He has not the sense in the first place. What he did, was simply the blundering clumsy conduct of a fool."

IX

Changes occurred in view of the altered relations between Franz and Margaret.

It came to be Perkins' nightly custom to formulate labored excuses that would enable him to retire to his own apartments, for as he said to Philip: "Just suppose it was one of us!"

Nor did the change stop here. Mrs. Perkins suddenly found it convenient to spend her evenings in the back parlor where the arrangement of lights was more to her taste and where she could sew without straining her eyes.

Perkins was treating himself to a few remarks one evening before taking Philip—who had just come in—up-stairs for a smoke:

"I think I got off a very good thing to-day," he was saying, "not too amusing, but very bright and to the point. When you take into account that it comes from a fellow who lays no claim to being a wit, why it's not half bad. If you are all dying to hear, I might be induced to repeat it." He did not wait for their entreaties however. "You see, it was this. It's quite complicated and calls for a lot of explanation. I was at Bessie's this afternoon and a Mrs. Cavendish came in. Philip and Franz know her, but, of course, you don't." This last was to Margaret. "Well, we were talking about family. Mrs. Cavendish is great on family—she has been separated from her husband— that is part of the story, and it's got to be remembered." Perkins came to a stand-still. "Now, isn't it strange that only the most gifted intellects can master the intricacies of a funny story. Really, you know, I am getting it all wrong. Oh, yes, this is it. Bessie was speaking of some one—I forget who, luckily that doesn't matter—and Mrs. Cavendish said—'He was a connection of mine by marriage.' And I said—to Bessie of course, 'I suppose she would call him a disconnection by divorce now.'.rdquo;

Philip turned to Margaret: "Have you met Bessie yet?"

"No; Ballard refuses to bring her to the house."

Perkins shook his head. "My mother and Bessie don't get on."

"Is it settled, Perkins?" Philip asked laughingly.

"I suppose it is. You see a fellow hasn't a ghost of a chance when a girl and her mother regularly set out to marry him. When that's the case he might just as well beg them to name the day—for they are bound to divide the spoils. Yes," with placid resignation, "I really suppose I am as good as done for. I know it from the way their cook treats me. When the cook treats you with a deference you suppose she would only bestow on the heavenly host, you may be altogether positive your intentions have been discussed in the kitchen by members of the family."

Philip turned from Perkins to gaze gloomily into the fire. He was wondering, as he had many times of late, how he would ever summon the resolution to tell Mr. Gerard of his altered fortunes.

Perkins, surveying the faces of his friends with an angelic smile upon his own freckled features, noted his abstraction.

"What's the matter, Philip?" he asked. "Nothing. I am simply in the depths to-night. I fear I am not very desirable to have about in my present mood."

"Is it the work?" asked Margaret.

"It's everything!" He roused himself with an effort. "Utter and complete dissatisfaction with my surroundings for one thing—the feeling that I am dying with dry rot. I suppose to you it seems fresh and interesting. You can't fancy what it is to those who have to live here. The narrowness and meagerness of it all!"

"It's not so bad," Perkins said. "The town has lots of intelligent and charming people and if you didn't go about with a chip on your shoulder, you would find them out."

"I detest intelligence," Philip retorted. "We have filled up the valleys by pulling down the mountains—when we get a dead level the millennium will be reached. All that will be left for the unfortunates who live then to do, will be to lie down and long for death."

"I say," said Perkins interrupting him, "what's wrong with intelligence, anyhow?"

"Everything's wrong with it. I can respect ignorance. As with any deformity it has its own pathetic dignity, but this thin spread of middle-class intelligence, which is one part enlightenment to nine parts of stupid prejudice, goes far to make me an ardent supporter of gaggings, clubbings and burnings at the stake."

Margaret laughed: "Is intelligence so dreadful as that?"

"I think it is——" then he stopped abruptly, for the door opened and Geoffrey Ballard appeared upon the threshold.

With an attempt at dignity he moved toward his sister's chair. No one spoke. The surprise was too intense. But they observed that he walked as though tired.

Margaret shrank from him, her face paling. Every particle of happy color had fled from it when he entered the room. As Geoff bent and kissed her, Franz came to his feet with what sounded like a smothered oath upon his lips. After the perfunctory greetings with his sister were disposed of, Geoff swung around languidly to the others. First, he shook hands with Perkins with much cordiality. Next he saluted Philip:

"I am very glad to see you again, Mr. Southard," he said.

"Thanks awfully," growled Philip. He resented this intrusion. Besides he was not in a good humor. He didn't propose to be decent to a man he disliked. That was asking too much.

Silently and avoiding the danger of words, Franz and Geoff acknowledged each other's existence. They consoled themselves with looking their hate.

While they were thus engaged, Perkins stood on tiptoe at Philip's side and said in a hoarse whisper: "What business has he coming here sticking in and spoiling our fun! Damn him! Why doesn't he stay away? I should like to punch his head for him jolly good and well. That's what I would! I came mighty near doing it, too, when he shook hands with me." And Perkins bristled pugnaciously.

Such was the prodigal's return and such his welcome.

Not many days elapsed before there dawned upon him a premonition of what had happened during his absence, and a chilly and uncomfortable premonition it was.

Most assuredly an understanding had been established between Margaret and the German. Whether it was love or a deepened friendship, he could not decide and he was reluctant to inquire. Until now he had never felt the least wish to familiarize himself with the emotions that swayed her, and he did not know just how to begin.

Geoff finally hit upon Perkins as a likely source of information. He sought him out and asked to be enlightened as to the relationship between his sister and "that Dutchman,"—and Perkins informed him,—becoming more and more pleased as gloom spread over the face of his questioner. Geoff was seriously alarmed. But if any one thought that after selling his sister at so great an advantage to himself as he had done he was going to sit supinely down and not endeavor to save the purchase money, they did him a rank injustice.

He began to urge upon his sister the advisability of their being domiciled elsewhere. He didn't demand any radical move to start with, simply that they obtain a house. This he urged on the grounds that they were wearing out their welcome at the Perkinses.

"We can't impose upon their good nature much longer, you know," he said. "And since you are so very well satisfied here, don't you think we had better settle ourselves in some more permanent fashion?"

Margaret demurred, but what he said about the Perkinses made an impression upon her.

"I think," Geoff continued, "you would enjoy a home of your own, where you could be mistress. Russell could, of course, relieve you of every burden. She is fully competent to order a much more extensive establishment than you will care to maintain. I find there is just such a place as you would fancy. It is furnished and ready for occupancy. The owner is holding some political office in Washington, his family is with him, and their home is for rent, providing a proper tenant can be found."

He did not think it worth while to explain that he had learned the chief reason why the house stood vacant was that the location was unhealthful, especially during the winter months. He was positive he should experience no ill effects from this and he could afford to take a few risks with his sister.

"I wish you would think it over, Margaret," he urged.

"Why can't you remain here?" said Margaret. And her glance wandered wistfully over the room. He was asking a great deal. She was very happy.

"I don't begin to have your knack at getting on with people. I trust you will not speak of this until you know what you will do."

All this while Geoff was wonderfully circumspect. Never before had he been so considerate or kind. He seemed to have undergone a thorough reformation. He knew if he did not accomplish what he was striving for he would find himself face to face with ruin. This steadied him astonishingly. He showed no inclination to leave and for the moment conquered his tendencies to dissipation. He even ceased to be disagreeable to either Perkins or Philip, but he made it his duty to see that the interviews his sister had alone with Becker were few and far between—and as brief as possible.

So it happened, when one afternoon in December Margaret announced she had taken the lease of a house and intended going into it immediately,—that Perkins and his mother listened to her in horror-stricken amazement. They could scarcely believe it.

"What!" cried Perkins: "what! leave us, you know! A house of your own! Why, you can have all of this one if you will only include mother and me in the bargain."

"What place is it?" Mrs. Perkins asked.

Margaret turned to her brother: "What did you say the name was, Geoff?"

Geoff braced himself mentally as he answered: "The Springer property."

He was tolerably sure they knew the house and its reputation. Nor was he in error. What people in a town of ten thousand or less don't know of their neighbors' affairs isn't worth mentioning. They knew all there was to know of the house in question.

"Why, look here!" Perkins stuttered, his words falling over one another in their haste for utterance. "You can't go there, you know. It will never do, you see. The house is damp as all get out from cellar to garret, and it's so mildewy in some of the rooms that the paper won't stick to the walls. I have been there lots of times and have seen it. Why, I say, you should just see the Springer children. They are sick all the time. You can't go there. We won't let you." And he fell to pacing the floor, his thumbs tucked in his waistcoat, as was his wont when nervous or excited.

Geoff watched him from between narrowed lids. There was a steely glitter in the look, and a baleful twitching at the corners of his mouth, as though he had it strong within him to express a good deal more than was policy just then.

"You have been most kind to us," he said; "you overwhelm us with your goodness. Still I know my sister will be better contented in her own home. As for the dampness of which you speak, I will see to that. It is a small matter and can be readily overcome."

"Aren't you contented here?" Mrs. Perkins asked quickly, turning to Margaret. "You know we will do anything for you—anything."

Margaret seized both her hands and clasped them to her breast, then raised them to her lips while her eyes glistened: "I have never been so happy. Not in all my life. Oh, you are so dear and kind! How shall I ever thank you for all you've done for me!"

"We can not possibly add to the sense of gratitude beneath which we are already struggling," Geoff interposed. He spoke coldly and insolently. He wished to stop this burst of sentiment or else it might go to dangerous lengths. He succeeded in mortally offending Perkins, who said hotly and with the bottled-up acrimony of many days in his tones:

"Why do you cut in when my mother and Margaret are talking! You are always cutting in where you haven't any right to."

This outburst quieted things down for the moment and no more was said about Madame Dennie's plans for the future, but in two minds at least the thought of her pending departure was uppermost.

When Geoff quitted the library a few minutes later, Mrs. Perkins, excusing herself to Margaret, followed promptly in his wake, and at once returned to the charge with unabated zeal.

"Are you going to take that child there and selfishly jeopardize her health? Are you? Answer me."

"That's exactly what I am going to do, my dear Mrs. Perkins, and the sooner the better, if you will allow me to say so."

"Then," said Mrs. Perkins, "you are the most contemptible—the most thoroughly contemptible of living creatures! That's what I think of you, and I am the easier for having said it!"

"Don't you think, my dear Mrs. Perkins, that you rather strain the case?" Geoff retorted. "After all, one's own business is about the only business one should undertake."

Mrs. Perkins flushed, but she put a check upon herself. "I positively decline to quarrel with you. I don't, for I see through you. I won't quarrel no matter what you do and you needn't try to make me."

"Your conception of what constitutes incompatibility would prove entertaining," Geoff replied. "I have the impression that that stage of disagreement has already been reached. The only course open for my sister is to leave."

Mrs. Perkins fairly gasped at the deftness with which he made their dislike of him embrace Margaret as well, but being of an emotional temperament she trusted herself to speak no further and retired to her own rooms where she could weep in solitude.

And so it was decided that Margaret should leave the Perkinses.

When the day came—and it came quickly, as Geoff's patience was all but exhausted—she wept as she passed out through the wide doors that had opened so hospitably to receive her.

"We shall see a great deal of each other, shall we not?" she said to Mrs. Perkins. "You will come to me whenever you can? I fear the cold will keep me somewhat confined, but you won't mind it as I shall, and you will come often to see me?"

Perkins and his mother went down to see that she was properly installed in her home, and then sadly took their leave of her just as the night came on. Geoff, being inordinately elated by his success, was absent, celebrating his victory in a spree.

In spite of the fires and a superheated furnace below stairs, the house had a musty odor and the big rooms held a damp chill that could not be warmed out of them.

Finally Geoff came in, with unsteady step and bloodshot eyes, to add what he could to the load resting on the poor little shoulders, which for years had been so weighted down with care and weariness. He found her lonely, miserable and in tears. This exhibition of weakness, as he termed it, he took in very bad part.

The initial dinner was a meal long remembered, with Geoff, stupid and maudlin from too much drink, constantly going to sleep and as constantly waking to growl his complaints.

When it was finished, he took himself from his sister's sight, while Margaret waited for Perkins and Franz to come as they had said they would.

Eight o'clock brought them and the evening was passed pleasantly enough.

Madame Dennie had been suffering from a cold for some days, and the next morning she was quite ill. Her brother took no notice of this, and for several days did nothing but press forward to the goal at which he aimed. He pursued his former tactics with the utmost industry, seeing that his sister never had a moment alone with her friends; and wishing to discourage their devotion, was aggressive and rude to such an extent that Philip made just one call on Margaret and then in unmistakable language announced his intention of not repeating the experiment.

"I don't intend to walk half-way across the town simply for the delirious joy of letting that fellow insult me!" And he kept to his word.

To be sure, with Perkins and Franz, it was different. They were blind to affronts and proof against the insufferable. For Margaret's sake they were willing to endure the unendurable, but the ordeal was too much for them to live down without an inward revolt at least.

Franz became habitually morose and sullen. Perkins waxed shockingly profane and his mother spent most of her time on the verge of tears; and all this while Margaret's condition grew rapidly worse.

When brother and sister were alone it was the eternal harping on the one theme. Geoff wished her to go East with him—anywhere. He gave her no peace. Morning, noon and night, he stuck to the dreary round of argument and objection.

This continued for a week. Margaret's cold developed into an alarming cough. She was confined to her room and could see no one but Mrs. Perkins and Russell.

Having space for deliberation, Perkins was seized with a brilliant conception: a project that anticipated nothing less than the getting of Geoff drunk and starting him on what Perkins called "a protracted spree."

He reasoned that a man of his cousin's inclinations could only hold up so far in combating the unholy charms of a properly presented temptation.

But Perkins was not called upon to assume the tempter's rtle. Geoff accomplished his downfall himself.

There was one fatal quality in all his plotting. He invariably gave out before the final blow was dealt.

He now exemplified this by going away when there was most cause for his remaining. He could not stand the quiet longer. He would have one bout, he told himself,—just one. When it was over with he would return and Margaret should go with him where he pleased. He felt almost safe in leaving: she was so ill.

X

Then," said Philip shortly, "if I understand you aright, you wish me to discontinue my visits?"

Mr. Gerard was rather taken aback by the directness with which Philip put it. To be sure that was what it amounted to, but—"You see, you keep other men at a distance: you take up most of the leisure she has to devote to society. I don't mean to be hard. I trust you appreciate the delicacy of my position— the peculiarity of it. I want to be fair to you and at the same time just to Barbara. It occurs to me that I can only accomplish this by having you——" He was very much mixed—very red and very miserable.

The cause of all his annoyance stood before him—cool and collected, but it was the calm of desperation.

The comfort of knowing this was, however, denied to Mr. Gerard. He took up the tangled thread of his discourse. "My dear boy, you must know I don't want to seem hard"—getting a fresh start—"I don't want to interfere with your happiness, but where my daughter is concerned I must be just. I can't be remiss in my duty there. Now I leave it to you—to your sense of fairness. You know what I think—do what you consider right."

"I suppose you can not understand just how I got rid of my money," Philip said grimly.

"I confess I can't," Mr. Gerard replied nervously. "Your admission has been a great surprise to me. It was only a month or so ago that you had quite a large sum saved and now you inform me it's all gone, and you don't tell me where."

"I can not, Mr. Gerard."

"Of course—of course. That is your business. I appreciate that—I ask for no explanation—and I do like your frankness in coming to me at once," but there was small favor in the glance he bestowed upon Philip. "If it's gone— why——-" he came to a stop again.

"It is gone. Every penny of it." Philip said relentlessly.

"It's very unusual, very."

"And you had rather I slow up on my visits?"

"I leave it entirely with you, as I said before. I don't understand and I am not satisfied. I—really it may be as well for you to keep away. But do whatever you think proper."

"You put it to me in such shape that there is just one thing I can do, and that is keep away and stay away."

"My dear boy, I——"

Philip cut him short by turning on his heel. "You have no objection to my calling this afternoon?"

"Oh, no. Not at all. It's right that you should."

"Thank you," said Philip, and took himself off, leaving Mr. Gerard puffing and agitated in the door of his office.

Philip was glad that he had carried off the honors of the interview where calmness and dispassion were involved, but he knew that the triumph was a small one, and that Mr. Gerard's turn would come later, when he himself could but compress his lips and suffer.

He was thinking of this and bitter revolt was in his heart when he presented himself to Barbara. His face told plainly what he felt. Indeed, it was so apparent that she silently followed him into the parlor.

He threw his hat down upon a chair and stood in the center of the room looking at her, wondering how it would be possible to exist, deprived of her companionship.

"What is it, Philip? Why don't you tell me?" she at last found courage to ask.

"It's what I have known would happen all along. Your father——"

"What has my father done?" she interrupted him.

"He has told me I must stop coming here."

Barbara's eyes blazed. Her diminutive figure was drawn wrathfully up to its fullest height. "Has he dared to do that—has he dared!"

"I felt in honor bound to tell him I had been compelled to spend my savings. He said—he was very kind—that a continuation of my attentions would compromise you, and since my future was very uncertain——"

"My life is mine—it belongs to me!" she interposed. "And if I choose to give it to you, it's mine to give. I know what I need better than he does."

"I wish I could have told him how the money went. He evidently attributes my poverty to wild and reckless extravagance. I could see it completely finished me off in his estimation. I wish I could have told—but I couldn't. I can't even tell you."

"It's nobody's affair but your own, and if we are satisfied I don't see what it is to him."

"Just the same, Barbara, he has made it his affair. He is your father, and it is his privilege." Her little foot tapped the floor angrily. His submission offended her.

"It's all right, Barbara."

"It's not all right," she burst out. "Is it all right that our happiness should be wrecked?"

"I don't say that. I refer to his requesting me to cease coming here. He evidently regards me as not the proper sort of person."

"What are you going to do?"

"There is but one thing I can do."

"And that?"

"Respect his wishes."

"If you do, what is going to become of me?"

Philip put his hand to his aching head. That was more than he could tell. He had thought of it, too. His personal pain and anxiety gave him no concern. He had become accustomed to it, but it would be so hard for her. She had not his training in disappointment. What could he do?

"What will become of me?" she repeated, with tears in her eyes.

"As soon as I have the money it will be as it was before. The separation will be but temporary—unless you forget me."

"I shall never forget you. I love you."

"Then as soon as I succeed even partially, I shall come back to you. I shall work so hard, it shan't be for long. I *will* succeed." And he set his teeth. "I know I shall and it will be no ordinary success when it does come. You have faith in me?"

"Yes! yes! but that's so far off! Think of the time we have already waited."

"I know, dear, but I am making every effort. I know, too, that despite all his efforts a man may fail—absolutely—and through no fault of his own. He may get down and never rise, though he struggle ever so hard. There is a savage remorseless quality to life, a cruel indifference to work and worth. This risk we are compelled to take. In any business or profession it would be the same. It does not apply alone to one who thinks he can write——"

He was striding back and forth across the room. "Yet I can't bring myself to believe that I am to be one of the failures, all I want is time—time! I know I can do so much. You must have faith in me, Barbara!"

"It has been so long," she said sadly, going to his side and clasping both her hands about his arm, "and I am afraid. I don't quite know of what—but I am afraid."

"Can't you be brave just a little longer—just a little longer?"

"I try to be—I really do, but——"

"But what?"

"I am afraid he wants me to marry Mr. Shel-den. He does not say so, but I know." And she began to cry again, clinging to Philip the while. "I know it! I know it! and unless you save me I shall be forced into it. I can't stand black looks and constant coercion. I shall yield. I know I shall, and my whole life will be ruined."

"So that's it, is it?" Philip's voice was hoarse and dry. "So that's it? That's what it signifies? He wants to get me out of the road, does he?" And after a brief pause: "Do you like him in the least, Barbara?"

"I hate him."

"He has money and all that sort of thing."

"It's nothing to me. I can only care for you."

"Has your father made any positive statement of his preference, Barbara?"

She shook her head. "Of course he does not speak of it, but I know."

"Well, I'll go in for work harder than ever, dear—we need not despair, for we are sure of each other."

"But—but—if I don't see you——"

"Can't you keep your love alive and not see me?"

"I suppose so, but you are so different from me. You don't feel the same."

"I feel with my whole soul, Barbara. Can I do more?"

"It breaks my heart to think I am not to see you." She glanced up into his face. "Not to see you at all—why how shall I manage to endure it?" Her eyes grew wide, filled with a pathetic grief that made him desperate. "And now scarcely a day passes, that I do not catch a glimpse of you."

"It can't be for long, Barbara."

"It may be forever." This was said in a stifled voice.

"It's not as if I were going away—not as if I were to leave the town. We shall see each other constantly."

"It's worse than if you were going away. It's a great deal worse. Then I could make up my mind to it and could, I suppose, bear it somehow."

"Dear," he spoke softly, "dearest, please look up. I want to talk to you. Can't you listen to me? Please, dear, it's not so bad. It might be worse."

"It's bad enough!" without lifting her head from where it rested upon his arm. "It couldn't be worse. I couldn't suffer more."

"Can't you be hopeful? Can't you try?"

"I do try."

"It is coming nearer all the while. I am making money—I shall make more. Don't you believe in my ability?"

"It's not that. I am confident of the future, but the present is so horrible, with all manner of doubt. Do you," looking up and letting her glance meet his for a moment, "do you honestly think it will ever be as we hope?"

"Yes. It can not be otherwise. It only means patience—only a little waiting."

"Tell me what papa said."

"He asked me to stop coming here until such time as I am in a position to be accepted formally as your intended husband."

"And when will that be?" shaking her head.

"It can't be so very far off and it comes closer with every day. If I could only give you some of my hope—if I only could!"

"You do—but—"

"I do, but it fails in its mission."

"Tell me what he said."

"It all amounted to this. I must forego the pleasure of seeing you, except very infrequently."

"Is it good-by you are saying to me? Is it? Is it?"

"I fear it is. You must forgive me, but I have to show some little pride, and there is but one course open to me. It's not choice, but necessity that influences me in my decision."

"Does he want to make me hate him! I shall." She gave way utterly to her emotions and Philip did the best he could to soothe her as she stood within the protecting circle of his arms.

"I have exhausted my patience. I am tired—tired. How do I know it will ever come. It has been years already," she said at last.

"It is no more doubtful than anything else would be. I am putting forth all my energy."

"I am tired. I am tired."

"I have this to reproach myself with. I thought in the beginning success would come sooner. I have kept on and on, and now I am as far from it as ever. It has been four years, Barbara, four years. I am so sorry, dear, so sorry."

"If you go I shall never see you again. Something will happen. I shall be driven into something dreadful. I shall be at papa's mercy, and I haven't any strength of character. He can do what he likes when you are gone, and I shall give in. I always do."

Her whole attitude was one of weak complaint. It was fast forcing Philip to the verge of madness. As if she divined what his thoughts were, she said: "You don't respect me. You think I don't amount to anything."

"I love you!" he said gravely. "And now I must go."

"You are not going!—not yet!—not yet!"

"I shall write you every day when I don't happen to see you, so you will know how I get on."

"Yes! yes! but are you going?"

"I must go sometime and it's better over with. We shall write each other and we shall meet quite often at various places. I shall go where I know you will be."

She was crying violently.

"You must not leave me! You must not, Philip!"

But he moved slowly to the door.

"I can't tell you how hard I shall work. Just be brave and good as you have been from the start and it will come out all right."

"I can't wait forever—and I need you now."

"You will have to, dearest."

"Doesn't it make you furious?"

"What, Barbara?"

"Furious, that he can interfere with us. It's our life—our love. We only ask to be left alone. Oh—I can't bear it!"

"I'm afraid we must bear it for a while. We won't be altogether separated— we will see each other now and then!"

"No! no! what will such meetings be—with people about—people who will stare at us with silly senseless curiosity!"

"Good-by for the present, dear—for to-day."

"No—no!"

"We shall meet often. Try to think of that."

"I am not brave and I invariably give in. He knows it. I shall have no peace if you go like this. Promise me you will come back!"

"I can not, Barbara."

"Then the blame for whatever follows falls on you. You go willingly."

"You are unjust."

"You go willingly," she insisted. "You desert me. You leave me for him to torture into doing what he wants! Is it nothing to you?"

"I love you," he answered simply.

"And if we drift apart?"

"I don't know what you mean. How can we drift apart?"

"People do."

"Are we like them?"

"Are we?"

"I thought we were not," he said.

"Why should you think that?" she answered. "I don't know. Perhaps we are the same as the rest. Perhaps I only imagine the difference."

"You are going?" she said in alarm as he moved toward the door.

"Yes, Barbara."

But Barbara threw herself down into a chair and commenced to cry afresh. This drew Philip back to her side in an instant.

"Won't you say good-by, Barbara, just for the present? Won't you say good-by, dear?" He sought to remove the hand she held before her face.

She gave him no answer and he turned from her, at first irresolute and then with more decision, for his mind was made up. After all, her sense of resentment would lighten her grief for the moment. It would be easier to bear because of it.

He stepped into the hall, the door closed, and Barbara heard his footsteps growing fainter. He was gone!

Curled up in the easy chair she sobbed out her sorrow and anger, for it was a mingling of both. At last she raised her head and looked about. She was still sobbing brokenly.

Suddenly she sat erect. It was growing late. She remembered that her father was to bring Mr. Shelden home with him to tea.

"I hate him!" she thought. "I hate everybody, but I shall have to see him and be agreeable, and I suppose I look like a perfect fright with my eyes all red. Of course while he is here, I shall have to pretend that I am enjoying myself, and my head hurts and I am miserable. I want Philip, and no one else!"

In proof of which she commenced to weep.

And so for an hour or more she lay curled up in the chair, a doleful little heap.

XI

I told them they must have a doctor," Perkins explained to Franz, "and in spite of my mother's objections I called one in. Mother has been dosing her for a week now."

Young Perkins and his mother practically lived with Margaret, now that Geoff was gone, and it was on the second day of their installment as members of her household, when Perkins, asserting himself in defiance of the paternal mandate, announced his intention of summoning a physician—"Right off, and with no more dependence on luck," by which it is to be inferred that his mother's remedies did not inspire him with much confidence.

"He is with her?" Franz inquired, having just come in.

"Yes, if it hadn't been for my interference, I am certain my mother would have kept on dosing Margaret with her nasty home-made concoctions until doomsday. Poor Margaret would never have rebelled: she would have swallowed the stuff until it killed her rather than wound my mother by showing lack of faith."

At this juncture they were joined by the doctor, a gray puffy man, reeking of stale tobacco smoke and staler drugs, who took the ills flesh is heir to as a personal grievance.

"Well?" Perkins interrogated him.

The doctor emitted a sound that could have been either a grunt or groan: "It won't do," he said gloomily; "she must be sent South. She has not the stamina for this climate. It's using her up. Unless something is done she will not live through the winter, I'll stake my reputation."

"Then she should go to Florida?" Perkins questioned.

"I said she must be sent South,—if you are interested in keeping her alive —and I suppose you are."

"Good lord, yes!" Perkins gasped.

"I don't say her illness is critical at its present stage, but if you are going to do what I recommend, don't put it off. I don't want to be blamed. Good night."

He snorted angrily at the inoffensive Perkins, picked up his hat and medicine-case and departed, leaving the young men staring apprehensively at each other.

Perkins jerked his head in the direction the doctor had gone. "He's a confounded fool! That's what he is. If he had waited a minute, I'd have said so. He doesn't have to scare us to death."

Franz was busy with his thoughts. How could she go and how could she stay threatened by danger? The problem swung between the two alternatives and refused to be solved.

Suddenly Perkins cried joyously: "I've got it, Franz! You must marry her right off and take her South yourself—otherwise she will be left to the mercy of her brother. You love her,—I know all about it, old fellow. I saw it by accident and I take just stacks of interest in you young people."

He put his hand on Franz's shoulder. His demeanor was both patronizing and affectionate. He looked as cupid might, grown to sturdy manhood, so thrilled was he by his purpose.

"If you are the least diffident, I'll adjust it. I'd. dearly love to, and won't it be a jolly little earthquake for Mr. Geoffrey Ballard,—won't it?" And he hopped around gleefully, proving there can be two good and sufficient reasons for a man's acts, namely—to please himself, and to annoy his fellow: and who shall determine which is sweeter?

Franz had felt his heart leap at the suggestion, but what would Margaret say?

Perkins plunged ahead vigorously: "What will you do; will you wait for Geoff to come and spoil it all?"

Before Franz could answer Margaret herself entered the room, accompanied by Mrs. Perkins. Instinctively they turned to her. Never had she looked so slight and fragile.

With an anxious throb of his heart Franz started toward her with outstretched hands. Perkins was no fool. He stepped into the hall, motioning his mother to follow. Then he shut the door, remarking: "I guess they would appreciate being by themselves," and he winked with peculiar emphasis.

Left with Margaret, Franz arranged a chair for her. She watched his rather clumsy placing of wraps and pillows with an amused smile.

"You will make a baby of me, and I shall be a bother always," she said. She was pathetically grateful for the slightest display of love or devotion.

"How do you feel, Margaret?" Franz asked.

Margaret reclined languidly in her seat. The excitement of getting down-stairs had passed and she felt tired and weak.

"Tell me about yourself, Franz," she said. "I haven't seen you in days. To-night I insisted that they should let me dress, I wished to see you so much."

"What did the doctor tell you, Margaret?"

"That I must go South, but"—hastily—"I can not do that—I can not leave you!"

"But, if it is for the best, dear?"

"Surely it can not be best for me to be cut off from my friends, when they are so few—" She spoke in a frightened voice, as if appalled at the idea. "I should simply die of loneliness." She glanced up at him appealingly, her lips quivering. "You would not have me go, would you, Franz? I am such a coward. What would become of me, without you?"

"I shall go with you, Margaret, if I may," he said softly. "It all rests with you, dear. The grief of your going, if you went alone, would be quite as hard for me to bear as for you."

For a space she was silent, then her reserve gave way entirely.

"If I go, Franz, it must be with you. I can not leave myself open to my brother's persecutions—I can not endure them! The doctor said—but he told you, too?"

"Yes."

"I wish to live"—clasping and unclasping her hands nervously. "I never before minded what happened to me, life is so hard—but your love has changed everything. I wish to live for your sake—not for mine."

"Are you willing to trust yourself to me?" Franz gently interposed.

Margaret's head half rested on the chair-back, half upon his shoulder. Her eyes were closed and the hands he held within his own burned feverishly. At last she whispered:

"Take me with you. It is best we go together. I am sick—sick—and he is killing me. If you would have me, you must take me now…."

The next day as Philip was at work, Franz entered his room unannounced. Seeing who it was, Philip put down his pen, turning from the pile of manuscript over which he had been toiling.

"Are you busy, Philip?" Franz asked.

"Not very. Why?"

"Because I should like a moment's talk with you."

Philip nodded.

"Just knock those books off a corner of the bed and sit down—dump them on the floor. What is it, old fellow?"

Franz, having complied with the suggestion, said: "You know that Margaret is ill?"

"I knew she had a cold. I hope it's not serious."

"Her physician advises that she spend the remainder of the winter in the South. This she will do as soon as she recovers sufficiently."

Again Philip nodded.

"It's very unexpected, isn't it? I should consider it risky."

"She is not to go alone."

"Oh, I presume Mrs. Perkins is to go with her?"

"It would not be paying much of a compliment to your intelligence if I thought to surprise you by saying that I love Margaret."

"Precious little," Philip admitted laconically.

"Well, I shall surprise you. We are to be married immediately. The situation is so grave as to permit of no delay. Her health and the probable reappearance of her brother make it necessary."

"Bless me! I never figured on this." Philip looked his amazement. "What will you do then, Franz?"

"When she is able to travel, I suppose it means Florida, or the Bermudas."

Philip had risen and gathered himself together while making the circuit of the room.

"I declare, I didn't congratulate you, did I? To be sure, old fellow, the thought of losing you is not agreeable."

"If you will, Philip, you can be of great service to me."

"I was about to volunteer," said Philip heartily, "but you swept me squarely off my feet."

On the authority of Perkins—"It was a mighty jolly wedding."

230

The ceremony was performed in Margaret's own room and during its progress she lay upon a lounge, looking as fair as the lilies-of-the-valley in her hands, which Perkins had given her, after liberally bedewing them with his tears dropped in sentimental secrecy.

The sun was sinking far across the white fields, and the gold of its dying flames stole in through the windows, lighting up the room, as Franz, standing at Margaret's side, gave her his name and the protection of his love.

Mrs. Perkins and Franz's mother wept profusely, and Perkins disgraced himself in his own estimation by sobbing aloud in stifled tones be vainly sought to suppress on peril of choking. He finally retreated to the hall, where he encountered Russell with a limp handkerchief—"making an ass of herself, too."

A little later Philip drew the curtains in front of the windows to exclude the darkening sky and Perkins said, "When you get screwed up to it a wedding is really more festive than a funeral, though they seem to have much in common. Now I am in a measure familiar with the ordeal, I venture to predict this has been the most blissful day I shall ever know—when one of my dearest friends is married to another of my dearest friends."

Here he had difficulty with his words.

"Doubtless you all think me a driveling idiot, but I feel like I don't know what—and I can't really help it."

Everybody laughed at this and Philip shook hands with him, saying he was the finest fellow in the world, while Margaret bestowed upon him a generous share of her bouquet. The gift bore with it a grateful little speech that caused him to weep afresh.

It was very late, indeed, when they separated.

"I assure you," Perkins informed Philip when they had reached the Perkins home, "I assure you, it has been the most satisfactory event in my life, and it's a source of stupendous joy for me to reflect that my dear cousin Geoff is destined to undergo a severe mental shock in consequence. I think I am entitled to all the comfort I can get."

Philip smiled appreciatively.

"What a funny little fellow you are! Such a good chap, too," he added.

"Well, I am glad she has Franz to look after her, and he will have the means to go on with his studies," continued Perkins.

"He is fortunate," Philip replied. "We so seldom get what we want—generally it's what we don't want that comes to us."

Perkins looked at him curiously, his head well to one side and his chubby hands buried in the depths of his trousers pockets.

"I say—what's up? Aren't you happy?"

"I am blue, and not so decent as I should be. I am always and everlastingly thinking of myself. I am wretched—but you know what's wrong with me, so don't discuss it. I can't stand it."

"As you prefer, Philip. Still, don't you believe it will be all right in the end?"

"It's not the future that troubles me. It's what may occur while I am flat on my back. I am fairly desperate!"

Perkins gazed at him sorrowfully. Philip added:

"I can't seem very generous to you when I flop into the dumps on no greater provocation than seeing those who are contented and at peace. My nature is not sweetened by adversity, it's being pickled in it." He struck the floor savagely with the heel of his shoe. "I feel like running off from everything, and if I could include my miserable self among what I left behind, I'd not remain undecided."

"I hope you won't go any place, Philip!" Perkins said in alarm. "What the dickens will become of me? It will be absolutely forsaken when Franz and Margaret go."

"You will see all you want of me. I shall unquestionably stay for a time at least."

"Why—have you been actually thinking of leaving?"

Philip smiled grimly.

"Don't distress yourself; you can safely depend on having all you desire of my cheerful company. And now if you'll help me into my overcoat, I'll start home."

No sooner was Philip gone than Perkins took from his waistcoat pocket, where he had secreted them, the lilies-of-the-valley Margaret had given him. As he gazed at them a telltale moisture mounted to his eyes. He could only shake his head mournfully and deposit them again—not next his heart—but near an equally important organ and one he knew more of, even though he was in doubt as to its exact location.

Poor Perkins! He was learning that a disinterested love has its griefs. It's not unmitigated bliss to witness another's rapture.

XII

Time jogged forward. The year grew to its fullest age and died—the old giving birth to the new, and as the days went on Philip worked at his task, worked and struggled with what courage he could find.

He had at first seen Barbara quite often, but the frequency of their meetings gradually lessened. This, he knew, was the result of her father's interference.

Had his ears been open to the current gossip of the town, he might have been shocked by a rumor that even his mother forbore to tell him. He toiled away through the days, running his race with chance and fate, and when hope was once more beginning to burn within him, the blow fell. Spread out on the table before him was her letter. For the hundredth time he read it.

"You will hate me, but I told you how it would be. My father is determined that I marry Mr. Shelden. He is determined, and I have decided to do as he wishes. You will despise me, but I have tried to be hopeful and true to you—I have tried so hard, so very hard, Philip. I can only see that the future is doubtful and uncertain. Perhaps it is best as it is. If you achieve the success you deserve, I am unworthy to enjoy it with you. If you fail—you know I am not suited to poverty. I believe in your goodness, in your generosity, most firmly, as I have from the start, and I feel it will comfort you, when I say that the thought of marrying Mr. Shelden does not distress me in the least. I am not altogether unhappy that I am so soon to be his wife."

Again and again Philip read it, until the words were jumbled together in meaningless confusion.

"No, she is not entirely unhappy—I can see that," he thought. "What will she gain? A house on the best street; a man twice her age, and her father's blessing. Bah! It isn't much, though it counts for more than I."

He turned and gazed out of the window. How many times he had done so when his day's work was finished and he was happy, tired, satisfied. He was looking on a different world —a world he had never viewed before. The coldness was only cold. There was no contrasting thought of warmth and cheer. It was bleak and lonely—only that!

He raised the letter to his lips suddenly and kissed it.

"I loved her!" he thought. "I still love her—and I hope she is happy." He drew forward a sheet of note-paper, took up his pen, and dipping it in the ink, began to write an answer to her letter—his farewell to her and love, and the hope born and created of love.

When the letter was written, he put her letter—the last he should ever receive—with others of hers that he had kept.

"When she is his wife, I shall burn them," he muttered. "Till then, I shall keep them here. It can do no harm."

He marveled how he got through the days that followed. They came and found him, unable to write, wretched, but so composed his mother imagined his grief less than it was. But he was madly restless. There was no peace for him save in movement. Night after night he tramped the streets. Day after day, with a gun on his shoulder, he roamed the woods, about the town and by the river. The gun served for an excuse. It was never fired. In fact it was never even loaded.

He could not work—and work was usually his refuge in periods of distress. Now it was changed. He could only await the day she would marry Shelden.

"When it is over with it will be the same as if I had not loved her," he assured himself.

One afternoon as he was going toward his home, he came on Geoffrey Ballard face to face. Not the splendid creature to whom he had been accustomed, but Geoff, the seedy and disreputable.

Geoff had just arrived. He had been wandering through back streets and alleyways for an hour or more, waiting until the darkness of evening should settle down that he might slink unobserved into his sister's presence and demand money sufficient to make himself presentable.

There was a moment of defiant silence on the part of the prodigal met by a contemptuous indifference from Philip. Then Geoff spoke:

"I am glad to see you, Mr. Southard."

"Are you? Well, you don't look it."

Geoff would have passed, but Philip detained him.

"Hold on! I have something to tell you." Geoff came to a stand. "Have you heard from your sister during your absence? If you haven't there is a surprise in store for you. She has been dangerously ill and she is married to Becker. That was two or three weeks ago. They are preparing to go South, as soon as she is able to take the journey. Hold on!"—but Geoff moved rapidly away.

His sister married—and to the German! It put all other considerations out of his mind.

Perhaps Philip had lied. This was the meager hope with which he endeavored to sustain himself. He entered the house, and brushing past

Russell, whom he encountered on the stairs, ran up to his sister's room. She was in bed and alone.

"Geoff!" she cried in alarm.

His face was purple with rage; he could not control his voice as he poured forth a volley of incoherent abuse, from which she shrank, frightened and shuddering.

"Is it so? Are you married?" He was a trifle calmer when he asked the question.

"Yes, Geoff."

She answered steadily, but her cheeks were colorless. She feared him more than she even admitted to herself. Still it was well to have it over with. Franz was not by.... If he would only stay away until Geoff was through was her prayer.

"This is the advantage you took of my absence!"

"Oh, hush, Geoff,—" she implored. "He will hear you! It will be the same as it has always been—you have the claim on me you have always had—there is no change. I've only got a little happiness,—surely you don't begrudge me that!" Perhaps she appreciated the weakness of her plea, for she continued with dignity. "You forget yourself,—and what is due me—-"

As she spoke, Franz entered. He had caught the sound of Geoff's high-pitched voice in the room below.

"You don't seem to realize that your sister is ill," he said coldly. For Margaret's sake he was prepared to endure much. "If you have any reproaches to make you must choose another occasion. She is not in condition to listen to you at present."

The German's quiet demeanor sobered Geoff on the instant. "I have nothing to do with you," he answered sullenly. "You have only done what any man would in your position, I suppose. It was an opportunity and you made the most of it. I am not blaming you, but"—turning hotly to the bed where Margaret lay—"I blame her for having no better sense than to do a thing like this without consulting me. It was my right, as her brother, to know!"

"But you were not here," Margaret interposed. She was anxious to draw all the trouble that was brewing upon herself. Geoff's mood boded harm.

He paid no heed to her. He twirled a cane of flexible rattan he carried between thumb and forefinger, and glared at Becker. Stupidity, anger and partial drunkenness were in the glance.

"I say to you," Franz began evenly and quietly, "I say to you that your sister is sick, and I insist upon your leaving the room."

"I have nothing to do with you, Becker, though you did sneak into my place. For a fellow such as you it was a chance not apt to come again." Franz flushed scarlet, but he managed to speak without perceptible emotion. "Whatever you may wish to tell your sister must be deferred. This is not the time."

He deliberately pushed Geoff from the room, closing the door after them.

In the hall they confronted each other. Franz was sternly self-possessed. He would exercise all the tolerance at his command, at no matter what cost to his pride.

Within the room they had just quitted, Margaret lay breathless and listening, but when there penetrated to her ears the echo of Geoff's insulting speech, she arose with a dizzy aching head and with trembling fingers began to dress.

The two men were standing at the head of the stairs. Geoff was saying sneeringly: "For a fellow of your stamp you have done well. I can congratulate you even if I can't my sister."

Franz was silent. He simply looked from underneath straight brows at his tormentor, biting his lips.

"You have done a fine thing for yourself. My sister's money will find more uses than ever. Of course, it was the main attraction."

Still Franz was silent.

"Why don't you deny the truth of what I say?" Geoff insisted. "Why don't you tell me I lie, you fool?"

"If you speak to me like that again, I'll not be responsible for what I do," said Franz evenly.

"I congratulate you—you have done a fine thing for yourself. It means ease and plenty." He stretched out his hand mockingly.

Franz struck the extended hand roughly with his fist. "What you insinuate is a lie! You are a coward to get behind the advantage you have of me—a coward!"

Geoff dropped back a step. With his cane he hit Franz lightly at first, and then made as if to repeat the blow.

Forgetting everything but his hate for the man before him, Franz put out his hand to take Geoff by the throat. It was then the cane descended, striking him across the temples. Instantly foot and hand alike were stayed. He reeled as though he would fall,—putting up both hands to his eyes.

Geoff saw the door of his sister's room swing open, and turning with an oath from Franz, who stood swaying unsteadily, he ran down the stairs.

In the hall Franz lurched from side to side, his hands to his face. "Franz," Margaret called, "Franz, dear! what did he do?"

With staggering uncertain steps he started toward her.

"Franz!" she called. "Dear Franz! what is it?"

He gave no answer. He only groped his way nearer, and she saw the cruel red welts just above his eyes. He had come almost to her, when he sank to his knees at her feet.

"Franz, dear!" she cried, "what is it? Are you hurt, my love? Are you hurt?"

She put her cool palm against his forehead, and kneeling beside him slipped an arm around his neck. She felt him tremble as though every nerve and muscle in his body were wrenched and torn.

As she clung to him a chill stole into her own heart. She, too, could only crouch and cower and shudder.

Finally he spoke in strange hushed accents. "Margaret, I can't see! It is all black—black as night in front of me!"

She pressed close in his arms, and with her little hand she chafed his brow where the red line burned and stung.

He stood erect once more and slowly turned about as if in quest of something.

"Margaret, how does the light come? Is it there?" He faced the wall—the window at his back.

She had moved with him, her glance fastened upon his eyes.

They were fixed in a stony glare.

"Where is the window?" he asked appealingly.

She was sobbing now.

"Margaret, I can't see—I am blind—blind!"

He felt her fall lax in his embrace. The sobs ceased abruptly.

She was unconscious.

XIII

Franz knew that Margaret must die.

She weakened visibly with the moments that had the single mission—to kill.

He knew but too well what passed before him in his darkened world. He knew that since his blindness, she had sunk through stupor to stupor, each to drag her farther and farther from him.

There were intervals—seconds that might have been ages, when she would sit erect and call his name, but there were no conscious periods.

She was sinking by slow degrees, and the blind man held a dark vigil.

In the still room the other watchers came and went noiselessly, with the question continually on their lips: "Is she better?"

During those long days, when it was neither life nor death, Philip came frequently to make his inquiries, to be confronted by the vision of Mrs. Perkins' tear-stained countenance or, what was worse—to encounter Perkins.

He would wander in their company aimlessly from room to room, or with them listen at her door, seeing in his fancy Franz sitting, a blind sentinel, counting the minutes that stole up out of the lap of time to bear her away.

It was the evening of the fourth day. The doctor had just left the sick chamber to be met at the foot of the stairs by the three anxious friends.

"What are the chances?" Philip asked.

He shook his head. Then addressing Philip: "It may be well for you to stay here to-night. She is failing rapidly."

Philip looked at him stupidly.

Perkins seized the doctor by the shoulder almost savagely: "Why don't you save her?" he demanded. "Why don't you?"

"I am doing all I can. The cure should have commenced weeks ago. I said then what should be done."

He pushed past them, glad of the opportunity to escape that their momentary panic afforded; but Philip followed him from the house, and as the doctor turned—a lighted match between his fingers, for he was arranging to make his walk home comfortable with a cigar, Philip said, "Do you mean she will die? Is there no hope?"

"None whatever."

"How soon will it be?" Philip questioned with a stolid curiosity which was a source of astonishment to himself.

"In an hour or so, I think."

Philip twice essayed to speak and failed. The doctor puffed reflectively at his cigar. He added: "She was never strong, and the shock of Becker's blindness will prove too much for her. She was in no condition to meet it."

Philip mopped his brow. It was damp and clammy. Of a sudden he dripped at every pore. "What do you mean to do?" he asked.

"I'll drop in later. I would remain if it wasn't for an old party up on the edge of town who can't last. His folks have sent for me a dozen times to-day. He insists he won't die unless I come to help him off, and I guess the family's afraid he will stick to his word." And the man of pills laughed softly at his modest little joke. "I am of no use here. All has been done that can be—only keep an eye on Becker. He doesn't take it right. He is too undemonstrative. Good night."

And he strode up the street, leaving an odor of tobacco smoke in his wake.

Philip went into the house, shutting the door quietly behind him. It was all like a hideous nightmare, and he felt himself as unreal as all the rest. He found Perkins seated on the lowest step of the stairs. His face was buried in his hands.

"What else did he say?" Perkins asked, shifting his position, and looking up.

"It was merely a repetition of his former statement."

"I wish it were I!" Perkins blurted out. "I wish it were! Why can't we do something for her—for him! You love her, too, don't you?"

"Yes, I love her; maybe not with your unselfish devotion, but I have your desire to be of service."

Perkins shook his head. "It's all up," he sobbed. "Think of it—Margaret dying!"

Philip regarded his friend pityingly, and took to pacing back and forth in front of him.

Imperceptibly he moderated his step until he no more than tiptoed up and down the hall.

Perkins, worn and wretched with four nights of sleeplessness, slumbered against the newel post, his hands idly folded in his lap, his hair roughened and disordered, his dress creased and crumpled, his whole attitude one of utter dejection.

The solitary gas-jet in the center of the hall burned feebly.

The light, stealing through the colored globe, imparted to Perkins' features a semblance of shrunken ghastliness. More than once Philip had a compelling impulse to turn it up, and had stepped to the chandelier to do so only to be resisted by an invisible force that possessed him, a chilling apathy that revolted at any change.

The least noise had a powerful fascination for him. The ticking of a clock —and numberless clocks appeared to be ticking with jarring clangor, some close by, some far off in the distance—or the footfall of an occasional belated wayfarer on the street without, would cause him to pause and listen breathlessly with a vague unexplainable fear. His sensations were so distressing that for the sake of personal contact he wedged in at Perkins' elbow on the steps. In spite of his care he aroused his companion, who stirred fretfully to ask sleepily: "What is it? Do they want me?"

"I wished to sit down. I didn't intend to disturb you."

"Oh! that's all right." And almost immediately Perkins was dozing as before.

In the room above, the watcher and watched kept their place.

Franz clasped her hands fast in both of his, as though through sheer physical strength he would keep her with him. As yet she had indicated by no sign that she understood what was going on about her. It was always the same tired tossing, but with greater weakness there slowly succeeded greater calm.

With a fixed rapt look Franz's gaze sought her face and never wavered; it preserved its direction as steadily from beneath his broad straight brows as though he really saw.

She turned restlessly for the thousandth time, and as he had a thousand times already, he whispered softly, "Margaret."

Hitherto his words had fallen on deaf ears, now the head moved upon the pillow—the sweet wan face was raised to his.

"Margaret," he said, "Margaret, do you hear me? My little wife! My little wife!" As he spoke her eyes opened.

The room was unlighted save for the night-lamp burning on the table, and peering at her in the gloom with those sunken sightless eyes of his, was her husband.

She remembered all. "Franz! Franz!" she cried, in a voice so faint as scarcely to be audible. "It was not a dream? I meant you should have so much,—say you forgive me!"

"You must not grieve, dear," he said tenderly. "You must not think of me now."

"It was all so beautiful until he came," she said dreamily; "I have been so happy with you, dear, so happy."

There was infinite regret and infinite tenderness in her all but inarticulate speech.

They were silent for a while, then Margaret said: "It is good-by we are saying, Franz. Who would imagine there would be so little to say?"

Franz bent over her, desolation in his soul.

"What was that?" she asked, her voice fainter than before.

"I thought it very quiet, dear," he answered. "Perhaps it is the wind."

"How many days ago was it?" she questioned.

"You mean when you were taken ill, dear? It was four days ago."

"So many days ago as that? Where are the others?"

"They are here. My mother, Mrs. Perkins, Ballard and Philip. Would you like to see them, dear?"

"Only you, Franz. Take my love to them."

Her voice had become the gentlest of murmurs, but the small white hand continued to stroke his face, though with a faltering movement. Then the soft caress stopped; a sigh escaped her; she appeared to slip from his grasp—to shrink within his arms.

"Margaret!" he said. "Margaret!" and his lips were ashen and tremulous.

He allowed her to fall limply to the pillow.

He waited a moment, then springing to his feet he started for the door. And as he groped his way, there burst from his quivering lips a great cry. "Margaret! Margaret!"

XIV

I t was the second evening after Margaret's death, and the night of Barbara's marriage to Shelden.

To Philip the day had come, as all days must, where one exists for them alone, with no other interest in their passing than that they go swiftly. What was in store for him he wondered. Even supposing he eventually succeeded, it would be the bitter satire of success. What could fame or money give him!— he was robbed of every inspiration. At least he could turn to his work for forgetfulness. That was something, even if it yielded him no further recompense. He looked at his watch. "It must soon be over with. They must soon be married," he thought, and slipping into his hat and coat started downstairs. His mother heard him and came into the hall.

"Are you going out, Philip?" she asked.

"Yes, dear. I want to see Franz. I haven't been there to-day. I'll not be out late."

"It's very cold."

"I shall not care."

She put up her lips to kiss him, then pressed her cheek to his. "I'm so sorry, Philip!" she whispered. It was the only expression of pity she had ventured.

"Don't, mother. I can't endure it. Not now—not yet."

With a hasty good-by he hurried off.

Ten minutes later and he stood with Perkins before the door leading into the room where Margaret lay.

"Where is Franz?" Philip asked.

Perkins nodded toward the door. "We can't induce him to leave her," he said.

"Why should you seek to? Poor fellow!"

They were silent, gazing at each other, a depth of sorrow in their glance. Finally Perkins said, with a show of control:

"Have you seen her, Philip?"

"No."

"Why?"

"I had decided to keep the memory I have of her unchanged. It is as I saw her when they were married. She was so happy, poor little thing!"

"There is more than happiness in her face now," Perkins observed thoughtfully. "Do you believe in a hereafter?"

"What odds can it be? It's in the present our lot is cast."

"Don't you like to think you are destined to meet those you love again?"

Philip placed his hand irresolutely upon the knob.

"I shall go in. Perhaps I shall be able to determine what I do believe."

As he entered the room, a rush of cold air met him, for the windows were partially raised—the outer shutters only being closed. The dim light filled the apartment with shadowy indistinctness.

Slowly and overpoweringly objects became plain in the somberness of his surroundings.

Margaret lay upon a couch in the center of the room. She might have been asleep.

At her side sat Franz, regardless of the stinging gusts of wind that came in between the shutters.

Philip stepped to the couch and looked down upon the beautiful face, then he moved back quietly, and would have quitted the room, but Franz detained him by saying: "Is it you, Perkins?"

"It is I," Philip answered.

Franz arose instantly, putting out his hand, and Philip clasped it eagerly.

Without the wind sighed drearily. The sound was depressing.

The naked branches of a tree growing in a corner of the yard lashed the house incessantly. The single lamp burned with a flickering flame.

"What is it?" Franz questioned, for twice Philip had essayed to speak.

"I am so sorry, Franz. So sorry," he cried in broken tones.

"I know you are," Franz answered simply.

"There is this that I want to tell you, Franz, if I may," Philip continued.

"Yes?"

"Barbara is to be married to-night." He came to an abrupt stop. "I have determined to go East," he went on presently. "It will mean greater opportunity. A garbled version of that affair of Anson's has got abroad and my mother is equally anxious to break up here. What I wished to ask you is, won't you join me, dear old fellow?"

"And allow my blindness to be your affliction?"

"You are more to me than I can express. First my mother—then you, and after you—Perkins."

Franz swept his hand across his forehead.

"Wait! How can I think of the future? My very world is ended! Wait."

Philip stole out of the room and from the house. It was snowing heavily. The ground was already covered. It had been bare at supper-time. He kept on up the street until he was opposite the Gerards.

The house was brilliantly lighted, but the wedding party was still absent at the church. He must see her once more!

So he waited in the cold, half hidden by the falling snow that clung to him and that drifted about the quiet and empty streets.

Yes, Franz should live with him and his mother. Comfort was possible with favoring circumstances where happiness was not.

Presently, disturbing his reverie, the dull rumble of wheels was audible, muffled and deadened by the fall of snow.

The carriages rolled into view.

He saw the many figures moving about, as the guests streamed into the house, and straining his eyes he saw Barbara. She stood in the open door, and as she turned to answer some one who had spoken on the walk—her voice reached him, gay and bright.

The guests had disappeared, yet he waited. He would wait until she entered her carriage to be driven to the station. It could not be very long, and then he, too, would forget.

Suddenly the doors swung back. He saw her, attended by her friends, clinging to her husband's arm, and then—she was whirled away and it was over.

Turning he went directly home and to his room, and took from the drawer the bundle of letters. One by one he burned them—and as the last letter left his hand, far off in the distance pealed the shrill shriek of the whistle that announced the approach of the train.

The sound drew him to the window. He opened it and leaned upon the ledge.

He heard the shrill whistle once again, the creaking of the wheels upon the frosted rails, the ringing of a bell—and she was gone! gone!

A desperate sense of wrong and injury—of pain and grief swept over him.

He turned from the white night and threw himself upon the bed,—abject, lonely, miserable! If he could only die—if he only could! but it was the sickness not of death, but of life, that was on him.

For a time he was unable to think or to throw off the stupor possessing him.

His mother came into the room, but he did not look up.

She closed the window, saying: "Philip, if you intend to lie there, you must be wrapped up, or you will take cold."

He did not speak, and she added: "It's late. It's almost midnight. Won't you go to bed?"

He shook his head.

"My poor boy! my poor boy!—I am so sorry!"

"The worst is over with," he said.

"Can't I help you? It hurts me to see you so. I wish——"

"Please go. You can't help me—nothing can. Please go!" His voice was full of entreaty.

"How could she treat you so, Philip!"

"It wasn't her fault. It was mine. I didn't trust myself. I didn't trust her. I was a coward! She would have taken any risk had I asked it of her, but I was afraid, and this is my punishment."

"Won't you let me spread a blanket over you?"

"No, no. I'll get up in a few moments." He lifted his white drawn face to hers: "Please go, mother. Please go. I—I—can't talk about it." Reluctantly his mother left him to his solitude. For a while he rested motionless on the bed, then he came to his feet and went to the table, taking his seat beside it, his elbows propped upon its blotted and discolored top. He pictured his altered life. There remained to him one solace if he willed it. He could cheat time by work, and so, perhaps, win fame to fill the place of love, and for the rest—the world could go hang!

So he pictured his future, a future vastly less successful than the reality was destined to be, and when he had built his new ideal—buttressed it with hope and courage—he picked up his pen, cleared it of the black rust that had gathered on its point, and commenced to write—to finish the work he had abandoned when the blow fell.

All through the night and into the dawn, to and fro across the long pages, with a cheerful little murmur of approval, the pen scratched and labored.

THE END